Wonderful to take this epic e:
Newfoundland Seaman, and Laur
much immersive and gritty detail, so many smells! we get the personalities and dynamics that come with any grand adventure, as well as fresh insight into the complex and sometimes tortured character of Meriwether Lewis. Bravo!
--Peter Heller, author of *The Dog Stars*, *The Painter*, and *Hell or High Water.*

Laura Lee Yates is as sagacious as Seaman himself, recording details of the expedition that only Lewis's canine companion's keen nose and sharp ears would notice. The story of the expedition is deftly woven into Seaman's observations as he endures all the hardships and privations, but also enjoys the discoveries and triumphs that the members of the Corps of Discovery experienced. A fresh look and a very enjoyable read for the armchair historian, dog lover, or Lewis and Clark enthusiast.
--Todd Weber, living history presenter and educational tour guide

"Laura Lee's gripping account of the Lewis & Clark Expedition is simply quite amazing."
--Milo Chavez, age 11

"Laura Lee Yates draws on her love for history, her sense of humor, and her affection for animals in this romping version of the Lewis and Clark Expedition, told through the eyes of Lewis' trusty dog. This antic read gives a much-deserved nod to history's often forgotten four-legged participants."
—Lisa Jones, author of the memoir *Broken: A Love Story*

Being an amateur historian, I never expected to read about the "Voyage of Discovery" from the viewpoint of a dog. What a difference perspective makes! The author does not play loosely with the events or timeline...this history focuses much more on the emotions of the participants. If you want to live the search for the Northwest Passage, read *Bound for the Western Sea!*"
—. "Preacher" (aka D. Pohlman), longtime buckskinner and columnist for The Territorial Dispatch

BOUND FOR THE WESTERN SEA:

The Canine Account of the Lewis & Clark Expedition

A novel
by Laura Lee Yates

BOUND FOR THE WESTERN SEA
by Laura Lee Yates

Copyright © 2016 by Laura Lee Yates

For more about this author please visit http://LauraLeeYates.com

Undaunted Press

224 Clark Ave

Paonia, CO 81428

Ordering Information: Quantity sales. Special discounts are available on quantity purchases by corporations, associations, and others. For details, contact the publisher at the address above.

ISBN-13: 978-0-9973491-0-8

1. Main category—[Historical Fiction]—Other categories—|Dogs] —[Lewis & Clark]

Cover Artwork and Design by Mary C Simmons

DEDICATION

For Harry, whose true heart shares the journey...

For all the dogs, past, present, and future: childhood pets Laddie, Duke, and Liz, and the ones who loved me more than I loved myself—half-Newfoundland Cody, awarded Best of Mutt, rapscallion Bogey, glorious Fleury, who journeyed with me on my own voyage of discovery, and sweet Venus, who shares a birthday with Meriwether Lewis and teaches me about joy, exuberance, and breathing deep.

And for Seaman, whose great heart and generosity of spirit made it all possible.

William Clark's Map of the Expedition

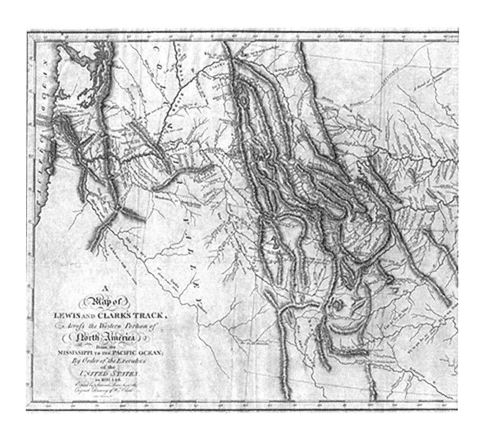

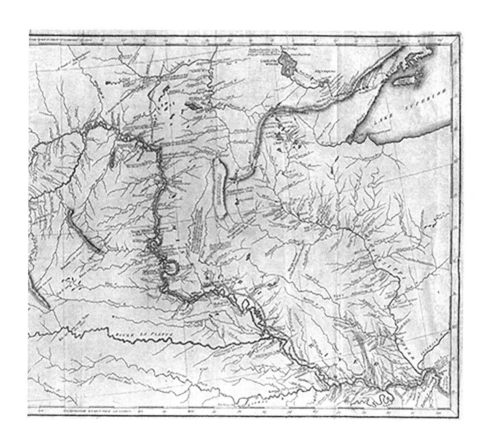

CHAPTER ONE

On the winter night in 1802 when I was born, my grandmother, who was a wise old bitch, reported that a fiery star flew across the Newfoundland sky and vanished into the West. With a snort and a shake of her graying muzzle she predicted for me the life of a rover. But my travels surpassed her wildest dreams, for my journey with the Corps of Discovery was the grandest any canine has ever known.

Now I stand in the White Pirogue, leaning out so far that Cruzatte has to shift position in the canoe to balance my weight as he paddles toward the mouth of Maria's River. Instead of scolding, old Cruzatte, half-French and half-Omaha Indian, winks at me, which looks peculiar since he has only the one eye. (I never learned what happened to the other.) "I know how you feel, beeg dog. It will be good when we are all together again." He swigs from a jug, only water now, since the whiskey is long gone. "I am sorry that I thought about eating you, Seaman. It was only once, when we had no meat for days, and I was so hungry. But you are one of us. You even learned to like my music, no?"

Though I can appreciate how Cruzatte's screeching fiddle cheers the men after a day of danger and hardship, I could never *like* it.

I continue to test the air, sifting through the fragrances of bark and leaves and river, a whiff of beaver, a trace of elk—never the scent I seek. Nobody sings or laughs as we speed downstream. We've faced a thousand dangers together, but now the Corps is divided, trying to accomplish too many different tasks all at the same time—and I don't like it one bit. Splitting up feels wrong, especially with my Master off in Blackfeet country where I can't keep watch over him. It's true that my hind leg throbs, injured for the second time when Meriwether's gelding tumbled off the Lolo Trail and struck me with a hoof as I leapt to the rescue, but limping or not I would have kept up, somehow. My Master doesn't have Will Clark nearby, either, to keep him steady. The men who accompany Meriwether have proved themselves over and over, facing grizzlies and rattlers and Teton Sioux—but my Master assigned only three to his own detachment, which is charged with exploring the territory beyond Maria's River. Our Indian friends avoid crossing paths with the fierce Blackfeet, and I wish Meriwether would, too. But he wanted one last exploration into uncharted territory, another chance to astonish The President with an amazing discovery. As if he hasn't done enough.

The sun climbs, flashing off the river and making all of us hot and squinty. Private Goodrich, seated in the front of the pirogue, stops paddling to wipe his brow, and then offers me a sliver of dried meat. I give it a sniff but turn away to stare back across the water.

"You must be worried sick to be snubbin' good buff," he says. "We'll all feel a sight better when we have the Captain back in the boat, all in one piece with tales to tell. I'll hook you a fat trout when we reach the rendezvous point."

Goodrich's hand ruffles my ears. Hard to believe there was a time when I didn't value the private, our very best fisherman and a loyal soldier, when I wondered if the young Shoshone Bird Woman still remembered her way home, if the farm boys would ever learn to hit a target. Those days before we became the Corps of Discovery seem long ago and faraway.

My own story began in a land of waves and rocky beaches, before I sampled the delights of buffalo and beavertail and *boudin blanc*, before I found my true Master...

Traveling flows in my bloodline. My illustrious ancestor Oolum stood beside Leif Erickson when the first dragon ship sailed to the coast of Newfoundland eight hundred years ago. Soon that new country harbored a race of canines that bore Oolum's stamp: massive size and strength, webbed paws and thick, oily black fur to withstand icy waters. Countless generations later I joined the ranks of these Newfoundland dogs, along with four sisters. Within weeks I was gnawing at deer bones and cods' heads while my littermates contented themselves with milk. One morning my first master, a boat-builder who hailed from France, lifted me to the back of a horse and held me in his lap for a jolting journey. The distant rumble I'd heard from birth rose to a growl, loud, ferocious, until it roared, sucked a breath, and roared again. Then I caught my first glimpse of the sea, and felt very small. But when the master set me down on a sandy spot between boulders I couldn't resist following the retreating foam, and when it turned and rushed toward me it knocked me from my paws, rolling me in an icy grip. Once I floundered to the surface and my legs sorted themselves out, I forged across the water. The Master laughed as he plucked me from the sea.

"Just as I thought—an able-bodied seaman, like your fathers before you!"

The boat-builder had promised the pick of the pups to the Royal Governor who owned my sire, and when I turned nine weeks old I left my family to begin my training. An old Scot named Fergus taught me and other pups of my breed the ocean rescue of both objects and men. I needed little schooling, since the ways of the water come naturally to those of Newfoundland blood, and Fergus said I was "well-christened."

A man named Tucker, shaped much like an upright flour barrel on stubby legs, arrived from America. He inspected each male puppy before concentrating on me, poking and prodding, prying my mouth open to peer at my teeth. Old Fergus had trained me well, for I held myself still, all but my tail. Later we set out in the boat. I returned the cork life-ring each time it was thrown, and the next morning the American tied a rope around my neck and hitched it to the back of a wagon. My paws got sore as we followed a road that wound its way to the shore and into the regional capital, St. John's, and then headed straight toward a double-masted vessel. Men scrambled up ropes overhead.

"'Bout time you got here!" a voice shouted. "Get aboard before we miss the tide!"

The Aurora was no coastal fishing boat like those I knew, but a graceful oceangoing ship for the transport of cargo and the occasional passenger. Wind filled her sails. Though it was a strange thing to watch my homeland grow distant and small, I reminded myself that this journey might lead me to my true Master. As a pup, I'd listened to my elders' tales of comradeship and devotion between dog and man, beginning with Oolum and Leif Erickson and on through the story of my grandmother's courage when she'd plunged into a stormy sea to save her Master. Would I have the opportunity to continue this tradition of service and become a hero? Fortunately, Tucker was only acting as go-between for his brother, a river man in a place called Pittsburgh, for I couldn't imagine Tucker being involved with anything heroic. He spent his time below except for irregular visits to feed and water me, and couldn't reach the rail to piss without staggering, unlike the sailors, who dashed or strolled from place to place, as comfortable among the ropes as squirrels in the branches of trees. Tucker's absence left me with the run of the <u>Aurora</u>. In her hold, crates and casks wafted wonderful fishy odors, sharp oily scents, or mysterious, pungent fragrances I longed to sample. But after an initial exploration, I preferred to spend my time on deck, where the briny air tasted new every moment and I could watch the sailors at their work. One of them—a generous fellow who tossed me a whole herring—had skin almost as dark as my own fur.

That same afternoon I spotted a rocky outcropping protruding from the sea. It kept rising, on and on, then sprayed a delicious-smelling fountain high above the surface. "Thar she blows!" someone shouted. The <u>Aurora</u> was not a whaling ship, but some of our sailors, including the dark man called Nigger, had served aboard those vessels and yearned to pursue and kill the great beast. I liked it just where it was, plunging deep into the ocean, mighty beyond any creature in my dreams.

We reached someplace big and noisy called Boston, then continued south. When the <u>Aurora</u> reached a city named Philadelphia, Tucker tied the rope around my neck once more, mounted a mare, and set out to the west. Mile after mile, with no midday meal, I followed, and by afternoon I was breathing hard and my tongue felt too big for my muzzle. The old mare plodded along, carting her heavy burden without complaint, while Tucker sipped from a flask he kept at the ready, occasionally breaking into song, the same two tunes over and over—something frisky about a chap called "Yankee Doodle" alternating with a solemn piece about God. My grandmother had cautioned me about God, who was something like the Great Mystery, only with a lot more rules for humans to follow. "I gather He is quite a fierce individual," the old bitch had explained, "for I heard Cook telling one of the carpenters that God would send him into the Hellfires for eternity." She'd shuddered. "Don't worry, little one, the Great Mystery has his eye on you, and as long as you are the best dog you can be, after your time on Earth is over you will be reunited with your true Master on the Dog Star."

Each night, when we set up camp along the trail or bedded down at a roadside inn, I would lick my paws clean, worrying thorns from my fur before they could embed in flesh. One evening we traveled even later than usual and "Yankee Doodle" rang out with extra vigor. We trudged along a low ridge top and began to see lights flickering below. The scent of water and mud and human waste drifted on the breeze. "Hope yer worth all the trouble I been to, mutt," Tucker said, "goin' to a foreign country an' dealin' with damned aristocrats an' pukin' my guts into the ocean. Now that my debt's paid an' we're back in Pittsburgh, I can do as I please without my brother or his wife buttin' in."

Soon we reached the brick home of my new master, where a sharp-faced woman informed Tucker that his brother was away, but she'd take the dog, and that was the last I ever saw of Tucker. The woman scowled at me where I sat on the porch. "Seaman, huh? Well, you look like you could eat us out of house and home."

I was promptly shunted to a warehouse half-filled with bins and barrels, given an ample but nearly tasteless dish of food beside a bucket of warmish water, and locked in all alone. For the first time, I found myself wishing I'd never left Newfoundland. I could smell the river nearby, but it made no sound, no rhythm of wave against shore. The air in the warehouse felt stale and damp. It threatened to be a very long night.

The morning dawned hot. I waited hours, more or less patiently, for someone to retrieve me, but after barking myself hoarse to no avail, I scrambled atop a barrel and managed to squeeze through a window left ajar. Hours ago I'd drained my bucket dry, so I followed my nose toward the river, where I waded in and drank my fill, even though it tasted musty. Then I struck out upstream, my legs propelling me through the current with ease, paddling past more warehouses, an inn, several taverns; workmen hammered on half-finished boats, sweat dripping from their faces. When the river grew sluggish, I shook myself and explored overland. Wagons, riders, and folks on foot crowded Pittsburgh's streets. As I trotted in the general direction of my new home I detoured into a doorway exuding the scent of baking bread, but unfortunately the proprietor, a fine-smelling female, shooed me out with a broom and a scolding.

"There he is!" a voice shrieked. I spotted the sharp-faced woman, puffing like a worn-out hound, pointing me out to a man beside her.

"Seaman! Come, boy!" the fellow called, and I dashed forward just as I'd been taught, then sat gazing up at him, which wasn't far, for he wasn't a tall man, nor heavy. "Oh, yer the handsomest dog, an' smart, too." He stroked my head.

"Perhaps that brother of yours did something right for a change," the woman said. But she didn't look pleased. "Well, now you have your fancy pet—at great expense, and don't think I don't know it—but he's not to dirty my clean house!"

The man knelt down and wrapped both arms around my neck, his pale hair tickling my nose. "Let's get you some vittles, eh, Seaman?"

And I walked by the side of my new master, thinking things had turned out fine after all.

Though my next meal was a considerable improvement over the previous one, I was still relegated to the warehouse for the night. Apparently my master, who was also called Tucker— Mister Tucker by his wife—was not the master of his house, for it became clear that Missus Tucker ruled that dwelling and all matters on land, which explained how little time we spent in the city of Pittsburgh. Early the next morning we boarded a squat wooden vessel called a keelboat and headed for New Orleans.

The slow-moving Ohio provided ever-changing aromas: ripe fruit and farm animals, then the intoxicating fragrance of deer, which sometimes fell to the guns of the boatmen, supplying us with delicious meat. I had little to do other than provide company for my master and learn the tricks he delighted in teaching. "Shake!" he would say, and I'd offer a paw; "Roll over!" he'd command, motioning with his arm, and I'd flop down on my right side and flip to the left, giving my back a good scratching in the process. Even though the men addressed my master as Captain Tucker, a burly fellow called Curly with no hair at all kept the keelboat moving downriver and supervised the loading and unloading of cargo at various points along the way. My new master was a bit of a disappointment, but I tried not to think about things like glory and devotion. I'd grown still more, surpassing my mother and nearing the height of my sire, and not long after the Ohio entered the broad Mississippi, on a night when the frogs sang, I mated for the first time with a sleek young bitch.

Sometimes we encountered small boats carrying longhaired men and women that the sailors called Injuns. As we floated downriver I began to see darker-skinned folk who resembled the fish-tossing sailor on the <u>Aurora</u>. I'd thought all humans looked pretty much alike, with their two legs, two arms, and nondescript features, but now I realized that they could be as different looking as one dog from another. In New Orleans, my master spent most of the week in an upstairs room with a woman little older than a child, her face round and dark and smooth, not pointed and pale and wizened as last year's apple like the face of his wife. I found myself content to eat large amounts of delicious food (especially shrimp, tails and all) and nap on the shady front porch, with occasional forays to the waterfront. During my only expedition into the heart of the city I reached a place called Congo Square, which reeked with a sour odor of fear and hopelessness. Money changed hands, and a little black boy sobbed as he was dragged away. I tucked my tail and slunk off. Since this new country had no King and said all men were created equal, how could one human buy another? Most of the dark-skinned people I met plodded along with their heads hanging. Why did a black dog like me delight so many people when they looked down on that color in their own kind?

Our return voyage progressed slowly, for we traveled against the current. Our arrival in Pittsburgh meant banishment to the warehouse again, though I made friends with several neighborhood dogs and enjoyed romping about that city, especially after snow blanketed the ground. Soon ice blocked the river and any hopes of another voyage faded. Winter passed, and with it my first birthday. Then the ice broke up and farmers hurried to the city bearing home-cured hams, woven cloth, and barrels of spirits. With a sigh of relief, Captain Tucker waved goodbye to his wife and we headed south. The countryside sped by, for the Ohio ran high, and in no time the keelboat reached the confluence and sped down the Mississippi to New Orleans, where the mistress displayed a rounded belly beneath her dress.

"We'll be back long before the baby's born," Captain Tucker promised as we boarded for the return trip upriver.

But in Pittsburgh, the ranting of Mrs. Tucker reached me even in the warehouse, and soon the master joined me, carrying a pile of blankets and a lantern. "She's found me out, Seaman. The money to start the business came from her father, and he holds all our assets in his name. I'm ruined! What will become of my child?" I could only offer the comfort of a warm body, and soon his tears matted the hair on my ears. As the night wore away he slept beneath his blankets, snoring so loudly that I remained awake until dawn.

The next day I was sold to a man who owned a nail factory at the other end of the city and never saw Captain Tucker again.

My new master, Mr. O'Connor, worked harder than anyone I'd ever met, laboring by day beside the blazing forges just like his men, taking time out only to conduct his dealings with those delivering iron or purchasing his finished goods. Yet when the day ended, he always found time to scratch my ears and toss a stick into the river. I never lacked companionship, for Mr. O'Connor had three sons and two daughters. The two oldest boys taught me to retrieve woodcocks that they shot from the air (all it really took was a bit of urging until I understood what they wanted) but the little girls and the youngest boy occupied most of my time, for though they swam like young otters I felt responsible for their safety, half-hoping one might need rescuing. My current master had started the first nail factory in America and was an admirable fellow with a fine family, I had plenty to eat (though sometimes I yearned for a dozen shrimp) and a soft place to sleep beside the bed of the two little girls. But I was now a year-and-a-half-old and had never done anything remotely heroic. Would I become a fat lazy dog, content to drowse away my days on land? Was this the destiny foretold by the star that had blazed into the western sky on the night of my birth?

In early July of that year 1803, news reached Pittsburgh about something called the "Louisiana Purchase." Mr. O'Connor was thrilled because somehow it made America twice as big as before, which puzzled me, since as far as I knew the Great Mystery had stopped creating land quite awhile back.

Later that month, a stranger from Virginia arrived in the city, boarding at a nearby inn while he awaited the completion of a large keelboat. The yard of the boat-builder adjoined the nail factory and the O'Connor home, so I saw this stranger often, for he came every day to observe the progress on his specially-designed vessel, checking each timber and detail of construction. His military uniform always looked clean, he never slouched, and he didn't smoke, chew, or spit tobacco: very unlike the soldiers I'd encountered about the city. At first we only gazed at each other from a distance, but one hot afternoon when I was supervising the young O'Connors, we found ourselves on the riverbank at the same time, hoping to catch a breeze. The stranger was a tall fellow with short soft-looking hair of a palish shade, deep-set eyes, a kind smile and a rather long nose, which might have explained why he seemed more attuned to the scents about him than the average human, for he plucked a blossom and sniffed it carefully, almost as another dog might do, before placing it between the pages of a book he carried with him. The stranger introduced himself as Captain Meriwether Lewis, asking that the children call him Meri. He smelled exactly right, like fields and fresh water.

The title "Captain" intrigued me, so I began to pay more attention to the keelboat. It was a low-slung vessel without the grace of an oceangoing ship, but looked sturdy. Sometimes the man in charge gave off that unmistakable odor of spirits and the men lolled about, vexing Meriwether so much that he would clench his fists and stride away muttering. I discovered that it soothed him to bury his fingers deep in my thick fur. I would lean into his legs, relishing the strength and sensitivity of his hands, and pant a little in pleasure. After a couple of days, he began to talk to me when we were alone. The Captain was a little funny about it at first, but pretty soon he told me how it helped to have someone to tell his secrets to without fear of them being repeated. He worried about the days passing without forward progress, about the river falling, and about someone called "The President" whom he feared disappointing. Yet other times, usually on outings with the O'Connor children, Meriwether seemed almost like a carefree boy, swinging the little ones in circles, flinging tree branches far out into the river and cheering when I trotted back with the stick dragging through the mud, his light hair tousled and his smile bright as sunshine.

With each sunset I would hear the Captain murmur, "Still no word from Will Clark...," until a day at the end of the month when an envelope arrived. He tore into it and scanned the contents without breathing, then tossed his hat into the air. "Clark's agreed, Seaman! He says in his letter, *'This is an undertaking fraught with difficulties, but my friend, I assure you that no man lives with whom I would prefer to undertake such a trip as yourself.'*" Meriwether snatched up his hat, plunking it on his head with no regard for the weeds straggling from its brim. "Will Clark spells abominably, but there's not a better man alive, and if something happens to me he'll carry on until the job is done. Come, let's light a fire under that cursed boat-builder!"

I couldn't imagine how a fire could solve the problem, but the letter buoyed Meriwether's spirits for several days. Work on the keelboat advanced and the Captain drilled with the gang of soldiers who lived in two nearby tents, marching the fellows back and forth and setting up targets for them to shoot

13

at with brand-new rifles. The smell of gunpowder—not so different from a good ripe egg—hung in the air. I especially liked George Shannon, an earnest Ohioan who was the youngest of the bunch and the worst shot.

Though the Captain had promised to meet his friend Will Clark downriver by the end of the month, the boat-builder stopped trying to hide his drinking when the workmen had only planked one side of the new keelboat. I remembered my grandmother warning about the power that spirits could wield over the hearts and minds of men. First Meriwether cajoled the builder, and then threatened. He muttered about abandoning "that damned keelboat," but Mr. O'Connor convinced the Captain that he'd be unable to obtain a decent substitute downriver. Far into the night the two men talked about plans for Meriwether's voyage, while I stretched out on the floor between them. Everyone in Pittsburgh had heard that Captain Lewis intended to travel the far reaches of the Mississippi, but to Mr. O'Connor Meriwether spoke of his true mission: an exploration of the Missouri River to its source, and a search for a waterway to the Pacific Ocean. The Northwest Passage, he called it.

"Eleven years I've dreamed of this!" Meriwether said. "Even before I joined up during the Whiskey Rebellion, I wanted to journey to the West. When I was a boy, the long days I spent in the woods were the best times of my life." I could almost picture that youngster when I watched him speak fast, his eyes shining. "I grew up not far from Monticello, and when President Jefferson appointed me as his personal secretary, I was honored, of course, but I missed the frontier and yearned to be more than a glorified pen pusher. Oh, it was fine to live in the White House and meet important people, but I longed to explore the unknown half of our continent. Then The President sent me to Philadelphia to study with the finest minds in science." Meriwether smiled, but now it made him look sad. "My father died during the Revolution when I was young, and I had to manage the family lands when I would have preferred studying, so it was thrilling to learn medicine, astronomy, botany and zoology—though sometimes I thought my brain would explode from all the knowledge I tried to cram into my head during that short period." Meriwether laughed, a sound that made my tail beat the floor. He reached down and tousled my ears. "But I wanted to be prepared for this great venture. Our country needs a way to the western sea. Why should we let the British and French control the fur trade? We need to know far more of the peoples who inhabit the Western lands."

The more I heard about the prospective journey, the more excited I grew. Even though I knew Mr. O'Connor could never leave his busy factory and his family, I began to have strange dreams: one night a great shaggy creature with horns bellowed and shook the ground about me until I woke panting; another time, a winsome bitch howled from across a rushing stream. Some nights I scented the salt of the sea and heard its roar.

Eventually Meriwether's persistence in the boatyard showed results, for the keelboat neared completion. After work had ceased for the day, the children delighted in scrambling about onboard, plaguing Meriwether with questions about where he was going and were there really wild Indians who wore nothing but one animal skin apiece as clothes? The youngsters had taken to calling him "Uncle Meri," and when August neared its end and the Captain's departure became imminent, the O'Connors planned a farewell picnic. That evening, as the family gathered and I retrieved sticks from the river, I tested the sky for Meriwether's scent. Finally, he rode up on his horse with a wicker basket tied behind his saddle. The children crowded around the poor gelding, who twitched his ears but didn't kick. From the basket came a frantic whining and scrabbling that I recognized immediately. I'd pressed forward with the others, but now retreated and lay down on the grass with my head between my paws, the last shred of secret hope vanquished. Even though I'd known that my dreams made no sense, I'd started believing that Meriwether was my true Master. Now he'd chosen some puppy to accompany him on his voyage.

When he lifted the squirming bundle from the basket, the little girls squealed with delight. "Pedigreed spaniel," Meriwether said, "descended from the best bird dogs. Make a fine hunter when he's older."

The oldest boy received the spotted puppy from the Captain's hands, holding it high above the heads of the smaller children, who all reached up to touch the silky fur. Meriwether dismounted and strode over to Mr. O'Connor. "I know this is a lot to ask..." He held out a coin larger than any I'd ever seen. "Would twenty dollars and the spaniel convince you to trade Seaman? We'll need a good dog to warn us of danger, and the pup's too young for a long journey."

"Nobody pays that much for a dog." Mr. O'Connor shook his head, watching the children fondle the puppy. I didn't move a muscle. Then Mr. O'Connor chuckled. "You're a clever fellow, Lewis. I suppose it's my patriotic duty.... Seaman is yours. May he bring you luck."

Mr. O'Connor stuck out his hand, and from that moment on I was Meriwether's dog.

CHAPTER TWO

On the morning of the last day of August we were ready to board the keelboat. The smaller children cried as they hugged me goodbye, and their mother presented a fine bit of beef from her apron pocket. When Mr. O'Connor approached, I offered him my paw, which he shook solemnly, though his eyes seemed more twinkly than usual. "You've been a good dog, Seaman. Serve your Master well." That was when I realized Mr. O'Connor was not only a hard-working man but also a wise one, for he understood that he had never been my true Master.

The spaniel pup wriggled in the youngest girl's arms, and I nodded at him, confident that in time he would make a fine companion for the O'Connor clan. Then I joined Meriwether onboard the keelboat and we cast off for adventure.

Fifty-five feet long and quite narrow, the wooden vessel bore eleven benches for rowers and a jointed mast that could carry two sails. Meriwether's cabin huddled under an elevated deck in the stern, but the bow deck offered the best view, allowing the pilot or my new Master a place to watch for sandbars or submerged trees in the river, which was flowing at a record low, and it provided me a fine vantage point for spotting interesting creatures. Meriwether often consulted the book he used for pressing his flowers, a volume called The Navigator that foretold the hazards of the voyage. This part of the river was full of islands which drew up sand, gravel, and driftwood that threatened to block our progress, and the entire crew would climb down into the water, lift all the cargo onto their backs, carry it downstream, and then drag the boat over or between the obstacles until we reached a place where the vessel would float freely. As the soldiers sweated and strained under the hot sun I heard one of them grumble that he hadn't joined the Army to work like a mule. But Meriwether tugged and struggled harder than any of them, with George Shannon always nearby, and that young fellow never complained either, even when he slipped and landed facedown in the mud. The going grew so difficult that the boat mired. My Master and I located a farmer whose sturdy oxen were able to pull the vessel free.

I admired Meriwether more everyday. He was always the first man awake, cursing the fog that often delayed our departure, helping prepare breakfast and writing in his journal, and then rowing beside the crew. With all the starts and stops, leaks and rainstorms, it took us eight days to reach Wheeling, Virginia, where we rested for two nights. Back on the river again, it poured rain, and Meriwether worked by lantern light to protect our cargo, especially the goods he'd purchased as gifts for the Indians we'd meet farther West. Soon he was soaked to the skin, and I worried he might catch a cold, an ailment to which humans seem prone, probably because they continue to wear clothes after they're wet and don't stop to shake off. When my Master quit it was past midnight. Instead of camping onshore we slept in the cabin, which was crowded and stuffy but easily warmed by our body heat, and the next morning the Captain seemed good as new. That day Meriwether said we covered twenty-four miles, our best progress to date.

The following day we journeyed even farther, and it was a day I will remember forever. I'd often hunted squirrels on land, where they always eluded me by climbing trees, but on that September afternoon hundreds of black squirrels chose to migrate across the river to the south side. When I pricked my ears, Meriwether urged me into the water, where I had no trouble catching up to one of the creatures. A quick snap and the black squirrel hung limp in my jaws. I swam back to the boat and deposited the body at my Master's feet to the cheering of the men. But it was Meriwether's praise that really mattered. I repeated my performance over and over until we had passed beyond the migration. That night we feasted on fried squirrel.

"I have written about you in my journal," my Master told me later, as he dipped his quill in its inkwell. "I am explaining that you are of the Newfoundland breed, and very active, strong, and docile. Your squirrel hunting exploits will be reported to President Jefferson himself."

The President was a mysterious figure. Meriwether spoke of him with great love and admiration, yet I sensed something like fear in my Master's attitude as well. It was almost as if The President was God and Meriwether might get sent to burn in the Hellfires if he didn't measure up. Yet The President had chosen Meriwether out of all the men in America, first as his personal secretary, then to lead this expedition up the Missouri and all the way to the other ocean. Why was my Master so worried?

Finally, we reached Marietta, Ohio, where Meriwether dismissed two men he'd taken on trial. George Shannon, the youngster who worked hard but seldom hit the target during practice, remained with us, and a stranger dressed all in fragrant buckskins joined up, a Kentuckian named John Colter. Colter borrowed one of the new rifle and knocked a bird out of a distant tree with a single shot.

"Pretty fair weapon, Cap'n, never seen one quite like it. Put this together yerself?"

"I designed the modifications and had it manufactured at Harpers Ferry for this expedition. More should arrive soon."

Colter stroked his beard and nodded. "Count me in."

The water grew deeper and we could utilize the sails, soon reaching the series of rapids called the Falls of the Ohio, which we traversed without difficulty before tying up at the settlement of Clarksville in Indiana. There, wearing his freshly-brushed uniform and cocked hat, Meriwether set off for the home of General George Rogers Clark, where we were to meet up with the General's brother, the Will who had sent the letter and was to serve as my Master's partner during our voyage into the uncharted West.

How we ate! I know our meeting with the famous General George Rogers Clark and with my Master's new partner Will (who I liked right away) was the important event, but the food was noteworthy, too. No waiting on the porch or in the kitchen at the Clarks' home: I was welcomed into the dining room along with the General's own hunting hound, and my plate contained a good portion of venison, goose, duck, beef, fish and three kinds of sausages. I decided to take the opportunity to bury a cache, for you never knew when an extra bit of food might come in handy, but before I could hoist my bulging belly off the floor, Meriwether said, "A toast to the finest meal I've enjoyed since I left President Jefferson's side!" If The President was going to be part of the conversation, it was best if I stayed at my Captain's side.

The General lifted his glass. "No matter where we end up, Virginians know how to set a table. We don't have French wines, but let York pour you some more Kentucky whiskey."

I ate so much that I had a hard time staying alert during the hours that followed. After dinner the various members of the Clark household took their leave until only the General, Will, and the massive fellow named York remained. York spent most of his time fetching bottles from the cellar and refilling glasses. He was about as black as me, with hair like the wool of a sheep, almost as if he were of a different breed from the others. The Clarks were also large men, and side-by-side Will and my Master were equally tall and upright, though Will Clark carried more meat on his bones and had brighter waving hair. The General, who was a leader during the American Revolution, still looked strong and hearty. Twenty years earlier he'd considered undertaking just such a journey as we now planned. "Maybe you'll find the Northwest Passage—think of it! You boys'll be the greatest heroes of the day."

Will Clark rolled his eyes at Meriwether whenever his brother called them "boys," but the General had useful advice about exploring the wilderness, and the three of them grew so absorbed in poring over maps and perusing books that I stretched out under the table and took a nap at Meriwether's feet.

If we'd lingered longer than two weeks with the Clarks I would soon have outweighed my sire, for the meals continued lavish. Our presence pleased the General's white-muzzled hunting hound, a savvy character named Old Bay, who said the grub was always good but even better with company around. Old Bay, who'd served with George Rogers Clark for many years, asked me why The President hadn't rewarded his Master for all the important work he'd done; I told him I had no idea but would keep an ear to the wind. My Master remained slim and looked quite dashing in his uniform, so the ladies said, and Meriwether delighted in the company of those frilly young women who wore too much scent as if to cover up their own individual odors, whose voices trilled things like, "Oh, Captain Lewis, you quite take my breath away!" One of Old Bay's granddaughters, a lithe creature named Eulalie, took a fancy to me, and we enjoyed a pair of nights together near the end of the stay in Clarksville.

We didn't spend all our time socializing, however, for the crucial task of choosing men for the journey occupied much of the partners' attentions. Word had spread of our expedition, and more than a hundred individuals showed up in Clarksville, hoping to enlist in the Corps of Discovery, as it had come to be called. Meriwether and Will Clark soon weeded out the hopeless ones, leaving dozens of young fellows looking for adventure and land of their own, which would be awarded to each man who served during the expedition. Together my Master and his friend Will analyzed the hunting skills, physical strength, and personal character of every applicant, eliminating several men for drunkenness. Meriwether proposed young but hardworking George Shannon, who'd finally learned to hit a target, and sharp-shooting John Colter as members of our company. Seven men recruited by Clark were chosen, and these nine were sworn in as the first enlisted men in the Corps of Discovery. York was to accompany us as well, though he didn't have to enlist in the Army. He journeyed everywhere with Clark, much as I did with my own Master, since Clark owned him. I remembered Congo Square with a shudder.

"You boys take care now, and come back with your scalps attached to your heads," the General said, shaking Meriwether's hand as we prepared to board the keelboat.

"I hear some of them Injuns are partial to dog meat," Old Bay told me with a sly grin.

I snorted at his little joke. "Too bad you're not coming with us—the way you folks eat, you'd make a fine meal."

The Ohio cooperated with our downriver voyage, flowing strong and steady, and in two weeks we reached Fort Massac on the Illinois bank. There Meriwether hoped to recruit more men and pick up eight volunteers from an army camp in Tennessee. But only two of the local soldiers suited and nobody could tell us the whereabouts of the Tennesseans. "More delays," my Master complained, slapping at one of the many mosquitoes that infested the place.

Fortunately, we met up with a woodsman named George Drouillard, known as a skilled hunter and trapper. Drouillard could speak French as well as English plus a couple of Indian tongues and the sign language spoken with the hands. His long hair was black and shiny as a raven's wing. Drouillard was what humans call a half-breed, his father a French Canadian who had married a Shawnee. I liked his clean outdoorsy smell. Often mixed-breeds gained the best traits of both their parents.

"I can offer you twenty-five dollars a month and all the excitement a man could want," Meriwether told him.

Drouillard hesitated. "Don't really see myself in the Army, not meaning any offense. Like to come and go as I please out in the woods, and all that marching and saluting seems like a waste of time."

Meriwether laughed. "I don't think we'll spend much of our time that way, but it's not necessary that you enlist. I'm authorized by The President to hire a few civilians as interpreters and guides, and you're just the sort we had in mind." When Drouillard didn't respond, the Captain sighed. "Can I at least persuade you to search out my missing fellows from Tennessee and bring them to our winter headquarters? We intend to camp on the east bank of the Missouri not far from St. Louis. We could pay you thirty dollars in cash."

Drouillard nodded. "Have to think on the rest."

I was glad when we left gloomy Fort Massac behind, but my joy at being back on the river soon changed to concern. That night, my Master grew so cold he woke me with his trembling, and I lay closer beside him, hoping my own warmth would help, but he shook and moaned for a couple of hours before growing feverish, tossing in his blankets with sweat on his brow. Once he groaned, "Tell The President I did my best... Clark can take them through...." I felt helpless. Will Clark had chosen to sleep aboard the keelboat that night, and young Shannon, who slept nearest to our tent, never roused during the long hours, snoring softly until dawn, when Meriwether seemed to rally. He dosed himself from his store of medical supplies, then spent a long while relieving himself, which seemed to make him feel well enough to travel. That day we progressed with frequent stops for him to disembark and visit the woods.

"How bad is it?" Clark asked during a private moment.

Meriwether offered a sickly smile. "I've survived worse attacks. Malaria will never carry me off. Rush's pills sped things along—they don't call them 'Thunderbolts' for nothing. Let's get moving, Captain, I'm not an invalid, and we want to make the Mississippi before dark."

We reached the confluence of the Ohio and Mississippi just at sunset, and under Clark's command the men set up a fine camp onshore, with my Master under strict orders to rest. Meriwether didn't even write in his journal, a rare occurrence. I hadn't known that my Master suffered from the malaria disease, and now I understood the wisdom of having Clark along as his equal partner. If one of the Captains was ill or injured, the other could take over. Turned out I'd underestimated Clark's cleverness (probably because it was hard for me to admit that anyone was half as smart as my own Master), for at the confluence, Clark found all sorts of important tasks for the crew that necessitated a six-day stay. He persuaded Meriwether that this was the perfect opportunity for passing on the surveying techniques and methods of celestial observation that my Master had acquired during his sojourn in Philadelphia. Using an instrument called a sextant, the two of them practiced "shooting the sun," only without guns. Together the Captains would consult charts that somehow enabled them to determine our latitude. Humans seem to feel more secure when they have a method to determine exactly where they are, while any dog understands that perfectly well without tools or books. On clear nights, the three of us would stay out under the stars, and Meriwether would make calculations using the movement of the moon across the sky. He knew the names of many of those distant lights, calling them Regulus and Antares and Aldeberan. "See that one?" he asked, pointing at the brightest of all. "It's Sirius, the Dog Star, part of Canis Major."

I slipped my head under Meriwether's other hand and leaned into him as he fondled my ears, both of us gazing into the heavens. My grandmother had shown me that very same star in the sky over Newfoundland. She had explained that when our time on earth was done, we would cross over to live on the Dog Star forever. Viewing it from the confluence of those rivers made me realize that no matter how far I journeyed, I would never be far from home.

One morning we loaded into a pirogue, which was a special kind of canoe with a mast for raising sail, and crossed the Mississippi to make more observations. There we discovered a hunting encampment of Delaware and Shawnee Indians. My hackles rose. "Now's when we could use George Drouillard," Meriwether said. But the Indians seemed quite friendly, so I relaxed. Since they understood some English, Meriwether explained that instead of the Spanish King, President Jefferson who lived in a city called Washington was now the Great Father of all the tribes. The Indians didn't look very interested. One of the Shawnees, a muscular fellow with a strange haircut, seemed far more intrigued with me; the two camp dogs were scrawny creatures that skulked on the outskirts, and I figured the Shawnee appreciated my size and strength. Even before my Master had finished his speech, the fellow began rummaging among his goods, locating three furs which he offered to Meriwether, gesturing at me and interrupting in broken English.

"Appears this Shawnee's taken a fancy to your dog," Clark said, "and wants to trade three prime beaver pelts. In case you don't know, Meriwether, that's a mighty fair offer. Pelts like those are worth close to eighteen dollars."

Meriwether placed a hand on my back and I felt it tighten on my fur. He shook his head no. "Seaman is not for sale at any price." To Clark, he muttered, "Bold rascal! I paid twenty dollars for this dog back in Pittsburgh and I'm not about to part with him now. He'll prove his true worth, given time." Meriwether continued his speech in a loud voice, keeping a close watch over the Shawnee.

With Meriwether recovered from his bout of malaria and the men in high spirits, we loaded the keelboat and two pirogues and headed up the Mississippi. We'd seemed a sizable crew, but the power of that mighty river tested the strength and will of the men. All the vessels were undermanned, especially the keelboat, and we were forced to zigzag back and forth, using any slack water downstream from a point of land to make headway. "Eight hours of steady rowing and we've only covered ten-and-a-half miles," Meriwether lamented. "At this rate we'll be graybeards before we reach the Pacific."

"We need more muscle," Clark said. "My brother insisted we'd stir up the Indians if we showed too much force, but that's a chance we'll have to take."

It took eight days to reach the army post at Kaskaskia, and by that time Meriwether had lost all patience with our slow upstream progress. Once the Captains had recruited reinforcements, Meriwether purchased a sturdy gray mare and we started for St. Louis with me near the horse's side, while Clark led the little fleet toward the mouth of the Wood River, where we planned to camp for the winter.

The following weeks passed quickly. Meriwether met with the important citizens of St. Louis, studied maps, and wrote often and at length to President Jefferson. He purchased supplies from the local merchants: corn, flour, biscuits, fine-smelling pork, salt, candles, lard, tools and twenty-one barrels of Indian goods. The boats were going to be a lot more crowded when we finally headed up the Missouri, but I was glad to smell all that food. In mid-December George Drouillard appeared with eight soldiers from Tennessee. My Master was happy to see the half-Shawnee woodsman though not so thrilled by the new fellows—"not a hunter among them—" but he sent them on to Clark at the winter quarters on the Wood River. Meriwether also entrusted Drouillard with the delivery of a bronze cannon and four blunderbusses that Captain Clark had requested, for the more he heard about a tribe of fierce upriver Indians called the Teton Sioux, the more Clark insisted that we needed a greater show of force.

Meriwether seemed far more worried about the lack of news regarding his partner's commission. In public, he always addressed Clark as "Captain," but so far, Will had no official rank, even though at one time he'd served as my Master's superior officer. It was one of those human concerns that didn't seem important to me but tormented Meriwether. "I gave Will my word," he said. I'd come to know that meant everything to my Master.

At the end of January of 1804 we crossed over to camp on the Wood River. Clark had devised improvements to the keelboat, mounting the cannon on a swivel in the bow and building storage lockers along the sides with lids that could be raised to provide a shield in case of attack. The company now amounted to more than forty. Drouillard had agreed to join the expedition as a hunter and interpreter but had gone off to settle his affairs. "You've accomplished a great deal," Meriwether congratulated his friend as we surveyed the keelboat. "But what's this York tells me about you being ill?"

Clark glared at the black man, who hung his head. "York shouldn't have worried you. Just my old digestive disorder, aggravated by the cold—damn this dismal hole! My toes are fine."

"No frostbite, then?" Meriwether asked.

"It was a near thing," Clark admitted. "I have the men keeping a close watch on their extremities. Now that we've finished the huts and the work on the boats, they're getting restless. We don't have ammunition to waste on a lot of shooting practice, which they love, so I try to keep them busy drilling, which they hate."

"Well, that needn't be your concern for awhile," Meriwether told him. "It's my turn to deal with the men, while you head off to St. Louis, and just in time for the Chouteaus' ball. The young ladies have been pestering me unmercifully: 'When *is* that red-headed friend of yours coming to the city, Captain Lewis?'" He gave Clark a little shove toward the shore. "Go on, Will, you look as if you could use a bit of fun."

Being on the loose at Wood River bested hanging about in the city while the humans talked. Rabbits required chasing, the riverbanks needed exploration, and the men any diversion I could provide, for Clark was right: the soldiers were restless as four-month-old pups. Most delighted in putting me through my repertoire of tricks, tossing sticks, or simply slipping me treats. Among my favorites were young, clean-shaven Shannon and his friend Charles Floyd, a Kentuckian whose father had served with George Rogers Clark. One of the soldiers, though, muttered that "a pet dog has no place in the Army." Short but solid as a bulldog, Patrick Gass had fought Indians and had supervised the construction of the huts at our Wood River camp as well as the new joinery on the keelboat. He was well-liked by the men, but the bearded Irishman never offered me a friendly word. Gass worked hard and clearly respected my Master, however, so I resigned myself to the man's disfavor. The soldier I liked least was a fellow named Moses Reed, who always saluted Meriwether with a flourish but looked surly when my Master wasn't watching. As I kept a closer eye on him, I discovered that the fellow often invented excuses to shirk his fair share of the labor.

When we returned to St. Louis to meet with Will Clark, Meriwether placed Sergeant John Ordway, an experienced soldier he'd met before, in command. We returned a week later to chaos: two of the men had refused to follow Ordway's lead, calling the sergeant a "damn Yankee," and four had gone off "hunting," but when they returned, even a human could smell that they'd spent their time drinking a lot of whiskey. Meriwether soon made it clear that the men would obey Ordway when the Captains were absent—or suffer serious consequences.

During the first week of March we returned to the city, where Meriwether served as the chief official witness to the transfer of Upper Louisiana from the French to us Americans, which puzzled me since nothing seemed to change. Clark returned to Wood River, but we remained for three more weeks in St. Louis purchasing additional supplies. By the time we crossed back, the ice had melted, great flocks of ducks and geese winged overhead, and the first mosquitoes began to buzz around me, for it seemed dogs were their preferred meal. When we reached camp, we learned that John Shields, the only married man with the expedition and the oldest of our soldiers, had threatened to kill Ordway and return to Kentucky, while Colter had disobeyed a direct order, loading his rifle and saying he was going to shoot the sergeant. The Captains put both men on trial for mutiny, but Shields and Colter asked to be forgiven, promising to do better; I suspected Colter's superior marksmanship and the fact that Shields was our most accomplished gunsmith had a lot to do with their pardons. Two days later, when the Captains chose the permanent party—the true Corps of Discovery who would man the keelboat up the Missouri River, cross the Rocky Mountains, and continue all the way to the distant sea—Colter and Shields were among the twenty-five sworn in as members of the expedition. My friend Floyd and his cousin Nat Pryor got appointed sergeants along with Ordway. Drouillard, who hadn't yet returned, York, and I never had to swear to anything.

With April, the days grew warmer and the mosquitoes worse, with all of us itching to be off up the Missouri, but the Captains still had business to complete in St. Louis. Clark returned to the camp at Wood River while Meriwether went on shopping, purchasing flags, cheesecloth netting, shirts for the men, nails, red and blue ribbon, additional Indian goods and, I was happy to note, more food. While we were in St. Louis staying at the home of the Choteaus, word finally arrived about Clark's commission.

"<u>Lieutenant</u>?" Meriwether looked as if someone had struck him across the face. He sank down on the bed, the letter limp in his hand. Then he crumpled the paper and threw it into a corner of the room. Did he expect me to fetch it? "Improper? Clark carrying rank equal to mine improper?" I'd never heard Meriwether so agitated. "For God's sake, Will Clark was my superior officer and taught me most of what I know about soldiering. Now the man is my partner. I gave him my word! Why didn't The President do something? How am I going to explain this to Will?" Meriwether strode over to the desk and poured himself a glass of brandy, drank it without stopping, and slammed the glass down on the desk. "No one must know. I'll confess the truth to Will, of course, but we leave soon and there's no need for others to learn of this news. We will go on as before." With that, he sat and began to write.

I never heard the two men discuss the discrepancy in military rank, and the other men never knew.

While we were in St. Louis, arranging to send the chief of the Osage tribe to Washington to visit The President, whom the headman called "Great Father Jefferson," Clark was packing up the camp at Wood River and readying the boats for our journey. Drouillard had returned to the city and aided Meriwether in selecting seven *voyageurs*, expert rivermen of French descent who would be invaluable on the trip up the Missouri. The Captains still worried that we had insufficient stores and Indian goods, but on May 14th, the vessels headed for St. Charles on the Missouri River, where we were to meet them. Finally, on May 20th, Meriwether mounted his horse. A number of officials and citizens of St. Louis accompanied us on our journey. By suppertime we rejoined Clark and the crew and we spent that night on the keelboat, everyone too excited to sleep much. The next morning Meriwether hired two of the St. Charles locals, fragrant half-breeds named Cruzatte and Labiche who were the sons of French fathers and Indian mothers, and Meriwether swore them into the Army. A score of the crew attended some kind of religious service, perhaps worried about burning in the Hellfires, while the Captains and the rest finished last-minute preparations despite thunder, lightning, and deluge of rain. At last, to the cheering of the crowd assembled on shore, we boarded our vessels and shoved off. As we turned the bow of the keelboat into the stream, the Voyage of Discovery truly began.

CHAPTER THREE

"Feels good to stretch the old legs," Meriwether said, as we traveled the riverbank on that second morning of our journey. His fingers rumpled my ears. "Didn't think you were going to float the whole way, did you, Seaman? Will Clark's the better waterman, so he's the one to manage the keelboat while we continue our scientific studies onshore." My Master stooped to study a flower blooming in the shade of the trees. "Another unknown specimen! The President will be pleased." I'd hoped Meriwether might forget about impressing Jefferson, but now I wondered if the man would haunt us for the entire trip to the Pacific.

We'd journeyed only a few miles the first day, camping on the north side of the Missouri. The French-speaking crew members on the Red Pirogue, who weren't enlisted in the army, laughed and sang and occasionally swore as they'd muscled their way upriver, and our proximity to St. Charles that first night had proved too tempting to some of those *voyageurs*—several had returned to their homes for one last visit, but I knew they'd return, for they weren't about to miss this chance to see uncharted territory with a force considered large enough to discourage marauders. Those who manned the White Pirogue, business-like Corporal Warfington and the six soldiers slated to return to St. Louis that fall, had been too tired to go anywhere.

Our time on shore passed uneventfully, with my Master's long stride eating up the miles, halting so he could sketch an unfamiliar bird or inspect signs of excavation by an unseen creature with powerful claws and a distinctive odor, allowing the three vessels to keep up. I swam sometimes in the Missouri, its strong current a challenge that made me appreciate the labors of the rowers in the keelboat, which carried most of our cargo and all the men of the permanent Corps of Discovery except Drouillard and a big Kentuckian named Willard, who were scouting the other side of the river. In the shallower water, the men used poles to push the keelboat upriver or else strained on towing-ropes, their feet slipping in the mud.

As evening approached, Meriwether chose the night's campsite at the foot of a tall cliff, and soon the others joined us. Will Clark removed his hat to push a damp strand of hair off his forehead. "I calculate we covered eighteen miles. Not a bad day's accomplishment. The men worked hard—including the *voyageurs* who rejoined us this afternoon." Clark grinned. "Reckon they'll never show much spit and polish, but we'll be glad to have those Frenchies on our side if it comes to a fight."

Meriwether stopped writing in his journal and frowned. "You've spent time around Indians, Will, fighting and making peace, and you really are concerned about those reports we've received on the Sioux upriver."

"The Kickapoos I spoke with at our Wood River camp avoid

them like the plague." Clark shrugged. "Here so near the mouth we'll only meet up with civilized tribes, but it won't be long until we can expect to contact hostiles."

"Then we need to make sure we're prepared," Meriwether said. "Let's allow the men a good night's rest, but hold a surprise inspection tomorrow: find out if they're keeping their arms at the ready and in good condition. Seems I remember a red-haired lieutenant used just such tactics with his rifle company."

"And I seem to remember one young ensign who always kept his weapons in fine condition, even if he was a little the worse for wear after a night drinking and squiring the ladies." Clark nodded. "These fellows will make good soldiers, too, given a little time and seasoning. Speaking of seasoning, what's for supper?"

The answer arrived with a small party of the same Kickapoo Indians Clark had conversed with back at our winter camp. The young men had promised to supply us with fresh meat during the first leg of our journey, and that evening they delivered four deer. Meriwether was so pleased that he gave the Kickapoos two quarts of whiskey in exchange, which seemed like a good trade to me but was a lot more than the Kickapoos had expected, judging by the expression on their faces. I studied them carefully, sniffing and listening and watching, trying to figure out what made Indians different than white people. They dressed much like our men in flannel shirts and buckskin leggings, and some of them even spoke French, which the Captains didn't understand but was the same language the *voyageurs* preferred; I could make out the sense of their speech after my weeks with my first master and my time in New Orleans. Again the Kickapoos warned us about the Sioux. Perhaps when we met up with that tribe I'd figure out what made Indians different.

The next morning, after we'd traveled a short distance, the Captains decided to stop off and visit a cave called The Tavern that they'd heard about in St. Charles. Accompanied by York, young Shannon, and Sergeant Floyd, we explored an immense cavern, dim light filtering from an opening high above our heads. Indian drawings that Meriwether called pictographs covered most of one wall. Paintings that humans call "Art" had never impressed me, but these drawings showed important things like deer and other animals hunted for food without confusing matters by a lot of unnecessary background. The pictographs fascinated Meriwether, and he continued to follow the trail of drawings along a sort of tunnel, with the light growing stronger until we exited the far side of the cavern. Far, far below us, the Missouri glistened in the sunlight. The men looked like bugs on the shore, the boats like leaves. The pictographs continued, but the tunnel became merely a ledge, so I stepped carefully, for the footing looked and felt treacherous. I couldn't smell any humans or animals other than us, as if no one had traveled this route for many years. Whoever had drawn these figures had not returned. We'd intruded in a place we were not welcome, and I whined in warning.

"It's all right, Seaman, the going's too tricky for a critter with four feet," Meriwether said. "There are more drawings higher up this wall. You stay, and I'll be right down." He edged his way forward, and then began to climb. I knew perfectly well what stay meant and had no desire to proceed, but didn't want him going on without me. "This looks like a fine place to carve my name and the date on the wall." Meriwether drew his knife from its sheath. As his body twisted, one of his boots slipped, a piece of rock crumbled underfoot and gave way, and then my Master was sliding beyond the ledge and over the precipice. In desperation I crouched to lunge toward him, but before I could move, Meriwether's blade plunged into the wall and halted his descent. He clung there, at least three body-lengths below the ragged stone of the trail. "Stay, Seaman! If you move the whole thing may collapse. I can make it."

Remaining still was the hardest thing I'd ever done. Every muscle yearned to rescue my Master from this danger, but my training ran deep. Meriwether's boots found a purchase on the wall, while his free hand located a crack deep enough to allow him to withdraw the knife and then thrust it in higher. I quivered as he lifted his body, his boots seeking a new hold. Foot by foot, Meriwether continued to climb, angling slightly toward me. My legs trembled.

"We ought to be moving on!" Clark's voice echoed from somewhere in the cavern behind me.

"A minute!" Meriwether called back. "I'm preoccupied just now!"

Nobody could help my Master. If the others tried to rescue him, the ledge might give way and all of us would fall to our deaths on the rocks far below. I swallowed another whine. It was up to Meriwether alone.

His ascent continued. My Master's breathing grew labored. His blade dug deep, rasping into grit. Just a few more feet. Again his boot slipped, but the knife held. Higher, higher he climbed, until at last he reached the ledge ahead of me and lifted his body to safety. Now I barked in joy!

Meriwether crawled to me on his hands and knees, then

wrapped both arms around my neck. "Here I am, Seaman, safe and sound. You're a good and a wise dog. I was the foolish one." He let go of me and stood up. "Let's get out of this place. I've had enough adventure for today."

When we rejoined the others, who were on their way to find us, Meriwether related his near-escape. "We heard Seaman bark," said Sergeant Floyd, "and he rarely makes a sound."

"I could have fallen three hundred feet," Meriwether confessed. "Seaman sensed the danger. Some dogs have an uncanny knack that way."

Clark didn't speak until we'd nearly reached the boats and the men had gone ahead. Then he grasped my Master's arm. "That was nearly a disaster, Meri. If one of the men had behaved that foolishly, I'd assign him a punishment so unpleasant he wouldn't make the same mistake again. Lucky for you we're partners in this endeavor." He released his grip. "But please remember this is a military expedition and not a lark."

Meriwether looked as ashamed as a dog caught pissing in his master's parlor. "You're quite right. It won't happen again." Then he smiled. "They're wonderful pictographs, though. And Seaman behaved like a champion."

The water grew rougher that day, and we proceeded with caution, Meriwether content to travel in the boat. After we camped for the night, the men faced the surprise inspection of their arms and battle readiness with mixed results: those traveling aboard the keelboat and the soldiers from the White Pirogue fared far better than the *voyageurs* that manned the Red. "Wipe that foolish grin off your face!" Meriwether shouted at La Liberté, who slouched against a willow tree. "This is a military expedition, and whether you're enlisted or not you'll do what's best for the group!"

I noticed that Clark busied himself on the keelboat, hiding a smile.

Two rainy nights later we reached La Charette, the last tiny settlement of whites on the river. Though the French folk who lived there were poor, they pitied our bedraggled condition and sent milk and eggs, delivered by a trader who offered more of the familiar warnings about the Sioux. We'd survived a near-capsizing at a rapids called the Devil's Racegrounds, which had worried Meriwether greatly for he feared the loss of his scientific instruments, our supplies, and the written records of our expedition, and the following day, the Captains issued orders stressing alertness, organizing our enlisted men into three squads under Sergeants Ordway, Pryor, and my friend Floyd, who were also to keep journals of our voyage. Each day in turn, Ordway would issue hominy and lard, then salt pork and flour, followed by cornmeal and pork, then back to the hominy, unless our hunters brought in fresh meat. I tried hard not to think about the meals of the past, yet couldn't help remembering those lovely sausages at General Clark's home. Fortunately, Drouillard, Colter, and some of the others were crack shots, and we often feasted on fresh venison during the days that followed. One day York swam out to an island (I wanted to follow him, but wasn't sure I could trust Meriwether on his own) where the black man picked a batch of fresh greens and cooked them up for our supper. In the past I might have nudged them aside, but now they tasted delicious.

Instead of incessant rain we had to deal with the growing heat of June. Stifling air along the river drove the men to abandon their heavy shirts, and Meriwether doctored several severe cases of sunburn. Some of the men developed painful boils that oozed pus, Clark came down with an aching throat and head, and many of the soldiers suffered from runny bowels that Meriwether called dysentery. York and Sergeant Floyd helped my Master with the nursing; despite their immense size, York's hands were gentle, and Floyd never grew impatient with his comrades. I remained healthy, but mosquitoes plagued me all day long. We purchased three hundred pounds of bear grease from a trader traveling down the river and the men slathered themselves with it, but the grease didn't deter the bloodthirsty insects that swarmed about my head, drinking from the tender skin of my face. Fortunately, Meriwether had the foresight to purchase yards of cheesecloth that allowed us to sleep in our tents relatively unmolested.

When we purchased the bear grease, we also recruited an interpreter from the trading party. Pierre Dorion had fought with General Clark during the Revolutionary War, and then headed west to live among the Yankton Sioux, where he'd married and become fluent in that language as well as French and English. The Captains persuaded the old man to journey with us until we encountered the Yanktons. They hoped Dorion would in turn persuade a few of the chiefs to travel east to meet with President Jefferson.

Some nights, when a breeze and smoke from our fires combined to keep the wretched mosquitoes at bay, Pierre Cruzatte would play his fiddle. Cruzatte had lost an eye and had poor vision in the one that remained, but his fingers were nimble as they raced up and down the strings while he plied his bow. The noise sounded a lot like a wounded screech owl, but the soldiers relished it. After particularly difficult days the men each received a double ration of whiskey, and one night a number of them began to dance, cavorting about like children, arguing who would take the women's part while one of the *voyageurs* beat upon a tambourine. Breathing as hard as the dancers, Cruzatte paused between songs, mopping his forehead. He and another of the half-breeds, the man named Labiche, had enlisted for the whole journey and served aboard the keelboat, watching for submerged trees and keeping the vessel headed in the right direction. "Won't be long until we'll see real females again," he said, winking his single eye at George Shannon. "I been as far as the Nebraska country, and the farther north you go and the colder it gets, the warmer the women."

"Wild Indians, you mean?"

Colter grinned. "Ever had a girl, Georgie? Well, you're in for a treat. I hear those Mandan females know how to make a man—or even a lad—feel mighty welcome. They'll put some hair on that purty face."

Shannon's cheeks changed color the way some humans do, but he grinned back at Colter, and when the music started up again he took the man's part in a reel while Colter danced as his partner.

I'd figured the mosquitoes couldn't get much worse, but I was wrong. We breathed them and swallowed them. They darted into eyes and down ears, where their high-pitched whine rose to shrieking. Clouds of gnats joined in the torment, and ticks attached themselves to any available skin. When we camped for the evenings, Floyd and Shannon would help Meriwether sort through my heavy fur, which didn't deter the vermin but only provided camouflage. The swollen ticks sizzled when the men threw them in the fire.

Several of the privates, including the Irish carpenter Patrick Gass and a Kentuckian named Joe Whitehouse, had begun keeping written records as did the three sergeants, and some nights there were so many men scribbling on paper that they had to huddle around the inkwells taking turns with the quill pens. Why men couldn't just remember things I would never understand. But each species has its strengths and weaknesses, my grandmother had explained, and we should be tolerant of our differences.

Despite the pesky mosquitoes and the difficulties of traveling upstream, avoiding all the snags and keeping from being buried by the crumbling banks of the Missouri, things went along pretty smoothly until near the end of the month. I was making my rounds, marking the perimeter of our camp as I did at least twice each night, when I observed one of the privates hunched over the whiskey barrel. He was a Maryland man named Collins who'd already caused trouble by stealing a farmer's hog back near Fort Dubois. Collins was chortling as he straightened up and offered a mug to another man whose face was hidden from me. The private was supposed to be guarding the whiskey, not drinking it! It belonged to everybody in the party, and though the stuff smelled vile to me, the men said it helped them relax after a hard day on the river. Meriwether had calculated that with a ration for each man our 120 gallons would last for 104 days.

"What's going on over there?" Floyd's cousin Sergeant Pryor strode toward the two soldiers. "Are you drunk, Collins? Dammit, man, that doesn't belong to you!"

Soon the camp was in an uproar. The Captains had to restrain Colter and others who threatened to tear Collins and the other soldier, Hugh Hall, "limb from limb."

"We'll convene a court-martial at eleven o'clock in the morning," Clark announced. "All of you get on back to your blankets. I'll stand Collins' watch."

If the men hadn't been so tired from fighting the current all day, I don't believe they would have slept anymore that night, but eventually the outraged muttering quieted. The Captains, however, never did sleep, with Clark on sentry duty in place of Collins, and Meriwether restless in his bed. I guess my Master was concerned that discipline had broken down so soon, though I'm sure the muggy weather didn't help his mood. At last he rose, built up the fire, and wrote in his journal. I kept him company as long as I could stay awake, but must admit I dropped off before dawn.

At the appointed hour, with Sergeant Pryor presiding and four of the privates acting as a "jury of their peers," Collins pleaded "Not Guilty!" to "*getting drunk on his post this morning out of whiskey put under his charge as a sentinel, and for suffering Hugh Hall to draw whiskey out of the said barrel intended for the party.*" Of course the men found him guilty, since as Colter said, they'd "caught the bastard red-handed." Collins was sentenced to "*One hundred lashes, well laid on,*" while Hall, quick to plead "Guilty!" was to receive half as many. All the enlisted men carried out the sentence, some more forcefully than others. George Shannon looked pale and scared, while York, who didn't have to participate in the whipping, flinched as if he felt each blow on his own black skin. As the blood began to drip from Collins' naked back Meriwether's fingers quivered within my fur. I'd seen children thrashed for misbehaving, horses whipped for refusing to cross a stream, and a dog walloped by his master for stealing a haunch of venison, but nothing like this methodical flaying of men by their fellows. When Collins and then Hall gasped and cried out, I wanted to run away. Drouillard had disappeared into the woods after the first lash, but it was my duty to stay beside my Master. Later, when no one was watching, I tried licking the bloody welts on Hall's back, but he pushed me away. That afternoon Hall and Collins groaned as they plied their oars. When we camped that evening, Meriwether salved the backs of both men, but all through that night and the two that followed I heard them moaning in their beds.

Now we entered a land lush with ripening fruit and thick with deer, "as plenty as hogs about a farm," Clark described them. Every day grew hotter than the last. When I accompanied Meriwether on land my tongue hung out, and even riding in the keelboat I found myself panting. One morning we woke at daybreak to the firing of a cannon, with the Field brothers grinning outside our tent.

"Happy Fourth of July, sirs," said Joe, a year older than Reuben and usually the spokesman for the pair. "Thought we'd start the day off with a bang."

"Who told you to waste ammunition?" growled Clark, who looked like he was trying not to laugh. "Why don't you do something useful, like picking raspberries for breakfast?"

I tramped the riverbank with Shannon, Floyd, and the two brothers, who all filled their caps with the fruit, staining their fingers and faces and singing the same tune fat Tucker had repeated over and over on our trip to Pittsburgh, the one about "Yankee Doodle." The men were just beginning a new song when suddenly Joe bellowed.

"Goddamn snake bit me on the leg!"

The creature had already slithered away into the brush, but I smelled the rattler scent and knew Joe was in real danger. Reuben and Floyd grasped him under the arms and half-carried him back to camp, Joe's face already twisted in agony. While Meriwether searched among his medicines and the others were debating what to do, George Drouillard drew his skinning knife and slashed across the fang marks just above Joe's ankle, then clasped the leg and sucked, pausing only to spit blood and pungent venom into the dirt, again and again until Meriwether had brewed a poultice of bark from South America. It was hard to decide which smelled worse: snake poison or that poultice.

"Okay, Drouillard, you can leave off suckin' me dry," Joe managed to say, trying to smile but ending in a grimace. "Guess now we're blood brothers—" He gasped and choked a little as Meriwether applied the poultice. "Does that make me part Injun too?"

The hunter wiped his mouth on his sleeve. "Funny-lookin' Shawnee you'd be with those blond whiskers. My old auntie would pull every hair growing from your chin."

Joe winced as Meriwether wrapped the poultice tighter. "Think I'll wait 'til some other day for that. Meantime, where's those berries I picked?'

"I got 'em," said brother Reuben, "but they're pretty well crushed. Maybe we should just make 'em into wine?"

"We'll have to celebrate Independence Day later," said Clark, clapping Reuben on the shoulder. "Now it's time to eat breakfast and be on our way. Guess we'll let you off rowing, Mr. Field."

"Oooh, my big toe hurts," Colter sniveled, hobbling in a circle. "Think a skeeter bit me."

While Joe Field huddled under a cottonwood, drinking a

foul-smelling tea concocted by Meriwether, Clark and Reuben rigged a piece of canvas on the bow deck so the wounded man could catch the breeze and still stay out of the sun. By the time we shoved off, Joe insisted on walking to the keelboat on his own, but once he'd settled I saw him wipe tears from his cheeks. That night he turned down the double ration of whiskey issued in honor of the holiday. "But everybody remember it's owed me," he said, sprawling next to the river. I could tell Meriwether was worried, and the two of us sat beside Joe for hours, along with his brother, Floyd, and young Shannon, who hadn't scrubbed the berry stains from his face. Joe hardly stirred when they shot off the cannon at sunset, but his breathing grew more regular and Meriwether pronounced him out of danger. Only then did my Master down his own ration of whiskey. "Well, fellows, we'd better get some rest, too. I guess we'll never forget this first Fourth of July celebration West of the Mississippi."

That night, Meriwether writhed in his sleep, several times muttering, "I gave my word." Joe Field seemed much improved by morning except for his bruised leg, the ankle still so swollen he couldn't wear a moccasin, and Meriwether looked cheerful despite the dark circles under his eyes. Yet he watched the men more carefully than before, much like a hen after she's nearly lost a chick to a cat. It was almost impossible to keep an eye on so many humans, but I resolved to try harder. If we were to make it to the sea and back again, it would take all of us working together.

CHAPTER FOUR

Sometimes that river reminded me of a pudgy old collie, broad and sluggish after a big meal, but around the next bend it could turn skinny and quick as a Pittsburgh ratter. One morning the wind and rain grew so wild the men had to leap into the water to try and save the boats, those who couldn't swim holding on for dear life even though the Missouri was shallow enough at that point for them to touch bottom; fortunately they made effective ballast and the boat and its cargo were preserved.

Joe recovered from his snakebite, and a week after his brush with death he returned from hunting with brother Reuben, who'd slung his kill, a hefty doe, over his shoulders, while Joe clutched a furry bundle in his arms. "Look what I found, Cap'n Lewis—a friend fer Seaman." The bundle wiggled and a head popped up, its muzzle tied shut with a leather thong. "Didn't wanna be bit ag'in so soon. Little critter's purty wild. Found him pokin' 'round the carcass of this deer Reuben shot and decided to bring him back. Sure is scrawny—not doin' too good on his own."

The wolfling's eyes were white-rimmed with fear, but I could tell he would have munched his captor if he had the chance. After Joe set him on the ground, I approached slowly, hoping to comfort, not alarm, but the wolf pup growled and struggled to snap his jaws.

"He's a fierce little creature," said Meriwether, "and a different species, I believe, from eastern wolves. After supper I must get my notebook and take measurements."

The cooks had the evening meal prepared, so Joe tied the wolf pup to a cottonwood tree beside the river and cut the leather thong with his knife, leaving the creature in my care. "They mean you no harm," I said. "These are a good bunch of fellows—"

"Humans! You be slave—you be traitor!" His snarling was guttural and primitive, but I could understand the meaning. "My ma dead now, but she say humans forget they be animals too—kill without eating."

His words shocked me. I'd never conversed with a wild canine, though I'd often heard their howls and marked their scent, and seen pelts hanging on a fence or cut into winter clothing. Men called wolves "varmints," a threat to their livestock. I'd never thought much about our kinship.

"Here's your dinner, Seaman, and a dish for the little one," said Meriwether, setting a meal of fresh-cut venison on the ground. The wolfling snapped at my Master's hand but missed. Meriwether shook his head. "I don't think Joe will have much luck taming this pup, but I suppose we'll let him try. It's young yet. The Indians have dogs that look much like wolves, but it seems they remain half-wild, not true companions."

After Meriwether had returned to the others, the wolfling sniffed the meat, curling his lip. "I take no food from humans. I not be slave—like you and that man."

"We're partners," I told him. "I choose to be with him. When I was even younger than you, my grandmother explained to me how thousands of years ago, the first Dog made the choice to become Man's companion, and now—"

"If you go away, he let you? You be slave."

The wolf pup turned his back, worrying the rope with baby teeth too small to damage the thick hemp. I chewed my meal, sorry I couldn't make him understand. Wolves had made a different choice. In some ways we were alike, but we lived differently, saw the world through different eyes. Maybe that was the way white men differed from Indians.

After supper Joe retrieved the wolfling, who continued to try and bite him, and I went off for a stroll with Meriwether, accompanied by Sergeant Floyd and Private Shannon, who'd both become interested in the Captain's study of plants. They discovered a type of wild cherry unknown in the east (quite delicious for a fruit) and stayed out until almost dark adding samples of foliage to the pages of Meriwether's field notebook. By the time we returned, the light had grown too dim for study of the little wolf, and I retired with my Master to the tent shared with Clark, York, and also Drouillard on the nights when he wasn't out hunting. Once I heard a mournful howl and considered another attempt at befriending the wild creature, then decided to wait until morning. But before that night ended, the camp was once again roused by the sergeant on duty. This time it was Ordway who had discovered a member of his squad, Private Willard, asleep while serving as a sentinel.

"What if we were in Sioux territory?" Clark said, speaking privately with Meriwether. "We could all be scalped without warning, the mission ended almost before it's begun."

"You're right." My Master's face looked like stone in the moonlight. "We'll have to try him tomorrow by military law. This time it's you and I who must serve as officials of the court. Willard's been a good man—no trouble at Wood River, strong, and talented as a blacksmith. But this is a serious offense."

My Master was agitated during much of the night, and I got worried. Had his malaria returned? Or sometimes Meriwether's bowels rebelled after he sampled a newly-discovered plant; I could nearly always tell by the smell when a weed wouldn't agree with me, but my Master would taste anything. Finally, after a deep sigh, Meriwether settled into sleep.

At dawn I delivered a hunk of deer liver I'd chewed to a pulp to the wolfling. He wouldn't even lift his head to smell the meat. The Captains had already planned to spend a day of rest at this spot, so Meriwether used the morning to make calculations and scribble in his journal, while Joe and Reuben dragged the wolf pup around by the rope, trying to tempt the wild thing with choice tidbits and kind words. He only growled at them and bared needle teeth. Though I would have enjoyed a ramble in the surrounding countryside with Shannon and Floyd or the visit to an Indian mound with Clark and some of the others, my Master seemed so troubled that I remained within reach. Often his left hand would bury itself in my fur, kneading the loose flesh around my neck.

During the noon meal, I heard Sergeant Pryor talking to Patrick Gass, and caught the words: "punishable by death." Surely they wouldn't kill Alexander Willard, that big quiet man with the strong hands, lonesome for his two sisters back home yet eager to journey to the Western Sea? I felt a shiver all the way to my tail, even though the day was hot and sultry.

When Sergeant Ordway presented his evidence, accusing Willard of *"lying down and sleeping on his post whilst a sentinel,"* the Private bit his lip until it bled, then answered, "Guilty of lying down but not of going to sleep." As the Captains deliberated, the enlisted men kept their distance without any conversation passing between them. The sky had clouded, and I could hear thunder in the distance.

"The Court," Meriwether read, *"after duly considering the evidence, are of the opinion that the prisoner Alexander Willard is guilty of every part of the charge exhibited against him. It being a breach of the Rules of War, as well as tending to the probable destruction of the party, do sentence him to receive One Hundred Lashes on his bare back at four different times in equal proportion."*

"The punishment will commence this evening at sunset," Clark said, "and continue to be inflicted by the Guard every evening until completed."

Willard never uttered a sound during his whipping. Afterwards, even though the men had enjoyed a rare day free from rowing against the current, no one felt like singing or joking, and Cruzatte's fiddle never left its case. I visited the wolfling, tied once again under the cottonwood tree, figuring he'd be terrified by the punishment he'd witnessed, but he said, "Man broke pack law. Wolf leader kill so pack survive."

A few hours past dark, soon after it began to rain, I left the tent, but instead of heading into the woods as I'd planned, I gnawed the rope until the wolfling was free. He stared into my eyes for just an instant, then loped away and vanished into the night.

CHAPTER FIVE

Back on the Missouri, we almost lost the keelboat when a gale drove it onto a sandbar, dashing waves over the windward side. As soon as the storm allowed, we continued, the men straining at their oars to make forward progress, when suddenly the wind died and the water grew calm as a pond. Soon we reached the mouth of the Platte River, its rapid current bearing a great quantity of sand. The Captains chose to paddle up in the White Pirogue with a few of the men. We watched for Indian sign, since the Otos reportedly lived on one side and Pawnees on the other, but the only scent along the Platte was old, with soggy ashes in the fire circles. That afternoon the Captains dispatched Drouillard, the most expert hand talker, and old Cruzatte, also half-Indian, out onto the prairie in search of tribesmen, sending along several twists of tobacco called carrots as peace offerings. Many of our own men valued tobacco almost as much as whiskey, with some, like Clark and Drouillard and the *voyageurs*, fondest of smoking it in a pipe, while others, including the Field brothers, Ordway, and Patrick Gass, preferred to chew the stuff. Gass seemed to enjoy spitting more than chewing and I was careful to stay out of his way.

One afternoon we raised sail and scooted up the Missouri on a gentle breeze, but by evening it had stilled again and the mosquitoes attacked in force. I didn't understand why they swarmed around some of the men (and me) and left others alone. By dark Shannon's eyes had swollen nearly shut.

Next day it was back to rowing, and the slow pace allowed Goodrich, a Massachusetts man who was our canniest fisher-man, the chance to hook a string of plump, whiskery catfish. The Captains had just settled down to a tasty evening meal when Drouillard and Cruzatte rode in with a mounted Indian. The man was of the Missouri tribe, but a terrible disease called smallpox had killed off almost all of them, so now he lived with the Otos. He approved of the fried catfish, eating with relish and wiping greasy fingers on his leggings, which smelled delicious. He, in turn, seemed to find me quite fascinating, and when Meriwether had me bow and then roll over the man slapped his thighs and laughed deep in his belly. "Good, good!" he said, which was about the extent of his English, used to de-scribe everything he saw and tasted. One of the *voyageurs*, La Liberté, could speak Oto, for he'd lived with the tribe for a time, and after the meal the Captains sent him off with the Indian with instructions to invite the chiefs for a council. I suppose it made practical sense, but La Liberté wasn't the man I'd have chosen for an important task, since he was lazy and didn't bother to hide his lack of interest in our mission.

We stayed put, hoping for a parley with the Indians. On both sides of the river open prairie spread out in every direction, wave after wave of grass, and my Master was as excited as a youngster about all the new plants and animals. When Joe Field killed a peculiar-looking creature and delivered it to camp, Meriwether was at it immediately with his instruments. I'd scented one of these fellows before at the mouth of a large tunnel.

"Body like a beaver, head like a dog," Clark said, though the pointed snout wasn't anything like my own broad muzzle. "Tail and hair like a ground hog."

"And inside, his organs resemble those of a domestic hog—but look at these!" Meriwether waved the striped creature's front paw, armed with claws stout enough to do serious damage. "I believe he's a small, short-legged member of the bear species. I'll stuff him today and send him back to President Jefferson!"

For the rest of the day, Meriwether refused to leave the cabin of the keelboat, intent on "preserving the specimen." I'd have preferred to taste the thing, but it was easy enough to be philosophical since the Field brothers began hauling in wild geese and several large turkeys and I was assigned to dispose of their innards. Since that first day of August also marked Captain Clark's thirty-fourth birthday, the evening's dinner was almost as tasty as that long-ago feast at the home of his brother: venison, elk, and even succulent beavertail—which Meriwether loved—topped off with a dessert of cherries, plums, raspberries, currants and grapes for the humans. (I was too full for even a bite of fruit.)

That afternoon a small party of Oto and Missouri Indians rode in with an interpreter and pitched camp nearby. The Captains sent fresh meat, cornmeal, and an invitation to attend a council the following day. The Otos, who were mostly some sort of minor chiefs, responded by sending us watermelons they'd grown, which the men devoured with enthusiasm but I found bland. Though the Indians were few in number, Clark made sure that "every man was on his guard and ready for any thing." I patrolled the camp, sniffing for intruders. La Liberté was nowhere to be found.

The Captains had named our camp "Council Bluff" and borrowed the keelboat's mainsail to set up an awning on the grass above the river. I liked these Indians, especially the youngest, a smiley fellow named Hospitality, and they all listened politely as Meriwether, wearing his full-dress uniform and cocked hat, spoke for a long time, calling them the "Children of the Great Chief of the seventeen great nations of America," who was really President Jefferson. A couple of the chiefs made their own speeches, saying they were happy to find a father they could depend on, and all the Indians smoked tobacco with the Captains, which Clark seemed to enjoy and Meriwether managed to tolerate without coughing. It was all very peaceful, and when we went our separate ways I heard Shannon saying, "These wild Indians seem like pretty easy-going fellows to me." But Dorion, the old man who had lived with the Yankton Sioux, only smiled.

Every day we moved upriver. Moses Reed said he'd left his knife at Council Bluff and doubled back to find it. When he didn't return, speculation arose whether he and La Liberté had lost their way or deserted. Most all the men were dedicated to the Captains now, and loyal to the expedition, but not La Liberté or surly Moses Reed. Drouillard and three privates were sent after the missing men, with instructions to bring them back—peaceably if they could, or else put them to death. That night in our tent, the partners spoke in low voices.

"I figure the deserters will cooperate once they're face-to-face with Drouillard's rifle," Clark said, blowing out the light. "But more than ever, we must keep discipline. All our lives may depend upon it. Go to sleep, Meri, and hope for the best."

More sandbars, dead snags, mosquitoes, rattlers. Then the search party returned with Moses Reed, eight Indians, and the Otos' interpreter. They had also caught La Liberté, but he'd tricked them and escaped. As soon as the Captains greeted the Oto and Missouri chiefs, including their head man Little Thief, they proceeded with Reed's trial. The prisoner confessed to deserting and stealing an Army rifle, asking the Captains for leniency. While the Captains conferred, the chiefs waited with the rest of us. Even with the morale of the whole expedition at stake, part of me wished Reed had made good his escape. I didn't want his blood on my Master's hands, keeping him awake nights. Finally Clark announced the sentence: Reed would run the gauntlet four times, and "*each man armed with nine switches shall punish him, amounting to five hundred lashes, well-laid on. In addition, he is expelled from the permanent party.*"

When Cruzatte, who spoke some Oto, explained the sentence to the chiefs, their eyes widened and they began to speak so rapidly that the half-breed threw up his hands in despair. Little Thief hurried to Meriwether's side and grasped his arm. "He wants you to pardon Reed," Cruzatte explained.

"Indians might use that kind of treatment on an enemy," Drouillard told the Captains, "but not one of their own. They never strike their children, and they aren't going to understand this."

"You'll have to make them understand," Clark said. "This man is a deserter from the United States Army."

Drouillard didn't speak for a bit. He'd grown up with his mother's Shawnee people, and though he spoke English better than many of the soldiers, who all admired his hunting ability, Drouillard kept some distance between himself and the others, except from Cruzatte, who was also half-Indian. "I'll try my best," he said at last.

It took awhile, but the chiefs eventually shrugged their shoulders and the sentence was carried out, though young Hospitality looked as if he wanted to cry too, when Reed began to whimper under the blows. I held my ground, determined not to cower, but my skin shuddered. All of us were glad when it was finished, and the Indians returned to their own camp, promising to rejoin us the next morning for another council.

A few hours later, the camp's mood changed, for it was Meriwether's thirtieth birthday and the Captains had issued an extra ration of whiskey. Cruzatte agreed to play his fiddle, and most of the men danced around the campfire, glad to banish the events of the day, though Drouillard took his rifle and strode onto the prairie. Floyd, who hadn't been himself for several days, sat with his back against a tree, not drinking, his face drawn. Sometimes he would clasp his belly, closing his eyes, and when Meriwether left the fire to write in his journal I curled up beside the young sergeant.

"You're a grand dog, Seaman," Floyd murmured. "I had a little foxhound bitch at home, half your size, with a nose that wouldn't quit. Hope my kid brother is taking good care of her." He stroked my back, and then doubled over. Maybe he needed to take one of Rush's Thunderbolts. "Think I'll crawl into my blanket now."

When Floyd stood up, he staggered, and Shannon left off dancing to rush to his side. "You're ill! Let me call Cap'n Lewis."

"All right," Floyd said. "Maybe he needs to bleed me."

Clark held Floyd's arm steady as Meriwether drew the tool called a lancet across Floyd's flesh, letting the blood flow freely and catching it in a dish. "I suspect a bad case of bilious colic," my Master said. He patted Floyd on the shoulder. "No duty for you, Sergeant. You're to head right to your blanket and stay there."

After Shannon and Floyd's cousin Nat Pryor helped the patient off to bed, Clark said, "Not much of a birthday for you, Meri. Did you ever imagine this was how you'd spend your thirtieth?"

"I never thought of Floyd being sick, of course, nor the business with Reed... But I've wanted this adventure for such a long time. Ever since I applied to lead an expedition West eleven years ago—wasn't I the cocky nineteen-year-old, thinking I could lead men across the continent!" Meriwether fondled my ears. "Thank God The President saw fit to have me train with the best men in the sciences, even if for a short time, and allowed me to choose the best soldier in America as my partner."

"We make a good team," Clark said. "I believe the rest of the men will see this through to the end. In most cases, we chose well."

Meriwether nodded. "Seaman and I need a walk before turning in."

The men were still celebrating around the fire as we ambled along the river, Cruzatte's fiddle squealing behind us, frogs chorusing ahead, and mosquitoes mercifully absent. I scented Drouillard's trail off to the south. Through the trees drifted smoke from the fires of the Oto and Missouri chiefs. Cruzatte had described the farms of the Otos, where they grew watermelons and squash, beans and corn, in addition to hunting deer and buffalo. They'd traded with white men for years, but Meriwether said that settlers would be moving west, either sooner or later, planting crops of their own and building houses. The Otos had opened their land to the Missouris after the smallpox epidemic, but how would they feel about sharing with white families?

"We're very solemn tonight," Meriwether said, his hand resting on my shoulder. "I suppose I've always found birthdays a time for reflection, a chance to look back at what I've accomplished over the past year and wonder what lies ahead for the next twelve months, where we'll all end up.... Sometimes I feel like time is my enemy, that I won't have a chance to achieve my dreams."

Was Floyd's illness making Meriwether gloomy? I could also smell the ration of whiskey on his breath, which didn't make my Master giddy and loud, the way it did most of the men, but turned him inward instead. Most of the time Meriwether seemed happy, absorbed in exploring the new countryside, in recording each newly-discovered plant or animal. But sometimes he disappeared into the dark, to a place inside him where I couldn't follow.

"Time to head back, Seaman. Another big day tomorrow. The President wants all the Indians we meet to accept American influence peacefully. By the time we reach the coast, I imagine I'll have my speech down pat, but better go over my notes again. Wouldn't do to stammer, even if they don't understand the words."

The chiefs showed up for breakfast. Humans set great store by finery, so all our men wore their uniforms, but Chief Big Horse wore nothing at all. Drouillard explained that the chief was trying to show how poor and needy he was. After the meal, everyone except Floyd and York, who tended the ailing sergeant, gathered near the keelboat, where the striped flag of the United States rippled in the breeze as the Captains escorted the chiefs to places of honor under the awning made from the mainsail. Then Meriwether began his "Great Father" speech, an expanded version of the one he'd given last time, talking a lot about the Otos making peace with the Omaha Indians instead of fighting them. When my Master hung a silver medal on a ribbon around Little Thief's neck, the chief grinned. The medal showed a picture of President Jefferson on one side and two clasped hands on the other. Little Thief and the other Indians also received a canister of powder, fifty balls of shot, and a bottle of whiskey. Then Meriwether demonstrated the use of magnets—which are a lot more powerful than they look—showed the Indians a compass, and shot off his treasured air gun, which seemed to impress the Otos, though I was pretty sure they would have preferred more presents. But Little Thief agreed to visit Washington in the spring and the Captains seemed satisfied with the council. Everyone was in a fine mood after the chiefs had ridden away, until we returned to camp and found Sergeant Floyd delirious.

"I been keepin' him cool," York said, "an' tryin' to get him to drink the medicine, but he's awful sick, like a horse when his gut's all twisted inside."

The Captains treated Floyd all that night, with Shannon, Nat Pryor, and York always nearby to help and many of the men coming to inquire if there was anything they could do. Meriwether kept ransacking his chest of medicines as if looking again might reveal something he'd missed, but Floyd couldn't keep anything down, not even water. When we all boarded the keelboat the next day, York carried the young sergeant on-board. The Captains had made a bed for him in the cabin, but Floyd said he preferred to remain outside where he could feel the breeze off the water. He seemed to rally for an hour or so as we worked our way upstream, but then began groaning, until he grew motionless.

"His pulse is so weak I'm afraid to bleed him again," Meriwether said. "I keep wondering what Dr. Rush in Philadelphia would do, but I can think of nothing more. This is beyond my skill."

"It's all right." Floyd's voice was weak but very calm. "Captain Clark, I am going away. I want you to write me a letter." He took a deep breath, exhaled very slowly, and then his face relaxed. He looked so young, the age of the oldest of the O'Connor boys, sleeping safe in Pittsburgh.

We buried Sergeant Charles Floyd on a bluff above a small river, with a cedar post to mark his grave carved with his name and the date: August 20, 1804. The Captains each spoke, saying we had lost a brother soldier, a man of much merit. They named the bluff and river after Floyd.

Then we proceeded on.

CHAPTER SIX

Two days upriver, the men elected Patrick Gass as sergeant in the place of my friend Floyd. The squad needed a leader and Gass was an experienced soldier who'd fought Indians, who worked hard and got along well with the soldiers and both Captains. But the Irish carpenter was no favorite of mine, since he had no use for me, never offering a pat or a tidbit, and often eyed York with suspicion, as if the black man were plotting trouble and it was up to the Irishman to prevent it. The rest of the permanent party had learned to value York's amazing physical strength and good nature, but those characteristics only seemed to irritate Gass. Once he'd come upon York sorting through our goods and demanded, "What are you about?"

"Fetchin' some powder for Cap'n Clark," York had replied.

"See that you give it to him straightaway when you find it," Gass had growled. "I don't approve of darkies havin' to do with guns."

Though Drouillard was our most consistent hunter, it was Joe Field who raced into camp the next day, hollering that he'd shot the first buffalo. Meriwether could hardly contain himself, detailing a dozen men to accompany him to the kill and haul the body back—after he completed his initial observations and measurements, of course. When we reached the carcass it was all I could do to keep from tearing into that great mound of flesh, especially after Meriwether cut into the belly and I scented the life-giving contents of its innards. I doubt any dog of the Newfoundland breed had ever smelled anything quite so tantalizing (barring the fragrance of a bitch in season) and I began to drool so freely that the hair on my chest grew wet and Joe offered me the sleeve of his shirt to wipe my jowls. It was good to hear everyone laugh again, even at my expense. That evening's meal was one I can still taste in memory, and I pitied all the poor Eastern dogs who would never taste the hump of a buffalo.

Meriwether, however, declined more than a bite or two of the meat, for he said he was beginning to feel unwell, and even before I'd downed my fill he decided to lie down in the tent. In his scientific zeal, my Master had begun a collection of what he called "minerals," and that day he'd encountered an intriguing substance. "I was convinced the stuff was either cobalt or arsenic," he explained to Clark, who hovered over him, "so I decided to taste it to make my determination. I suppose I also breathed its fumes during the collecting process." Meriwether looked pale and wild-eyed. "Now we know that it's arsenic. If you'll excuse me—" He scurried from the tent and spewed the contents of his stomach into the bushes. Luckily he recovered promptly.

Soon George Shannon had the chance to be camp hero, for one evening he brought down the largest elk we'd yet encountered with a lucky shot he might never duplicate. Colter insisted Shannon eat the creature's heart raw, but after a few bites the young private slipped the rest to me, which I devoured with zest. Since Shannon had brought down such a prize, Captain Clark appointed him to stay with Drouillard and locate the two horses that had strayed from camp, and then catch the keelboat upriver. The next morning Shannon waved goodbye as the boats glided from the shore, smiling big because he didn't have to row against the strong wind and the current.

Hoping it would get the attention of the Sioux, the Captains lit a prairie fire, and in the afternoon a young Indian swam out to the Red Pirogue. Dorion was able to talk to the boy, who turned out to be an Omaha, and we pulled into the bank to meet two of his friends. They said they could lead us to a Yankton Sioux village, so the Captains dispatched Dorion, Nat Pryor, and one of the *voyageurs* to go with the Indians and let the Sioux know we would meet them at a place called Calumet Bluff. There we set up a fine camp, and soon Drouillard tramped in looking hot and dusty. "I don't suppose Shannon's gotten here ahead of me? I lost the trail of the bay gelding when he crossed the river, and Shannon insisted on following the other by himself. Now all three of them are who-knows-where. If that young fellow's trying to hide his trail, he's doing a damn good job—but I fear he's just plain lost."

"You look worn-out, Drouillard, sit down and have a bite to eat with us," Meriwether said.

"He's not really... what you'd call a first-rate hunter."

Clark nodded. "At least there's no fear the lad's deserted. Hopefully he won't stumble upon the Indians before we do. We'll send a couple of men out to look for the private, but we need you in camp in case the Sioux contact us before Dorion returns."

Gass's squad worked with the Frenchmen to repair damage to the Red Pirogue while the rest of the men hunted and jerked meat, all the while watching for signs of Shannon or the Sioux. I could have followed the missing man's scent, but what if the Indians showed up while I was gone and Meriwether needed me? We were all getting worried that Shannon had been injured.

"Prob'ly shot hisself in the foot," Colter said.

The following day, the little search party returned without the young private, but they'd figured out from his tracks that Shannon had managed to locate the horses and had gotten ahead of us, riding hard because he thought he was behind.

"Let me go," Colter volunteered. "By now the pilgrim's all turned around and mighty hungry, so I'll load up some vittles and hustle after 'im."

"All right," Meriwether agreed. "I'd send Seaman with you, but with Shannon on horseback and this heat... Well, good luck, Colter, and be careful. We don't want to lose you, too."

I felt like hiding my head under my paws. The sun had overpowered me during an exploration of a high hill called Spirit Mound that the Indians claimed was haunted by eighteen-inch-high devils, and though the Captains hadn't run into any danger, only swirling flocks of birds and some bats, I felt ashamed that I'd been sent back to the river to recuperate. Now my friend Shannon was missing, hungry and alone, and I was considered unfit to help find him.

Meriwether kept busy at his journal, but often he would gaze off in one direction or another. "Reed in disgrace, Floyd dead—now Shannon's gone and Colter off after him. That's close to ten percent of our fighting strength, and we find ourselves in Sioux country." He scratched behind my ear. "I don't like it, Seaman. The President puts more importance on our dealings with the Sioux than with any other tribe. They control the river." Jefferson again: he was still on our trail. "America needs open trade routes. We can't let France and England keep us bottled up along the coast. Our destiny is far greater—I've known that for years. For awhile I thought we'd have to fight Napoleon to keep New Orleans open, ally ourselves with the damn British. Now the Louisiana Territory is ours, but it's just on paper. We have to prove ourselves." Meriwether sighed and picked up his pen, scribbling away on paper of his own, while I lay there panting in the heat, no use to anybody.

Late that afternoon I wandered down to the river for a drink just as Nat Pryor and Dorion appeared across the water accompanied by a party of Indians. There had to be twice as many of them as there were of us and I let out a warning that brought my Master from his tent in a hurry. Sergeant Pryor waved his hand and everything looked peaceable, so Clark dispatched the repaired Red Pirogue, which returned with the sergeant, old Pierre Dorion, and a young man who looked a lot like him and turned out to be his son, a trader with the Yanktons and half-Sioux himself.

"There's five chiefs and close to seventy warriors," Pryor reported, "all real friendly. They got some idea I was a kind of chief, too, so they started carryin' me into their camp on a buffalo robe like I was a king or somethin'. The village is real handsome, with painted hides stretched over poles, tall an' big enough around to hold more than a dozen people."

"Tipis!" Meriwether said. "You may be the first American to see a real Plains Indian tipi, Sergeant Pryor. Be sure to report all about it in your journal."

"Yes, sir. These sure are stout, good-looking fellows. They fixed us a fine feast of a fat—" he glanced over at me, and then looked away— "of dog. An' they're ready to parley."

I felt dizzy. I'd thought Old Bay was just teasing about Indians eating dog.

"It's good to meet you, young Dorion," Captain Clark was saying. "Let me get together some tobacco and a couple kettles full of corn for you to take back to add to their evening meal, with an invitation to join us tomorrow for a meeting."

In the morning the Captains ordered dress uniforms, the striped flag, even the firing of the swivel gun. The Yanktons wore their best gear, too, with plenty of feathers and fringe, led by four warriors wearing nothing but paint who were playing flutes or singing and shaking rattles made out of deer hooves. The Indians all sat down, listened to Meriwether's speech telling them they were the children of President Jefferson, their new father, then told Dorion they would respond the next morning. I could tell Meriwether wanted to get on with business but he stayed patient, presenting medals and loading one of the chiefs up with a fancy coat, cocked hat, and American flag. After the council was officially over for the day, the young warriors showed off their shooting with bows and arrows. Then Meriwether ran me through my tricks, which seemed to please the Yanktons, though I wondered if they were deciding whether I would taste better boiled or roasted. At dusk the men built three bonfires and the male Indians danced around, telling by their movements what great warriors they were. The women didn't dance, only made high-pitched trilling noises to urge on their men. At Dorion's suggestion, our fellows tossed out presents of tobacco, knives, and bells.

In the morning it was the Siouxs' turn to speak. The chief wore his new hat. He said the Indians were poor, had no ammunition for guns or nice clothes for their women. But he agreed that if Mr. Dorion accompanied him, he would go to Washington in the spring, which made Meriwether happy. The other Yanktons weren't flashy speakers, but they managed to get across the fact that they wanted powder and lead and maybe some whiskey, and the last chief warned the Captains that the Tetons up the river might not be such good listeners. So even though we'd survived our first tribe of Sioux, the real danger still lay ahead. When the Yanktons crossed the river to their own camp, the partners seemed pleased, but stayed up so late talking strategy that I struggled to keep my eyes open.

From all the reports the Captains had assembled, they figured we had about two hundred and fifty miles before meeting up with the next band of Sioux, the Tetons about whom we'd received so many warnings. At least we had a bit of breathing space and plenty to eat in the meantime. It was September, and we'd entered rolling terrain covered by short grass, with fewer trees along the river. Meriwether said it looked like "a beautiful bowling-green in fine order"—whatever that was. The hunters had no trouble bringing down elk and deer, so we devoured our fill. Buffalo became a common sight, and I yearned to eat another. All around the outskirts of the herds lurked wolves, which Meriwether called *"faithful shepherds, ready to take care of the wounded and maimed."* I hoped the young

wolfling had rejoined his kindred. We also spied a horned animal that looked like a cross between a goat and a deer, so fleet
of foot I abandoned chase after a few strides.

One day I accompanied the Captains onto a knoll where
we found ourselves surrounded by a village of small burrowing
creatures that disappeared down holes, only to pop their heads
up elsewhere, chattering to each other in voices that sounded
like barking to the men. I could tell they certainly weren't canines, but the *voyageurs* called them "little dogs." Meriwether
determined to capture one for President Jefferson, and soon
most of the men were spread out with shovels, trying to dig
their way into a burrow. I chose a spot of my own and dirt flew
from under my paws, but none of us got even close: the men
could tell by measuring with a stick, while my nose told me
that even buried to my hindquarters I had a long way to go.
The day had turned hot and the men were ready to abandon
the hunt for a "prairie dog," as Sergeant Ordway insisted on
calling them, but Meriwether wasn't about to quit. He ordered
the men to fill all our kettles and buckets with water and carry
them to the knoll, which they did without too much grum-
bling, then pour bucket after bucket down one tunnel. When
its inhabitant emerged, looking a bit soggy, Ordway killed it
with his shovel and Meriwether carried the animal back to the
keelboat in triumph. "When we get closer to Fort Mandan we'll
take a live specimen and ship him back to Washington for The
President!"

Next Meriwether decided to attempt his first buffalo. We
walked so far across the prairie that I began to wonder if I'd
ever taste water again. Then I caught scent, a little like cow,
only wild and magnificently pungent. My Master could tell by

the prick of my ears that we were onto something. "Good fellow, Seaman!" he whispered. "Take it slow and you'll be eating hump tonight."

We crept up the hillside. When we peered over the crest, hundreds of the beasts spread out below us: shaggy big bulls, horned cows and their calves, so much meat on the hoof that I began to tremble and would have bolted forward, but Meriwether placed a hand on my head. "Steady now." He raised his rifle, sighted, and pulled the trigger. The animals nearby started at the noise and smoke and thundered a short distance away, but a young bull had fallen to the ground and didn't move. Meriwether whooped. "Got him right between the eyes! That's why I wanted Harpers Ferry rifles!"

He was so excited we ran most of the way back to camp, where I was glad to refresh myself in the river, and some of the men followed us back to the kill, congratulating their Captain on his shooting. Normally he behaved a bit formally with the soldiers, but that day he seemed like one of a gang of boys (not unlike a litter of puppies), laughing and joking with the others as they butchered the carcass, even biting a hunk of the raw heart so the blood ran down his chin.

Meriwether killed another buffalo the next day, and Clark shot one, too, before handing his rifle to York. "Your turn. Not much different from hunting squirrels back home."

York grinned and stepped forward, sighting on the biggest bull, but shook his head. "Need somethin' tender. That ol' feller would wear out a whole set o' teeth." He chose another target, smaller and farther away, his movements sure, and made a clean drop. Later York shot a second buffalo, and that night he danced around the fire like one of the Yankton warriors, acting out his kills while the men cheered him on, all but Sergeant Gass, who spat tobacco juice into the dirt.

A couple afternoons farther, the hot wind carried a familiar scent downriver, one I hadn't smelled for three weeks and feared I never would again. George Shannon stood on the bank, looking like a ragged scarecrow. I sprang from the keelboat, and he waded into the water to meet me, laughing and crying at the same time. Shannon had his face in order by the time the Captains and men landed the boats, but he looked changed, the last baby-fat gone and his cheeks hollow.

"Feared you was gone for good!" Colter said. "I headed after you with food but couldn't catch up."

"Food—you mean <u>meat</u>? I nearly starved to death, ran out of balls, killed one rabbit by shooting a stick, but otherwise I just ate grapes for the last two weeks."

"You look it," Meriwether said. "Welcome back, private. Climb aboard and we'll start fattening you up."

"I did bring back one of the horses, sir. He's grazing just over the bluff. If somebody hadn't gotten here soon, though, I would have eaten him."

Colter shook his head. "Pilgrim, how a man could nearly starve in this land o' plenty is a real puzzlement!" He thumped Shannon on the back, nearly knocking him down. "You're nothin' but a sack o' bones. Reckon we better give you some more shootin' lessons."

Clark actually killed one of the fleet-footed goat-deer a few days later, and Meriwether was in his glory, studying its forked horns, measuring its cloven hooves, then stuffing the creature to send back to Washington, while I enjoyed all the entrails. That same afternoon Private Shields brought in another treasure for the Captain: the body of a white-tailed jackrabbit, unlike anything encountered in the East, also very tasty. With food so plentiful, it wasn't long before Shannon looked like himself again, though I noticed he didn't stray far from the keelboat.

In addition to a plague of mosquitoes, birds of an unfamiliar variety began to frequent our evening camps, quick to steal any meat left unattended. The black-and-white poachers that my Master called magpies annoyed me with their raucous voices and thieving ways, but they were careful to stay out of my reach. After a couple of tries, Meriwether brought one down, but his attempts to stuff it failed miserably. He vowed to take one alive for The President. Its squawking would serve Jefferson right for always worrying my Master. Another creature we heard often, yet rarely saw, smaller, quick-moving relations of the long-legged wolves we observed near the buffalo herds. These "prairie wolves," as the men chose to call them, yapped and yammered half the night, voices shrill and less understandable than those of their larger cousins. I never heard them say anything of interest, but perhaps their intelligence failed in the translation. Naturally the first one shot became an addition to Meriwether's growing collection of preserved creatures, bones, and skins, and I looked forward to the day when we could ship all those specimens off to Washington and clear space in the boat. For a brief time, we also had a live beaver aboard, an active little fellow with a powerful scent. Drouillard had found it wandering the riverbank and planned to keep it as a pet, but while the interpreter was off hunting one day the baby beaver escaped and the *voyageurs* caught and ate him. They offered me a scrap of the tail, which is almost as tasty as buffalo hump.

The weather grew windy, and some days we were able to raise the sails and scoot upriver, which was nice for the men, who didn't have to row or pole the boat but also meant we were getting closer to the Teton Sioux that much faster. One night we set up camp on a sandbar. Meriwether had chosen to sleep onboard the keelboat in order to work late on his specimens, so I made myself comfortable on the moonlit deck, letting the rocking motion of the water lull me to sleep. Sometime in the middle of the night a lurching woke me: the sharp sandbanks on both sides were peeling away, the boats in danger of over-turning as sections of bank collapsed and crashed into the river, water churning and straining the keelboat against its tow rope. I bounded to the cabin, but Meriwether was already on his feet, shouting a warning to the men on shore. They re-acted with astonishing speed, getting themselves and the gear aboard, and we untied and pushed off just moments before the former camp disappeared in a torrent of sand and clay. After that close call, we found another location, and every evening following I made certain we had not placed ourselves in that kind of danger again.

I'd survived the collapsing sandbank only to discover a new nemesis: prickly pear. As long as we stayed right along the riv-er we remained clear of the dastardly vegetation, but now the high plains that surrounded us sprouted with this new kind of cactus perfectly designed for lodging in my paws. Of course I couldn't bear to be left behind when Meriwether chose to tramp the prairie, but no matter how hard I tried to avoid them the sharp spines managed to pierce tender places. Each step drove them deeper. Shannon would help Meriwether remove my spines before they could fester, but the next day often meant another dose. Then Drouillard rigged me some buffalo-hide moccasins for which I was eternally grateful. They didn't deflect everything, though, and the men who hunted also suffered. We'd advanced far enough that the Tetons might appear any moment, and after we discovered several abandoned campsites Meriwether decided to remain aboard thereafter (fortunately for my poor paws).

One evening, after a twenty-mile day, we located a grove of cottonwoods and began to assemble camp. Some set up tents, the three cooks unloaded their gear, and others of us gathered firewood, which was one of my favorite jobs, though I could only manage one stick at a time. My mouth full of a particular-ly large branch, I could only whuff when I spotted three young Indians swimming across the river from the opposite side. But Drouillard, always alert, had spied them, too, and he notified the Captains and accompanied them to the water's edge. With Dorion left behind among the Yanktons and Cruzatte knowing only a little bit of Sioux, communication was primarily Drouil-lard's responsibility. Through hand signs, he determined that the boys were, in fact, Tetons, and a band of eighty lodges wait-ed at the mouth of the next river, with a second village of sixty lodges a little farther along. Clark gave the boys two carrots of tobacco and Drouillard explained that we would come to meet with their chiefs the following day. That night, nobody sang around the campfire. Drouillard acted calm as always, even though our success or failure might rest in his hands, but the *voyageurs* were jumpy as chickens that smell a fox near the henhouse, while the younger soldiers inspected their firearms over and over again. Meriwether reviewed his speech another time, concentrating on the part about the Sioux making peace with the Omahas, while Clark pored over his notes and maps, puffing on his pipe and exhaling into the confines of the tent so I could hardly breathe. When I went out to make my rounds and get some fresh air, I heard Shannon asking Colter what he should do if he dryballed his rifle.

"Don't," Colter said. "Listen, these Tetons probably ain't so much. You'll do fine. But be sure you empty your bladder before any shootin' starts."

Even with lots of soldiers on guard detail, I didn't sleep much that night and woke before dawn from a dream that I couldn't recall except that I felt so feverish I wanted to jump in the river. We ate our usual cold breakfast and loaded the boats without much talk among the men. Colter had hunting duty that day, which meant he traveled onshore aboard our last remaining horse, the one that had nearly become dinner for Shannon, and while Colter was doing his business in the bushes the horse disappeared. When we picked Colter up on-shore, he swore, "It had to be Tetons that stole it!", so when we spotted five braves beside the river Clark ordered our men to lower anchor and had Drouillard tell the Indians that Great Father Jefferson had sent the animal for their chief and it must be returned. They replied that they knew nothing of the horse. Drouillard believed they were telling the truth, so the Captains doled out some more tobacco.

We located a sturdy sandbar at the mouth of the Teton River and set out the awning and the flag, with the keelboat anchored so the swivel gun could protect the council site. Late that morning three chiefs and a lot of warriors and even a few women and children appeared, all dressed up except the na-ked children, and bearing buffalo meat. The Captains greeted them wearing their cocked hats and bright buttons and swords and presented the guests with a quantity of salted pork, which gave the Tetons the upper hand as far as I was concerned, given the superior taste of buffalo. After they finished the usual smoking, Meriwether launched into his "Children of the Great Father" speech. Even though Cruzatte tried translating, the Tetons just sat there. Drouillard fared a bit better, but concepts like "peace" and "brotherhood" and "Washington" didn't seem to make much of an impression, so Meriwether changed tactics. The soldiers began marching around, dressed in their uniforms, doing their best "About face!" and "Left flank!" and the like. Then Meriwether demonstrated his air gun. The Tetons stared off into space or scratched their faces. Next the Captains gave out the usual presents to the leaders: the head chief Black Buffalo, the Partisan, and Buffalo Medicine. Nobody needed to translate the Partisan's words, for a sneer expressed his contempt for the gifts. The others didn't look much happier. I moved out of the shade of the cottonwood trees and closer to Meriwether, though I'd been told to stay out of the way and had planned to be as inconspicuous as possible in case there wasn't enough meat for all the Indians. The Captains were conferring between themselves with Drouillard beside them.

"Invite the chiefs and some of their leading warriors to come aboard the keelboat," Clark said. "We'll show them the compasses and the magnifying glass."

I didn't like it, but knew I was supposed to stay put and could only watch from the shore as the White Pirogue ferried the party to the keelboat. There, nothing seemed to impress the Tetons until the Captains offered each of them whiskey. Even from that far away, I could tell the glasses weren't even half-full, which shouldn't have been enough to get anyone drunk, but suddenly the Partisan began reeling around, sniffing the empty bottle and staggering into Cruzatte as if he would fall down without somebody to hold him up. At that point Clark and some of the soldiers began to herd the Tetons into the pirogue. They resisted, but somehow everybody got loaded in, Tetons and Americans, and headed towards us, with Meriwether remaining on the keelboat. The Partisan started talking in a big voice, lifting up the medal around his neck and dropping it to his chest with disgust. His voice grew even louder, and then he grabbed the cocked hat that the Captains had given to Black Buffalo and flung it into the water, and as the pirogue reached the shore, three of the warriors seized the bowline and another hugged the mast and wouldn't let go: they'd chosen their own present.

I'd never seen Clark lose his temper before, but now he drew his sword. "All hands under arms!" he shouted.

In an instant, Meriwether stood poised beside the loaded swivel gun, ready to light its fuse, while Sergeants Ordway, Pryor and Gass manned the blunderbusses and the men threw up the hatchcovers as breastworks, prepared to fire their rifles. A few of the Indians directly in line with the swivel gun began to back away from the shore, but most aimed arrows or cocked their muskets. The Captains would be their first targets and I'd never bring down all of the Tetons in time to save my Master— but I could die trying. A snarl began in my belly and reached my lips.

Then Black Buffalo seized the rope from the three warriors and motioned the man holding the mast to go ashore. They obeyed, but the Partisan joined them and continued his ranting, drawn bows all around him pointed at our men. Clark's eyes blazed as he leaped into the water and waded onto the bank with Drouillard and some of our soldiers, sending two back with the pirogue.

"We have enough medicine on our boat to kill twenty of your nations in one day!" Clark shouted. Could Drouillard make the Tetons understand? "This expedition must and will go on. Our men are not squaws but warriors!"

The Partisan yelled back and waved a knife. I crouched to spring at him. But by that time, a dozen of our soldiers had crossed over from the keelboat, and more of the warriors began backing up. Clark stepped forward, transferring his saber to his other side and extending his hand to the chiefs.

But they refused him. And then Clark turned smartly, ordered the soldiers to join him, and waded out to the pirogue. "Come, Seaman!" he commanded.

As Drouillard and Cruzatte pulled me dripping into the boat, nearly upsetting it, I realized Black Buffalo and two warriors were wading behind me. They were talking and signaling that they wanted to come aboard. "The chief wishes to sleep with us on the keelboat," Cruzatte said, "and then come to his village so the women and children can see its wonders."

So we *had* made an impression. Clark agreed to the request, and the three Tetons joined us, all of us wet and still nervous about what was going to happen next but relieved nobody was dead. Out on the river, I could see the men hauling up the anchor and my Master's face, resolute in the sunlight.

The Captains led us a mile upriver to an island that we could defend from attack, ordered the boats tied together, and posted a heavy guard. That night, as I lay beside my Master, his rifle at the ready, I realized I hadn't thought about the Great Mystery for quite awhile. I guess crisis can make us look beyond ourselves, and I was so full of joy that Meriwether and all of our company had survived the confrontation that I needed to thank somebody. Black Buffalo had intervened at a desperate moment, but who could say that the Great Mystery hadn't been watching over us all from someplace high above the Missouri River? It comforted me to think so, and I listened to Meriwether breathe until the sun rose on another day.

CHAPTER SEVEN

In the morning, we rowed about four miles before reaching Black Buffalo's village, with canoes of Indians accompanying us all the way. The chief had invited Meriwether to meet his family, so with the interpreters and a few of our soldiers we walked among the tall pointed tipis of poles and buffalo hides. On the hillside grazed herds of horses, but I was far more interested in the village dogs, who looked well-fed—but then who would want to eat bones? I shuddered and concentrated on our mission: to make friends and allies of the Tetons and learn as much about them as possible. Meriwether was busy with Black Buffalo, so with careful courtesy I approached a grizzled bitch curled up in the shade.

"Greetings, Grandmother. I have journeyed a long way to meet you."

She eyed me with curiosity. "I hear your words, Black Stranger, and saw the chief gaze upon you with favor. Our kind seldom travel on the water with men, and never in a boat such as yours."

"We come from a land far to the east, near the place where the sun rises, and we journey to the Western Sea."

"What was wrong with the place where you lived before? Did the buffalo grow scarce?"

"Actually, we didn't have any buffalo at all."

"Ah, you seek better hunting grounds?"

"Not exactly." I was supposed to be asking the questions. "Do you think your masters will wish to trade with the Americans?"

The old bitch sighed. "I suppose. For us dogs, it only means more things to pull or carry when we move camp. See the places on my shoulders where the hair is worn away? That is the mark of the *travois* poles, and the loads grow heavier with each winter."

So the dogs in this village served their masters as beasts of burden and not just... I couldn't see how this information would help our mission but it eased my mind a little. "How many people live here?"

"Black Buffalo leads one hundred lodges, with many in each lodge. And now there are more slaves among us, women and young ones taken during the last raid on the Omahas."

"Where would I find these slaves?"

She inclined her muzzle toward the south end of the camp. Her eyes, cloudy with age, gazed at me. "You look strong and well-fed. The whites are good masters?"

"That man is mine." I felt proud to point out Meriwether, surrounded by a group of Teton women and children. "He is brave and kind, a leader of men and a pathfinder."

"That is good. Safe journey, Black Stranger, wherever you may go. And watch your step among the dogs of this village.

They will not like it when the young bitches twitch their tails to get your attention. I am old, but even last winter I would have invited you to share my heat."

I lowered my head. "You honor me, Grandmother." Backing away, I heard her chuckling.

The slaves were a wretched bunch, filthy and tattered. I encouraged the big-eyed children to pet me, rolling onto my back and pawing the air to make them laugh. Cruzatte joined us, and with his fluent Omaha learned of the raid two weeks before when the Sioux had killed seventy-five warriors.

Soon I located Meriwether, who had already started writing down Teton words for the vocabulary lists the Captains kept of every tribe we met. Late in the afternoon Clark and more of the soldiers and *voyageurs* joined us. At dusk, the warriors insisted on carrying both Captains on buffalo robes to an enormous lodge in the center of the village. I could smell the fragrance of roasting buffalo, but underneath that delicious aroma another odor filled me with dread. I hung back at the entrance to the council lodge. "Better that you wait outside, Seaman," said Meriwether. "These people see dogs in a different way, and it wouldn't do to offend them."

With relief I found a comfortable indentation in the earth that allowed me a good view of the entrance. I couldn't hear the talk, which was fine with me, but later, the music and singing carried well. The village dogs had gathered nearby, bitches flirting and males prowling hackles up without any provocation on my part. I didn't fancy being mauled by a dozen wolfish-looking characters much more than I liked the idea of being eaten, but if the rest of the Corps could hold its ground against odds, then I must, too. Head up, I remained on alert.

"Would you like something to eat?" the most forward of the females asked. Her speckled fur cloaked an agile form. "I have a nice buffalo rib buried not far away that I'd be happy to share with you."

"Thanks, but I'm on duty."

A burly fellow with one torn ear stalked forward. "Too important for the likes of us, are you? You'd cook up good and juicy. Maybe when the Partisan kills your white master he'll serve you for the victory feast."

Despite centuries of breeding and a disciplined upbringing, I felt my hackles bristle. But the last thing the Captains needed was a dogfight disturbing the proceedings. Trying to look casual, I stood, stretching to full height and giving my fur a little shake to emphasize my bulk and condition. "As I said before, I'm on duty." With measured steps, I joined several of our soldiers near the entrance to the council lodge.

The Tetons put on quite a show. The women uttered shrill cries and waved the hair of dead enemies during their dances. When it was the men's turn, one painted warrior didn't think he'd received enough presents from the soldiers and threw a tantrum, breaking a drum, throwing two more drums into the fire and then jostling past us into the night. Black Buffalo just shook his head, making his eagle feathers flash in the firelight, and the dancing continued. What I really wanted was to find a quiet place and collapse beside my Master since none of us had slept very well the last two nights, but I managed to stay attentive until the party broke up. Then Black Buffalo led two girls forward and presented them to the Captains. I'm no judge of human females, but these looked young, clean, and hopeful, and the chief proud to offer them to his white visitors.

Meriwether, who'd always seemed to appreciate a handsome girl, recoiled, shaking his head. Clark smiled, but he turned the women down, too, which didn't please Black Buffalo at all. Drouillard tried to smooth things over, and I could tell he would have been happy to stand in for the Captains, but eventually the chief shrugged and sent the girls away.

Unfortunately, Black Buffalo and the Partisan decided to spend the night with us instead, which meant I had to stay awake again. The Captains had a lot to talk about, anyway, for Cruzatte reported that the Omaha women had told him the Tetons planned to stop the expedition and take all our goods. Of course, as prisoners the Omahas had reason to stir things up, but that news didn't make it any easier to sleep. At least the Partisan was within nose range and not off plotting mischief.

The next day followed the same pattern, with another dance in the evening, and that night the Partisan and one of his warriors planned to sleep aboard. Clark and some of the soldiers climbed into the pirogue, headed for the keelboat while the Tetons waited with us for the next ferry. Maybe Labiche had drunk too much, for somehow the pirogue slammed into the anchor cable and broke it, so Clark called out, "All hands up! All hands up and at their oars!" Unfortunately, the Partisan had no idea what Clark's words meant, and when the soldiers onboard started running around and yelling, the Partisan figured the Omahas were attacking in revenge. Pretty soon two hundred Teton warriors lined the riverbank, armed for trouble and led by Black Buffalo. Eventually Drouillard convinced them it was a false alarm and the Indians went back to bed in their tipis, and we lay down, too, but it was another bad night for sleep.

In the morning, we tried to find the anchor. The Captains had just given up and ordered the expedition to proceed when the warriors reappeared with all their regalia—including weapons—and Black Buffalo asked the Captains to stay another day. At the same time several warriors grabbed the bowline. So we were right back where we started. Black Buffalo suggested we give the warriors some tobacco, the Captains got mad and refused, Drouillard tried to explain things so everybody could understand, and I was ready to bite the first Teton who threatened Meriwether. When it was Black Buffalo who approached I was sorry, for he seemed like a sensible fellow, but fortunately he was trying to make peace again, gesturing that my Master should go ahead and give the warriors the tobacco. I could tell Meriwether was tempted to shoot somebody, but he must have had old Jefferson in the back of his mind, telling him to make friends with the Tetons, so in the end he tossed the tobacco onshore and Black Buffalo jerked the rope out of the warriors' hands.

It was over.

As we passed a young Indian on shore, Clark shouted, "If you are for war or are determined to stop us, we are ready to defend ourselves!" making it plain that his temper was frayed. Later, when everything had settled down and the Captains had a chance to talk, Meriwether tried to blame himself, saying he'd let The President down, while Clark said it was the damned Tetons, calling them "vilest miscreants of a savage race" and "the pirates of the Missouri." I hoped we'd never see them again. The Captains worried the Indians might pursue, though, so at dusk we tied up to a tiny sandbar in the middle of the river. I felt sorry for all the men who got guard duty, but sandbar or no, I needed sleep and so did my Master, and the night passed without incident.

The Partisan and a couple of his men had followed us and signaled the next morning, hoping to come aboard, but the Captains had learned their lesson, so we took advantage of a strong south wind and sailed upriver for twenty miles. That night—again on a sandbar, which seemed the lesser risk—the Captains broke out the whiskey and the men relaxed, even bragged a little about how they'd stood off all those Indians (whose numbers seemed to multiply hourly) without firing a single shot. Shannon tried to talk as tough as Colter and the others, but he looked ready to drop. The air had turned cold. Above us geese were headed downriver, honking as they hurried toward warmer weather. Fall had arrived while we weren't looking. I wriggled closer to Meriwether and closed my eyes.

Those days in early October are some of the best I can recall. Frost banished the mosquitoes, the heat abated, and we'd left the Sioux behind. If I thought we'd seen a lot of buffalo before, they were nothing compared to the great herds that migrated across the river to winter grazing grounds. Deer, elk, and the speedy creatures I called loper-goats followed, with plenty of wolves to pick off stragglers and carrion birds to clean the bones, with more geese, swans, and ducks trumpeting and quacking in the sky overhead, all headed in the opposite direction from our little fleet. We were moving north toward winter, but that didn't seem to worry anyone when we had all we could eat and the sky remained cloudless. Meriwether spent most of his time onshore, striding along with me and sometimes with a small party of the men, Shannon and the Field brothers most often among them. Some days we covered thirty miles, all of us decked out in double-soled moccasins (though I made sure someone removed mine whenever the prickly pear allowed.) Except for Drouillard and maybe Colter, Meriwether could out-shoot everyone, particularly when he used his espontoon for a rifle-rest instead of as a walking stick or snake-killer, and he procured many specimens. His smile shone all day long.

Soon we began to pass abandoned villages of a tribe called the Arikara. Corn and squash and tall sunflowers still grew wild in fields beside the river. Smallpox had wiped out so many of the Arikara that now they all lived in three villages near the mouth of the Grand River. When we arrived there, Clark stayed behind to guard the boats while Meriwether chose Cruzatte, Sergeant Pryor, and the Field brothers to paddle us over in one of the pirogues. The Arikaras seemed friendly, and right away we met up with a trader named Gravelines who'd lived with the tribe for thirteen years and spoke their language plus French, English and even Sioux, so we could communicate with these Indians and avoid unnecessary trouble. Meriwether questioned the trader for two hours, and was so happy that he hired Grave-lines on the spot as an interpreter and told him to invite a del-egation to a council the next day. Then it started to rain, with wind howling and roaring. In the morning waves were crashing so hard against the keelboat that we figured the parley was off, but weather didn't stop the Arikaras, who crossed over to us in bowl-shaped boats made of buffalo hides and willow branch-es. The wind made it too noisy to talk, though, so the Cap-tains handed out some carrots of tobacco and told everybody to come back tomorrow. The Arikara chiefs had spotted York, however, and all that day Indians kept coming down to the riverbank, trying to get a peek at Clark's servant, for even though they'd traded for years with the French the Arikaras had never seen a black man before, and nobody as big as York.

Councils started the next morning. I liked these Indians better than any we'd met so far. For one thing, they appreciated the gifts from the Captains: red paint, looking glasses, four hundred sewing needles, cloth, beads, combs, scissors, knives and tomahawks, plus the usual medals and finery for the chiefs (which was a lot more than the Sioux received, for some reason, but apparently that had all been decided a long time before...) The Arikaras paid attention during Meriwether's Great Father speech, which they could actually understand with the trader translating, and liked the boom and smoke of the swivel gun. But when the Captains offered them whiskey, the Arikaras turned it down. Meriwether looked a bit ashamed when one of the Arikaras said he was "surprised that their Father should present to them a liquor which would make them act like fools." Even though the trader had said that no one of the chiefs was more important than the others, the Captains still appointed the leader of that village, a man named Crow at Rest, as head chief and gave him the most gifts. They followed up with the shooting of the air gun, which amazed the warriors and helped Meriwether recover his confidence after the refusal of the whiskey. The men liked the Arikaras, too, since during the afternoon the husbands encouraged the soldiers to mate with their wives. Apparently they thought power would rub off on them that way, and our men had been so long without females most were glad to give it a go. Clark described the women as "very fond of caressing our men." York was especially popular, and while he was in the lodge with one of the wives, her husband guarded the door so nobody would disturb them. Shannon seemed a little nervous, spending most of his time showing off me and my tricks to an admiring crowd, but he was just about ready to go off with a young woman who wore a short dress made out of sweet-scented loper-goat skins when Drouillard drew him aside.

"Private, I know this seems like a great idea about now, but you'd be regretting things soon enough. See how friendly these women are? Well, they were just as friendly to all the traders that have passed this way before, and you can bet that besides a few half-breed babies those fellows left behind their diseases. That young woman's wearing little enough clothes that I can pretty much tell for sure that you'd be visiting the Captain for medicine before we'd gone far upriver."

Shannon looked horrified. "Thanks for warning me."

Drouillard smiled. "Why don't we head back to the boat and relieve some of the fellows on duty? They won't listen to me, anyway, so they might as well have at it."

Fortunately dogs don't suffer from the same diseases, and since Meriwether seemed perfectly safe and absorbed in his note-taking, I spent an interlude in a cornfield with an eager little bitch. When we were resting beside each other, the Arikara female asked if I'd visited the Holy Dog. I asked what she meant. "Come on, I'll show you," she said, climbing to her feet.

I'd planned to return to duty, but was glad to follow, for she smelled delicious and this Holy Dog might be something important. We traveled a few miles along a creek before we came to three great stones at the edge of the prairie. Two of them were shaped like people, but the other was definitely a dog!

"A long, long time ago," the bitch told me, "a young warrior fell in love with a beautiful maiden, but her parents wouldn't let them get married. They were so sad that they came to this quiet place to mourn together, and the girl's dog came with them. After awhile they all began to turn to stone—first their feet and paws, then their legs, and they kept eating grapes to keep from being hungry until their mouths turned to stone, too. You can see the girl still holding grapes, even after all this time."

Sure enough, wild grapevines were growing from out of the creek bank and gleaming fruit nestled in the girl's stone hands. I felt small. The Great Mystery had visited this place.

"Sometimes the people come here and make offerings," she said, and I noticed a number of empty dishes on the ground, smelling of corn and beans but more strongly of raccoons, who are gluttons with no sensitivity about holy matters. I wanted to linger, but had already been away a long time, so together we returned to the village and parted ways.

The next morning, Crow at Rest announced that he was glad about his new Father and none of his people would be trying to stop our expedition. He hoped the Captains would be able to convince the Mandans upriver to make peace and even be friends with the Arikara. We visited the other two villages, since the Captains had offended the other chiefs by designating Crow at Rest the head man, and after more smoking and presents they said they wanted peace with the Mandans, too, and might be willing to go to Washington in the spring. One of them even agreed to journey with us to the Mandans as a peacemaker, so we'd accomplished our mission to the Arikaras and Meriwether was satisfied, writing in his journal with a flourish.

I'd pretty much forgotten about Moses Reed, the attempted-deserter, since the Captains had dismissed him from the permanent party and the keelboat and made him ride in the Red Pirogue. He'd been forced to work without honor or hope of reward, so it shouldn't have surprised any of us that he continued complaining and trying to win others over to his side. His main target was Private John Newman, and I guess Reed kept after him, saying how unfair things were and how the Captains were real sons-of-bitches (which is a stupid and impossible insult, if you think about it in canine terms). Eventually Newman came to believe Moses Reed, and that night the two of them started shouting treason at the Captains and got themselves arrested. There wasn't much more the Captains could do to Reed, since we didn't have room for a jail and they still didn't want to execute anybody, but they held a court-martial of Newman. Ten men appointed as the jury found him guilty. The Arikara traveling with us on the Red Pirogue cried when the whipping started, but the rest of our men were loyal to the Captains. This time even Shannon looked as if he felt the offender was getting what he deserved. The Captains also "discarded" Newman from our permanent party and made him ride with the *voyageurs*.

Nights grew cold enough that the men spent time preparing winter clothing, since they had to sew warmer coats while I simply grew one. Joe Whitehouse, who'd worked as a tailor back in Kentucky, helped those who'd never threaded a needle. Drouillard and a few others had carried along iron traps and they killed some beavers for their furs, apparently worth quite a bit of money to folks who made fancy hats. Lots more buffalo and elk migrated across the river, and we came upon a herd of loper-goats in the water, with Arikaras on either side shooting the animals with arrows and boys braining the loper-goats with sticks and dragging them to shore. I'd always wanted to catch one of those creatures, so I leapt into the water and swam toward the nearest buck. Now I was the speedy one, and when the buck tried to gore me, I evaded the pronged horns and broke its neck. As I grasped the loper-goat and began to swim back toward the keelboat, the men cheered.

"That's some dog!" Private Potts shouted.

Meriwether, Colter and Drouillard each killed a straggler, which I also hauled back to the boat, and we feasted in the company of some of the Indians, with Cruzatte screeching his fiddle late into the night.

As far as I was concerned, those days of tramping and hunting with my Master (and eating the yield) could have continued forever, though I felt sorry for Clark, who was down with a bad case of rheumatism in his neck, which Meriwether treated with a hot stone wrapped in flannel cloth. But our expedition had a larger purpose. Meriwether was looking forward to meeting with the Mandans. We'd passed some deserted villages with earth lodges full of bones where the smallpox had killed off nearly everyone, but we didn't meet our first live Mandans until just after the earliest snowfall, when we encountered a hunting party of two dozen warriors led by Chief Big White, who was fat and had light skin. We still had the trader Gravelines with us, so Meriwether had no difficulty talking with the chief and smoking tobacco, all very friendly. Two days later we set up camp just downstream from the first Mandan village, located on the west bank. I hadn't realized we'd be surrounded by so many Indians, for men, women, and children flocked to see us, and even though we hadn't had trouble with the Arikaras none of us had forgotten the Tetons, so Clark stayed onboard the keelboat while we walked with Chief Big White, Gravelines, and Drouillard to the first village, called Matootonha. A stockade of wooden stakes surrounded forty big lodges, each shaped like a half moon and covered with earth, making them roomy and warm inside. In the center of the village stood a wooden post, which Big White said represented Lone Man, a great Mandan hero. The Indians of Matootonha couldn't have been friendlier, and everybody was so eager to pet the "black bear-dog" that I was afraid my winter coat would be worn away. Many of the Mandans had skin like Big White, as fair as Meriwether's, which was now tanned by the sun, and some had pale hair and light eyes. My Master smoked more tobacco (avoiding any coughing) with the important men of the village, and when we headed back to camp he was so stirred up he could hardly walk in a dignified manner. "They seem like such a fine people! We'll hold a council with the leaders of all five villages, Mandans and Minitarees. I would have liked to make it to the headwaters of the Missouri, but it's time we choose a suitable site and build our winter quarters." He clapped Gravelines on the back and smiled at Drouillard. "And we can really talk to them. They'll be able to truly understand Jefferson's grand plan and give us advice about making our way over the Rocky Mountains to the Pacific. We'll find the Northwest Passage, I just know it! I can almost see that ocean now."

I was thrilled that Meriwether was in such high spirits, but I wished I could *smell* the ocean. Instead, a strong odor of dirty human lingered on the keelboat. No one else seemed to notice, but Clark explained that a French trader named Jessaume had visited. The man had lived with the Mandans and Minitarees for fifteen years and had married a Mandan woman. "Rene Jessaume's insolent, but cunning, too—claimed he served as a spy for my brother during the Revolution, but I don't believe his boasting. I'm convinced that he does know all the chiefs and important men, however, knows who would be offended if we give too many presents to the others, and knows who holds the real power. So I hired him as an interpreter."

Soon we met the chief of Rooptahee, the second Mandan village, located upriver on the opposite bank. Black Cat was older and darker-skinned than Big White and not fat at all, his laugh not so loud or frequent. Jessaume was with us when we accompanied Black Cat upstream to look for a place to build our winter quarters. The trader struck me as a sly sort, reminding me of a weasel, his clothes rank with the smell of old sweat; it had to be hard needing cloth and skins to keep warm and protected, but at least most of our men tried to keep somewhat clean. All that day we searched for a place with plenty of trees and lots of game, but didn't find a suitable location.

The next day the Captains held the official council, which some of the Minitarees (who were also called Big Bellies even though none of them were as fat as Big White) attended along with the Mandans, including the Minitaree head man, a famous war leader who had only a single eye, the same as Cruzatte. Old Chief One-Eye missed nothing, peering intently at the Captains, their uniforms, and of course the presents. Black Cat seemed ready to get on with things halfway through Meriwether's speech, yet my Master persevered, and then introduced the Arikara chief who'd come to make peace. The Indians talked some more, but it was obvious that things weren't going to be that simple.

Black Cat had taken a special liking to Will Clark, so the next day he invited the Captain to visit his lodge. Jessaume said Black Cat was the most powerful of all the Mandans, so Clark was eager to hear what he had to say. When he returned from Rooptahee, Meriwether's partner was chuckling and shaking his head. "First the chief said 'it would fill his heart with joy' to have peace with the Arikaras so his warriors could hunt and the women work in the fields without watching for enemies all the time. But then he talked about the presents. Not as much as expected—oh, he didn't mind personally, but his people just weren't satisfied. My God, we could have brought twice as much loot and it still wouldn't have been enough! But the old fellow did say he would go see President Jefferson in the spring."

We had a visitor in camp that day, too, a British trader named McCracken who spoke with a Scottish accent that reminded me of my old trainer Fergus. Down visiting from a British fort in Canada, McCracken hadn't heard about the big Louisiana Purchase that had doubled the size of America, so Meriwether explained it. I could tell my Master was trying to act friendly, but he didn't like anything or anyone British—partly because President Jefferson didn't but also because they had killed off so many people during the Revolution, and when my Master was just a little boy his own father had died on his way back to the fighting after a furlough. The British had been supplying most of the goods purchased by the Mandans, and part of our mission was to establish American trade relations with the tribes we met, so things were about to change. Meriwether managed to swallow his distaste and write a polite letter to Mc-Cracken's superior in the North West Company, explaining the new state of affairs.

In the beginning of November, we began to build our winter quarters. The Captains had chosen a location across the river from Matootonha, Big White's village. That same day, Meriwether paid off the *voyageurs* who had paddled the Red Pirogue, and some of them set to work building a boat so they could hurry home to St. Louis, while others decided to spend the winter with the Indians and return with Corporal Warfington on the keelboat in the spring. Gravelines and the Arikara chief headed downriver, along with a few of the Mandans, while Jessaume and his wife and child moved into our camp so he could act as an interpreter. The next day another trader appeared, a French-Canadian named Toussaint Charbonneau who hoped to hire on as an interpreter, too. He smelled about as bad as Jessaume and couldn't speak much English. Charbonneau brought along his two wives. The younger one, Bird Woman, was just a girl, but her belly was already big with a baby. I liked her bright eyes and wondered why such a clean young Indian lived with a stinky whiskery man like Charbonneau.

"I hear you go to Shoshone country," he said in a loud voice, as if that would make the Captains be able to understand his French. "My wife comes from there." He pushed Bird Woman forward. She stood very still, looking down at the ground. "This woman was captured by the Minitarees at some place called Three Forks, and then I won her from them in a bet. Her people have lots of horses, see? They know those Rocky Mountains.

And she speaks the Shoshone language. She's not worth much otherwise, but she would be a big help, see?"

When Cruzatte translated what Charbonneau had said, the Captains did see. Bird Woman could talk to the Shoshones, Charbonneau could talk to her in Minitaree, then to Cruzatte, Drouillard, or Labiche in French, and then one of the half-breeds could tell the Captains what was being said. Any conversation would take an awfully long time, but that was better than not being able to talk at all: we'd seen what happened with the Tetons. So they hired loudmouth smelly Charbonneau on the condition his young wife Bird Woman come along, too.

Sergeant Gass supervised the construction of the fort, subject to the Captains' orders, of course. He chose the best cottonwood trees and set the men to cutting and hauling. As the days grew colder, high walls began to rise in a shape like a wedge of flying geese, plus two rows of four huts each with a space in the middle. The soldiers built a walkway on the roof, chinked the logs, and began the third wall facing the river, its tall pickets digging deep into the ground. The Captains dubbed the place "Fort Mandan," and Clark said it was strong enough to hold off a cannonball.

Soon after we settled into the stockade, Big White visited with a fine gift: one hundred pounds of elk and buffalo meat carried from Matootonha by his wife. The Captains made sure the woman got a mirror and some scissors for her trouble. Other Mandans brought news that two Arikaras who had gone to the Tetons had returned battered, reporting that the Sioux were angry that the Mandans and Arikaras had made peace. The Minitarees were jealous that we had built near the Mandans, and the Mandans wanted us to promise we would do all our trading with them. But most of the time these Indians were pretty easy to get along with, and so were their dogs. I became friends with two big males, littermates who lived in Matootonha with Little Raven, who served as Big White's second-in-command.

"The sons of our master are the best hunters in the village," Gray Dog told me, "so we eat better than the others." He was the heavier of the two, with a wolf-like coat inherited from their wild sire, who had mated with one of the village bitches four springs before.

Spotted Dog scratched at his floppy ear. The other ear stood up straight. He looked more like their mother, they said, who had died during a bad winter. (I wondered if the Mandans had cooked her, but didn't ask.) "You look like you're eating good, too. Our master says that man Drouillard is a mighty hunter, even if he is half-white."

I nodded. "He's a fine tracker and a deadly shot. The Captains rely on him to keep us in meat."

"The young men of Matootonha want rifles like Drouillard's, but not just for hunting," Spotted Dog said. "They want to win glory in war."

"But the wars are over," I told them. "The chiefs made peace."

Gray Dog snorted. "The chiefs are old men. They already had their glory in battle, so peace sounds good. But the young men want to make a name for themselves. In war they prove their bravery, show they are leaders. When the old chiefs die, the tribe will need new chiefs. How would the people know who to choose without war?"

I considered Gray Dog's words. Americans chose their

leaders a different way, but Gray Dog was right: the chiefs had more to gain from peace, while the young men wanted to prove themselves in war. They wouldn't choose to follow Jefferson's peace plan. Would Meriwether understand that, or would he blame himself, believing he had let The President down?

The peace didn't last until the end of the month, when Arikara and Sioux raiders attacked a small Mandan hunting party. The Arikaras had already broken their promise. While Meriwether stayed behind to guard the fort with a few men, Clark led most of our soldiers across the frozen river to Matootonha, determined to help the Mandans punish the oath-breakers. But the Mandans decided the snow was too deep for pursuit. When Clark and the men returned, the Captain said, "One of the chiefs <u>laughed</u>. He told me they always knew the Arikaras were liars."

Meriwether looked shaken. For almost a week he seldom left the Captains' hut, huddled over his notes but writing only sporadically. York made sure I had plenty to eat and Shannon took me for romps in the snow, but I missed the companionship of my Master. I feared it might be a long, dark winter.

CHAPTER EIGHT

One morning Little Raven reported to the Captains that the Mandans had discovered a herd of buffalo only a few miles from the river and offered to loan us horses so some of our men could join in the hunt. Meriwether roused from his solitary mood with a spark in his eyes. "It would be good to get outdoors again, and Lord knows we could use the meat."

"The rheumatism in my neck is acting up, but you choose some of the men and go, Meri," Clark said. "You're spending too much time at your desk, losing your color already with winter still two weeks away. Take York, too. The Mandans think he's big medicine."

Meriwether gathered Drouillard, the Field brothers, Colter, Shannon, Pryor, Gass and seven more of the privates, including Robert Frazer, a Virginian like himself who had joined the permanent party to replace Moses Reed, and we all followed Little Raven across the river to Matootonha. The Mandans treasured their horses, sending them out to graze by day and bringing them into their lodges (along with their dogs) at night, where the horses munched on cottonwood sticks. Now the beasts snorted, clouds of steam billowing in the cold, and stamped their hooves. A few shied at the unfamiliar soldiers, but the men got mounted, grinning to be on horseback again, even without good saddles and bridles. York dwarfed the horse assigned to him, but the animal didn't seem to mind his burden, for Little Raven said he was Big White's own mount, accustomed to a heavy load. The chief had offered Meriwether one of his finest hunting horses, a tall mottled mare with pale eyes, and the horse reared and crowhopped until she realized she couldn't dislodge my Master. Our soldiers joined the waiting Mandans and all of us headed toward the hills, me ranging off to one side with Gray Dog and Spotted Dog where we wouldn't get kicked. We were lucky, since some of the other dogs had to pull sleds.

"Your man rides well," Gray Dog said, "for a white. Can he shoot?"

"You'll see," I told him, trotting proudly, my tail high.

The scouts signaled us to approach in silence. The scent of buffalo just ahead thrilled me so much I could hardly stand still, and the horses felt the excitement, too. The Indians had divided their party, some staying with the soldiers, two larger groups breaking off in either direction. When all were in position, a signal from Little Raven sent them racing over the hilltop at more speed than I could possibly attain, and I topped the crest just in time to see the first arrows fly into the nearest buffalo, sending the rest of the herd thundering with all of us in pursuit. Meriwether's mare outpaced the rest of the horses of the soldiers, but he hadn't yet fired a shot, for the mare twisted and turned to bring her rider closer to a target, then swerved to avoid the horns of an enraged bull. Clearly the mare knew her business, so I relaxed and enjoyed myself. The Mandans, the better riders even though I hated to admit it, guided their mounts with their knees, leaving both hands free to shoot their bows, sometimes releasing with such power that the point of the arrow emerged on the far side of its victim. Women had followed us, hurrying to butcher the animals before the local wolves could claim the meat, and with my friends the brothers I abandoned the chase to trail behind the squaws, feeding on the spoils.

"What an experience!" Meriwether said when he returned to the hilltop with the soldiers, horses and men all puffing and wild-eyed. "I can't remember when I've felt so alive. These Mandans are the finest horsemen I've ever seen." He patted the mare's neck. "Wasn't sure we'd survive all those horns and hooves—not to mention Private Shannon's shooting—but everyone's accounted for. Let's get the creatures butchered and hauled back to Fort Mandan!"

We couldn't carry all the meat from the ten animals killed, but I did my best not to leave any of the best portions for the wolves. That night we dined "better than kings," Private Gibson said, and the next morning Meriwether was at it again just after dawn with the men who hadn't had a chance the day before, joking with Little Raven that soon we'd all be as heavy as Big White. Our soldiers killed nine more buffalo, but the temperature dropped so fast that we took only the tongues before hurrying back to the fort. Though the cold scarcely troubled me other than the icicles that formed on my jowls, three of the men suffered frostbite, including poor York, who had taken too long doing his business. The Captains' thermometer read forty-five below zero. But Meriwether's smile had returned, and I believed, as Gray Dog said, that "Buffalo are big medicine."

The Mandans continued to be friendly, the women eager to spend time with our soldiers in exchange for a mirror and bright ribbons or a hank of beads. Even Shannon experienced the pleasures of the female sex with a young girl Drouillard pronounced "clean as a whistle." She was so taken with the young private that she refused the other men, much to their chagrin. I found my own companions among the local bitches but was careful to form no lasting attachments, knowing we would be on our way at winter's end. Though Meriwether declined to couple with the village women (and I believe Clark did, also) my Master remained cheerful as the Christmas holiday approached, spending as much time as possible questioning the older warriors about the country that lay to our west. The Captains would get down on the ground inside the lodges, where the Mandans would draw lines and squiggles in the dirt to show streams and mountains and valleys. Clark would then transfer the information to one of his maps. He was about as obsessed with his mapmaking as Meriwether with plants and animals, though we gathered few samples as the weather grew colder, for the plants had long since disappeared under deep snow, while most of the wild creatures were hibernating or at least hiding somewhere out of the weather. The Mandans spoke with awe about a great bear, far larger than any we had ever encountered and ferocious, and Meriwether was already looking forward to sending a skin to President Jefferson. The warriors had questions of their own, and it was funny to see the Captains trying to explain about museums and French wine, and of course the Indians were mightily interested in our weaponry as well as the bales of trade goods. We needed to reserve trinkets for tribes we would meet on our way West, however, so the

Captains were careful not to barter away too much. Only rarely did they rent the Mandans' horses.

Holidays seemed to mean a lot to the men, and on Christmas morning they woke the Captains by shooting a round each from their rifles and firing the swivel gun, which was mounted to protect the fort from attack. After downing a ration of whiskey, which put most everyone in a fine mood, some of the men went hunting, but most cleared away the tools and workbenches to make space for dancing. Meriwether had explained to the Mandans that Christmas was a special day of ritual for Americans, so the Indians had remained in their own village, but the wives of the interpreters Jessaume and Charbonneau giggled as the men capered about to the music of Cruzatte's fiddle and the *voyageurs'* tambourine. Dinner included a good portion of meat as well as hoarded dried apples and spices plus another round of spirits, followed by more dancing.

"Why don't we teach old Seaman a Virginia reel?" Colter asked, hat on backwards so its coontail flopped in his face. He took hold of my ears, teasing me away from the sidelines. I pranced a bit, joining into the spirit of the thing, and made everyone laugh so much that I began leaping about, and then even Meriwether joined in, his feet flying in a fancy pattern that ended with him spinning in a circle while everybody clapped in time.

Then we stepped back as others took up the dance. Meriwether tousled the fur on my back, breathing hard. "I must have looked like a fool out there," he muttered to Clark, who was smoking his pipe.

"It does the men good to see you acting human," Clark said. "Young Shannon thinks you walk on water, for God's sake. Did you notice he cut his hair just like yours? Said he was tired of trying to keep his long locks clean. The men need us as leaders, Meri, but it's not necessary to pretend we're stone statues."

"Meaning why don't I go off with that young Mandan girl? I don't see you slipping out to meet the niece of Black Cat's that's always following you about." Meriwether smiled. "Still dreaming about Miss Hancock back home?"

"Little Judy must be growing up fast," Clark said, blowing a ring of smoke. "She should be just about ready to wed by the time we get back."

"Will we ever see our loved ones again?" Meriwether wondered. "And will we find what we seek? Twelve years I've dreamed of this journey, but what's really out there? The map of the known world ends at Fort Mandan. The rest is just speculation."

"Trust you to turn a party into a time for worrying. Relax, Meri, it's Christmas! I'm sure your mother's fine, and President Jefferson, too, and soon enough we'll be back on the river, headed west into who knows what. That's the challenge, isn't it? What would be the point if we knew it all in advance?"

"You're right, of course," Meriwether agreed. "Still, I can't help but consider the odds that—"

"You're impossible!" Clark interrupted, giving my Master a push toward the table still laden with food. "Put some meat on your bones if you won't dance anymore, and try to act as if you're having a good time."

Meriwether nibbled a bit and passed me some select morsels, but we left the party early, and from our hut I could hear the music and sounds of merriment as my Master bent over his journals, his pen scratching across the pages.

A few days after the year 1805 began, the Mandans held a celebration of their own they called the buffalo dance. They invited us to the enormous lodge near the center of Matootonha, empty except for the village musicians, and seated us at the back. Gray Dog and his brother padded over to greet me, complete with our own ritual sniffing. "Your soldiers will enjoy this," Gray Dog said. "It's time to call the buffalo."

The musicians began beating their drums and shaking their rattles and chanting. Soon the old men of the village entered the lodge and sat in a circle. Then the younger men and their wives came in and sat behind them. After a lot of smoking, the drumming and chanting grew louder. One young husband led his wife to an old fellow with a wrinkled face but lots of beads and paraphernalia, begging the old man to mate with her. The girl wore nothing but a handsome buffalo robe, and the old fellow looked interested but had a hard time getting to his feet. Eventually the girl led him off to a place where they could mate in private.

"That way the husband gains the power of the old warrior," Gray Dog explained, "and the buffalo will be called closer."

Anything that might bring buffalo within range of our hunters sounded like a good idea to me. Other young men were pleading with other old men to take their wives, too. Then one of them approached Sergeant Ordway. "They believe your soldiers, though young, possess great power," Gray Dog said. "This should be a fine hunt."

Most of our men thought the whole thing was a great idea as soon as it was explained to them and the Captains didn't order them to remain seated. One by one, certain of the soldiers, and York, too, disappeared outside. Clark and Meriwether made their excuses to the chiefs, saying they had business back at the fort but the men were welcome to stay. We let ourselves out behind Joe Field, who was following a buffalo robe into the shadows.

A few days later Mandan scouts sighted buffalo not far from the village, and for the next week we ate very well.

Meriwether's mood seemed to darken with the days, but whenever he had an important task at hand the shadow lifted off his shoulders. Mandans and the occasional Minitaree would often appear at the fort for medical treatment, and my Master treated the abscess of one small child, forced himself to amputate the toes of a boy whose foot hadn't recovered after a bad case of frostbite, and dispensed Rush's Thunderbolts. The most common malady that plagued our men was called syphilis. Nearly all the men suffered at one time or another and Meriwether treated them with a pill called calomel that contained mercury, which was the same thing that made our thermometer tell how cold it was. Why that helped the men with syphilis I don't know, but they all recovered and were soon back at it with the Mandan girls.

Early one morning Toussaint Charbonneau banged on our door. "Captain, Captain!" he shouted. "Quick come!"

The belly of the young Shoshone girl called Bird Woman had grown very large that winter, and it was time for her child to be born. Our interpreter wanted Meriwether to deliver the baby. "He says it's half-white, after all," translated Drouillard.

"Hopefully it won't resemble the father," Meriwether murmured, washing his hands in a basin of water. I hoped it wouldn't smell or yell like him. I liked Bird Woman, who sometimes knelt close to my ear and spoke to me in her own tongue, which seemed to anger Charbonneau because he couldn't understand Shoshone; I couldn't either, but I liked the sound of her voice.

I'd never witnessed the birth of a baby, and it turned out my Master never had, either. "When I studied with Dr. Rush, we didn't spend any time on childbirth," Meriwether said. "Never thought the issue would come up. But when we get into the mountains, this girl may make all the difference. We must have horses to cross the Rocky Mountains, and her people can help us if only they will."

"Worry about the mountains later," Clark said. "Let's see what we can do for the poor little thing. She's not much older than Judy Hancock, hardly big enough to be a mother."

Bird Woman lay on a pile of furs in the interpreter's hut, her face shiny with sweat. She cried out when we entered and I trotted over to her. "This is no place for you, Seaman," Meriwether said, "go on, now." The girl clutched at my fur, trying to make the Captains understand that she wanted me to stay. "All right," my Master agreed, "he probably knows as much about this business as I do."

Those were long hours. I'd seen a litter of kittens born, and all eight of them came into the world with a lot less fuss than this one little human. When Bird Woman writhed, her hand grasped my fur so tight that I wanted to whimper, but there was already enough noise in the room, with old Charbonneau moaning a lot more than his wife and crying out to God to save his baby (with no mention of the mother) and how he would be a better man after this. I could tell the Captains wanted to order him outside, but he was the only one who could talk to Bird Woman and tell her to push, and since Charbonneau was there, Jessaume insisted on staying, too, because the Captains had hired him to be an interpreter first and he said he'd helped birth his own child. Between the two of them the room smelled so bad I didn't blame that baby for deciding to stay right where it was. The delay hurt Bird Woman, though, and soon tufts of my fur lay on the ground, so when Jessaume started talking about how the rattles of a big snake had saved his child, Meriwether was ready to listen. Among my Master's specimens was a whole set of rattles, and he sent York to fetch them, then crushed two of the segments into tiny pieces which he mixed in a cup of warm water.

"I don't see how this could cause any more pain than she's already feeling," Meriwether said, offering Bird Woman the cup, "but I can't see how it will do much good."

I figured it was a lot like the buffalo dance—worth a try—and about ten minutes later Bird Woman gripped my ruff so hard we both cried out and then the little boy slid into Meriwether's hands, not pretty but alive, and in a matter of moments he was yelling.

"I guess Charbonneau is the father, all right," Clark said.

Meriwether looked almost as exhausted as the mother, though he was grinning as he wrapped the black-haired baby in a clean piece of flannel. "This will make a fine tale for Dr. Rush, but I'm afraid rattlesnakes are in short supply in Philadelphia."

Charbonneau named the baby Jean Baptiste after his own father, though I'm sure that Bird Woman gave her child a secret Indian name. A lot of the men began letters to their families about that time. Meriwether wrote pages to his mother and brothers and sisters in addition to all his reports to President Jefferson. Charbonneau acted as if he'd produced the baby single-handed, all puffed-up like a banty rooster, but Bird Woman just smiled and murmured to the child in their own language, letting me sniff the tiny creature thoroughly, and Clark said I thought I was the baby's Godfather. But it had nothing to do with God. The Great Mystery had brought this baby into the world to share our adventure. Jean Baptiste Charbonneau was now a part of the Corps of Discovery.

As the winter dragged on, game grew scarce and we were almost out of fresh meat, but sometimes it was just too cold for hunting. When one of the men left a jug of spirits outside, it froze hard in fifteen minutes. The Captains hated to part with more of our preserved rations or trade goods, so John Shields set up a forge and bellows inside our fort and pretty soon he had a good business going with the Indians, sharpening their hoes and axes. Then he repaired the old firearms of the Mandans and Minitarees. Eventually he'd fixed and sharpened everything, so he began fashioning the heads for battle axes out of our burned-out iron stove. These were so popular with the Mandans that Shields couldn't keep up with demand, even after he recruited Private Willard to help at the forge. Then Meriwether had our blacksmiths cut the last of the sheet iron into small pieces that could be worked into arrow-points, each worth seven or eight gallons of corn. I still preferred meat, of course, but Mandan corn and squash helped fill an empty belly.

Of all the men, I probably saw the least of Drouillard, who spent most of his time away from the fort trying to supply us with fresh game. The half-Shawnee managed to locate elk nobody else could find, but one day he returned to the fort empty-handed and fuming. "It's the damn Sioux again, Cap'n Lewis. Four of us were near to twenty-five miles out when a big party came riding up and cut the horses from the sleigh. I figure a hundred, maybe more. One of their leaders left us with the oldest mare but made Goodrich and Frazer give up their knives. They tried to relieve us of our tomahawks, too, but we convinced them that wasn't a good idea."

Not much riled Drouillard, but he looked ready to chew up a few Sioux for supper and was the first to volunteer when Meriwether announced we would go after the thieves. Cruzatte and Colter set off for Matootonha to let the Mandans in on the plans, and at sunrise Big White showed up, then Black Cat with a few men from Rooptahee, all old warriors armed with bows and arrows and a couple of ancient muskets, since all the young men with the good guns were out hunting. We set out on the trail, the ground frozen so hard the ice cut my feet and those of some of the men, leaving a trail of blood on the snow. The tracks of the thieves were harder to follow, and pretty soon the Mandans gave up and went back to their warm lodges. Not Meriwether, of course. We made thirty miles that day. Luckily it was so cold that I could scarcely feel the lacerations on my paws, but all of us had sore eyes from the glare off the snow, and even though finding two abandoned tipis and old fire-rings meant the Sioux were way ahead of us, it gave us someplace to rest for the night. I licked my paws clean, munched my ration of dried meat, and settled down beside my Master, though it was hard to sleep with a dozen of us in one tipi. By morning it had snowed so much that neither Drouillard nor I could pick up the trail, so Meriwether turned the expedition into a hunting trip, using the tipis as our camp. We stayed out for a week. Meriwether enjoyed living in the tipi so much he announced that we would purchase one as Captains' quarters for the next part of our trip. I liked being away from Fort Mandan, too, and the time spent tramping about in the snow with my Master, but some of the men suffered in the weather and bemoaned the loss of their regular visits with Mandan girlfriends. We took thirty-six deer and fourteen elk, ate as much meat as we could swallow, and still hauled almost a ton back to the fort, according to Meriwether's calculations.

One morning we woke to rain, the first since fall. Meriwether's calendar showed it was the first day of spring, which cheered everyone. The ice in the Missouri started breaking up, with so many ducks, geese, and swans overhead we could hardly sight the sky. Then huge chunks of ice floated down carrying drowned buffalo. Though our men didn't like the ripe-tasting meat, it didn't bother the Mandans, and I feasted beside my friends Gray Dog and Spotted Dog.

All the men were eager to get back on the river, so nobody slacked off, not even the deserter Moses Reed. Clark supervised the men repairing the keelboat, which had been left in the water too long and damaged by ice, while Gass had a crew building canoes. Soldiers made jerky and sewed moccasins, everybody joked and laughed and sang. I found the village bitches particularly amorous. Meriwether allowed himself a little time for eating and sleeping, but every other moment he wrote. Those reports to The President consumed all of his attention, kept him awake, left his fingers constantly stained with ink. Apparently Jefferson had authored a book about the state of Virginia that Meriwether greatly admired, so my Master was determined to produce a document worthy of his hero. I wanted Meriwether out in the spring air, but instead he hunched over his desk, writing, writing. I resigned myself to his obsession but longed for our journey to resume.

At last it was early April and we had the two pirogues packed along with six new canoes. Corporal Warfington and his men, including Reed and Newman, dismissed from the permanent party, had loaded the keelboat for their trip back to St. Louis, prepared to fight their way through the Sioux with the Captains' precious reports and journals. They also carried the live animals—a prairie dog, three magpies, and a grouse, all recently captured to send back to The President. I was glad to see those noisy squawkers head the other way, though I pitied the little prairie dog (even though it really wasn't a canine) because it was lonely for others of its kind. Standing onshore at Meriwether's side, I watched the men say their farewells, then turn the keelboat downstream while the smaller vessels began the pull up the river. Then we headed upriver, too, neither of us sorry to bid Fort Mandan goodbye. Meriwether whistled a tune in time with his ground-eating strides.

Later we rejoined the others and spent the night in the new buffalo-hide tipi, along with Clark, Drouillard, the interpreter Charbonneau, his wife Bird Woman and the baby Jean-Baptiste. I never heard the little human cry, and he was a far more pleasant companion than his father, who snored almost as loudly as he spoke. We paid a last visit to Black Cat's village, where Meriwether smoked a farewell pipe, then returned to the river and waited for the boats to catch up. One of the canoes had taken on water and we had to dry out all its baggage. Late that afternoon a Mandan warrior and a young girl waved us toward the riverbank. I recognized the girl who'd taken a fancy to

Shannon. Now it seemed she wanted to accompany him on our journey. Meriwether knew that an unmarried female among all those soldiers could cause a lot of trouble, so he told her to go home, which seemed to relieve the private.

"Women have no place on a military expedition," muttered Patrick Gass, not looking at Bird Woman but making his feelings clear. The Captains believed the Shoshone girl could prove so important to the success of our mission that they were willing to risk dissension. She'd already added to our supper ration by digging with a stick into the hoards of wild artichokes gathered by mice. (I'd have preferred the mice themselves.)

Without the heavy keelboat, we made better progress against the current. The White Pirogue was smaller than the Red but more stable, so it carried our valuable instruments, medicines, the best of the trade goods, the journals and much of the gunpowder. Paddled by six of the privates, including three who confessed to being unable to swim (which I couldn't fathom) the White also transported Bird Woman with the baby on her back, Charbonneau, and at least one of the Captains, plus Drouillard on the rare days when he wasn't ashore hunting. Meriwether and Clark took turns traveling on shore. After eight days, we reached the last upstream point on the Missouri known to have been visited by white men. Meriwether stood in the prow of the pirogue, gazing into the uncharted West.

"On to the Rocky Mountains!" he cried, his eyes flashing. "On to the Pacific!"

CHAPTER NINE

At once Meriwether redoubled his efforts to procure specimens for The President. He soon discovered a plant he called a dwarf juniper and took cuttings for Jefferson, believing it would make a fine border for gardens. Then my Master shot a plump bird that he named a snow goose and preserved its skin, complete with white feathers, letting me take care of the insides. Shannon was thrilled when he brought Meriwether an unfamiliar bird the Captains called a "new kind of plover." But the enormous tracks we located in the damp earth along the river and deep claw marks on a nearby tree aroused the most interest. "These must be signs of the great bear the Mandans told us about," Meriwether said, his voice eager. "And here's some of its spoor! I can hardly wait to meet up with one of these fellows."

"The Mandans put on their paint and prepare to hunt these bears with the same rituals they use before a battle with the Sioux," Drouillard reminded him. "Might be best we steer clear of them."

"Most of the Indians have only bows and arrows," my Master pointed out. "These gentlemen will be no match for the Harpers Ferry rifles."

I was already convinced these bears were no gentlemen. The dung of other bears smelled of berries, bugs, and roots, but this one had left behind the unmistakable scent of digested flesh, and he was clearly big enough to be trouble. I would need to keep an especially close eye on Meriwether. Being a genius never seemed to keep him out of trouble.

We didn't encounter any live Indians, but one afternoon the two of us found a scaffold higher than my Master's head that held the skeletons of two dogs still in harnesses, and underneath a human wrapped in buffalo robes with a bow and quiver of arrows by his side.

"What a terrible reward," Meriwether said, "for the service these dogs gave to their Master. These people believe that if they sacrifice the animals, the poor creatures will continue to serve them in their spirit land." He shook his head sadly and turned away. I lingered a moment. Knowing how I would feel if something happened to Meriwether, perhaps someone had done these dogs a kindness. "Come, Seaman, leave that be! Don't worry, nothing like that will ever happen to you."

Wind made our voyaging more difficult. Sometimes we had to hunker down by day, for the canoes wouldn't withstand the waves. Blown sand flayed our faces, hurt our eyes, and damaged Meriwether's pocket watch so it stopped working. Then the weather turned cold, water freezing on the oars. We'd reached the conjunction of the Missouri with a river called the Yellowstone, where the land grew more trees and yielded some fine buffalo, not as lean as those we'd eaten so far, the calves providing fine "veal," as the Captains called it. We also enjoyed plenty of beaver tail, Meriwether's favorite delicacy, and the men gulped a ration of whiskey, which inspired Cruzatte to play his fiddle and led to dancing around the campfire. But the Captains were more interested in Drouillard's report of big-horns, a kind of sheep prized by the Minitarees. Our most skilled hunter couldn't get close enough for a shot, but he'd found one of the large curving horns on the ground.

A few mornings later we traveled onshore, with Shannon serving as Meriwether's assistant. The two of them became engrossed in their study of a particular type of flower, following the blooms downwind toward a thicket of underbrush. As we drew closer, I scented something unpleasant—something dangerous. When I growled, Meriwether glanced up to sight a gigantic creature emerging from the brush. "Good Lord, it must weigh three hundred pounds!" he whispered.

Fortunately, he'd instinctively raised his rifle, so when the bear took a few steps toward us my Master fired. In seconds, another of the beasts emerged from the thicket, snarling, and Shannon shot. Both bullets had struck their targets, but while the second bear turned and ran, the first stood on its hind legs like some awful giant human with grizzled fur, roaring its rage. Then it dropped to all fours and charged.

"Run!" Meriwether yelled.

We bounded toward the river as if the ground had caught fire beneath us, with Meriwether trying to reload as we ran, but I heard that roaring closer now, and turned, determined to buy enough time for my Master and our friend to escape. Blood gushed from the beast's chest when it stood, towering high above me, its beady eyes glaring, teeth bared, claws extended like terrible blades. It roared again, and from a place deep inside me rose an answering roar, not as loud as the bear's but fierce and defiant. This creature would not have my Master.

Then another shot rang out. The bear grunted, pawed at its skull, staggered, and fell with a crash only three feet away.

"Is it dead?" Shannon asked behind me, sounding as if he'd been running for miles.

"My first shot to the heart should have killed it," Meriwether said, coming to stand at my side, staring down at the body as he stroked my head. "Fortunately it was wounded badly and Seaman's stand was enough to slow it down so I could finish reloading. I hate to imagine what it could have done if it had caught one of us... Still, it isn't as formidable as we were led to believe, though I can see why the Minitarees are cautious. You did reload, Private? Pretty good shooting on your part—the practice is paying off. Let's examine this fellow more closely."

I kept a close watch for more of those bears in the days that followed, but instead observed herds of buffalo, elk, deer and loper-goats, flocks of waterfowl, lots of bald eagles and an unusual number of porcupines, which I carefully avoided. As usual, wolves followed the herds, as did their smaller brethren with the yapping night-song. It was Clark and Drouillard that encountered the next bear, which took five balls in its lungs and five more shots elsewhere before it fell. This one was far larger than the first, a male perhaps as heavy as six hundred pounds. Even Meriwether agreed it was a fearsome creature.

Up until that time, Charbonneau had only served as noisy baggage, but one evening, after Meriwether had killed a fine buffalo cow, he proved himself useful when he prepared a kind of sausage called "*boudin blanc.*" Meriwether couldn't simply enjoy eating them, as I certainly did: he had to write about them, documenting each step of the process from cleaning out the length of intestine to stuffing it with savory morsels and boiling it in a kettle, then frying it in bear fat. I believe our sausages equaled those served at the home of General George Rogers Clark, and Charbonneau rose in my estimation. I would have liked him more if he hadn't bragged about his accomplishment, however.

That night I fell asleep early, but woke from a dream that seemed somehow familiar and disturbing, though its memory faded as I came to full alert. The tipi was dark, my Master, the other men, Bird Woman and the baby all breathing quietly. I climbed to my feet and stretched, figuring I should make my circuit of our camp. Normally I patrolled the entire perimeter, marking boundaries, but I'd neglected my task because of an over-full belly. Everything seemed to be in order, however, the guards awake in their places. A fine grove of cottonwoods provided shelter for the soldiers, who slept in the open most nights. The river flowed nearby. Then I heard it, floating across the water just as in my dream: a sweet and seductive voice, coaxing me closer. It was a wild voice, a musical howl of promise and peril. "*Come to me*," it beckoned. Another world waited on the far side, and I felt its lure all the way to my paws. Yet I resisted, feeling my responsibility to not only my Master but to all those who traveled with us: strong and steady Clark, earnest young Shannon, the high-spirited Field brothers, Drouillard who did most of his talking with his hands and his rifle, faithful York, young Bird Woman and her baby, even Sergeant Gass who despised me but did his duty. These and all the others were members of my pack. We worked together toward a common goal.

I believe my resolve would have held if the wind hadn't changed, blowing that fragrance across the river. My nose seemed to have a direct connection with my paws, and in an instant I was dashing toward the water. As it buoyed me up I forgot everything except her, waiting on the other side.

I will never forget the time we spent together, tied in the embrace that perpetuates life. Though I'd known many females before her, our union was different, satisfying more than some momentary urge. She introduced me to a part of myself that I'd never known, a creature as wild as herself. Once she had belonged to an Assiniboin, a mighty warrior who had fallen in battle. She'd chosen life over death on the scaffold. "Now I am free," she said, her voice like the river, full of power and will. "I make my own choices. I call no man Master."

That word brought me back to the dog I'd always known, the Seaman who'd traveled from Newfoundland to Meriwether's side and on West. I made my own choices, too. "The sun's rising. I must go back. Come with me."

"I can't." Her voice deepened. "Stay with me."

We stared into each other's eyes. I liked the dog I saw reflected there—brave, adventurous, strong. He was me, but something was missing. "My people would welcome you, if you change your mind. I would welcome you."

Then I turned and walked toward the river. This time the water chilled me to my bones, but my legs carried me across. I didn't dare look back. But I could feel her eyes, watching.

Later that morning, when we stopped a few miles upriver, Shannon called, "Look, there's a wolf-dog at the edge of the trees!"

"Fine-looking bitch," Clark said, "but that means we double the guard tonight. We're on the edge of Assiniboin country, which could mean trouble."

"Here, girl!" Shannon called, but she faded into the trees. We never saw her again. But her fragrance lingered in my nostrils, and some nights I imagined her just across the water, calling, calling.

We survived a number of encounters with the grizzled bears, beasts so ferocious that Meriwether announced he would rather fight two Indians than one of these "gentlemen." Joe Field jumped off a twenty-foot bank into the river to escape a wounded male, but when it plunged into the water in pursuit, only Colter's perfect shot through the creature's brain saved Joe from a horrible death. That same day, both Captains chose to walk along the shore, a rare occurrence. I was enjoying their good-humored banter when a sudden gust of wind struck us, and also struck the White Pirogue, which had been sailing briskly upriver near the far bank. Charbonneau was acting as steersman, and the fierce gust rattled the interpreter so badly that he panicked and turned the White broadside to the wind. She laid over so hard that many of our goods were flung over the sides and the men who couldn't swim risked drowning. Charbonneau was crying out to his God to save them, Meriwether was yelling at Drouillard to take the helm and tearing off his coat to enter the water, and I was bounding toward the river. I hit with a splash and swam at top speed for the swamped pirogue, but Drouillard had her under control by the time I reached them. Instruments, medicine, and trade goods all bobbed around the boat, and I mouthed the nearest object and carried it to Bird Woman, who leaned over the side, the baby still on her back, to help rescue all she could while her husband cowered, clutching the mast. Meriwether saw that we had the situation in hand so he remained on shore, but when we'd recovered everything that floated and made our way to the bank my Master lit into Charbonneau using language as colorful as anything I ever heard on the Pittsburgh water-front. It turned out we only lost a small amount of medicine and a few kegs of gunpowder, but Charbonneau was forbidden to take the helm ever again. Meriwether was so impressed by Bird Woman's calm retrieval of our goods, however, that the Captains named a river after her. Once again we'd escaped actual disaster, but two days later Clark narrowly avoided a rattlesnake, then a burning tree almost fell on our tipi while we slept. The men began laying bets about what danger we'd encounter around the next bend.

Beaver abounded in that country, and I had a grand time retrieving any shot by members of our company, as nothing delighted Meriwether more than a meal of beavertail. Shannon's marksmanship truly had improved, and one morning he wounded a large male which was still able to swim toward its lodge. As usual, I pursued the creature, but when I approached it whirled, powerful teeth closing on my hind leg. The pain only urged me to snap the beaver's neck and head toward the hunters on shore. But my leg was reluctant to cooperate. Somehow I managed to flounder to the bank and drag myself and the beaver out of the water, where I collapsed onto my side.

"Captain, he's bleeding something terrible!" Shannon said.

I could feel Meriwether's hands on my leg and tried to flop

my tail, but it refused to work. "The beaver has cut the artery. I must stop the blood loss, and soon."

As others gathered around us, asking how they could help, their voices began to grow fainter, as if distance was coming between us. I couldn't feel my leg at all. Had they packed it in snow to numb the pain? No, it was May now, snow far behind us. I could smell spring in the air. Why couldn't I smell my Master? Where was Meriwether? I whined, and a voice whispered back: *It's going to be all right, Seaman, you're a brave dog.* Then it grew quiet, so quiet I let the silence float me away to the West....

... My leg felt as if a burning poker had stabbed it to the bone. I turned my head to bite at the pain, but couldn't reach it. Hands held me, lifted me and laid me in the boat. Meriwether's voice. I couldn't make out the words, but the sound was enough to calm me. We were together. He would save me if he could. Otherwise, I would join the Great Mystery and wait for him. The Dog Star glowed bright overhead....

"Seaman comin' 'round, Cap'n Lewis." When I opened my eyes, York's teeth gleamed against his dark skin. He patted my neck. "Thought you'd gone an' left us for good, but yore Massa done pulled you through."

Meriwether knelt at my side. He smelled wonderful. "Hey, old fellow. You almost let that beaver get the best of you." His hands smoothed my fur, gentle, and I wanted to lick those fingers that had saved my life. But I just couldn't lift my head. "Gave us quite a scare. Young Shannon couldn't believe anybody could lose that much blood and survive. You were more dead than alive for awhile there, but I believe we've rounded the bend. Try to take a little broth."

To please him, I managed to lap a few mouthfuls. It had a distinctive taste. Then I recognized the scent: beaver soup.

I missed out on things for awhile, riding along in the boat as baggage that often had to be hauled up the river by the tow-ropes. Once Charbonneau complained that my extra weight was breaking his back, but Drouillard shut him up, and that afternoon, the hunter killed our first big-horn and awarded me a meaty bone. At first Meriwether lingered nearby in case I needed him, and I could tell he was proud that he'd saved my life, but as I mended he started wandering off, nearly stepping on a rattler without me to protect him. My Master killed the serpent with his espontoon, but altogether I was feeling use-less with my gimpy leg. Bird Woman seemed to understand and began leaving the baby in my care, which delighted us both. Christened "Little Pomp" by a doting Clark, the child loved to tug on my ears or tail and gurgle.

After ten days of recuperation I still limped a bit but could hobble along onshore when the men had to use utilize the tow-ropes, and my appetite had returned to normal. We'd en-camped for the night and slept peacefully in our tipi, but I woke to the sound of splashing, then snorting and hoof beats too near for comfort. I scrambled to my feet and reached the entrance, where moonlight revealed the huge form of a buffalo bull, dripping wet, thundering toward our lodge from the di-rection of the river. I let out a bark and lunged forward as he approached, and the bull veered away, just missing the forms of soldiers rousing from sleep.

"Our dog is turning out to be a handy fellow to have around," someone said as the dust cleared. I couldn't believe the identity my ears assigned to the speaker and had to turn and stare. Patrick Gass was nodding and smiling. "Never thought I'd say it, but a Gass is nothing if not an honest man. The girl, too, when the boat swamped—why, this must be the best damned outfit west of the Missouri!"

The men had a laugh about that, since we were likely the only outfit, but I understood that Bird Woman and I had passed muster.

We entered a region with dry air but banks slicked by late rains, the river rocky with a current too swift to row or pole the boats. The men towed the vessels like mules, sliding in mud that sucked their moccasins off so they had to step barefoot among sharp stones. We nearly lost the White again when our last hemp rope broke. That night the Captains issued an extra ration of whiskey, but everyone was too tired to sing. Then we passed among white cliffs that towered high above the river which Meriwether described in glowing detail for his journal. I was more impressed by the following day's travel, which provided six elk, two buffalo, two deer and a bear that had nearly caught both Drouillard and Charbonneau before the half-Shawnee dispatched it with a crack shot to the head. Meriwether commandeered the elk skins toward covering the frame of a collapsible iron boat he'd designed back in the States and hauled along. Soon, he assured us, it would come in very handy.

An important decision now faced us. With the snow-covered peaks of the Rocky Mountains in view, we reached an unexpected river confluence, not mentioned by the Mandans or Minitarees in discussions of our route West. Where did the fork lead? Could it be the stream the Indians called "*The River That Scolds All Others*?" We believed we'd passed that several weeks back. Or was this the actual Missouri, our proper route toward the sea? If we chose the wrong fork, we could miss Bird Woman's Shoshone people and our chance for purchasing horses to cross the Rocky Mountains.

We set up camp to take readings and allow the Captains to make a decision. While most of the men tended their battered feet, I was happy to rest my leg and lie beside Meriwether while he speculated. The Captains had dispatched Sergeant Pryor to explore the right-hand fork, which had a muddy bottom and looked cloudy with sediment, while Gass led a party up the wider left fork, which appeared to Meriwether more the way a river fresh from the mountains ought to look, swift and clear over a bed of stones. They both reported back, but their information didn't settle anything, so the Captains decided they would each travel for no more than one-and-a-half days on separate forks before making their choice together. The men enjoyed a ration of whiskey, but Meriwether's share only made him more worried.

"We can't make a mistake now," he muttered, running his fingers absent-mindedly through my coat. "It wouldn't be fair to the men who've been working so hard without complaint, and it could mean the success or failure of our mission."

At the moment, I was more concerned that he might try to leave me behind in the morning. I sprang up and grabbed a nearby stick, growling and shaking it to tempt him to toss it for me. He obliged, and when I dashed back with the stick between my teeth, tail flailing at top speed, he chuckled. "All right, Seaman, you can go."

We left at dawn, heading up the right-hand fork with Drouillard, Pryor, and several of the privates. I wore the stout new pair of buffalo-hide moccasins Drouillard had fashioned for me, but prickly pear tormented us all and we had to clamber up and down through steep ravines. Even though I found myself favoring my bad leg, we still managed to cover more than thirty-two miles that day, according to Meriwether's calculations, which pleased him greatly. We sheltered for the night among the willows, which didn't keep the rain off the men, or me either, but they minded and I didn't. Even then my Master wrote in his journal, for he had two new birds to document. The next day he added an unknown kind of ground squirrel and a very tasty form of grouse to his list, and we traveled another thirty miles or so, enough to convince Meriwether that this branch of the river turned too much to the north to be the route we sought. We planned to return by raft, but those the men constructed couldn't handle the swift current, so we trudged back, my limp growing more pronounced with each mile. After another wet night, we nearly lost Private Windsor over a precipice, but that day the hunters shot six deer, which made me forget about my injured leg. We camped dry and Meriwether woke cheerful as the birds that sang all around us, and so certain that the river we followed was not the Missouri that he named it after his cousin Maria, because the stream was pretty and so was the girl. After another long march, we were all glad to collapse at the main encampment, where Clark was relieved to see us, since we'd been gone longer than expected.

The partners conferred, and after breakfast the whole camp discussed which fork to take. The Captains believed the left-hand branch correct, but Cruzatte, the most experienced boatman, disagreed and so did the rest of the men. However, all said they were ready to follow their leaders anywhere, and I felt the same. (I, of course, was also convinced that my Master was right.) The Captains decided Clark, the better waterman, would stay with the boats while Meriwether led a small party up the left fork. We hid the Red Pirogue and cached most of the heaviest baggage, leaving supplies for the return voyage, and that night Cruzatte fiddled for hours while the men danced. The only one around the fire who looked unhappy was Shannon, for Meriwether had chosen Drouillard, Gibson, Goodrich and Joe Field to accompany him while everyone else remained with the boats. That night Meriwether left his bed a number of times to do his business, dosing himself for dysentery, and Bird Woman was feverish, sick enough that Captain Clark bled her. No one in our tipi got much sleep.

In the morning Meriwether still felt poorly but wasn't about to let that change his plans. As soon as he hefted his pack, I was at his side, eager to begin this latest exploration. He placed a hand on my head. "Not this time, Seaman. Your leg needs rest. You <u>stay</u>." I couldn't believe my ears. He wasn't at his best, either, making him more in need of my protection. I whined in protest. "Keep an eye on Bird Woman and the baby," Meriwether said. "I'll be back before you know it."

I didn't like this at all. Drouillard and the others were good fellows, but they were only human (though Drouillard had proved himself as fine a tracker as many canines.) What if Meriwether took off on his own, as he was prone to do? He tended to get so focused on new plants and animals that he grew oblivious of danger. Even though we'd seen no Indian sign, this country was full of bears, snakes, and perhaps creatures we'd never seen before. Since Pittsburgh, we'd always stayed together. Who would protect him now?

That was one of the few times I wished I could talk so Meriwether would understand. Most of the time words seemed totally unnecessary, but now I longed to convince him to take me in spite of my limp, which was more pronounced since our last expedition. I could only watch Meriwether march away with the others in his wake. Now he was in the hands of the Great Mystery.

CHAPTER TEN

That was one of the longest weeks of my life. As we proceeded upriver, I sometimes wandered on shore with Shannon, but often rode in the remaining pirogue beside Bird Woman, who grew weaker each day. My presence comforted us both and provided a diversion for Pomp, now four months old. At that age, dogs already have their adult teeth, but human babies are still helpless; however, Pomp's lively curiosity needed an outlet, supplied by my ears, fur, and tail. Sometimes Charbonneau would hold his son, making faces so Pomp would chortle, but the men had plenty to do fighting the strong current and frequent rapids. Nights were cold, rattlesnakes abounded by day, and I felt almost as mopey as Shannon, even with a wealth of buffalo meat and fat geese for supper. When we reached the site of Meriwether's first camp, we found the skins and most of the meat of two bears, which made me anxious, though that didn't stop me from enjoying the bones. That afternoon Joe Field doubled back with a letter from Meriwether, telling us we were truly on the Missouri and to prepare for a long portage.

"I think those Minitarees played a joke on us, sir," Joe said, petting me as he reported to Captain Clark. "Wait'll you see the Missouri now. It's gonna take a whole lot more time than we figured to haul our baggage 'round the falls. Gives me blisters just thinkin' about it."

Meriwether had recovered from his dysentery and thus far stayed out of the reach of bears and the like, so I relaxed a little on his account, but Bird Woman continued to decline. Clark bled her again and applied a smelly poultice to her belly, which seemed to offer some relief, and he also tended to the ailments of the men, who toiled all day in the slick mud and sharp rocks to keep the boats progressing upriver.

Late one afternoon I caught a familiar scent and barked, then bounded from the bank so fast I slipped and landed on my belly, so when I reached Meriwether I was covered with muck, but he didn't seem to mind that it dirtied him, too. "All in one piece, Seaman," he said, "though I did have a few close calls. Drouillard said I should have brought you along, bad leg or not."

Drouillard rose even higher in my esteem. I shadowed Meriwether as he joined Clark beside the river. Will was nearly as relieved to see his partner as I was. "Welcome back, Meri. I want to hear everything, but first I'd like you to take a look at Bird Woman. I'm afraid my doctoring has only made her worse." Clark spoke a few words close to Meriwether's ear, and my Master frowned.

The men had landed the pirogue and carried Bird Woman into the shade of a few cottonwoods, where she huddled on her buffalo robe, face beaded with sweat. Meriwether's brow wrinkled. "Let's try some laudanum and a dose of the bark." As the two Captains unloaded medical supplies, he said, "Damn Charbonneau! I'm convinced your suspicions are correct and she's suffering some obstruction of her menses caused by venereal disease. If the poor girl dies, she leaves us with an infant and no way to communicate with the Shoshones. We can't let that happen."

Meriwether's party regaled us with tales around the fire about the incredible waterfalls they'd discovered. "Goodrich caught a passel of salmon trout," Gibson said, "finest I ever ate. Now, the Captain—" he broke off, glancing over at Meriwether.

My Master grinned. "I suppose I should confess my own misadventures. I'd gone off on my own and shot a fat buffalo, then grew so intrigued with the way its lifeblood poured from its nostrils that I didn't notice the bear until it had crept within twenty steps of my location. I started for a tree about three hundred yards away, trying to look casual and reload as I walked, but the bear opened his mouth and took off after me full speed, so I ran for the river and waded in, figuring I would try to keep him at bay with my espontoon. He looked prepared to come in after me, but suddenly changed his mind and dashed the other way. I can't believe I looked that formidable, so I have no explanation for his behavior." Meriwether smiled at Clark, who didn't smile back. "Then I encountered an unfamiliar brownish-yellow creature of the tiger kind. It crouched down as if to spring at me, but I managed to get off a good shot, not sure whether I hit it or not, but the creature disappeared into its den. Pretty soon I came on three bull buffalo which made straight for me, but they stopped about a hundred yards away, then turned tail and stampeded in the opposite direction. Well, by that time I was beginning to believe that all the beasts in the neighborhood were in league against me, but perhaps I was under some enchantment that kept them from doing me actual harm. The dream-like state didn't extend to my feet, however, and prickly pear convinced me that I was awake and better head back to camp."

"We sure were worried about the Captain," Goodrich added, "so we were mighty glad to see him limp in. An' the next afternoon he was takin' a little nap and woke up to find a big rattler sharin' the shade of the same tree!"

"I killed him with my espontoon," Meriwether told us.

"You should have taken more of us along with you," Shannon said.

"All I really needed was Seaman." Meriwether scratched behind my ears. "He would have warned of the dangers."

That night I gazed up at the sky, thanking the Great Mystery for watching over my Master in my place, and vowed to stick closer than ever to my Master's side.

Clark left at dawn with a party of soldiers to survey the river and the portage. Meriwether forced Bird Woman to drink water from a spring he'd discovered which smelled like ripe eggs, and she felt so much better the next day she even sipped a little buffalo broth. Gass and five men began to construct wheeled carts for transporting our goods, Shields and a few others men helped my Master unpack the frame of his collapsible iron boat, while the reminder of our party sought elk to complete the covering. The hunters killed plenty of deer but none of the larger species, so Meriwether had to make do with a couple of buffalo hides.

After a day or two, Bird Woman felt so good she dug some

of her favorite white roots and ate them raw, together with some dried fish, which she kindly shared with me. Soon she was moaning in pain again. Meriwether shouted at Charbonneau for allowing his wife to eat against orders and dosed the girl with more medicine, which broke the fever. Meanwhile the men began packing our baggage for the portage while Meriwether fussed with his iron boat, already christened the <u>Experiment</u>, and worried about the length of Clark's absence. When his partner finally returned, they walked out of camp together to discuss what lay ahead, looking very serious. "Good or bad, we must make the portage," Clark said. I was relieved when the Captains abandoned their secret plan of sending some men back to St. Louis. That always seemed like a bad idea to me, for whenever the party split up bad things happened.

Two days later the portage began. We set off on the north bank, hauling baggage and the iron boat frame in a canoe set upon one of the crude carts. The burden was so heavy the men struggled even on level ground. When the Captains called a halt, some of the fellows tumbled to the ground and fell asleep in an instant. We'd traveled almost to our intended campsite when the axle broke. Gass swore as he figured out a way to repair the cart, but it was so near dark the men just loaded as much as they could on their backs and headed for the site, where Clark had cached some meat. I was ranging ahead on scout with Meriwether when I detected an odor that meant trouble. My barking alerted the men, but it was too late: wolves had already devoured most of our dinner.

We stayed at that spot, near a place called White Bear Island, where Gass, Shields, and Joe Field helped Meriwether cover the iron boat and receive the baggage the others hauled nearly eighteen miles. I felt sorry for the soldiers laboring in the heat, their feet stabbed by prickly pear, hands blistered just as Joe had predicted, and the rest of their bodies battered from their ordeal. Whitehouse suffered some sort of sunstroke, and then drank too much water, getting so sick Meriwether had to bleed him with his penknife, the only tool at hand. But the soldiers stayed amazingly cheerful. My Master appointed himself the chef at Camp White Bear, where he cooked up tasty dumplings for everyone and poured the whiskey. That night I heard Joe Field telling Sergeant Gass that the Captain really was a fine fellow, which had always been obvious to me.

It took almost a week to get all our baggage as far as White Bear Island. The men had to mend their moccasins most every night. After a violent hailstorm pounded us, Meriwether measured one ice stone at seven inches around. Bears gave us so much trouble that nobody was allowed to travel alone, even to do their business. All night I patrolled the camp, barking at the monsters and rousing the guards, who would fire their guns and yell; luckily, I could manage a little sleep during the day. Work on the hide cover for the iron boat progressed, but Meriwether worried that we had no pitch to seal the hides, for it hadn't occurred to him that we'd run out of pine trees. Clark, Charbonneau, Bird Woman and the baby almost drowned during a flash flood. Though the men worked as hard as humanly possible, the portage seemed endless.

"It's been almost three months since we left Fort Mandan," Meriwether pointed out to Clark. "I fear we won't make it back there by next winter. Even if we find the Shoshones soon— "

"I don't like that line of thinking," Clark interrupted. "Concentrate on getting your boat done and leave speculation be."

"Sound practical advice, as always," my Master sighed. "What would I do without you?"

That night we ate a fine meal of buffalo, bacon, beans and Meriwether's suet dumplings, and the men downed the very last of our whiskey, for it was again the Fourth of July, Independence Day of 1805 for America. Most of the soldiers even summoned up the energy to dance to Cruzatte's screeching until a rainstorm struck, but they sheltered under the sails and continued to tell jokes and sing songs that made Meriwether murmur that it was just as well Bird Woman couldn't understand English.

In the morning we began to dry the iron boat in her covering, with some of the men pounding together charcoal, beeswax, and buffalo tallow, a mixture Meriwether had devised to seal the hides in place of pine pitch. The vessel was light and large enough to transport a lot of baggage, but I caught Clark eyeing her askance when he thought no one was watching.

The mosquitoes grew troublesome, but Meriwether scarcely noticed, for the Experiment was ready to enter the water. Five of the men carried her easily to the river, where she bobbed on the surface, appearing quite seaworthy. My Master looked pleased and ordered Sergeant Gass to attach the seats and oars he'd fashioned while the men loaded the canoes and prepared to depart. Just then the wind began blowing so hard they had to unload everything, and even so many of our goods got wet. The wind storm continued until evening, when we discovered the seams of the boat had separated and the Experiment was filling up with water.

"She will not answer," Meriwether said. "If I hadn't singed the elk skins, and if I'd thought to harvest pitch before we reached this country without pine trees... Well, it's too late to do anything about her now." He walked away from the river, shoulders slumped.

"There's a couple of cottonwoods large enough for dugout canoes not far away," Clark called after us. "At dawn I'll take some men and get started on them."

Though I acted as silly as I could, going so far as to steal Meriwether's hat and prance around with it in my jaws, nothing distracted my Master from his misery. "I let everyone down," he kept muttering. I gave up clowning and leaned into my Master's leg, but it was like I wasn't there at all. Was he thinking about The President, safe and comfortable back in Washington City while my Master was trying to lead the Corps to safety? Though Meriwether heaved a huge sigh and returned to camp, his dark mood lasted all night, but by morning he was back in action. (I never heard a word of criticism from any of the men.) We hunted and dried meat, fought off mosquitoes and swarms of black gnats. Pryor dislocated his shoulder and needed Meriwether to replace it in the joint. Eventually my Master dispatched everybody in canoes except Private Lepage, who was sick, and Bird Woman with Little Pomp, and they accompanied us the three miles by land until we met up with Clark and his builders, who were still hard at work on our new vessels.

On July fifteenth we embarked at last, all eight canoes loaded snug. Meriwether's spirits climbed with each mile, and when Drouillard shot a buffalo we stopped and ate it, my Master consuming a portion of the guts cooked over a blazing fire the way the Indians ate it without washing off all the good juices. The next day Bird Woman cooked us bread made from the bone marrow mixed with pounded seeds from the sunflowers which bloomed all around us, and Shannon and York picked berries for dessert. But even though we had lots to eat, the Captains were looking ahead, anxious to meet up with the Shoshones. Since they believed a party of our size might alarm the tribe, Clark decided to take a small detachment ahead. Onshore, Meriwether and I kept pace with the canoes, an easy task with the current so swift, and he shot a loper-goat, one of our favorite meats. Next day we spotted a fire not faraway, which my Master speculated could be the Shoshones. Soon we located an elk that Clark had left for us, along with a note that he would meet us farther along. At night it was hard to find a place to camp because of the prickly pear, and all of us had sore feet, but I didn't mind so much, for I spent as much time as possible in the water, chasing down geese which couldn't seem to get off the ground at that time of the year but were still capable of delivering nasty blows with their bills. Most of the men preferred the smaller birds, but York and I developed a taste for big old ganders, and when I delivered one of them the black man would slap my shoulder and say, "You must be 'bout the best goose dog in the West!"

As we progressed into the mountains, Bird Woman grew excited when she recognized particular peaks or small streams entering the river, though when we caught up to Clark he reported Indian sign but no Shoshones. His feet had swollen and blistered, but he was stubborn, just like Meriwether, and insisted on continuing his search in the morning with a new group of men while we remained with the boats. Meriwether helped keep the canoes moving, for he'd learned to "push a tolerable good pole," as Cruzatte put it, and I think it cheered the soldiers when the Captain joined their labor. But the men were so exhausted they never laughed or sang, with Shannon looking nearly as gaunt as he had after being lost in the wilderness. How much longer could they continue fighting the current? I couldn't add my extra weight to their burden, but a new pestilence called needle grass left its barbed seeds in my paws whenever I walked ashore.

Just when I felt I couldn't take one more step without howling, we reached the spot we'd been aiming for ever since we left Fort Mandan: the place where three rivers came together to form the Missouri, the exact spot where a Minitaree raiding party had kidnapped Bird Woman five years before. Now, I'm not much on scenery, but Three Forks looked fine to me, with a big meadow perfect for deer and elk, snowy mountains for bighorns, and lots of clear water for fish, waterbirds, and beavers. It would have made a fine Dog Star. There we found another note from Clark and decided to set up camp, but right away Meriwether was eager to explore. Even though my paws still hurt, I wasn't about to let him go wandering around by himself. The right-hand fork appeared most promising, so Meriwether christened that river the Jefferson, and named the other two forks after Mr. Madison and Mr. Gallatin, two of The President's friends.

When Clark showed up that afternoon he looked terrible, with a high fever and aching in every muscle. Meriwether prescribed rest and five doses of Rush's Thunderbolts, plus York kept a bucket filled with hot water so his master could soak his feet. By morning Clark looked himself again, but both the Captains were troubled. Where were the Shoshone? Everyone kept glancing over at Bird Woman, who tended Little Pomp as she always did, though sometimes her hands quivered. It must have seemed strange to be back in the place where her whole life had changed. When I'd left Newfoundland, I looked forward to finding my true Master, and eventually I'd met Meriwether, but she'd ended up with loudmouth Charbonneau. Now she had a baby and traveled with a pack of white men. What would her family think if they were still alive?

We rested for two days before starting up the Jefferson River. Meriwether chose to journey onshore, where we got so tangled in the maze of beaver dams and willow thickets and canals that we ended up camping alone that night. My Master shot a plump duck for me to retrieve and built a big fire to cook it, so we shared the duck (I could have eaten two myself) and settled down on a bed of willow branches, prepared for a peaceful night's sleep. Unfortunately, the fire didn't deter the bloodthirsty mosquitoes, so it wasn't as restful as it might have been, though Meriwether said I provided almost as much warmth as a buffalo robe.

We met up with the others for breakfast, then tramped further upriver. We found no buffalo sign, the deer were wary and even Goodrich couldn't lure the fish to bite, so we had no meat that night. Meriwether grew more fretful than ever to meet up with the Shoshones, so after a skimpy breakfast we set out inland with Drouillard, Charbonneau, and Sergeant Gass, who'd hurt his back in a fall but could walk all right. Once he'd decided I was an asset to the expedition, Gass had proven a good friend, though I still had to watch out for flying tobacco juice. Sun burned down at us, and by the time we neared the river again all of us drooped. But everyone rallied when we sighted a herd of elk. Meriwether and Drouillard each shot one, which made the whole camp happy. I also devoured the innards of a new type of pheasant that Meriwether recorded in his journal.

Our search for the Shoshones continued. We'd lost Shannon again, but he turned up only a couple of days later and had killed and skinned three deer, which earned him congratulations from Colter. When Bird Woman spotted a mountain that rose high and nearly flat-topped above the plain, she chattered to Charbonneau, who told Cruzatte what the girl had said. The old boatman explained to Meriwether that her people called that mountain the Beaver's Head, and it did look a lot like the one that bit me. But we didn't catch our first glimpse of a wild Shoshone until an afternoon when I scented a horse on a hill and Meriwether was able to identify its rider. Drouillard, McNeal, and Shields accompanied us that day, and we headed toward the Indian while he rode down toward us. When we got closer, Meriwether waved a blanket three times, a sign of friendship, and I waved my tail, but the Shoshone was outnumbered, and even though Meriwether left his rifle with McNeal, holding out a looking-glass and some other trinkets and calling out the word *Tab-ba-bone*, which was supposed to mean "white man," the Indian eyed Drouillard and Shields, who kept getting closer off to one side. Meriwether signaled those two to stop, but I guess Shields didn't understand, so he kept advancing. Meriwether tugged his sleeve up so the Shoshone could see the pale part of his skin and managed to get within a hundred paces when the Indian whirled his mount and galloped away.

Meriwether cursed and said, "There goes a chance at getting horses."

I couldn't blame the fellow for running. The Shoshones had only come to these mountains after being bullied by the Minitarees and the powerful Blackfeet and other tribes with guns.

142

Now they had to sneak out onto the plains to hunt buffalo, all the while watching for raiders who wanted to steal their women and children and kill the warriors. They lived a lot like rabbits, who can't defend themselves and have to rely on their wits. Suspicion kept them alive. Maybe they would all disappear into the higher mountains with their precious horses. No wonder Meriwether was mad at Shields for advancing.

We camped, and as soon as it was light Drouillard followed the horse's tracks. After he reported back, we started around the base of the mountain, which looked like a good route toward the West if only we could come up with horses to carry the baggage. We kept climbing, following the course of a little stream that Meriwether called "the most distant fountain of the waters of the mighty Missouri," though it didn't look anything like most of that river. McNeal stood with his feet straddling the stream. "Thank you, God, for getting us to this place where the water flows toward the east on one side and on the other, west to the Pacific," he said. Right then everybody seemed joyful, disappointment and pain and danger forgotten in this moment when we stood at the place Meriwether called the Continental Divide. That water was about the best I'd ever tasted, so cold I gave a little squeak with each swallow and made the men laugh.

Down we went, about twenty miles all told before we camped for the night. We headed out early in the morning on a trail that many feet, hooves, and paws had traveled before us, and it wasn't long before the breeze carried a fresh canine scent. My perked ears let Meriwether know something important lay ahead, and pretty soon we could all make out two women, a man, and three dogs. Meriwether told our fellows to stay put, exchanged his rifle and pack for the striped American flag, and walked forward, calling out *"Tab-ba-bone!"* But the Shoshones weren't taking any chances and ran off.

The dogs cowered yet held their ground. "We come as friends," I told them.

The largest, who had one notched ear and was two-thirds my height but mostly skin and hide, managed to meet my eyes. "Who are you?" he whined.

If Meriwether had waited, we might have gotten somewhere, but my Master was already rummaging in his pack. When he pulled out a silk scarf and stepped forward to tie it around the dog's neck, it was too much for the skinny creature, who turned tail, the others hard on his heels.

Instead of getting discouraged, Meriwether just kept going, and after less than a mile we topped a rise not far from three more females. One looked about Bird Woman's age, and she dashed off like a flushed rabbit, but the old grandmother and the little girl must have figured they were doomed, for they sank to the ground and lowered their heads. Meriwether walked right up, raised the old woman by the hand so she was standing next to him, and rolled his sleeve again so she could see his arm was pale even though his face and forearms were tanned dark as an Indian. I wagged and Meriwether spoke in a soft voice, calm as could be, telling her he was a white man and a friend, and even though she couldn't understand his words she began to look less scared and more interested, especially when Drouillard and the others joined us and Meriwether pulled out beads, mirrors, awls for sewing moccasins and some vermilion. Drouillard signed that she should call the other girl back, and pretty soon the runaway reappeared, thrilled with her own share of trinkets and smiling as Meriwether painted her face with the vermilion. I sidled close to the littler girl. Pretty soon her hands reached out to touch my head. When I nosed her fingers she giggled.

"See if they will take us to their camp," Meriwether said, and Drouillard signed the message to the grandmother, who agreed. We followed her, the little girl's fingers clutching my fur.

When we'd traveled two more miles the rumble of hoof beats warned us we were about to meet up with a lot more Indians, but Meriwether didn't look scared a bit. When those Indians rode up at a gallop, dust flying, horses snorting, the warriors all painted, my Master set down his rifle and picked up his flag. I felt prouder than ever to be his dog as Meriwether stepped forward to meet that Shoshone war party, their sixty men carrying bows and arrows and a few muskets while he was armed only with a piece of striped cloth. The man riding in the lead spoke to the old woman, who must have said all the right things, for the warrior dismounted and his followers did the same. Then the head warrior said, "*Ah-hi-e, ah-hi-e,*" and gave Meriwether a big hug, smearing bear grease and paint all over my Master's face, and then the other warriors wanted their turn, so pretty soon Meriwether looked fancier than any of them and as blissful as I could remember. When he pulled out his pipe to smoke with the Shoshones, the little girl's father picked her up and settled her on my back. Then all the men sat in a circle and the Indians took off their moccasins except for the little girl, who fondled my ears as we watched the others puff away, the pipe moving around three times, followed by the giving of presents. Instead of complaining like the Sioux, the Shoshones treasured every single bead. The head warrior was named Chief Ca-me-ah-wait, and he looked skinny but strong, reminding me of someone, though I couldn't think who that could be. He accepted the American flag, spoke to his warriors, and all of them mounted their horses except the chief and the little girl's father, who walked beside us toward the main encampment of the Shoshones, the little girl gripping my sides with her legs.

The Shoshones camped along a river they called the Lemhi, and as soon as the father lifted his little girl from my back I hurried down to the water for a long drink from that swift-running stream. I'd already acquired a retinue of village dogs, and a skinnier bunch I'd never seen. The bitches who still nursed pups were little more than skeletons. "Food scarce in these parts?"

Notch-Ear, clearly the leader, replied, "Little enough for the people, less for us. But soon we venture onto the plains for buffalo, and then we feast."

"*Buffalo, buffalo,*" the others murmured like a chant, as if the word itself could carry them to better times.

I found Meriwether and our men in the only hide tipi among a village of brush shelters, where my Master sat smoking with Ca-me-ah-wait and his warriors. Then Drouillard used hand signs to explain Meriwether's words: who we were, why we'd come, and where we were headed. The chief's eyes studied my Master's face. He wanted to believe we were friends, I think, but was afraid we might harm his people, who looked as if they needed a season of good meals. The women and children didn't have to worry about taking care of the whole tribe, though, and after the ceremony they clustered around Meriwether and the others, eager to meet the pale strangers and accept their gifts.

I guess they'd never looked into a mirror before, since they squealed when their own faces stared back at them. I knew the trinkets served an important purpose, but had other concerns. We hadn't eaten for twenty-four hours and my stomach growled so loudly that I worried someone might think me unfriendly. The men were hungry, too, and when Meriwether told Ca-me-ah-wait, the chief rustled up some cakes made from berries and chokecherries. The Shoshones didn't offer me anything, but most of our men slipped me some, which seemed to scandalize the locals, so I guess their dogs had to fend for themselves. The chief also gave Meriwether a tiny piece of salmon, not enough to fill anybody's belly, but my Master looked so excited it might have been a whole platter of fish.

"We must be nearing the Pacific!" he exclaimed. "Just a few more mountains and we'll reach the Columbia!"

All of us walked down to the river, where Ca-me-ah-wait and Drouillard signed back and forth. The chief explained that we still had a tough journey ahead of us, but Meriwether remained cheerful. We'd found the Shoshones and they had horses, which looked as if they were eating a lot better than the people or the dogs. If a salmon had made it East, my Master figured the Corps of Discovery could make it West.

The Shoshones gave a dance in our honor, but all the tension of that day, not to mention the long, hot march, had worn Meriwether down, so he chose to go to bed after a short time, settling down in one of the brush lodges on a pile of loper-goat skins. Those hides made me think of meat, but I belonged at my Master's side when we were surrounded by Indians. Not far away, Drouillard and the others continued dancing with many of the Shoshones, but Ca-me-ah-wait and some of his warriors had withdrawn from the party, too. Could we trust these Indians? I was glad when Meriwether fell asleep, but I lay awake for a long time, staring into the darkness and testing the air.

We spent the next morning at the Shoshone camp, giving Clark time to come up the river. The Shoshone horses and mules that grazed all around us numbered around four hundred, so we were hopeful they would spare some for our expedition. My Master spent much of the time writing in his journal, but suggested Drouillard and the privates go hunting. Chief Ca-me-ah-wait loaned them horses, so along with twenty of the braves, our men chased loper-goats for two hours, sometimes within view of our tent. By now I knew that I could never catch one of those fleet creatures on land, and even though the hunters did their best, they returned sweaty and empty-handed.

That afternoon, with Drouillard signing between Ca-me-ah-wait and Meriwether, we learned more about the route ahead. Our way lay north along a trail they called "Lolo" taken each year by a powerful tribe named the Nez Perce on their way to hunt buffalo. It led over the Shining Mountains—not just one ridge but many, and shining with snow—through rocks and fallen timber that held no game. This description didn't sound promising to me, and the knowledge that we had already left the buffalo behind was disappointing. The Shoshones could live better, the chief signed, if they had guns and powder, for then they could quit hiding in the mountains and live in buffalo country without having to fear their enemies.

"After we reach the Pacific and return to the Great Father in the United States," Meriwether said, "traders will bring an abundance of guns and every other article necessary to your defense and comfort."

That pleased Ca-me-ah-wait, who agreed to return with us the next morning to meet up with Clark. But when the time came, the warriors wouldn't budge. They suspected we'd allied ourselves with the terrible Blackfeet, who we hadn't even met (and I hoped we never would.) Meriwether told the chief that white men considered it disgraceful to tell falsehoods, and how could we bring the traders if we didn't complete our mission? The Shoshones still looked suspicious, so Meriwether challenged Ca-me-ah-wait by saying, "I hope there are still some among you who are not afraid to die."

The chief couldn't let that pass, so he vaulted onto his horse and gave a speech to the other Indians. Soon half-a-dozen warriors mounted their horses, including the little girl's father, who was called Raven Singer because he had such a harsh voice, and we started back the way we'd come. Some of the old women started crying as if they never expected to see those warriors again, but we hadn't gone far when more Shoshones joined in, until sixteen Indians rode along with us, including three women. That night we camped along the creek, with nothing to eat except some flour boiled in water. What we really needed was meat. At sunrise Meriwether dispatched Drouillard and Shields with their guns, which made the Indians nervous, so some of the Shoshones set out to spy on our hunters. The rest of us proceeded on, hungry and worried, and pretty soon one of the spies galloped back. Drouillard had shot a deer! That changed everything. Meriwether was riding double behind Raven Singer, who, along with all the other Shoshones, started whipping his horse. When I finally reached the kill, panting and ravenous, the Indians were devouring the innards like a pack of wolves, but they hadn't touched the meat. Meriwether reserved a hindquarter for us and gave the rest to Ca-me-ah-wait and his people, who didn't bother to build a fire, chewing the raw flesh as gratefully as I did. Our fellows cooked, Drouillard killed two more deer, and then Shields showed up with a loper-goat, so we resumed our journey with full bellies and even a little food for later.

When we drew close to the river, Ca-me-ah-wait signaled a halt. He presented each of our men with a fancy kind of collar called a tippet made out of the skins of white weasels. I'd never liked those sneaky little creatures, but I had to admit they made a fine decoration, and now Meriwether in his buckskins and decoration looked like an Indian, which might have been the reason Ca-me-ah-wait was so generous with his finery: if we were hooked up with the ferocious Blackfeet, they'd have a hard time telling the white men from the Shoshones. In return, Meriwether placed his cocked hat on the chief's head, and then Drouillard and Shields and McNeal all transferred their head-gear to various Indians. Raven Singer even tied a fringed collar of loper-goat skin and teeth around my neck. I thought we'd make quite a sight for Clark and the others when we met up at the river.

But when we reached the water there wasn't a boat in view, which was enough to rekindle the Shoshones' doubts. "Not out of the woods yet," Meriwether muttered. He had to think fast. He passed his Harpers Ferry rifle to Ca-me-ah-wait and said, "If the Blackfeet appear, you can use this to defend your people. And if I have deceived you, then you must make what use of the gun as you think proper. Men, do the same."

Now the Shoshones held all the rifles. If they wanted to kill us and keep the guns, it would be easy. Or they could just ride off into the mountains with all their horses, leaving us stranded.

"In the morning," Meriwether continued, his voice steady, "I will send the hand-talker Drouillard to get a note that waits for me at the forks. My co-chief, Captain Red-Hair Clark, will have written me, saying he is only delayed by the swift water."

It took Drouillard quite awhile to explain that speech to the Shoshones, since they didn't know any more about "notes" than they did about mirrors. I remembered Meriwether leaving a message for Clark tied to a cottonwood branch as he often did. Raven Talker agreed to go along with Drouillard in the morning.

"With the Red-Hair Captain comes a woman of your people," my Master explained, "taken in a raid by the Minitarees and rescued by a white man." I had a hard time picturing Charbonneau as Bird Woman's rescuer, but that seemed to interest the Indians, especially Ca-me-ah-wait. "Also you will meet a mighty black man strong as a bear, with short hair as woolly as a mountain sheep and skin as dark as night."

The Shoshones murmured among themselves, and I could tell Meriwether had made them curious. So we all settled down together to sleep, with Ca-me-ah-wait on one side of my Master and me on the other. Neither of us was taking any chances: he had to watch out for his people and I had to watch out for mine. Maybe I was starting to understand Indians.

We ate our leftover meat just after first light, waiting to hear what had happened when Drouillard and Raven Talker reached the river. Ca-me-ah-wait and Meriwether both tried to look calm, though all of us knew how much depended on the next few hours. It was hard to sit still. Then Raven Talker came riding back, his teeth glistening in the morning sunshine. "White-men-come!" he croaked, for Drouillard had taught him the words. Ca-me-ah-wait grasped Meriwether's arm and started babbling in Shoshone, and even though we couldn't understand a single word he said, we felt the same way. Everybody was talking and laughing, and I got so excited I started bouncing around like a puppy, fringe dancing about my neck. Then I caught Clark's familiar scent and barked!

It wasn't long before the Captain appeared with Bird Woman beside him, Pomp on his mother's back and Charbonneau wheezing and red-faced just behind. Ca-me-ah-wait hugged Clark, one of the young women with our party ran forward and hugged Bird Woman, some of the warriors hugged Charbonneau, and I sniffed everybody. Pretty soon all the humans were smeared with paint and bear grease and thrilled about it. It turned out that the woman, who was named Jumping Fish, had escaped the Minitarees the same day the raiders had captured Bird Woman, so they were old friends embracing and laughing together after five years in different parts of the world.

When everybody calmed down a little, we hurried to join up with the boats at the river. Shannon waved from the shore, Joe Field called, "Look at Seaman's fancy new collar!" and the Shoshones surrounded York, reaching out to touch his skin to see if he wore paint, too. One of the women stroked Sergeant Gass's whiskers, which didn't bother him one bit. Suspicion had vanished like smoke in wind.

Meriwether ordered the men to set up the sails as a canopy and everybody sat in the shade for a conference. He chose to use our translators instead of hand signs. Private Labiche explained my Master's English to Charbonneau in French, who then told his wife in Minitaree what the words meant. He liked being a center of attention, but Bird Woman acted shy about assuming such an important role in front of her own people. At first, when she spoke in Shoshone, she stared down at the ground and mumbled so softly we could hardly hear, but her voice grew less halting and stronger when she raised her head. She looked across the circle at Ca-me-ah-wait, wanting him to understand what Meriwether had said about peace, and suddenly she was running across that distance between them. She flung her arms around the chief's neck and threw her blanket over them both, sobbing. I'd never seen her cry before, so this meant something important. It turned out Ca-me-ah-wait was Bird Woman's brother, which started him crying, too. Meriwether got tears in his eyes and sank both shaking hands into my fur. Jumping Fish was holding the baby, so she carried him over and put him into the chief's arms, and when the baby reached up and poked his uncle in the chin, even tough Sergeant Gass started sniffling a little, though he tried to hide it.

Sometimes, when the best things happen, I can almost scent the hand of the Great Mystery.

CHAPTER ELEVEN

We did hold a council that day, though Bird Woman kept bursting into tears whenever she tried to translate the words of her own brother. At first Charbonneau looked as if he wanted to hit her for being a foolish girl, but after awhile he figured out their relationship could make him an important man among the Shoshones, so he retrieved his son and acted like a fond husband and father. The Captains needed Ca-me-ah-wait to understand that the success of our mission meant American goods for the Shoshones, including the weapons they needed to protect themselves and hunt buffalo. But to accomplish that, we needed horses and a guide to travel the Nez Perce trail through the Shining Mountains. In the morning, the chief said, we would return to the village, where he'd encourage his people to help us.

Everyone in the Corps of Discovery secretly sighed in relief at Ca-me-ah-wait's words, since nobody (especially me) wanted to be stuck in a place where everybody looked so hungry. The Captains gave one of the big Jefferson medals to the chief and littler ones to his two head warriors, and then presented Ca-me-ah-wait with a fancy uniform coat, leggings, a carrot of tobacco and lots of trinkets. Everybody in the Shoshone party got something, either paint, sewing awls, knives, beads or mirrors. Even those small items made the Shoshones act like the O'Connor children at Christmastime. When the Captains showed them our scientific gear and Meriwether shot off his air gun, their eyes grew big. Everybody wanted to touch York to see if his skin stayed black, and when my Master ran me through my tricks they pronounced me "Great Medicine." I liked these people, and their respect relieved a worry that had nagged at me ever since I watched them tear into that deer without cooking it. These people needed food, but now I figured I was safe from the stewpot, especially after Drouillard, Colter, and the Field brothers carried in four deer and a loper-goat for a feast. It gave me pleasure to share the innards with those hungry Shoshones. That night, even surrounded by all those Indians, Meriwether slept better than he had in a long time.

In the morning, Clark and about half of our men prepared for a scouting trip along the Salmon River, just in case it turned out we could use our canoes to paddle through the mountains instead of climbing them. Meriwether traded some of our Indian goods for four horses, looking as pleased with his bargains as did the Indians. Soon Clark headed off with all the Shoshones except the two head warriors, Bird Woman's friend Jumping Fish, and one other woman. We began packing our baggage for transport by land to the village. Drouillard killed a deer, Colter caught a beaver, and Goodrich and Thompson netted trout, so we enjoyed a fine day. Meriwether even found time to write in his journal, since he had a lot of news for President Jefferson. I hadn't realized it was my Master's thirty-first birthday until Shannon congratulated him. As Meriwether sat writing, he read aloud to me:

"*I reflected I had as yet done but little, very little indeed, to further the happiness of the human race, or to advance the information of the succeeding generation. I viewed with regret the many hours I have spent in indolence, and now sorely feel the want of that information which those hours would have given me had they been judiciously expended.*"

He scribbled more words with his pen, looking very serious even though he'd managed to find the Shoshones and everything looked promising for the future. I wished Clark was around, for he had a knack of saying just the right thing to prod Meriwether out of his darker moods. All I could do was poke my nose under my Master's arm and make him laugh.

"Oh, Seaman, sometimes I wish I could look at life the way you do, a single day at a time. But I can't manage it. Instead I can only resolve—what did I write? —'*in future, to live for man-kind, as I have heretofore lived for myself.*'" He stroked my fur, and I leaned into his legs, thinking that sometimes each of us wish to be more than we are, but that the Great Mystery has a plan we can't begin to understand.

Our half of the Corps of Discovery kept busy at the place Meriwether named Camp Fortunate, turning canoe paddles into wooden saddles, caching supplies to lighten the load, recording information about the Shoshones and studying the stars at night. It grew cold enough that ice formed in our buckets. While Goodrich and a party of anglers fished in the river, Drouillard and some of the others hunted hard to keep us all fed. The dog Notch-Ear belonged to one of the head warriors and spent his time in our vicinity, but we never grew close, for he was too preoccupied with his belly to provide much information. Now, I'm the first to admit that food is one of life's greatest pleasures, and I do miss it when I can't get it, but Notch-Ear's obsession became monotonous. *"Buffalo, buffalo,"* he would whisper, his dull eyes lighting up until he looked more wolf-like than ever.

Bird Woman and her baby, Charbonneau, Ca-me-ah-wait and about fifty of his warriors plus their women and children showed up in the middle of the fourth day along the river. We held a little council, gave out more presents, and fed them corn and beans. Meriwether offered the chief a few of the dried squash grown near Fort Mandan, and when they were boiled the chief said they were the best thing he'd ever tasted, except for the lump of sugar his sister had given him two days before. Of course, he'd never tasted General Clark's sausages, but how somebody would prefer any vegetable to a beavertail I couldn't imagine. Goodrich and his anglers had netted more than five hundred fish, so we divided those among the Indians, too, and Meriwether bought six more horses. When another band of Shoshones joined the party, he traded for three more mounts plus a mule, so now we'd assembled a small herd of our own. We even added a quiet mare just for Bird Woman and baby Pomp, which amazed her friend Jumping Fish. Most of those horses showed a lot more spirit than the dogs, and the mule's eyes held a calculating gleam.

We began the portage inland from the river, with the Shoshone women carrying loads as heavy as any of our men. The mule proved a wise and sturdy fellow. His name, he told me one morning in his peculiar accent, was Rockfoot. "I've traveled these mountains for years," he said, "and know every tree and creek. This is some hard country for flatlanders." Rockfoot turned his head from the trail to study me. "You look fit, not like these poor excuses for dogs, but you'll be a damn sight thinner before you reach the other side. Guess I will be, too. When all the Shoshone leave tomorrow for the buffalo, your white masters will be wandering these mountains, wondering how they'll ever reach home."

"No offense intended, but you must be mistaken," I told him. "Ca-me-ah-wait has promised us more horses, a guide— "

Rockfoot interrupted with a snort. "These people are hungry! They like you all fine, but if it comes down to a choice between food and friendship, which do you suppose it will be?" He turned his head back to the trail, picking his way through a jumble of boulders.

I worried about Rockfoot's words for the rest of the morning, but it was loudmouth Charbonneau who broke the news to Meriwether. Charbonneau liked being a big man among the Shoshones and privy to information through his wife. While we were downing a meager midday meal, he mentioned to Cruzatte that Bird Woman heard Ca-me-ah-wait tell one of the younger warriors to make sure the tribe was ready to leave the next day for buffalo country.

"When did you hear this?" Meriwether demanded as soon as he heard the news.

The interpreter translated, and Charbonneau scratched his whiskers. "Ah, let me think... Yesterday?"

"And you didn't think it worth mentioning until <u>now</u>?"

Charbonneau backstepped fast, since Meriwether looked ready to strangle him. I could see my Master struggling with his temper—not only with Charbonneau, but with the Shosho-nes. So much depended on them. When he'd mastered himself, Meriwether called Ca-me-ah-wait over for a smoke. Bird Wom-an looked nervous, stuck in the middle of both the translating and the conflict. It all came down to the fact that the Shosho-nes had promised to help us get ourselves and our baggage over the mountains and now Ca-me-ah-wait was going back on his word. When he heard that accusation, the chief didn't say anything for awhile. I felt sorry for him. His people needed buffalo, but he wanted to honor his promise. Finally, he told Meriwether he would keep his word. It sounded like something my own Master would say if the situation was reversed, and I wanted to lick Ca-me-ah-wait's hand in gratitude. But Meri-wether only nodded as if the chief had done exactly as he ex-pected. That night, though, when we stopped for the night, he gave the only deer Drouillard had killed to the Shoshone wom-en and children, while we went to bed hungry.

On empty bellies we continued our portage, stopping to drink from a spring that Meriwether believed was the birth-place of the Missouri, as clean and clear as water gets. One of the Shoshone women stopped off for an hour, and then re-joined us with a new baby, which impressed all our men, who liked to think themselves the tougher sex. (I'd rather fight any three dogs than one bitch defending her pups.) When we got close to the village, the chief asked Meriwether to fire off our rifles so his people would think about how good it would be to have guns someday, and our men were happy to oblige. The Shoshones had moved their camp a few miles to a level river bottom where the grass grew long and green for the horses. They escorted us to a skin lodge, already reserved for Meriwether's use, where Colter waited with a letter from Clark.

"That river ain't gonna do at all," Colter told Shannon while Meriwether was reading the note. "Whitewater that'd swallow a canoe whole and sheer cliffs on either side. It's overland for us, youngster, through mighty wild country. Don't go gettin' lost out there—you'd never find us again."

Clark's message confirmed Colter's theory, so right away Meriwether began bargaining with Ca-me-ah-wait for more horses. Those strong, swift animals were pretty much all these Indians owned worth anything and the Minitarees had raided the Shoshone herds not long before, so the chief wouldn't make any more promises; Ca-me-ah-wait's name translated to *He-who-never-walks*, and he wasn't about to begin now. Meriwether started worrying again—not that he'd ever really stopped—but he encouraged Cruzatte to play his fiddle, which cheered both our men and the Shoshones, who'd never heard such screechy music nor seen men dancing a reel. The Indian drummers played along, picking up the beat until the Shoshones started dancing, too, with Raven Talker jigging about with his little girl in his arms while Pomp clapped chubby hands. I felt like prancing myself, but stuck by Meriwether on the sidelines, eating a little of our parched corn.

The Shoshones came up with a guide for us, a fellow with an unpronounceable name Clark dubbed Old Toby, who'd traveled the Shining Mountains when he was younger. His three sons agreed to come along, too, and we managed to acquire twenty-eight horses plus Rockfoot the mule, so on the first day of September we set out north to cross the Rockies. I guess this was supposed to be the Northwest Passage, but if there was a trail you couldn't see it. I didn't like the dearth of animal scents ahead. We climbed, scrambled, and slid through thickets and downed trees, boulders, and sharp stones. I felt sorry for the horses, who had sore backs from the crude wooden saddles, but at least they could nibble on vegetation. Our hunters came up with three deer right off, but that didn't go far, and soon we were hungry again. Sometimes the men had to cut our way through with axes. It snowed, hailed, and sleeted, and two of Old Toby's sons disappeared. On the third morning, we had to wait until our baggage thawed before we could pack up. That evening we stumbled down the side of a mountain into a river valley, where we met up with four hundred friendly Indians called Flatheads, though I couldn't see why, since they looked pretty much like their allies the Shoshones only not as skinny. Our appearance worried them at first, especially since they thought York was a giant Indian wearing black paint, which meant war to them. They decided, however, that we were a pathetic bunch since our men wore no blankets, and their chief met us with buffalo robes. It shocked the chief when he discovered that all but York were white men with a few half-breeds thrown in, and that we only used blankets for sleeping. The Flatheads were generous with their berries, the only food at hand, with Shannon smuggling me a share. After the smoking and talking, we purchased more horses and traded some with sore backs for healthy, spirited animals, including a few mares with suckling colts. Rockfoot took a dislike to a fractious spotted stallion, which meant kicking and biting, but pretty soon they settled down and we parted from the Flatheads, who were off to meet up with the Shoshones and hunt buffalo. I envied Notch-Ear, who was about to feast, while it looked as if we were in for a long spell of short rations.

Hot days, cold nights, not enough to eat, but at least the terrain was easy. Off to the west, though, high snowcapped mountains loomed, and they *were* shining when the sun came out. Somehow we had to cross them. Old Toby said if we turned east we could make it back to the Missouri in only four days, when our route had taken seven weeks longer! I could tell Meriwether felt sick when he heard that, but he didn't let it show around the men. That night, he wrote fiercely in his journal, describing a new kind of woodpecker, pressing so hard his pen broke and he had to rummage for a new one.

We spent an extra day at a camp the Captains called Travelers Rest. Drouillard and the others came in with four deer, a beaver, and three grouse, while Colter returned without meat but something that meant more to Meriwether: three Nez Perce Indians. One of them agreed to escort us to his relatives only six days away, so everybody went to sleep encouraged and less hungry than usual. Unfortunately, the spotted stallion and one of the mares wandered off and it took so long to catch them the next morning that the Nez Perce guide changed his mind and left to catch up to his friends who were headed the other way. Only seven miles that day. We'd reached a kind of summit, so the route proved easy for a little while, but then the weather turned nasty, Old Toby got lost, and we floundered through fallen timber for hours, which didn't really bother me.

"Never liked trees much," Rockfoot muttered. "Give me an open meadow with plenty of grass..." Yet he was more sure-footed than the horses, who stumbled and balked, clambering down to the river to stand with their heads hanging, dejected because we'd ended up at a fishing camp where other horses had already eaten down the grass. To make their situation even worse, the men talked the Captains into killing one of the colts, which cooked up into a fine meal for us but nearly drove the mother out of her senses. Meriwether named that camp Colt Killed Creek.

The next day Old Toby figured out where we needed to go, but to get back on the Lolo Trail we had to climb a wooded slope so steep that three of the horses fell and slid a long way down. None were hurt, though Clark's field desk smashed to sticks that became kindling for the fire we started when we reached the summit, melting snow to boil the colt's bones into soup.

The next day was worse. We woke up covered with snow, which continued all day. Some of the men had worn out their moccasins, so they wrapped rags around their feet to protect against frostbite. Every time a man or horse brushed against a tree it dumped more snow. Always wet and cold, we had a hard time staying on the trail, and that evening had to kill a second colt, which meant another mare screaming all night, her milk bag swollen. The rest of the horses weren't much happier, desperate for grass, and many strayed that night in search of something to eat. After we had them all rounded up and packed, our little cavalcade trudged forward.

Rockfoot glared at me. "How can you look happy when everybody else—not just horses, but your men, too—are miserable? Can't you at least pretend?"

My tail sagged. Sure, I would have preferred a nice river for swimming and no ice balling up in my paws, but snow and fallen trees, rocks and slippery slopes really didn't bother me much. It was as if I'd been born for this adventure.

"I take it back," Rockfoot said, "a droopy Newfoundland is too depressing. Just keep wagging and we'll keep putting one hoof after another. I can tell that Captain of yours will never turn back, nor the others, neither."

Drouillard and his fellow hunters only shot three grouse, so we ate the last of the colts for supper. Everybody sat around the fire, not hungry now but knowing we were in real trouble. The Captains decided that Clark would travel ahead with six men, hoping to find a source of food. We followed in his wake, and that night ate a little of the "portable soup" Meriwether had concocted back east. Nobody really liked it much except me. Everyone was still hungry, some of the soldiers suffered from dysentery, and many had broken out in the sores of the syphilis.

Reduced to eating a little of the soup, some old bear fat, and even tallow candles, we struggled West. My belly kept clamoring and I grew light-headed. Even though I admired the Indian horses, who had even less to eat than I did but still pressed onward, I couldn't help wishing one of them might trip and break a leg so we could eat it. But that was up to the Great Mystery. When Private Frazer's pack mare fell a hundred yards into a creek, I was hopeful, but she was ready to continue with her load after only twenty minutes. Eventually we came upon most of a butchered stray horse that Clark had left for us, which was a lot chewier than the colts but with the same wonderful sweetish taste.

The next day we ate the very last of the horse meat, some crawdads Goodrich fished out of an icy creek, and a couple of pheasants. The others also devoured a lone prairie wolf shot by Meriwether. Hungry as I was, I just couldn't swallow a fellow canine. That was a bad time for all of us. Were we ever going to escape from those endless Shining Mountains? All the bones stood out in my Master's face, but he still walked with a straight back at the head of our group, so I was determined to stay at his side until I dropped in my tracks. I think the rest of the men felt pretty much the same way I did. If their Captain could keep going, then they could, too. Even though Meriwether didn't laugh and joke with the men the way Clark did, they admired and respected him. We'd proceed on, and if we died, we'd do it together.

Not long after that we met up with Reuben Field, part of Clark's advance party, who carried some dried fish and roots for us along with the news of a Nez Perce village only seven miles away. Somehow we summoned the strength to pick up our pace, descending into a level valley where we found eighteen lodges.

We had survived the crossing of the Shining Mountains.

The women at that first village fled into the woods at our approach, taking all the children with them, but the men welcomed us. Clark had gone on, and we met up at the next encampment in a reunion that felt like a big pack getting back together after time apart. I understood why Bird Woman had chosen to come along with the Corps of Discovery instead of staying with her own brother and her friend Jumping Fish. Even though Charbonneau treated her worse than the other men treated the horses, we were her family now. She proved herself useful once again, for a Shoshone boy lived with the Nez Perce, and he could tell her what these Indians said, and she could pass the words on to Charbonneau, who told Labiche, who told the Captains.

Clark warned us we'd be sorry if we consumed too much of the fish and the tasty bread made from the roots, but we were all too near starving to listen. Dogs possess a superior digestive system that allows us to eat almost anything, so I only developed potent gas and loose stools. The men really suffered, though, with explosive diarrhea, heaving, and bellies so bloated it was hard for them to breathe. Meriwether became the sickest of the lot. As soon as the first big council ended he staggered far enough away from the men so he could groan in agony, which made me feel worse than if I was vomiting myself. Our soldiers were so ill that the Nez Perce could have overpowered them and stolen all our guns and goods without any difficulty, though I would have taken a few warriors down with me. Instead, these Indians offered us their friendship. Of course, just like the other tribes we'd met, they realized we could offer future trade opportunities, but there was more to it than that. I'd made friends with a sweet-natured Nez Perce bitch who belonged to an old woman named Wat-ku-weis.

"A long time ago," the bitch told me, "Blackfoot raiders captured my mistress and carried her off to Canada, where they sold her to a white trader. The man and his friends treated her well, and when she rejoined her own people she often spoke of the kindness of whites. When your Captain we call Red-Hair Clark showed up, the warriors thought about killing all the white men." The bitch, whose Nez Perce name translated to Honey Tree, nuzzled my neck. "My mistress is old, but she is powerful. Wat-ku-weis said, 'These are the people who helped me. Do not hurt them.'"

I nuzzled back, grateful the warriors had enough sense to listen to a wise old woman. The Nez Perce showed respect for their elderly and treated their women and animals well, plus they smelled good. These were the best Indians we'd ever met.

As soon as our soldiers felt better, they began trading with the Nez Perce for food, bartering beads and cloth. We set up a special camp beside the Clearwater River for building canoes. The Nez Perce helped us hollow out logs using fire, which made the job go faster, and old Chief Twisted Hair and younger Chief Tetoharsky promised to ride along with us so we could make friends with other tribes who spoke similar languages. Despite feeling awful, Meriwether tried to aid Clark in the duties of the Captains, for they were eager to be back on the water, this time headed downstream. As soon as we branded our horses and cut their forelocks for easy identification, we loaded all our baggage into the newly-finished canoes. I was sorry I had no chance to say goodbye to Honey Tree or Rockfoot (though the last time I'd seen him he'd been too busy munching grass to talk) but it felt wonderful to be back on the water. That day's rapids and the near loss of the canoe piloted by Sergeant Gass proved too much for Old Toby and his son, however, for they left us abruptly as soon as we landed and were last seen running toward home without even our thanks, much less any payment.

Our campfire was crowded that evening, for a number of the Nez Perce had followed us on horseback. Twisted Hair and Tetoharsky joined hands with our soldiers and danced to Cruzatte's shrieking fiddle. But I had a hard time enjoying myself, for our Frenchmen, including Drouillard, had traded for dog meat and devoured it with relish. I'd come to view Drouillard as a hero, especially after he'd fashioned my first set of moccasins, so it confused me to see him chewing canine flesh—not prairie wolf this time, but a much closer relation. No sooner had I recovered from that shock than a Nez Perce woman stepped into the firelight. I'd noticed her before, her gaze often fixed on the

Captains in suspicion. She began singing, her voice so powerful that Cruzatte stopped scraping his fiddle to listen. Though none of us could understand her words, I heard the sorrow in her song and wished Honey Tree had accompanied us so she could translate. Had someone died? The woman swayed, began plucking the elk teeth sewn to her dress, offering them to our men, begging that they accept her gifts. Joe Field smiled and patted her hand after she gave him one of the teeth, but she didn't seem to see or feel him at all. Then she turned to Meriwether. My Master lingered beside the fire, but had hardly eaten any dinner, his innards still troubling him. With his face illuminated by the flames, he watched her unsteady approach. The woman staggered, and then ripped disks of white shell from her ears. She held out both hands to Meriwether. "No, you must keep them," he said, though I knew he treasured anything from the sea as a sign we had nearly completed our westward journey.

Her song rose higher as she stared at my Master, her eyes like a night without stars. Her fingers tightened on the disks. She crossed both arms across her chest, drew the shells down the bare skin of her arms. Blood welled up. Meriwether looked like he was going to be sick, his eyes fixed on the trails of blood glistening upon her arms. When she started to repeat the process, he lurched to his feet and left the fire. As I rose to follow, I saw Bird Woman's face wet with tears. Then I raced after my Master.

That night I feared dark dreams, but the rhythm of the water lulled me to sleep, and when I woke the sky was bright and it was time to ride the river toward the Western Sea.

CHAPTER TWELVE

For the first time since leaving Wood River, the Corps of Discovery ran with the current. After surviving two wild rapids, we reached the head of a torrent of whitewater, dark rocks rising above the boil.

"She ees rough, I think," Cruzatte said, "but we will get through."

Nobody wanted to begin portaging every rough stretch of water, and even Charbonneau and the others who couldn't swim urged the Captains to attempt the rapid.

"We can make it," Colter said, "ain't nothin' but water an' rocks."

That morning, the Captains had privately discussed the lateness of the season. We were well into October now and they didn't want winter to catch us before we reached the coast. I think our rush downstream exhilarated even Clark, normally the cautious one, so the Captains agreed to continue without a portage. I rode with Meriwether in the first canoe, and he shouted with laughter as we shot through the rapid without incident, as did the second vessel. The third canoe with Lab-iche at the helm struck a boulder, which ripped a hole in her side, but she limped through and then to the shore with all her party and baggage. A few Nez Perce fishermen walked over to welcome us, accompanied by three dogs. Those dogs acted as if they couldn't understand my greeting, and when I attempted the ritual sniffing they tucked their tails between their legs and skittered away. No manners, but they probably didn't know any better.

Twisted Hair spoke with the locals while I took the oppor-tunity to conduct my business away from the shore. When I returned, Meriwether and Droulliard had joined the Indians, and the half-Shawnee was hand-talking, the Nez Perce nod-ding and smiling. It felt safe to leave my Master and join the rest of the Corps, who had started a fire. A good meal was al-ways welcome, though I figured it would be nothing but fish and perhaps some roots. I settled down near Shannon, who was feeding sticks to the flames.

"Don't hold this against us," he said. "You eat things we can't stomach, and we need meat to keep us all going." He patted my head. "It doesn't mean we think any less of you, Seaman. You're one of us."

"The black dog ees worried?" Charbonneau asked in French, throwing an armful of branches on the fire. "Yes, he would make a fine supper for Charbonneau."

No wonder those dogs were skittish. They figured they might provide the next meal.

I couldn't watch. I left camp, waded into the river. But the rushing of water wasn't loud enough to cover the sound of the dog's death squeal.

I stood in that water, buffeted by the current, numbed by the cold. Maybe I'd stay there forever. And when Meriwether called me, I actually considered playing deaf. It's a ploy known to all canines, explained by my grandmother when I was an unweaned puppy. A ploy I'd never used. I couldn't imagine being dishonest to any master, but especially to Meriwether, who was always honorable and true. So I turned and started back, trying not to smell the aroma of roasting meat, trying not to wonder if that dog had once loved his Master. My paws felt heavy, each step an effort. But how could I blame them for filling their empty bellies? We'd come into new country, and our men had to learn new ways to survive.

Yet even on the Lolo Trail, I hadn't thought about eating *them*.

"I saved you a fish," Meriwether said. He knelt down and presented it, his eyes gazing into mine, his face gaunt and worried. I shuddered when I smelled his breath. But I accepted the fish, and when the boats were ready to set off again, I climbed in close beside my Master.

Soon the Clearwater entered a much larger river, one Twisted Hair identified by a weaving, side-to-side hand motion. "The Snake!" Meriwether exclaimed. "Not far to the Columbia!"

The men laughed and sang again, glad to be traveling without hauling on tow-ropes or poling against the current (and perhaps because they'd enjoyed their meal so much, though I tried not to think about that.) This Snake River, far wider than the Clearwater, had the power to propel us forward with immense speed. It also had fangs. Sharp rocks just beneath the surface gave little warning, and only the knowledge of Twisted Hair and Tetoharsky and the sharp eyes of Drouillard and

Clark riding at the fore of our little convoy kept us afloat. I felt sorry for one-eyed Cruzatte, who cursed his poor vision, for in this swift, unknown water he couldn't act as steersman and had to rely on others.

That night we landed at a Nez Perce fishing camp, where the men purchased roots, a few salmon—and more dogs. A couple of the men offered me hunks of the boiled meat, but honored my refusal to eat. All but Charbonneau. He delighted in dangling a strip of flesh in front of my nose and laughing. Once he even told me—in French, so most of the others wouldn't understand—that I was lucky they hadn't killed me on the Lolo Trail. I was glad when Colter told him to "Bugger off!" Clark was the only one of the Corps who wouldn't eat the dog flesh. It didn't agree with him, he said. I was careful to avoid the local canines, and they wanted no part of me, either, though we dogs are drawn to our own kind. There just wasn't any point making friends.

As we continued downstream, the Captains chose to run rapids that they might have portaged earlier in the season, though of course the low water made things more dangerous, not less. We just couldn't know how long the rest of the journey to the Pacific might take us, or when winter would strike. So we shipped water, dried out our goods, struck rocks, patched the canoes, and continued. Firewood grew scarce, and one evening the need to cook forced us to use some left behind by Nez Perce, though we'd never taken anything belonging to the Indians unless they offered it. Clark had shot a number of plump ducks called blue-wing teals and shared the roasted birds with me, leaving the others to their dog meat. It was the best meal I'd eaten in a long time.

My Master had finally recovered fully from his illness, and when we'd survived a fierce rapid and emerged safely into the Columbia he yelled, "On to the Western Sea!" and threw his hat in the air. I jumped into the water to retrieve it, and when I returned with it in my mouth, he laughed and jumped in to join me, which initiated quite an uproar, with Colter pushing Shannon overboard and the Field brothers tussling until they both fell in. My Master had grown so thin, but now he seemed strong and healthy again. Maybe the Great Mystery had intended those dogs as food for our expedition.

When the swimmers emerged from the river onto the bank, shaking themselves off in a pretty fair imitation of canines, we heard drums and singing, and soon two hundred Indians had formed a half-circle, dancing on around us in greeting. Meriwether tried to look dignified, even with water dribbling off his hat. Clark rescued him by climbing out of a canoe with a pipe in hand, and everybody settled down to smoke together. We spent the rest of that day and much of the next with those friendly Indians, a rich band calling themselves Sokulk, whose language sounded almost identical to that of the Nez Perce but which fascinated Meriwether, who immediately began compiling his usual vocabulary, aided by Chief Twisted Hair. Shannon wrinkled his nose at an odor even humans could smell: decaying salmon. Some of the fish flopped half-heartedly in the shallows, but in addition to the thousands drying on wooden scaffolds, many lay dead upon the water and the banks. I longed for a good roll, immersing myself in enticing aroma, but felt I should keep close to my Master, surrounded by Indians from a tribe we'd never met, no matter how friendly they seemed. Clark and our best hunters tramped off and pretty soon they returned with some grouse nearly as big as turkeys and more ducks, so we all ate our fill—especially since the others glutted themselves on dog meat which the Indians were happy to provide. These Indians were welcoming and generous, so I forced my tail to wag, struggling not to judge their eating habits.

The Sokulk made much of little Pomp, now eight months old, and enjoyed every trinket our men traded, especially a few mirrors from our dwindling stock, and they welcomed us into their nearby brush houses, where we met giggling children and many elders, including a blind woman more than a hundred years old. Many had sore eyes and rotted teeth.

"Is it the long days of glare off the water, do you suppose, and poor diet?" Meriwether speculated.

Shannon shrugged, trying to look wise when he probably had no more idea than I did. My Master just couldn't keep from analyzing things, trying to figure it all out—probably one of the reasons why President Jefferson had chosen him to lead this expedition. Meriwether still gave his speech whenever we met a new batch of Indians, but it was shorter, for he planned more serious diplomacy on our trip back up the Columbia. For now, we were focused on our progress West.

The Captains felt the fish had decayed too much for us to eat them (though the ones I swallowed did me no lasting harm), so they rifled through our stores for enough trade goods to purchase forty Sokulk dogs. Most the Indians butchered before we left, but half-a-dozen were loaded into one of the canoes, their muzzles tied shut, eyes rolling. The men went out of their way to pet me and offer tidbits of Indian bread. That canoe kept to the rear while I rode with Meriwether at the head of our little flotilla, trying my hardest not to think about our new cargo.

The next day we met a powerful chief named Yellept and his band of Wallawallas. After the smoking, the Captains presented him with a medal, but when he asked us to stay awhile the partners explained we had to hurry along, promising to spend a few days the following spring. Later we passed several canoes of Indians headed upriver, numerous lodges, and Indians drying fish. The downriver travel affected our men like whiskey, and they plunged their paddles into the water and stroked hard, anxious to proceed even faster.

We stopped so Clark and a few of the soldiers could climb a cliff that towered above the river. When the captain waved, we could see the grin on his face from all that way. As soon as he got close enough, he shouted, "I sighted a snow-covered peak to the west! Must be the mountain mentioned by Vancouver! Not much farther and we'll reach the ocean!"

Though I was glad to see my Master and the rest of the Corps members so excited, I knew we had a long way to go, for the air still smelled stale, even on the river, with no fresh scent of the sea. Prickly pear, my old nemesis, bristled just beyond the banks, which were barren and treeless. We could scarcely gather enough wood to cook supper, and for breakfast had to purchase dry willow from the local tribe. When they first saw us, some of the Indians looked worried, but Bird Woman and Pomp set their minds at ease, for no war party would bring along a woman and child. One of the fellows wore a sailor's jacket, sparking more hope of the coast. As the locals traded us roots and acorns, they spoke of two dangerous rapids ahead. All our men who couldn't swim traveled on land, carrying the Captains' papers and our scientific instruments. These Indians had noses pierced with a piece of shell, but they weren't Nez

Perce, which was confusing, nor did they seem to like us much, though they were willing enough to sell us wood to cook our meal. Private Collins also served the batch of beer he'd brewed from quamash roots. It smelled a lot worse than rotten fish but the men downed it gleefully and danced with more vigor than Cruzatte's bow had stimulated in a long while; I guess a thousand miles without liquor improved the taste and potency. I would have enjoyed myself more if I hadn't felt so much like a prize steer on parade. When the Indians marveled at my size, I could feel them calculating how many meals I might provide.

Very early in the morning, Meriwether and Clark both left camp to explore the shore downriver, for they wanted to scout the hazards ahead. My Master got distracted studying the wapato roots dug by the local Indians, so his partner went on ahead. Soon Meriwether looked up and exclaimed, "Lord, that's a mighty fellow!" An immense dark bird, its wingspan greater than any eagle, soared high above us. Meriwether snapped off a shot, but the creature continued to soar unconcerned. My Master reloaded, I was pleased to note, but let the bird be, still marveling at its dimensions. "I believe it's a type of vulture not known to science!"

When we caught up to Clark, the Captain's expression was grim. "Come take a look."

It looked impossible. For nearly four miles, water boiled through narrow chutes and falls, breaking over boulders that would smash a canoe to splinters. Yet after the two had conferred, the partners decided only one twenty-foot section required an actual portage. We could hire Indians and their horses to transport our heaviest goods—as long as our soldiers kept an eye on them—and line the canoes down with our elk skin ropes. Indians lined the banks to watch us dare the river, shaking their heads. Would our luck hold? I chose to travel on-shore, able to keep an eye on the boats and ready to leap into the churning water if necessary. When one canoe broke free from its ropes, it was caught downstream, and the passengers emerged onto the shore, laughter a little wobbly but grinning with pride.

The elation didn't last long: fleas saw to that. I had known those vermin in Pittsburgh, of course, but here along the Columbia, among the dried grass and fish skins, the creatures thrived with a vigor that no amount of scratching could thwart. The men stripped naked, trying to get at them, raising welts with their fingernails, their legs pimpled with bites. York was a favorite meal, and though you couldn't see the tormentors on his dark flesh, he twitched and writhed under their onslaught. Fleas are a bane of canine existence, and even my thick, oily undercoat couldn't turn them back, instead providing concealment. I bit and scratched myself raw, too plagued to enjoy dinner. I found some relief in the water, however, and then followed Meriwether and Drouillard to the nearby village. My Master seemed untroubled by the pestilence. "It's much better if you just ignore them," he informed me. "Digging at yourself only makes it worse."

In the village, everyone scratched, an accepted part of life. The local dogs, though fat and yappy, were a dispirited lot, but between fleas and frying they had little to celebrate. Meriwether became fascinated by a pine canoe, wide in the middle but tapering at both ends and crafted by the Chinook Indians just downriver. "It's so light," he sighed, "and easy to portage. But those crosspieces must make it stout enough to withstand a real beating."

I admired the bold raven carved on the bow, but didn't like what the Indians signed about the Chinooks themselves. Rivals of the Nez Perce, they spoke a different language than that of Twisted Hair and Tetoharsky. I had noticed that the chiefs already stuck close to our soldiers and their Harpers Ferry rifles. Meriwether found these local Indians helpful, though, with information about river conditions and willingness to trade food—which translated to some dried fish and eight of the plump little dogs. "I'll send men for them later," Meriwether said. "Drouillard, ask if the owner of the canoe might be willing to barter for one of our vessels, and some goods, if necessary."

Meriwether had learned some of the sign language himself, but now he left it in more experienced hands, which meant this was really important, even though my Master tried not to look particularly interested. The owner of the craft was stout and jolly. For the raven-bowed vessel he had traded a horse.

"To a white man downriver, or so he tells me," Drouillard reported. "He says it is such a very fine canoe, so why would he want one of ours?"

From the pack he carried for just such a purpose Meriwether withdrew a few strands of beads and a man's striped shirt. The Indian's big smile didn't change. My Master added a mirror, then two lengths of shiny ribbon. When he still received no response, Meriwether held up a hatchet. Now the Indian showed even more teeth and gathered up his new treasures.

"Tell the fellow to come down to the river and we'll have one of the canoes unloaded," Meriwether said. Instead of leaving his new acquisition for the men to retrieve, he picked up the carved bow while Drouillard hefted the stern. "Like a feather!" my Master whispered, his eyes shining. "Ah, Seaman, the <u>Raven</u> will fly all the way to the Pacific. I can almost smell the saltwater now!"

Clark admired the new canoe with enthusiasm and Sergeant Gass pronounced it "a damn fine piece of workmanship." Meriwether's jubilance lasted until later in the evening, when Twisted Hair informed Drouillard that he had heard from the local Indians that the Chinooks downriver intended to kill us. That prompted the Captains to call a surprise inspection, but the men had learned their lessons well, and Clark found all the weapons in good order, issuing each of the Corps enough ammunition to fire one hundred rounds. Even though a powerful and potentially hostile force waited downriver, our soldiers weren't worried. "We faced down the Tetons," Sergeant Ordway said, "and the Chinooks can't be bad as those rascals."

Our Nez Perce guides didn't look comforted, and in the morning Twisted Hair announced that they were of no further service to us since the tribes ahead spoke a different language, making the chiefs useless as interpreters, and they'd never traveled any further west.

"Just stay with us a couple more days, until we pass through the Narrows," Meriwether signed. To Clark he said, "That will give us an opportunity to try and affect a peace between the Nez Perce and the Chinooks."

I respected Twisted Hair, who always offered me a friendly pat without any indication of sizing me up for the pot. Now the old chief found it impossible to say no in the face of Meriwether's determination.

The next stretch of river looked treacherous. The passage narrowed between cliffs, forcing a tremendous boil of water into a space only forty-five feet wide. It was time for the non-swimmers to portage again, carrying the valuables while the captains and the strongest swimmers prepared to run the chute. Once more patrolling the shore, I had to weave my way through hundreds of Indians that had gathered, apparently to watch the white men capsize and drown. They sounded like a flock of hungry chickens clucking after food. Several times I dodged hands that lingered too long on my body. I already had a dislike for these Chinooks who purportedly had plans to stop our progress, and the Nez Perce chiefs had chosen to risk the dangerous river rather than come among these rivals. When I saw a group of Indians hurrying to the end of the white-water, eager to snatch any goods that floated free of capsized boats, I longed to scatter them by barking (and perhaps a few well-placed nips) but now our little fleet was ready to attempt the chute. Meriwether rode in the lead canoe with Drouillard manning a paddle just behind him, the <u>Raven</u> swooping into the swirl of water with the other dugouts not far behind. My legs tensed to spring into the torrent, but to the amazement of the Chinooks our vessels all survived. Onshore, Charbonneau thumped the nearest Indian on the back.

"Nothing can stop the mighty Corps of Discovery!" he shouted, and for once I agreed with him.

We all loaded back into the canoes for several miles of calm water. Meriwether could hardly sit still, ecstatic about the <u>Ra-ven</u>'s performance. Then he spotted a village of wooden hous-es. "First since we left St. Charles! I think it's time we attempt another bit of diplomacy."

Scaffolds of drying fish bordered the bank. Clark estimated close to ten thousand pounds. The dogs in the vicinity were a mangy, cringing bunch that cowered when an important-look-ing man strode toward us, his forehead sloping back from his eyebrows to his oily hair. Like all these people, he wore few clothes, but around his neck hung so many strings of shells that he clattered with each step. The Captains greeted the fellow with sign language and held something of a council, though nobody understood a word spoken out loud, and I wasn't sure Drouillard's signing came across very well either. Perhaps we'd traveled too far for the hand messages to make sense. Everybody smiled, smoked, and scratched, the two Nez Perce chiefs looking uncomfortable the whole time, though that could have been from the fleas. At least the Captains had tried to bring peace.

The next section of river was called the Long Narrows, and again we divided our forces, the non-swimmers carrying our treasures, and again the boats survived, astonishing this batch of Indians. We made camp on a rocky promontory that wasn't comfortable but looked safe from attack. There we remained for three days to repair minor damage to all the canoes except the Raven, which remained unscathed, to dry out our goods, and allow Drouillard a chance to hunt and Meriwether to study the stars so Clark could update his map. We said our goodbyes to Twisted Hair and Tetoharsky, promising to visit them the following spring when we returned for our horses and Rockfoot the mule.

Though the Captains wanted us on friendly terms with the local Indians, the Chinooks made that difficult, for they just couldn't keep their hands off our belongings. Colter, the Field brothers, and Sergeant Gass got so irritated they wanted to fire a few rounds at the thieves, but we all restrained ourselves, though nobody discouraged me from growling if I caught someone skulking near our goods. Once I lunged at a fellow who ventured too near my Master's precious field notes, and the men applauded the sharp click of my teeth near the Indian's retreating rear. "That's our Seaman!" Gass said. "He won't let 'em steal nothin' if he has anything to say about it."

One night, however, a pair of chiefs and fifteen of their men canoed from across the river to bring us deer meat and root cakes. Out came the medals and trinkets, followed by Cruzatte's fiddle. The Chinooks enjoyed the music, but York made the biggest impression, leaping about in a wild dance wearing a grin and not much else. Drouillard and the hunters had shot five deer and Goodrich provided a new type of trout which he fried in a little bear oil. "Private, I do believe that is the finest fish I ever tasted," Clark said, and I had to agree.

The Indians spent the night with us at Fort Rock Camp, which meant I didn't get a wink of sleep, but the hours passed uneventfully. When we parted in the morning, Meriwether said we'd made a good start on American-Chinook relations.

Next came a four-mile stretch of the Columbia so wild we sometimes had to portage not only our baggage but the canoes themselves. But after that, everything changed. Though the Pacific was still far away, the power of its tides reached all the way up the river. Instead of bare banks, we gazed upon forests of towering trees. Winging overhead and swimming in the pools and eddies were all kinds of waterfowl, which sometimes fell to our guns, giving me a chance to retrieve and something to eat besides fish and wapato roots. One new type of duck thrilled Meriwether so much that he wouldn't swallow a bite of dinner until he'd recorded its description and measurements. Now the sky tasted different. Some mornings mist hung so heavy that we had to delay our start. But the Chinooks hadn't changed, clucking and plentiful and eager to pick up our goods without trading. Apparently their influence extended all the way to the coast, and I wasn't looking forward to having these people as neighbors all winter. But the cool wet climate agreed with me. When I sniffed the air, it reminded of my very first home in Newfoundland. I seldom looked back unless a scent stirred my memory, and now I thought of my blood kin. Had my wise grandmother, already gray-muzzled when I was born, gone to the Dog Star? Had my sisters whelped litters of their own? I was nearly four years old now, probably half again bigger than the bitch who'd birthed me. Then my Master's rifle boomed and I leaped into the broad Columbia flowing West toward the future.

We met other tribes of Indians besides Chinooks, including the Skilloots, who spoke the same kind of language but didn't show any interest in dog meat and acted quite sociable. Many wore sailor coats or overalls and carried metal weapons, indicating their trading relationship with white men from coastal vessels, and they even spoke some English words, including "musket" and "damn rascal" and "son-of-a-bitch." We smoked with them in the usual friendly manner, but then Clark's favorite pipe tomahawk came up missing, and while we were searching the Skilloots, someone stole Drouillard's blanket coat that he called a *capote*. Our men found the *capote*, but the pipe never turned up. Though Clark managed to hold his anger in check, those Indians got the message and left, and after that encounter the Captains posted extra guards.

Only a little way downriver we encountered a fleet of canoes that made the <u>Raven</u> look plain and puny. The largest bore a carved bear on her bow and the image of a man on her stern. Clark really wanted that boat but was still fuming over his lost pipe and wasn't about to do any business with the Chinooks until it became absolutely necessary. When it came time for us to camp, we had to settle for a rocky beach that the men found "wet and disagreeable." I rather liked it, though, especially since we enjoyed tasty swan and goose for supper. From a nearby island, flocks kept quacking and honking and trumpeting, making my stomach growl as the night wore on. Nobody slept much, and then we woke to fog rich with the tang of salt. When the visibility cleared enough to proceed, I rode in the bow of the <u>Raven</u>, nose to the wind, my ears blown back. Not far now.

Then it stormed. During a walk onshore with the hunting party I pitied the men, their hair and whiskers and tattered clothes dripping, but the trees, taller than any I'd ever seen, protected us from the worst of the rain. The undergrowth swelled with such vigor that our hunters abandoned their efforts, and the Captains ended up buying fish, root bread, and three butchered dogs (it wasn't quite so bad when the canines were already dead...) from some Indians called Wahkiakums, who lived in a village with wooden houses and traded us the skins of two otters for some fish hooks. "Look at these pelts," Meriwether gloated on our way back to the boats. "They make beaver look coarse! I've never felt anything so soft. Sea otter will change the American fur trade."

He continued to finger the pelts until I couldn't help feeling a little jealous. Nobody petted me much these days or wanted me leaning up against them, since Colter said I smelled like a big wet dog, which of course was true. Except for Drouillard, who joined me daily for a dip in the river, they all needed baths, but did I complain?

After another rainy night huddled among stones the men grumbled under their breath as they plied their paddles, tide working against our progress, the salt scent strong in my nostrils. By noon even the men could smell it. Everyone stroked harder, hoping to be the first to sight the sea.

Then sharp-eyed Clark cried, "Ocean in view!"

But rain poured down. Though we paddled thirty-four miles that day by Meriwether's reckoning, we didn't seem to get anywhere, for we'd entered a big bay. Hall, Wiser, and especially poor Bird Woman kept retching over the side from seasickness. Luckily Little Pomp proved a better sailor, chuckling whenever a wave rocked the boat. That night steep banks kept us pinned to the bay so we had to perch on rocks, and when high tide reached us, everyone scrambled to save the baggage and canoes. With the wind and waves, we couldn't go anywhere the next day, so there we were, trying to fend off floating trees longer than a whale, so wet even I could feel it on my skin and nothing to drink except puddles of rainwater, unless you were as foolish as Charbonneau, who drank so much from the bay that all the salt made him puke.

Low tide allowed us to proceed to a hollow at the mouth of a stream, so at least we weren't thirsty anymore, but everybody looked completely bedraggled and half the men had runny noses. I longed to go off exploring with the advance party of Colter, Shannon, and Willard, but remained at Meriwether's side, which was difficult to do, since the delay had him pacing even in that constrained space, as frustrated as a dog on a rope too short to reach his dish. Finally Colter returned. "There's a sandy beach just a little way round the point," he reported, "but the waves won't quit an' our boat couldn't make it any farther. Chinooks kept skimmin' right by us, though, in their fancy big canoes. We landed by a couple Injun huts an' tried a little fishin', but no luck, an' then I found my gig an' basket gone. Got it back, but I guess that's why they know the words 'damn rascals.'"

Meriwether determined to take a small party in search of the white men that some Chinooks had told us lived at the mouth of the river, so Colter and four others transported us in the <u>Raven</u> to the sandy beach, landing us just before dark. We huddled there, wood too wet to build a fire, with Drouillard, the Field brothers, and Frazer.

"Wish we had some whiskey," Reuben said.

"Wish we had some women," Joe said.

I would have liked a nice buffalo tongue or beaver tail or leg of loper-goat, but all we had was dried fish and soggy root bread and not much of that. Frazer kept sneezing and Joe's ragged buckskins had nearly rotted away. But Meriwether was still focused on getting to the ocean itself, which was loud in our ears but still out of sight, and until he could say we'd reached the Pacific he wasn't about to give in to discomfort. My Master seldom spoke much about himself, not even to Clark or to me, but that night he seldom stopped talking.

"Did you men know the first time I met William Clark he was wearing two pounds of flour and a half-pound of tallow in his hair?"

"The Captain?" Frazer asked, his hoarse voice cracking in surprise.

"Well, he was only a lieutenant then." Meriwether laid a hand on my head, and when I sidled closer he seemed glad of the contact. "General Wayne wanted each of us in his four sub-legions to look alike. We all wore bearskins—hot in the summer, but wouldn't one be nice right now?— and Clark's men each sported a green plume, but that wasn't enough for Mad Anthony. He assigned all the black-haired fellows to the First and the Third, and the rest of us had to wear wigs or powder with flour so we'd match each other. When they transferred me to the Fourth my sandy hair was deemed satisfactory just as it was, but poor Clark, our leader, had to use the full Army ration of flour and tallow to tame his blazing red locks to match the rest of us." Meriwether laughed along with the men. "I guess it gave those Injuns a shock when they'd scalp a fellow and his hair changed color right in their hands."

"Did you lose a lot of soldiers?" Reuben asked.

"Not many," Meriwether said. "Clark was an exceptional leader even then. Quite fond of surprise inspections."

"So he hasn't changed much," Joe said.

"A good man just gets better." Meriwether stroked my back, then eased an itchy, hard-to-reach spot between my shoulder blades. "I'm convinced William could have had the same kind of brilliant career as his brother, the General, if his health hadn't gotten in the way. I feared it might keep him from this expedition, too, but his stomach troubles and rheumatism eased up, thank goodness."

"My mother's people called George Rogers Clark 'Long Knife," Drouillard said, startling everyone, for he seldom spoke unless translating or making a report. "A bad enemy but a good friend."

"That's something you could say about any great man," Meriwether agreed. "Thomas Jefferson, now—nobody could have been a better neighbor to my family—he was like an uncle to me when my father died—and he's the best President this nation could ask for. But ask a rabid Federalist about Virginia Tom and you'll think the Devil's a fine fellow in comparison."

Politics and Jefferson both confused me. I figured the Republicans and the Federalists must be something like two rival packs of canines, each wanting the pick of the females. Jefferson had fought his way to the top of one pack, and now these Federalist fellows were circling, hoping to bring him down.

"My brother's a Federalist," Frazer said, "but he lives up in New York. Me, I remember seeing a bit of Mr. Jefferson when I was growing up. Once he showed me the bone of some giant critter he said used to live in Virginia a long time ago. Told me it had tusks like a wild boar and horns like a bull."

"The mammoth!" Meriwether exclaimed. "The President hoped we might come across some of the living creatures on our way across the continent. I'm afraid that dream has gone the way of the Northwest Passage. He'll have to be satisfied with grizzly bears, herds of buffalo, and a whole lot of wild and beautiful country. We've seen some sights, haven't we? One day our great nation will stretch all the way from the Atlantic to the Pacific. And you men will be part of history, the ones who blazed the trail."

I'd never fully understood the power of words. That could have been one of the most miserable nights of the whole trip, but the time passed fast because my Master kept everybody talking and laughing, and the men forgot they were cold and wet and didn't have any whiskey or women, and I was so proud of my Master I didn't mind waiting to reach the sea, even though its fragrance taunted me like a squirrel one branch too high. And as soon as the sun rose we set off in search of Shannon and Willard and the mighty Pacific, knowing nothing could stand in our way.

CHAPTER THIRTEEN

The Western Sea! Though clouds and rain hid all but the first lines of breakers from view, we had truly arrived. I wasted no time, charging into the waves. Bitten by beaver, stabbed by thorns, starving, thirsty, and so tired I'd wondered how one paw could follow the others, my body now became weightless, carried in the arms of the Great Mystery, for surely no other force held the power of endless tides. But my blood-line and experience gave me power of my own, and my legs struck out for deeper water.

"Looks like ol' Seaman's headed for China!" Joe Field yelled, and I turned back toward shore.

Meriwether laughed and waded in a few steps himself. "We made it, men—overland to the Pacific!"

Frazer and the Field brothers splashed in the shallows, while Drouillard hunkered down on the wet sand, loading up his pipe for a ceremonial smoke, though how he would light it in the wind I couldn't imagine. Meriwether stood, legs braced, gazing off to the west, a hand shielding his eyes, trying to pierce the drizzle and fog that hung over the water. Was he looking for a ship or the next horizon? Then he sank to his knees, the surf soaking him to his chest, and his cheeks glistened with tears. When I paddled over to lick his face, he wrapped both arms around me, his body trembling as he murmured, "All the way to the Pacific."

To the north, waves thundered against rocks. It was November of 1805, and according to Clark's calculations, we had traveled 4,142 miles from the mouth of the Missouri. But to me it felt more like some great circle, ocean to ocean, as if I'd come home.

We still had exploring to do. We set off up the coast, where we soon found Shannon, Willard, and a party of five Chinooks, with two of the Indians holding Harpers Ferry rifles. From the strange way they all stared at our approach I couldn't tell who was the most surprised, but the guns immediately returned to the hands of the soldiers. Shannon strode toward us, a smile breaking over his face like sun after storm. "Are we glad to see you, Captain! We spent the night alongside of these skunks, and this morning they helped themselves to our guns. I just finished telling them—well, using hand signs—that we're part of a whole regiment that would shoot them as thieves." He waved his rifle. "And here you are!"

We joined Willard and the Indians, who didn't look at all sorry about the robbery, only curious. "You look terrible, private," Meriwether said. "Could those be more fleabites I see?"

Willard scratched at the spots on his cheeks. "These Chinooks don't seem to mind keepin' company with the little critters, sir, but I guess fleas prefer my white flesh if they can get it."

"Captain Clark should be coming around the point with the rest of our party as soon as there's a break in the weather, so take these scoundrels with you and meet up with the Captain at the sandy beach. We'll reconnoiter further north and rejoin you at a later date. Drouillard, please sign to these Indians that we expect them to go along with Shannon and Willard and *keep their hands to themselves*. We'll let Clark and the larger party impress upon them the consequences of any more such actions. I gather you didn't encounter any other white men?"

That place was called "Cape Disappointment," which made sense since we didn't find a ship or any traders, but Meriwether didn't seem worried at all, and it felt wonderful to be traveling on my own four paws with the sea on our left. I acted as foolish as a pup, chasing after shorebirds and foam. Before we returned to the others, Meriwether carved his name on a mighty tree. "For posterity," he said. I was just about as proud as he was that we had made it all the way to the Pacific, but all I could do was lift my leg on the trunk, knowing rain would soon wash my scent away.

We all met up back at the beach camp, where we spent a wet week. Two Chinook chiefs and their followers smoked with the Captains, accepting medals and an American flag without much expression, but our men showed a lot more enthusiasm when a fellow named Delashelwilt arrived with his wife, who appeared to be in charge of six young women, daughters and nieces eager to spend time with soldiers. I never figured out what made particular girls appealing, but I could tell Meriwether didn't think much of these Chinooks. They didn't wear a lot of clothes, which made the whole business a lot simpler, and bore strange decorations on their skin like those I'd observed on sailors. Just above their feet some kind of cord dug into flesh so their legs bulged above, as if to show how meaty they were, though I was pretty sure these people didn't eat each other.

Across the bay lived another tribe called the Clatsops. Some of them paddled over one day to display two robes made of the pelts of sea otters. I liked the tangy scent of those furs and the Captains liked their feel. "I suppose I'll have to come up with something special to purchase one," Clark said. From our dwindling supply of trade goods, he set out a watch and a handkerchief, and then added a bunch of beads and an American dollar. The Clatsop pointed to the beads and shook his head. "Blue!" he said. Indians preferred "chief beads," the color of the sky. But we'd already traded ours away, and in the end the Clatsops recrossed the bay with their robes, sure they could get a better deal from the men on the ship that arrived each spring.

"They drive a tough bargain," Clark lamented. "You'd think they were canny Yankee traders."

Sergeant Ordway, who hailed from New Hampshire, nodded and grinned. "Must have learned from the sea captains, sir."

"At least they didn't steal anything," Meriwether said, "a pleasant change from the other tribes of the Columbia."

We survived the storms in makeshift shelters cobbled together from old planks we'd found at an abandoned Chinook village (complete with fleas), but now we needed to choose a better location and construct winter quarters. The Clatsops had reported more deer on the north side of the river, but plenty of elk on the south side where they lived, which was good enough for me.

"Upriver the climate would be more severe," Meriwether said, "and on the coast we'll find a good source of salt, which I've sorely missed."

Clark snorted. "Salt water isn't healthy. But we'd have a better chance of meeting up with a trading vessel so we could purchase the supplies we need."

"And then we could send the field notes and journals back to President Jefferson," my Master said, always concerned that something might happen to those precious documents.

After a lot more talking back and forth, they decided to put the matter to a vote. Everybody got a say, including York and Bird Woman. Sergeant Gass frowned when he heard that. "Never heard of such a thing."

"First time for everything," Sergeant Pryor said. "Most cap'ns wouldn't care what any of us thought. This is new territory—might as well have new ways."

But it didn't really matter in the end, since all but Private Shields the blacksmith voted to cross over to the south side and look for a suitable site. About half believed that if we couldn't find a good place, we should move up the river towards the Narrows, while the others wanted to stay along the coast. Bird Woman preferred to live wherever she could dig roots. Nobody asked, but I was in favor of the elk.

We found an easier crossing over to the south side and stopped along the mouth of another river, where the weather turned nasty. After three days of inaction, Meriwether had enough of pacing around camp. "Since I'm wet anyway, I might as well get out there and accomplish something. I'll take five men in the Raven and look for a place with plenty of game."

When I stuck my nose under his hand, he laughed. "And Seaman will come along, of course."

We rounded the place called Tongue Point, set up a tent, and sent out the hunters. They returned with four deer, ducks, and some plump geese, which made for a tasty dinner, even without any elk. The next morning we rose with the sun, heading up one river and then another in search of a good spot. The waterways provided home for all kinds of birds, including enormous long-legged waders with sharp beaks whose hoarse voices reminded me of the Shoshone Raven Talker. Finally, on a small bluff above the line of the tides, we located a good spring about three miles from the coast and two hundred feet from a nice river, with plenty of tall trees for building. Best of all, Drouillard and Colter killed six elk and five deer. That settled it.

Clark headed out with a party of soldiers in search of a good salt camp while we remained behind to bring in a supply of meat and prepare for construction of the fort. The men were in pretty poor shape, some with tumors, others with dysentery, boils, and strained muscles. I felt just fine, and with an important task to complete Meriwether thrived, though none of us slept very well on account of the fleas. When Clark and his group returned after three days, our men still hadn't finished cutting all the trees we needed. Gass fussed over the timber, concerned we hadn't found any wood that split as well as he liked for the roofs, but work commenced on a smokehouse, since we had no other way to preserve meat in a climate where it had rained all but three days in a month. Humans think meat is spoiled just when it's becoming ripe.

Two canoes of Clatsops, led by Chief Coboway, soon paddled up for a visit, bringing roots and the pelt of a young sea otter. I didn't think much of a kind of dried thistle they provided, but after roasting in the fire the wapato roots tasted a lot like potato. We offered the Clatsops some fishhooks and a bag of Shoshone tobacco, plus the usual medal for Coboway. I think the Indians had hoped for more, but they spent the night peacefully, and then glided back down the river toward their village.

Fort Clatsop grew more slowly than Meriwether liked, for keeping the camp fed drained a lot of manpower and the wind and rain seldom quit. By mid-December, the builders had started chinking the gaps between the logs. Eventually Sergeant Gass found wood he deemed acceptable for roofing and two days before Christmas the Captains' hut was far enough along that we moved on in. Joe Field finished lashing together new writing tables on Christmas Eve, the same day the men occupied their three sleeping rooms across the parade grounds, even though that side of the fort still had no roof. Charbonneau plus Bird Woman and Little Pomp had their own quarters on our side. Altogether the fort measured fifty feet square.

Next morning the men woke us to the firing of all the guns, a shout, and then a song about a king named Wenceslas, who seemed quite popular, though nobody had liked George, the last king over America. The Captains gave out tobacco as presents for the men who smoked or chewed, while the others received handkerchiefs. Nobody danced, since the mud in our little courtyard sucked at the men's feet and caked on my paws, and they didn't have even a sip of whiskey, only water from our spring. Though I enjoyed the dinner of elk and fish (both quite ripe) and a few roots, I suppose it wasn't much of a feast. A lot of the men started remembering other Christmases, mostly with their families, but Shannon even started talking about Fort Mandan with a little catch in his voice, and then we went to bed early. Fleas kept us scratching all night.

On the 30th of December, the roofs and the men's bunks were completed. That day the Captains told the visiting Clatsops that we would close our gates each night and at sunset all Indians had to leave the fort. A sentinel would patrol constantly, for we just couldn't trust the local people, especially the Chinooks, who had muskets obtained from the traders and "sticky fingers," as Colter said with a growl. The men even instigated a password: *"No Chinook!"*

The New Year of 1806 seemed to agree with Meriwether, who was already looking forward to the next, when he expected to be home with his family and, of course, The President. "In Washington," he told me, "you'll be the toast of the town, the only canine member of the Corps of Discovery. The President's house has the best food, the best wine, and the best music. You'll enjoy our visits there."

I wasn't so sure.

Ridding the blankets of fleas became York's daily assignment, which he conducted with a ferocity that made me glad he was on my side. The constant drizzle and damp bothered York more than most of the others, for his nose always ran and the low-hanging smoke troubled his eyes. Here on the coast the Indians had seen lots of black sailors, so he didn't make as much of an impression with the Chinook girls. "You an' me's a lot alike, Seaman," York told me one day. "We did fine on the trail, even when it was tough goin'. Here I'm only a slave ag'in, an' both our Massas always settin' at those desks writin' away.

Wish I had me a nice gal with skin the color o' molasses. An' you could have a purty lil' spotted hound to keep you warm. That what I wishes."

York was right. I missed the daily adventures of the journey West, and the notion of a sweet hound bitch sounded fine. The nearest Clatsop village was only a few miles, but the local dogs acted afraid of me. All they seemed to care about was eating, which was important, but when they grew fat... I certainly didn't want to produce pups for the pot.

Sometimes, when Meriwether huddled over his new desk, it seemed safe for me to leave him alone, and I would head down to the river. Besides the waterbirds and the fish, sea otters sometimes ventured near, studying me with bright eyes in round whiskery faces. If I couldn't protect Meriwether from danger, I felt useless. Gathering a few sticks of firewood just wasn't enough. But the Captains coveted the sea otter furs, and so I would try, time after time, to catch the little beasts unaware; they would always vanish below the surface before my jaws could close on them. Seals, the other animals that intrigued me, were so watchful that I could only admire them from a distance. Humans had always praised my swimming ability, but those seals had a kinship with the water that I lacked.

During one of those visits, Charbonneau sauntered to the bank nearby and unbuttoned his trousers to piss in the river. He leaned back, grunting with pleasure, and then he was slipping in the mud, sliding off the steep bank and into the swift current.

"Help me!" he shrieked in French, before a wave filled his mouth.

I didn't hesitate. Instinct took over, and I was in that river swimming toward Charbonneau in moments. The current dragged him downstream, but I managed to maneuver past and circle back, positioning myself so he could grab my tail. But in his panic the fool lurched forward to grasp the ruff of my neck and both of us floundered. He was dragging me down, making it impossible for me to swim or even stay afloat. When he yelled "Save me!" right in my ear, it was all I could do to restrain from biting a little sense into him. Thankfully Charbonneau lost his grip, gurgling in terror, and I gained enough distance from him that my tail was the only thing he could clutch. It felt as if he would wrench that appendage from my hindquarters but I clenched my teeth against the pain and struck out for the shore. Charbonneau's feet struck bottom. He let go and clawed his way onto the shore, lying there panting.

Maybe if I'd stopped to think about it I'd have realized Bird Woman would be better off without this loudmouthed smelly old half-breed bullying her. But centuries of breeding wouldn't be denied, and so I'd rescued about the last man I would have chosen. I even followed him back to Fort Clatsop, just to make sure he didn't get into any more trouble.

Labiche was on guard duty. "You went in zee river?" he asked in French, his eyes wide with disbelief. "But you cannot swim!"

"Just waded in to rinse dirt from my clothes," Charbonneau said. "Some of us like to look our best."

And he never said one word about the rescue.

Though I didn't think much of the local Indians, at least their visits to the fort budged Meriwether from his desk. He never gave them his "Great Father Jefferson" speech, since this Oregon Country wasn't part of the United States, but he did want to compile a vocabulary and write down all the details of their cultures, like the way they flattened the heads of their babies. Both the Captains admired the Chinook canoes and filled pages of their journals with drawings. The Clatsops brought roots and dried berries, which our men welcomed as a change from elk meat they considered spoiled, but the Clatsop women kept their distance. Even though they lived just across the river, the Chinook females behaved very differently.

"They just can't keep their hands off us," Colter said, and it was true, as long as the soldiers came up with suitable presents. What would happen, I wondered, when we ran out of trade goods?

With the fort completed, the Captains decided we could spare a few men to make salt at the coast, assigning my friend Joe Field along with Bratton and Gibson. Drouillard headed our party of hunters, which had to range farther and farther to kill enough elk, which often "spoiled" before they could haul it back to the fort. I ended up with a lot of meat nobody else wanted and could imagine myself growing plump and lazy if it continued. Pretty soon Meriwether was busy doctoring the men for syphilis again. It affected Goodrich the worst, so he couldn't wear pants for a few days, but that didn't stop our men from mating with the Chinook girls.

"Nothin' else to do," Reuben Field muttered. "Wonder how Brother Joe's gettin' along with no females at all?"

The Captains kept away from the Chinook girls, just as they had with the other tribes. When I heard Meriwether stirring under his blankets, I knew he was doing more than scratching at fleas. Sometimes I wished my Master would just give in and find a female, but instead he wrote. He'd grown pale again and his deep-set eyes looked tired.

"The boredom's hard on all of us," Meriwether confided to Clark one evening. "The men have already made enough moccasins to recross the country with pairs left over. They're sick of feeding the smokehouse fire—'women's work', Labiche calls it, but how else can we preserve the elk? And they're already tired of eating it every day. Boiled elk, dried elk, elk soup, leftover elk. When we get some fresh enough to roast, that's a feast, even with nothing else." He sighed. "Sometimes I think we've built ourselves a prison, not a fort. Spring can't come soon enough."

The Captains had set April 1 as our departure date, knowing snow would linger late in the mountains and prevent any earlier passage. Before then, we would face a lot of gray days.

Once we heard about a whale that had beached itself to the south. I longed to see the great beast, but Clark was to lead that expedition, leaving us to hold the fort. As the party assembled, Charbonneau strode over to speak to the Captains through Cruzatte. "My wife she is a foolish girl," he said. "All last night she keep me awake, talking about the fish on the beach. If I do not ask you for her to go along on this trip, I will never get any sleep."

Clark beckoned Bird Woman to his side, and with the help of Cruzatte, asked why she wanted to join the party.

"She says she has traveled a long way," Cruzatte translated, "to see zee great waters, and now that a monstrous fish is to be seen, she thinks it very hard she is not permitted to see either one."

Clark laughed. "That would be very hard. Let her come along, then, and Pomp, too. It's time they both see the Pacific."

It was awfully quiet with so many off in search of whale meat and elk meat and salt. Though Little Pomp never cried, his attempts at talking and his laughter had livened up the fort, and I was glad when the party returned four days later. Indians had already stripped the whale carcass, but Bird Woman signed that she'd climbed inside the great skeleton, and Clark had purchased three hundred pounds of blubber and some oil. Some of the men thought the blubber tasted like beaver, which Drouillard and Colter trapped occasionally, but I couldn't agree. Whale blubber tasted like the deeps of the sea.

Later we sampled another local food, for the rivers began to swarm with fish called hooligans, which the Clatsops netted and sold, showing our men how to spear the little fish in rows and roast them over the fire, the fat dripping and sizzling with a scent that made me drool. Meriwether liked them so well he traded for them whenever he could.

Although the men grumbled about the cold it didn't really feel like winter, for we never had any snow, only day after day of rain accompanied by wind. If we didn't keep a good fire going, leather grew mold. Sometimes I felt a little moldy myself. At least I didn't mind the wet, but the incessant dripping from the roofs and trees was a sound I wouldn't miss one bit. Each week made all of us more restless. Pomp learned to walk, and I helped Bird Woman keep him out of trouble, for he had to learn that hot metal burned, blades cut, and his father had a short temper. "Can't you keep that brat out of my way?" Charbonneau shouted. "You're no good as a wife! Why did I have to bring you along, and not my other woman, who knows how to take care of a man?"

"Shut yer yap!" Labiche snapped. "You're zee only one with a female at all."

Shannon looked like he wanted to say something to Charbonneau, too, but instead he scooped little Pomp into his arms. "Roll over, Seaman!" he commanded, and I obliged, which made the both of them laugh, so I kicked my paws in the air and howled.

I wished I could make my Master laugh as easily. Sometimes he would walk with me down to the river, skipping flat stones across its surface, but he never joined the hunting parties. "Let the men have their fun," he said. "I have my reports to write. They have so little."

As time crept along, the men had even less, for the visits of the Chinook girls and the "old baud"—as the Captains called Delashelwilt's wife—required a toll. When Meriwether caught Collins bartering away a knife, he made a new rule: no trading away the weapons. Instead, the Captains supplied each soldier with a small supply of ribbon.

A stocky smiling fellow called Chief Cuscalar became something of a friend to Clark, sharing the hospitality of his village during a rare visit the Captain made among the coastal Indians, and Clark occasionally sent presents to the chief. One time Cuscalar and his two wives visited us, bringing roots and woven mats. Clark thought they were a gift, but later the chief asked for three metal files in return, which we couldn't spare, so Cuscalar upped his side of the bargain by offering his wives to the Captains. Neither he nor the females took the refusal well.

"They'll trade anything for what they want!" Meriwether

said after the disgruntled chief strode away with his wives in tow.

"I suppose he meant it as an honor." Clark shrugged. "All this expedition needs is a pair of Captains with the pox."

In February, some of the Clatsops stole six elk from Drouillard's cache. Up until that time I'd preferred the Clatsops to the thieving Chinooks, but robbing a cache (especially of elk) was unforgivable. When Chief Coboway sent three dogs to replace the stolen meat I had to leave the fort, unable to witness the execution and consumption of fellow canines. Down at the river, as I lay on the bank envying the grace of the seals with the rain dripping off the ends of my ears, I wished with all my heart that it was April.

Time is in the hands of the Great Mystery, however. Even though a few flowers had gone into bloom and the days had lengthened, the wind blew harder than ever, driving the storms sideways. Even the conical woven hat Meriwether had purchased from the Indians couldn't deflect the rain from his face. The endless progression of gray days seemed to sap the life from him, and that shadow I'd sensed before grew until it was almost like a second Meriwether, a dark presence that brooded over the writing desk like the wide-winged carrion bird. Clark had brought down one of the creatures we'd spotted when we first reached this Oregon Country, and its immense stuffed form haunted one corner of our room in the fort. I seriously considered dragging the monster outside, tearing off its head and wings until it was only a pile of feathers, but it was one of Meriwether's most valued specimens, so I let it be. Clark tried to draw Meriwether out of his gloom: challenging him to a shooting contest, even though he knew my Master was the better shot, then borrowing Pomp from Bird Woman and bringing the boy to our room, where my tail became a target for those chubby little fingers. Sometimes Clark spoke of the future, when Meriwether would receive the The President's praise for a job well done, but even the mention of Jefferson failed to stimulate much interest. My Master spent far too much time huddled with his journal, writing, scratching out passages, swearing. Once he even ripped a page free and fed it to the fire, destroying his own words, something he'd never done before. That worried me.

The only time the shadow really lifted came on the occasions when Shannon lured Meriwether from the fort for a scientific exploration of the countryside. The experience of our journey West had transformed the Corps' youngest member into an able frontiersman. Under the tutelage of Drouillard and Colter, Shannon had become one of our better hunters, and he remedied the boredom of life at Fort Clatsop by spending much of his time stalking elk. During his travels, Shannon always kept an eye out for interesting specimens, birds or plants that might be new to science. Then he reported back to Meriwether.

"All right, lad," my Master might agree, "show me your discovery."

Then we would tramp the coastal hills or penetrate the mossy woods, and Meriwether would bend down to examine a tiny cone or a set of delicate leaves. "I'm afraid this one's already known," he would usually say. But sometimes a light sparked in Meriwether's eyes and his fingers quivered as they plucked a sample. "A new form of lily," he would exult, and Shannon's smile would match that of my Master, and my tail would wag so hard I couldn't stand in one spot. Those were the good days.

As March progressed, the Captains stepped up preparations for our return journey, deciding we would depart sooner than planned, which roused a cheer from the men. Shields had all the rifles functioning perfectly, we had plenty of dry powder and new moccasins to spare, but we needed at least one more Indian canoe, preferably several. When Drouillard returned from a Clatsop village with a trio of Indians and a single vessel, the Captains rummaged through all our trade goods. But everything the locals wanted that we could spare had already fallen into their hands. In the end, Meriwether produced his fancy dress uniform coat, only a little the worse for wear. Even gilt braid and a whole carrot of tobacco didn't tempt the Clatsops, however, and they left the fort carrying their canoe.

"I do not like these fellows," Charbonneau said in French. "They steal our elk and more, I think, if we let them. We should let one of their boats stick to our fingers."

"We can't trust them, that's sure," said Labiche in English. "Maybe Charbonneau is right and we should take a canoe as payment. Six elk are worth a lot more than three dogs."

I kept waiting for the Captains to say something, sure they would never agree with loudmouth Charbonneau. We had never taken anything that wasn't offered except a bit of firewood. But we needed another canoe, and when four of the men, including Charbonneau, left Fort Clatsop the next morning, nobody stopped them. Chief Coboway paid a visit that day, smoking with the Captains. This time he'd only brought a few of his men and left his wives at home, signing that his ears hurt from the females' chatter. Maybe if the Captains could have talked to Coboway in a common language, explaining how badly we needed another boat, things would have been different. Perhaps the four men had merely gone hunting, though Charbonneau was so noisy he could seldom get close enough for a good shot at anything. I'd never learned to like the smell of tobacco, so I left the fort, following the old scent of a meadow mouse even though I knew its maker had long since vanished into some hole. The day was dismal as usual, which matched my mood. How long until our departure? I wanted my Master away from this place that we'd worked so hard to reach.

"*Sacre bleu!*" Charbonneau said, peering at me from dense underbrush. "It's only zee dog! The canoe will be safe here after all, until zee Clatsops have gone home. She's one fine vessel, and we need her more than they do. We deserve thees canoe."

Private Collins stepped out of the brush and reached a hand to pet me, but I shrank back in confusion. Indians stole horses from one another, but weren't our people supposed to be showing them a better way to live? I turned and ran away from the trees, past the fort and down to the river. A pair of geese rose from the water, honking at my intrusion. As they winged their way inland, I wished we could follow them, go away before it was too late.

That night, after the Captains had settled into their bunks and blown out the candles, Meriwether said, "I'm sorry for this day. Should we have ordered them to stay away from the Clatsops' canoes?"

"I didn't like fooling old Coboway, acting as if nothing was going on," Clark said. "But what choice do we have? The only things these Indians want are rifles and powder, and we swore we would never give them to any tribe."

"And so we break a different vow, our agreement that we

would never take anything not given or purchased." Meriwether didn't speak for a long moment, his fingers digging into the fur of my neck. "Tonight I was too ashamed to write the whole truth in my journal. Even my own foolishness, when I walked unheeding into danger—at least those were honest mistakes. This feels like a betrayal of everything we set out to do."

"Try to be philosophical about it," Clark said. "We didn't want this to happen, but it's done. The Clatsops can craft another canoe. We plan to leave the fort in Coboway's hands. That should make up for it."

"It's not what it does to them, it's what it does to us." My Master's hand slid from my fur.

No one slept well in our room that night, including the fleas. It felt almost good to scratch and bite at something within my reach.

CHAPTER FOURTEEN

"It's a fine thing to be on the move!" Colter puffed, paddling hard from his position in the <u>Raven</u>. "Never thought I'd tire of eatin' elk meat, but a hump of buffalo would sure taste good, and to git some, I don't even mind the work o' goin' up-river."

"Amen!" said Joe Field, reaching up to scratch at his chin, bereft of whiskers for the first time in months. "Reckon ol' Seaman was the only one among us who really liked it there. I swear he's fatter than ever—better watch out for hungry Chinooks."

I had put on a little bulk, but was confident that the journey ahead would shed the excess pounds. Those first days on the river had acted like a tonic on Meriwether, who often manned a paddle, anxious to speed us on our way against the strong current, whether toward home or simply away from Fort Clatsop. He'd written out several copies of the names of every man in our party and posted the list in our little room before turning the buildings over to Coboway, also giving the chief one of the lists which the Indian seemed to treasure. Each mile from the coast seemed to lighten my Master's mood, though I found I missed the sound of the surf. We'd brought along many reminders of our dreary time at the coast, however, not only the stolen vessel, now carrying some of our men and baggage, but scores of fleas and lingering cases of syphilis, though the men had finally agreed to swear and honor an oath of celibacy, which was a word I'd never heard before but apparently meant no more business for the "old baud" and her girls. Before we'd departed, the Captains had even presented old Delashelwilt with a certificate of "Good Deportment."

Though we'd already towed the canoes through several rapids, the men retained their good humor, but Meriwether started his worrying again after one of the many Indians gathered along the riverbank used hand signs to inform Drouillard that the salmon were late this year and the tribes upriver were starving. All the way to Nez Perce country we could expect to find few deer or elk, probably no loper-goats, and certainly no buffalo. If we waited for the salmon to run up the Columbia we might not make it back to the Missouri before it froze in the fall, and if we missed the Nez Perce, who crossed the mountains as soon as the snow melted each spring, we'd probably be horseless again, for the Captains had entrusted our little herd to the family of Chief Twisted Hair. I suppose Meriwether did have good reasons to worry, but sometimes I wondered why he couldn't be a little more like his partner Clark, who joked with the men rather than brooding in silence. I guess it's hard to be a genius.

The solution to the food dilemma was right there along the bank, yipping and cowering. Drouillard managed to purchase enough for us to keep moving. "I guess Seaman and I will just have to get by on roots," said Clark, the only man in our party who still wouldn't eat dog meat. I figured by the time we reached the Nez Perce my paunch would be long gone.

As we continued upriver, we began to see more Indians. Some of the poor people were gaunt and hollow-eyed, but others looked like they seldom missed a meal. Those fellows kept hanging about, looking for something to steal. One night, Sergeant Gass caught an old man sneaking around camp and whipped him with a willow switch before sending him on his way. That was the first time anyone in our party had struck an Indian, but nobody felt very bad about it, and when another Chinook attempted to steal Colter's tomahawk, I was surprised the man escaped intact. Every portage kept me busy guarding against theft, and when we reached the Narrows, Meriwether assigned men with rifles to help, since I couldn't be everywhere at once, no matter how hard I tried. The trail along the river was slippery and narrow. An Indian flung rocks down upon us, which only glanced off my thick fur but drew a spot of blood on McNeal's shoulder, while Shields had to draw his knife to fend off a pair of Watlalas that threatened him. When we reached our stopping place for the night, everyone was exhausted and edgy. Meriwether was too busy surveying a crack in one of the canoes to pay me any mind, so on sore paws I limped off to do my business. Sharp rocks jabbed with every step until I located a sandy depression where I could nap in peace. Why stay awake for a supper of roots, anyway? I flopped down with my head on my paws and closed my eyes.

I woke to the pinch of a rope tight around my muzzle, more rope around my neck, and the prick of a blade at my hindquarters. I sprang up, but the noose tightened around my throat until I could hardly catch breath. Two dark faces leered at me from either side, tugging on the ropes. Was this a nightmare? No, the blade prodding the flesh beside my tail was all too real, and I could scent my own blood over the rank smell of the Indians around me. Why had I gone off by myself, let down my guard? Another poke from the knife and I lurched forward, trying to escape the pain, which delighted the Indians, who loosened the stranglehold around my neck. When I balked, the ropes tightened again until I gasped for air. The blade jabbed. I jumped forward again, and the Indians kept me moving, away from the camp, from the Corps of Discovery, from Meriwether. I tried to howl, but the rope around my muzzle was drawn so tight I only managed a whine. Was this what the Great Mystery had planned for me? Each step brought me closer to a horrible fate. I could almost feel the flames of a fire, smell my own flesh cooking. I tried to turn my head to look back toward camp, but the Indian at the rear made a stabbing motion. The rope that bound my muzzle slacked for just a moment, though, and I pawed at it, gaining enough space to manage a single woof before it snugged again. Then the grip around my neck squeezed so tightly I struggled to see through a dark fog. Was that the song of the sea roaring in my ears? My paws seemed to float, gliding faster and faster. I was diving deep, deeper than any seal, as deep as a whale, away from the blades of humans that wanted to flay my flesh from my bones. There in the dark, where it was cold and quiet, I would be safe. But I was alone. Where was my Master? Then the water rushed away and left me gasping, lying on solid ground.

"He's breathing."

I opened my eyes to Shannon's face only a foot away. Colter and Drouillard stood on either side of him, rifles at the ready. The Watlalas had vanished. Maybe it was all a terrible dream.

"Thank God you heard him bark, Drouillard!" Colter said. "The Cap'n woulda had all our hides if them redskins got away with ol' Seaman. They woulda had themselves a real feast."

I shivered, still lying on my side, and Drouillard crouched beside me and placed a hand on my head. "I doubt they wanted to eat the big fellow. More likely they planned to use him to upgrade their stock. Dog like this is worth more as a breeding animal."

I struggled to stand, shaking off a rope that lay across my back. The skin beside my tail smarted where the knife had jabbed me. It was no dream.

"Captain Lewis needs to hear about this," Shannon said.

"I wouldn't be in those Injuns moccasins fer nothin'," said Colter. "The Cap'ns don't want trouble, but Seaman's part of the Corps. Come on, boy, let's hustle you on back to camp."

When we arrived at the encampment, set well above the river for defense, everyone crowded around, the men petting me and all speaking at once while Bird Woman cleaned the cut beside my tail and applied a salve that stung at first but grew soothing. Then the men all stopped talking. The Field brothers stepped apart to let the Captains through. "What's going on here?" Meriwether demanded. "Why hasn't anyone started a fire?"

"Seaman had a little Injun trouble," Colter said. "Got kidnapped by three o' these river fellers."

Drouillard nodded. "From the Watlala band. But Seaman's all right, sir. They had him trussed up and used a knife to keep him moving, but the sight of Colter, Shannon, and me and three Harpers Ferry rifles persuaded 'em to release your dog."

Meriwether knelt, his fingers gentle as they parted my fur and examined my wound. I could feel his hands tense, and when he stood up abruptly, his eyes burned like hot coals. "Keep your rifles at the ready, men! I believe they're trying to bait us into taking some foolish action. Well, I'll be damned if we're going to violate our mission for a few renegades, but they must understand we won't allow any more interference! Come, Seaman."

We walked off a little way from the others, leaving Clark to argue with the hotheads who wanted to punish the Watlalas. I kept my ribs right up against Meriwether's leg. His fingers stroked my ears, but I could tell he wasn't relaxing. "How dare they? I promised The President we wouldn't raise a hand except in our own defense, but they keep provoking us with their thievery and their insults—it's more than a man should have to bear! These river Indians are the worst of their race, sneaky, underhanded, without a speck of honor." He took a deep breath, exhaled hard. "The President doesn't understand. He expects too much..."

There wasn't a thing I could do except stay close by his side so he wouldn't feel quite so alone. The shadow might be stronger than I was, a weight that bowed his shoulders, but I would struggle against that darkness as long as I could draw breath. The Great Mystery had kept me around for a reason. We still had a job to do, much of a continent to recross. We'd followed the sun West, but now each day's rising would light our way home.

"At least they brought you back," Meriwether said, standing straighter again. "You know, Goodrich hooked a new type of trout. I'd planned to stuff it, but I believe it would serve better as a meal for you. Science will just have to wait its turn."

That fish with no seasoning at all tasted even better than a salmon fried in bear grease.

The next morning an Indian appeared outside our camp, unarmed, wearing a striped blanket and little else. "Friend!" he said.

After Drouillard had spoken with him in hand signs, we found out he was a chief of the Watlala band. He planned to act as our escort through the Cascades in payment for my kidnapping. Apparently the three young men had gone against his wishes. But I suspected him, nonetheless, and stayed as far away as I could and still keep watch during all the time it took to haul our lighter canoes and baggage to the calmer water above the rapids. The next day, rain pouring down on us as usual, Clark went ahead with a few men, hoping to buy horses, while we attempted to transport the heaviest of the dugouts through the Narrows. York had remained behind to help with the heavy work. The muscles in his mighty arms strained, trying to hold onto the canoe, but the vessel tore free from his grip and catapulted end over end into the white torrent.

"I's sorry she got away," York said, his big hands bleeding. "We gonna' go after her?"

"She'll be nothing but kindling after that wild ride," Meriwether told him. "We'll make do with what we have. We always do."

Meriwether was able to trade four elk skins and two of our buffalo robes for a couple of small canoes. I looked away, feeling queasy as they loaded the carcasses of three dogs aboard one of the boats.

After a wet camp, we continued. Soon men from the advance party returned with a note from Clark. "Tell him to offer them twice as much!" Meriwether said, scribbling furiously on the reverse side of the paper. "We must have at least five horses. I want all of us off this river and I want it soon!"

In the end, we traded away our two largest iron kettles for four horses. We had never bartered them before, which showed how desperate the Captains had become. Fortunately, salmon finally arrived in the river, and though more Indians had appeared than ever, they became busy with their fishing and seemed less interested in us. But tomahawks and knives continued to vanish every night until Meriwether became so angry he couldn't eat breakfast. "That does it! We're abandoning the canoes and traveling overland to join Clark. I can't tolerate these river Indians a moment longer. And we won't leave a particle for their benefit."

At Meriwether's command, the men piled all the boats and poles and paddles together. Then he set the pile ablaze. We all watched it burn, my Master's face flushed from the flames. Then he shouted, "Leave that be, you villain!" An Indian had edged in close to grab a piece of iron that had fallen from one of the poles. Meriwether lunged toward him, heedless of the fire, and grasped the man's arm so hard the iron fell between them, clanging against a rock. My Master had never struck anyone, not even when Charbonneau let two of our precious horses escape, but now he cursed and battered the man with his espontoon, letting all his fury and frustration out on this one Indian, who cringed and tried to shield his face. "Get him out of here!" he told Colter, shoving the fellow away from the fire. A number of Indians had gathered to watch, and Meriwether swung his espontoon in their general direction. "I'll shoot the first one of you who tries to steal from us again. We aren't afraid to fight you. I have it in my power to kill you all and set fire to your houses!"

Though the Indians couldn't understand his words, they backed away from his fury. Shannon's mouth was hanging open, but he held his rifle in both hands and so did the rest of our men. I think some of them hoped the Indians would make an aggressive move, give them an excuse to take action after all the frustrations. I felt a growl building in my chest. But the sight of Meriwether silhouetted against the fire and all our Harpers Ferry rifles cowed those river Indians. Some of them even hung their heads. Meriwether stood perfectly still, the espontoon held before him. His eyes flamed the same way they had when he'd found out about my kidnapping. Then all the fire went out. He looked older, somehow, which for some reason made me think of the General back in Clarksville.

"It's not my wish to treat with you unfairly. You have stolen our knives and tomahawks, but since we do not know who the thieves are among you, we will let our property go rather than harm the innocent."

He turned as I'd seen the men do during their parades and strode away. I padded after him. Maybe those people were nice enough folks—good to their families and neighbors (though not to their dogs) with their own way of life that we just didn't understand. But if I never encountered another river Indian in my life it would be too soon.

CHAPTER FIFTEEN

I'd forgotten how sore paws could get. Soon all the men limped except Private Bratton, who was too crippled to walk and rode one of the pack animals. Meriwether's left ankle had swollen to twice its normal size, but each night he soaked it in a cold stream and managed to hobble on the next day. At last we reached the village of Chief Yellept and his Wallawallas, where it was like greeting old friends. When the Captains accepted the invitation to camp nearby for a few days, I let out a whimper, just a little one, as I lowered myself to the ground. "I know how you feel," Shannon whispered. I guess we'd all been trying to hide how much we hurt.

The Wallawallas spoke a language that reminded me of Nez Perce, not like the clucking of the Chinooks and their kin, and when we discovered a captive Shoshone woman in the village, Bird Woman could converse with her, relay to Charbonneau, then on through Drouillard or Labiche to the Captains. Chief Yellept was able to tell us about a shortcut to the Lolo Trail over the mountains, brought us fish and fuel, and presented Clark with a white crested-neck stallion. The chief would have liked one of our kettles as a return gift, but since we'd no more to spare he was satisfied with Clark's sword plus balls and powder. By the time we departed, we'd assembled a herd of twenty-three horses, mostly young and feisty, with Clark's white stallion the orneriest of the lot. We would have made better time if the weather had cooperated, but it began to rain, then hail, then snow. We were out of food again after a poor supper, wondering where we'd find our next meal, when we encountered Chief Tetoharsky and a small band of his Nez Perce, who provided us with some bread made of a plant a lot like a parsnip and offered to lead us to Twisted Hair's village, where we'd left our horses the previous autumn; maybe old Rockfoot the mule could kick some sense into the unruly Wallawalla horses. We crossed the Snake River and tramped along the Clearwater, hungry again. The Nez Perce didn't have much to eat at that time of the year, but on our previous visit Clark had treated the legs of an old man who hadn't walked for a long time. The fellow had made a miraculous recovery and now he greeted us by hopping from one foot to the other. Since these Indians had decided Clark was "Big Medicine," they were glad to trade us all the food they could in exchange for his services.

I liked these people a lot, since they'd proved themselves honest and friendly and never ate dogs. The local canines didn't cower and slink, trotting right up to our soldiers to be petted, but I could see the men sizing them up, hoping for meat instead of the roots and a few fish that had made up our recent meals. Unfortunately, the Nez Perce were willing to sell what they wouldn't eat themselves, and when Labiche offered to barter his calico shirt for a plump little bitch, the bidding began.

Run away, I wanted to tell these trusting canines. This was far worse than with the packs among the Chinooks, who were destined for short, unhappy lives. Our men weren't starving. They didn't need these dogs. Was this the hand of the Great Mystery at work, or simply greed? But I didn't make a sound. Maybe I'd become too good a soldier.

"Come on, Seaman," Shannon said. "Let's go for a walk."

No matter how far I went, then or years later, I would never forget the surprised yelp from the first dog that fell under the knife.

Thankfully we soon left that village, traveling until we met up with a Nez Perce band led by Chief Cut Nose, a squat fellow who bore a scar from battling the Shoshone. When we learned that he held one of that nation captive, Bird Woman was eager to talk to the man, who said his name was Flint Necklace. Soon she began to look uneasy. "The Shoshone captive says one of the elders of this village believes we are bad men," Drouillard translated from Charbonneau, "who have come to kill them."

We all acted as friendly as we could, and since the dogs in that village were skinny from a hard winter, I could assure them in good conscience that we harbored no ill intentions. Not a single bitch was in season, but they had good bone structure and sweet dispositions, so I began to hope that I might find a willing female sometime soon. The Captains traded for a couple of horses which they planned to eat if necessary.

As we continued our journey up the Clearwater, we could see the Bitterroot Mountains covered with snow, which affirmed what Tetoharsky had warned: late storms still blocked the trails over the mountains. We ended up eating those Nez Perce horses, their entrails so grassy that my portion tasted more like vegetables than meat, but very welcome. Cut Nose and the Shoshone prisoner Flint Necklace had both accompanied us, and the scar-faced chief kept gesturing for Cruzatte to play his fiddle, when all the old half-breed wanted to do was rest. Flint Necklace had a lot more dignity than his master, and Bird Woman let him hold Pomp when she dug for roots.

All of us had looked forward to reaching Twisted Hair's lodge, but when we arrived, we were disappointed: our horses and old Rockfoot weren't waiting for us. Cut Nose and our old friend Twisted Hair started arguing right off, and even though we couldn't understand what they were shouting, it was enough to make the Captains decide to move on to a good water source before setting up camp, with no chance to follow up on the tantalizing scent I'd detected.... Clark invited both the chiefs to join us for a council, glad to have Flint Necklace to interpret, but that evening the Shoshone explained to Bird Woman that this feud between the chiefs was not his affair and he wanted no part of it, so we still had to rely on hand signs to find out what had caused the dispute. First Drouillard got Twisted Hair's side of the story, how Cut Nose had gotten jealous when he got back from his autumn raiding and found out Americans had made friends with one of his rival chiefs. Cut Nose made it clear he considered himself a lot more important than old Twisted Hair, who had guided us all the way to the Narrows. The two chiefs started yelling again and stalked off to their respective camps on either side of us. Drouillard was so disgusted he went hunting, but when he came back was ready to give it another try. The Captains invited Twisted Hair for a smoke, and finally we were able to make some sense out of what had occurred. When Cut Nose had returned from his raiding, he'd wanted to be boss, insisting that he was the one who should be taking care of our herd, and Twisted Hair had grown so tired of hearing about it that he didn't want to have anything more to do with our horses and had let them run wild. Then Clark invited Cut Nose to smoke. That chief said Twisted Hair was a "bad old man with two faces." But our horses were fine, he told us with a scowl at his rival, all living with his good friend Chief Broken Arm up the river.

The next day we traveled through snow, the fractious Wallawalla horses slipping and sliding on the narrow trail, until we reached the lodge of Broken Arm, which was the biggest building we'd seen in a long time, built of sticks and woven mats. We regained about half of our saddles and horses, plus Rockfoot the mule, nearly as bony as before. The Captains offered to trade one of our skinny horses for one of Broken Arm's plump colts, knowing if they ate only roots the men would all be sick again, but instead the chief gave us <u>two</u> colts and wanted nothing in return. For the first time in a long while, we feasted until we were full, and Cruzatte produced his fiddle without any urging, playing well into the night. Some of that screeching I only heard from a distance, though, for a female had switched her silvery hindquarters at me when we first arrived, wafting an unmistakable invitation.

The Captains passed out a couple of medals, and now all the Nez Perce seemed to get along fine. Clark kept busy treating his Indian patients, some with rheumatism and three dozen or so with sore eyes, and that left Meriwether time to work on his vocabulary and study the customs of the Nez Perce. We were all relieved to be in the company of these generous, friendly people after our tribulations along the river. Three bitches had come into breeding season, so I kept busy, too. Here I could relax, without feeling the need to guard our goods or worrying that I might provide the next meal. The canines were a cheerful lot, their greatest peril in being gambled away from one owner to another, for the Nez Perce delighted in a wagering game that involved a stick hidden in the hands. Twisted Hair and his big family camped near us, and the wife of one of his sons often slipped me portions of a savory stew.

Since snow still blanketed the mountains, the Captains planned a two-day council for the middle of May. All the important Nez Perce chiefs of that area rode in. Most had never seen a white man before, and York's black skin was again a source of amazement. Word had also circulated about the "Black Bear Dog," and several warriors brought bitches with them, eager to breed bigger, stronger puppies, which didn't bother me a bit though it did irritate some of the local males; one gray wolfish fellow, formerly the top dog, bared his teeth at me whenever we met, but that was as far as it went.

The Captains began the first day of the great council by drawing a map with charcoal on a stretched buffalo hide, followed by the usual smoking and gift-giving, though our store of presents was by now rather pathetic. My Master gave a long speech, which took even longer to translate to Nez Perce from Shoshone from Minitaree from French from English. But at least Meriwether could get across his message of peace, trading posts, and sending delegations to Washington. Then he brought out the air gun and our scientific curiosities. Broken Arm especially liked the spyglass, saying its magic could keep a closer watch on his wives. Our men demonstrated the range and accuracy of our guns, and that day Meriwether outshot even Drouillard, hitting the target twice from 220 yards away. That really impressed the Nez Perce, who took to calling him "Chief Long Eye," just as they called Clark "Chief Red Hair."

The second day the Nez Perce spoke, with all the chiefs and elders getting a say. Their people, nearly four thousand strong, wanted a chance to trade for guns and ammunition in order to hunt buffalo and protect themselves from the Blackfeet, who didn't get along with anybody. Broken Arm stirred up a mush made of roots, which he invited each man to eat if they accepted the decision of friendship reached in council. The women wailed, worried we might turn out to be dangerous to the tribe, but the men swallowed every bite of that mush.

"This was a good day's work," Meriwether said, after we'd finished celebrating with the Nez Perce and bedded down for what was left of the night. "I believe these may be the finest people we've encountered on our travels."

"It's a good thing," said Clark, yawning as he tugged his blanket over his shoulders. "From what they say, we won't be able to get over the Bitterroots for at least a month."

Meriwether sighed. "I suppose we'll just have to wait. It irks me, though."

"Don't you think I feel the same way?" Clark asked. "I lie here thinking about Judy Hancock back home, growing to a fine young lady, suitors knocking at her door—believe me, Meri, I'm at least as eager to get back as you are, but it can't be helped."

Meriwether stroked the top of my head. "All right, I'll try to be patient. The President will just have to wait."

That night Jefferson entered my dream, but all I could recall when I woke up was that The President was twice as tall as other men.

Since we planned to stay awhile, the Captains moved our camp to a spot along the Clearwater River where we could fatten our horses, catch fish, and have access to better hunting. At Long Camp we lashed together some brush huts, which leaked whenever it rained. The Nez Perce were in and out of our camp and we made frequent visits to their nearby villages. The women were "*clean and comely,*" according to what Meriwether wrote in his journal, and the Captains had no objection to the men trading for their services. When brass buttons became popular with the tribe, all the soldiers' uniform coats were stripped bare. The Captains got a little worried about what might become the next item of barter, so they gathered up the rest of our trade goods and divided them among the soldiers. Everybody got one moccasin awl, a knitting pin, a little bit of vermilion paint, two needles, some thread and a yard of ribbon.

"Ain't much," Colter said, "so those with more in the way of looks and charm'll have an edge."

"That leaves you out," Joe Field told him, "but you can always go huntin'. Maybe one o' them beaver pelts will make some girl shut her eyes and forget your ugly mug."

They pretended to tussle, growling like grizzlies, and then laughed together. Our men had learned to get along better than I ever expected. Sometimes they'd even share one girl between them. They were pretty crafty about coming up with trade items, like making more moccasin awls out of links of worn-out chain. The Nez Perce girls weren't greedy, but we were rapidly running out of goods. Then meat became harder to find. So the Captains sacrificed their brass buttons and made up little packets of medicines which they entrusted to York and McNeal, our best traders. The two returned with three bushels of roots and some bread, which was a good bargain, but York wore such a big grin that the men speculated he'd gotten even more in the way of payment.

"Can't help it if these little gals wanna touch my black hide," he told them. "Me an' Seaman are mighty pop'lar in these parts."

Poor Bratton had been ailing for a long time. At Long Camp, the Captains built a sweat bath, and when the private was able to walk without pain for the first time in months, they also used it to treat a chief who couldn't move his arms or legs. They gave the chief some laudanum, too, and pretty soon the old man could use his hands and wiggle his toes.

Meriwether worried that the men weren't getting enough exercise to prepare them for the climb over the mountains, so the Captains began organizing competitions. Reuben Field could run faster than any of our soldiers, but one tall Nez Perce was so fleet that he usually finished ahead of the pack. Sometimes I raced along with them, but Newfoundlands aren't really built for speed. However, a game that Meriwether called "Prison Base" was a lot like something the O'Connor children had called "Keep-Away," and I'd had lots of practice at that one. Sometimes I'd steal the elk-hide ball from both sides and Nez Perce and Corps members would run themselves silly trying to catch me.

Clark wanted to muscle up our horses, too, so our men rode in races alongside the Indians. Our men had considered themselves good horsemen, but those Nez Perce could outride anybody I ever saw. Meriwether admired the horses so much that Broken Arm gave him a gray stallion with black flecks on his rump that my Master named Silver. That horse was handsome but cantankerous.

"All he thinks about is mares," Rockfoot told me, "mares, mares, and more mares. Us mules keep our minds on business. The only way that crazy fool will be of any use is if they cut him."

I'd heard about this cutting before. Meriwether called it "castrating," when they sliced off a horse's balls so he'd behave and so only the best stallions could mate. The thought made me cringe, but most of our horses were males and just about useless as it was, especially when mares came in season. Then it was all snorting and prancing and whinnying, with Silver the worst of the bunch. So when Meriwether decided to go ahead with the castrating, I understood the necessity and kept my tail high, though I harbored a secret urge to keep it tucked around my parts. Drouillard used the white men's method on Silver and another of the stallions, while Broken Arm's son demonstrated the Nez Perce way on several more. I declined to observe the details, but Silver didn't heal up fast like the horses treated by the son of Broken Arm. He hung his head and stopped eating, until finally Meriwether had to shoot him. Silver served us in his own way, though, by providing a fine meal.

About that same time Little Pomp got sick. Now a toddler, he was cutting teeth, and one of them abscessed, infecting his ear. Both Captains treated the boy, supervised by the worried mother. Bird Woman never complained about anything, even when she didn't get enough to eat for herself, but she'd always made sure she had enough milk to keep her son healthy and collected a store of clean moss or cattail fluff to catch his drop-pings. I think she reminded the men of their own mothers, even though she was younger than any of them, and they all took turns visiting Little Pomp when he was sick, trying to distract him from the pain and fever. Sergeant Gass whittled a clever toy that danced when you pulled a leather cord, and Shannon ran me though all my tricks at least twice a day, which never failed to amuse Pomp and his special friends among the young Nez Perce. It took awhile for the swelling to go down, but then Pomp was back to normal, poking his fingers into everything.

Every day Meriwether would stare up at the Bitterroots, hoping the snow had miraculously melted away. Clark didn't seem as restless, regardless of what he said. Sometimes he re-turned to our little hut with faint traces of a scent I recognized. Even though Meriwether tended to sniff at every new plant, in-cluding the many he'd discovered during our stay with the Nez Perce, he didn't seem to notice the fragrance at all, and the Captains never talked about it. I wished my Master would fol-low his partner's example. I'm sure he would have slept better instead of tossing and turning all night as he so often did.

As June progressed, the men began assembling a store of roots and bread for our trip over the mountains. The Nez Perce warned us that the snow was still too deep, but the Captains felt it was time for us to move on, so Broken Arm and all our other friends held a big farewell party with lots of racing and games. That night, Cruzatte fiddled for hours, accompanied by the Indian musicians, while everybody danced.

If the soldiers hadn't been so eager to get home, I think they might have been sad to leave, but when we'd loaded our horses everybody was smiling except York. The tribe had invited him to stay, and I could tell a part of him hated to leave. The Nez Perce treated him like a warrior, not a slave. It was so different between York and his master than between Meriwether and me. I knew York loved Clark, but he resented him, too. Being a human is more complicated than being a dog.

Our time with the Nez Perce had given me another chance to try and figure out the difference between Indians and white people, which had puzzled me since the beginning of our journey. Sometimes I thought it was a lot like dogs and wolves: relations who'd taken different paths a long time ago. I preferred the tribes that the Captains called "wild" Indians, who'd never met up with whites, to Indians like the Chinooks who'd traded with British and American sea captains for a long time. Before that, maybe the Chinooks weren't so bad, either. The Nez Perce had seemed happy with things the way they were before, but now they wanted guns and powder. Would that really make their lives better? Only the Great Mystery knew the answer to that question, though Rockfoot had his own opinion: "White people remind me of beavers, trying to change the flow of things when they ought to leave 'em be."

Some of the Nez Perce rode along when we left Long Camp, planning to dig for roots at a place called Weippe Prairie. Rain had slicked the trail, but the Captains were more worried about feeding the Indians as well as ourselves. Luckily, so many burrowing squirrels surrounded our evening encampment that we killed enough for supper. Meriwether liked them a lot, so I went back out and waylaid a few more when they ventured out of their holes.

The next day we started climbing the Lolo Trail, though it was so buried by snow that it was hard to tell if we were on it or off. That night Meriwether looked glum, and Clark tried to cheer him up, saying it was sure to be better tomorrow. But it wasn't. Drouillard reckoned the drifts measured as deep as fifteen feet. The horses floundered, the men shivered, I kept stopping to bite away ice balls that clogged the pads of my paws and left bloody tracks through the snow. All of us remembered passing this way the previous autumn, wondering if we would ever find shelter and something to eat. Meriwether and Clark spoke together in hushed voices, and then announced something we'd never heard during our journey: we were going to retreat. Everybody got dejected, but it made sense, so we stumbled back to Weippe Prairie, home of the burrowing squirrels and roots that Bird Woman dug with a stick. But soon Drouillard and Shannon located a brother of Cut Nose and two other Nez Perce who agreed to guide as far as Traveler's Rest, so after waiting for a few days, we tried again. The Indians wore nothing but moccasins and an elk skin apiece, but the cold air didn't trouble them any more than it did me. They kept us moving at a good pace, though at one point they insisted on stopping to smoke a pipe. When food grew scarce, Labiche invented an edible new concoction made of bear oil boiled with roots, and the horses munched any bit of grass our guides found for them. As we progressed, the hunting got better and soon we had almost enough deer meat to satisfy our appetites. When we reached the hot springs we'd discovered last autumn, all the men stripped off their clothes and jumped shouting into the water. I didn't like the steam rising off the surface, so I refused all enticements to join in, but when the Nez Perce scrambled out of the hot pool and jumped into the icy water of the nearby creek, I leapt in with them.

The next day we'd almost reached Travelers Rest when Meriwether's mount slipped while crossing a steep hillside. I heard the gelding's squeal of alarm just behind me, but by that time he already had both hind legs over the edge, and the horse fell, toppling my Master from the saddle. Careless of flailing hooves I sprang after him, terrified the gelding would crush Meriwether before I could reach him. Something struck my hind leg with a force that knocked me down, and then I was tumbling, too, unable to help Meriwether, who clutched at a tree branch that stopped his fall as I continued to crash downward, expecting that clumsy horse to land on me at any moment. Then I slammed into a fallen tree trunk which knocked the wind from me. The gelding had lodged against another tree and had already struggled to its feet by the time our men scrambled down the slope to assist Meriwether. Shannon and York helped me to stand.

"Is Seaman all right?" Meriwether called, coughing a little as he rubbed his chest.

I attempted a few steps. The beaver-bit leg had taken the blow from the hoof, and when I put weight on it I had to swallow a whimper.

"Looks near as battered as you do, sir," Shannon told him, "but I don't think anything's broken."

Meriwether and I both managed to hobble up the slope, but it required ropes and a lot of swearing to get the gelding back on the trail. Those final miles to Traveler's Rest on the last day of June seemed to take forever, but at last I could collapse, too sore to want any dinner, my head in Meriwether's lap.

CHAPTER SIXTEEN

A single night's sleep and Meriwether was back on his feet, ignoring aches and pains which had to be as bad or worse than mine. My leg felt like it had been run over by a herd of buffalo but I hid the limp as best I could, knowing something big was in the wind. When the Captains called everyone together to explain their plans for the next part of our journey, it was even worse than I expected: the partners had decided to divide our forces. Meriwether planned to lead a detachment over to the Great Falls, where he would leave Private Thompson and the ailing Goodrich and McNeal to prepare for a portage of our canoes and baggage while the rest of the party explored Maria's River. Most of the Corps would go with Clark to the head of Jefferson's River where we'd left our canoes and a cache of goods. Sergeant Ordway and nine men were to head downriver in those vessels while the rest of Clark's group would explore the Yellowstone River country, then build a new canoe and paddle down to the Missouri. Meanwhile, Sergeant Pryor and three of the privates would deliver the rest of the horses to the Mandans and contact British agent Hugh Heney with a proposal.

I didn't like the plan at all. I'd overheard the Captains discussing it privately for weeks, but couldn't believe they would go through with it. The Corps needed to stay together. I felt that in every bruised bone of my body. Now the Captains proposed dividing our force, making each small unit vulnerable, and Meriwether was talking about wandering into Blackfeet country, which was the last place anyone ought to be headed.

"My foray up Maria's River does involve risk," Meriwether said, his face grim. "But it's territory we need to explore, and contact with this tribe of Indians could be crucial to peace on the plains and unobstructed American trade. I ask no man to go with me by my order. I'll take only volunteers."

When nearly all the men stepped forward, Meriwether's smile lit up his face. "You're a fine group, and I thank you all for your confidence in me. But I can only take six men. Drouillard, I'll need your hand talk if we meet the Blackfeet. Reuben and Joe... Sergeant Gass, you'll be my next-in-command." He scanned the eager faces before him. "Privates Frazer and Werner."

I understood how Shannon must feel, left out when he wanted with all his heart to follow Meriwether into danger. After the Captains explained more about the intricacies of the plan and the meeting broke up, my Master sought out the young private. "Do you understand why I didn't choose you as one of my party?"

"No, sir, I don't!" said Shannon, his face flushed. "I've worked hard to become a better hunter and frontiersman— "

"And you've succeeded," Meriwether interrupted him,

"which is one of the reasons I passed you by. I can't leave Captain Clark without the means to feed his party. But there are other reasons, George. You're becoming something of an amateur botanist—no one has brought me more new specimens than yourself. Now, I wouldn't want this getting back to anyone, but Captain Clark, fine leader that he is, will be so focused on his mapping and of course taking care of his men, and Bird Woman and Little Pomp, too, that he could step right on the rarest lily on the continent without noticing." Meriwether smiled. "I'm counting on you to document the blossom before that happens. Even more important, when we send Sergeant Pryor to the Mandans I want you along. You've a fine head on your shoulders, as long as you know what direction you're headed."

Shannon tried to smile back. Even all that praise didn't make up for being excluded. "I'll do my very best, sir. But I'd rather go with you into Blackfeet territory."

Meriwether placed a hand on the private's shoulder. "We each have a duty to perform. My mission is no more important and probably no more dangerous. We'll all join up and be headed down the Missouri for home before you know it."

"I hope you're right, sir."

I hoped so, too.

The Captains set Shields to repairing our damaged rifles and sent out all our hunters in search of meat, not just for our stay at Traveler's Rest but also to preserve for Captain Clark's journey into country that was low on game. Our Nez Perce guides, at ease during our crossing of the mountains, now looked nervous. The last thing they wanted was to encounter their sworn enemies the Blackfeet, but they agreed to accompany our party for two more days. Meriwether spent much of the afternoon composing a long letter to Hugh Heney, hoping to convince the British trader to come over to the American side and act as our emissary to the Sioux. Though I was content to lie by my Master's side and rest my leg, a short ramble before supper cheered us both, for Meriwether sighted a wealth of bird species while I had a good splash in the creek. The exercise stimulated our appetites for a fine meal of venison. Unfortunately mosquitoes accompanied us on every endeavor.

On the morning of July the third, Clark set out with his party, Little Pomp grinning back at us from his cradleboard. He'd grown into a heavy load for Bird Woman, but she seemed happy about returning to the region she'd traveled as a child. Our group started down the river with nine men and the Indians, stopping to build rafts when our Nez Perce guides told us we needed to cross to the opposite bank. We hadn't journeyed far before we started seeing abandoned lodges that the Nez Perce identified as belonging to their enemies. Even though our guides were strong young warriors I could smell their tension, but Meriwether looked more fascinated than concerned. When we stopped for the night we had to kindle large fires, for the mosquitoes grew so bloodthirsty that the horses became frantic and could only rest if they huddled in the smoke. Rockfoot stamped and swatted at the tormentors with his skimpy tail, long ears twitching.

The next day, as Meriwether expressed his gratitude to our guides, the Nez Perce looked sad. Drouillard had grown especially friendly with them, and they warned him to stay away from the Blackfeet, but of course that tribe inhabited the very direction we planned to travel. "They're worried their enemies will cut us off," Drouillard said, "and fear they will never see 'Chief Long Eye' again."

"They've been good friends to us," said Meriwether. "Though we may not share the same trail, the Great Father will hear of the goodness of the Nez Perce people."

That was Independence Day 1806, but instead of holding any sort of celebration, we headed east, and after five miles reached the lively stream that the Nez Perce had called "River of the Road to Buffalo." I liked the sound of the name and sniffed, hoping to catch the thrilling scent.

"You're starting to drool," Rockfoot pointed out. "We got some ways to go yet. I been this way before. Oh, after a time we'll come across all the hump you can swallow, but don't be surprised if we meet up with Indians who don't think you have any business in their territory. That master of yours ain't met any Blackfeet yet, but before this little adventure ends he'll probably get his chance. Glad I'll be staying at the Falls to help with the portage. It'll be hard work, but I'm used to that, an' it beats roasting over a Blackfeet fire."

When we finally stopped for the night, Drouillard said Minitarees had camped at the same spot a couple of months earlier, but he couldn't positively identify the fresh tracks he spotted the next day.

"They sure own a whole passel of horses," Joe Field said, "whoever they are."

That part of the country grew thick timber interspersed with open meadows between high stony mountains. All along that river, beavers labored at their dams. A couple of days later, we turned north, as the Nez Perce had recommended, following a creek. With all the willow brush, we couldn't see far ahead.

I moved closer to the side of Meriwether's mount. The gelding, the same creature who'd fallen from the trail, had recovered and settled down well, but I didn't trust him to safeguard my Master. Nor did I like the lack of visibility. When I heard a shot ring out ahead of us and off to the west, my hackles rose, but Meriwether said, "Sounds like Reuben's rifle. He was foraging that way."

Sure enough, Reuben Field soon galloped in, his mare sweating and rolling her eyes. "A moose, Cap'n! But I only grazed him, an' he charged straight at us. Worthless horse wouldn't stand her ground!"

"She just showed good sense," Meriwether said, "a wounded moose is nothing to trifle with. You stay nearby, Seaman, I don't want you messing with that fellow. We have plenty of meat, and soon we'll reach prime buffalo country."

The creek dwindled to a trickle, woods giving way to more open territory that allowed us to spot approaching danger. We climbed the ridge until we could see the great plains rolling below us without an end in sight. Meriwether took a deep breath, his eyes scanning the expanse of grass below. Then he urged his horse forward. "And just like that, we're back on American soil," he said. "Almost home."

Even if I wasn't born in the United States, I'd learned to love the country where I'd spent most of my life. I'd surely seen more of it than any dog in history. It was good to be back—even though we still had a long way to go—and the aroma of buffalo floated on the breeze. All the next day I could scent the creatures and we saw plenty of droppings, but it wasn't until the ninth of July that Joe Field brought down a fat bull. Even with the drizzle, we relished that meat, happy to be back in the "Land o' Plenty," as Sergeant Gass called it. The next day, our hunters brought in five deer, three elk, and a bear. I'd been on the lookout for those "monstrous gentlemen," remembering our frequent encounters the previous summer. We also saw whole packs of wolves ranging about, for they followed the buffalo, and now herds peppered the prairie. I could smell the mating scents, but it was the roaring of the bulls that kept the horses restless all night. We feasted on hump and tongue until I thought I'd pop.

"I believe this as close to Paradise as we'll come in this life," Meriwether said. "I estimate ten thousand buffalo within a two-mile radius of this spot, the air is fresh and clear after the rain—what more could we ask?"

To be safely through Blackfeet territory, I thought, though at the moment the concern seemed less pressing. We'd constructed bull boats from hides and willow, and in the morning would cross to our cache. Even the mosquitoes seemed satiated, for that night they left us in peace.

When we rose with the dawn, things had changed. Werner and Thompson returned from rounding up our horses to report that seven of the seventeen were missing. Meriwether figured an Indian hunting party had stolen them and sent Drouillard in pursuit, though what my Master expected one man—even that one—to do if he found them I couldn't figure. The rest of the men crossed the river in the clumsy bull boats while I swam along with our reduced herd, which included Rockfoot. "Sometimes it pays to look old and slow," he said, "that way you don't get stolen."

Back at the site of our camp during the long portage of summer 1805, Meriwether supervised the opening of our cache. Soon it became clear that spring runoff had saturated the area, and when we uncovered the plant specimens Meriwether groaned. "Ruined! All those weeks and months of collecting, drying... I should have chosen a better site. We can only pray that the seals around the papers and maps have kept out the moisture." He scarcely breathed until we'd dug up the leather bundles sealed with candle tallow and opened each one. Fortunately, the papers had fared better.

That night the mosquitoes returned in force and no amount of smoke would deter them. "Durn pests!" Gass cursed. "How've they survived all this time without Irish flesh to feed 'em?"

While we waited for Drouillard to return, we began preparing for the upcoming portage. Meriwether designed a scaffold hidden within the thick brush of a tiny island, for when it came to his precious documents he wouldn't take any chances, hoping to safeguard the papers in case the small party remaining behind was attacked. I began to hope that he'd change his mind altogether and call off the expedition up Maria's River. Instead, citing the loss of the horses, he reduced the size of his party, deciding to leave six men behind at White Bear Island to give the portage party a better chance of defending itself. That left only three men to accompany us into the heart of Blackfeet country. Maybe only two, for Drouillard was still missing, which worried Meriwether, though he tried to hide it even from me. Then our interpreter rode in, shaking his head. "Took me two days to figure out where they crossed the river. These are wily fellows, Captain, probably about fifteen lodges, though what tribe they're from I can't say for sure. I trailed them a bit, but they had too much of a start on me."

"We're glad to have you back," Meriwether said, "horses or

not. Sorry you won't get much chance to rest up, but we head out in the morning, just you and me and the Field brothers. The rest will remain behind. We'll take six of the horses."

And me. Surely I was included in the exploring party. I wouldn't be of much use during the portage and Meriwether needed me to keep an eye on him.

While the others packed the necessities of our journey, Meriwether conferred with Sergeant Gass, who would command the party at White Bear Island. I'd grown to like the Irish carpenter, who turned cranky whenever we ran out of tobacco but had proven himself a loyal and valuable member of the Corps. He listened to every word Meriwether said, taking notes, asking questions, nodding as he heard his Captain's replies. "I'll take good care of the men, sir," he said. "Goodrich and McNeal won't be much help, what with recovering from their frolics with the Clatsop girls, but the men are all hard workers and you're leaving us some good horseflesh. That stubborn old mule is worth twice the average."

"Sometimes he reminds me of an Irish sergeant I know," said Meriwether. "But we won't make our farewells yet. Thought you might ride with us to the Falls. I promised Private Frazer he could go that far, since he missed it last time, and I don't want him riding back alone."

"Thank'ee, sir. I've looked forward to seeing that place again."

"I have great trust in you, Patrick," my Master said. "I know you'll get the job done."

That was a bad night. We almost lost Hugh McNeal to a grizzly, there were so many bulls bellowing that it sounded like one gigantic, long-winded creature who wouldn't stay quiet, wolves howled all around us and mosquitoes tortured me until I couldn't help adding my own howling to the din.

In the morning we set out for the Falls. Our view of the plains transfixed Meriwether. Buffalo grazed everywhere with their watchful attendants the wolves. I'd have found the situation more exciting if my leg hadn't plagued me so much. I'd hoped a few days' rest would help, but instead the leg seemed stiffer and more painful than before, and after we'd journeyed a couple of miles I could no longer hide my limp. By the time we reached the Falls, I was hobbling. That place was like a miracle, though. Meriwether talked about how inadequate he felt trying to describe those torrents, "one of the most beautiful objects in nature." The water raged, billowed, hissed, roared, a living thing touched by the hand of the Great Mystery. I forgot my sore leg and my worries about the Blackfeet and walked right into an eddy below a great cascade, where fountains of spray danced in the air. When Meriwether waded in beside me and placed a hand on my head, I knew that this moment was worth any danger or hardship. "I couldn't have come all this way without you." His fingers stilled. "We've been true companions, which makes it that much harder for me to leave you behind."

I didn't believe my ears. He couldn't mean it.

"You've tried so hard to keep up, but the trail we follow now is long and difficult, and we'll be riding fast. Your leg would never stand the strain." His words drained away every spark of magic from that place. I only felt wet, and cold, and miserable. "I'm sending you back with Frazer and Sergeant Gass. The men will take good care of you, and I count on you to keep watch over them. They can't smell or hear or sense danger the way you can."

What about you, I wanted to howl, w*ho will keep watch over you*? But instead I followed him from the water, for even if I could speak words he'd understand, they wouldn't change his mind. I lay down with my head between my paws, watching my Master give his last-minute instructions to the men, shake hands with Sergeant Gass. When he mounted his horse, that same foolish gelding who'd fallen and reinjured my leg, I rose and took a few steps toward him.

"No, Seaman, you <u>stay</u>!" he said. "I'll be back soon. I promise." Then he wheeled the horse, urging it to a trot.

"We'll see to the Cap'n!" Joe Field called. "We won't let no grizzly nor Blackfeet hurt 'im." After a jaunty wave, he hurried his horses after Reuben's and Drouillard's, and the four of them disappeared over the rise, two pack animals jogging behind.

I stood there, just looking, until Sergeant Gass walked over and patted my neck. "We'll all be back together, laddie, the Captain gave you his word. In the meantime, there's work to do. Come on now."

I don't remember one thing about the trip back to White Bear Island, or much of anything about the next couple of days except someone saying, "Never saw ol' Seaman turn down buffalo tongue before. Guess his leg's botherin' him worse than we thought."

"You gotta to eat somethin'," Private McNeal pleaded, waving a hunk of meat in front of my nose. "It's been two days, an' Cap'n Lewis'll skin us alive if yer only hide an' bones when he gets back."

"Leave the dog be," Sergeant Gass said. "He'll eat when he's ready. Seaman's too smart to starve himself to death."

Gass was right. I'd paid little attention to the men working around me, repairing the crude carts for the portage or dressing skins, but now it was time I did my share for the Corps. I sniffed at the meat: prime hump, raw and bloody, too good to waste.

"What did I tell you? That's the best dog in the Army," Gass said. "He's just been resting his bad leg. By the time the Captain rejoins us, Seaman will be good as new."

Gass's confidence, both in me and in the success of Meriwether's mission, was contagious. Maybe those Blackfeet weren't so terrible. After all, our men had their Harpers Ferry rifles, Drouillard's skills, and Meriwether's ingenuity and determination. Maybe they'd miss Indians altogether, or just meet up with some Minitarees. I gnawed at the meat, suddenly ravenous.

Sergeant Ordway and his nine men arrived the next day by canoe. "Hope you saved me a few buff!" Colter called, digging his paddle into the bank. "Here we were barrelin' down the river with the critters all round us an' the Sarge wouldn't let me shoot nary a one."

"What would we have done with one of those enormous beasts?" Ordway asked, climbing out like his back hurt but smiling just the same. "But now you'll get all the hunting you can stand. It's your job to keep this whole camp supplied with meat while the rest of us do the real work."

Cruzatte groaned. "We will rest today, no? My legs are bent so they may never go straight again."

"An old water rat like you?" Gass asked, extending a hand to help Cruzatte rise from the canoe. "Good to have all you fellows with us. It will give the skeeters some other targets, an' we could use a bit of fiddle music. Plenty of buffalo cooking right now, and something even better." He spat into the dirt. "We dug up the cache of tobacco."

Labiche whooped as he beached the second vessel. "Now if we only had whiskey!"

"Won't be long," Willard said beside him. "After this portage, it's downriver to St Louis."

While the men from Ordway's party rested up, Gass and his crew finished repairing the carts, which had failed to meet the carpenter's standard of excellence. Thompson and Werner hitched Rockfoot to the largest of the rigs. The wheels wobbled a little but rolled just fine. "We'll be stopping to replace those axles before we're halfway there," Gass grumbled. "That willow's not stout enough for the job."

"Beats haulin' the canoes an' the gear ourselves," Werner said. "I like this ol' mule better all the time." He slapped Rockfoot on the rump, and then jumped out of the way of a hind hoof.

The next days passed slowly, but keeping busy helped prevent me from worrying constantly about Meriwether. I guess in some ways I'd grown a lot like my Master: better with a goal out there ahead of me. Just as Gass had predicted, the axles kept breaking down, and the mosquitoes were so thick you couldn't breathe without one flying down your throat. So many bears prowled around us that I had to patrol each night, sounding the alarm if any ventured too close to camp. Once, I got to thinking about what might be happening to Meriwether and nearly followed his trail. But we each had duties of our own.

All day long the sergeants kept the men at their tasks,

though with everyone eager to reach home they didn't need much prompting. Some mornings, as my leg healed, I'd head out with Colter in search of meat. I think he loved buffalo almost as much as I did. "Look at that big bull! Why, he's too handsome to shoot—he'll see to it them sweet cows make lots more baby buffs. Let's you an' me head over that hill an' see if we can't find us somethin' a little more toothsome."

From the rise overlooking another section of prairie, we watched a pack of wolves take turns chasing down a loper-goat. "Lots o' fellows don't like wolves, but you gotta admire the way they do business. That goat's too fast for one alone, but they work together to tire 'im out an' bring 'im down. I seen wolves do the same thing with the buffs. They can only do it if they work together. Kinda like us fellas in the Corps of Discovery."

Colter was right. Our soldiers were truly like a pack now, with the Captains as the leaders and everyone doing their part. We watched until the wolves brought that goat down. We didn't seem to worry them a bit. I guess they hadn't been around guns enough to know that a good rifle could kill from a long distance. The wolves were a part of the Indians' world, but that was changing now, and I feared it would go hard for them.

That was the same day Wiser cut his leg bad so badly he had to ride in a canoe aboard one of the carts. What with Goodrich and McNeal dosing themselves with mercury and now another private lame, the others had to work twice as hard, but nobody complained, or not much. The Frenchmen sang as they carted the goods, and some nights Cruzatte played his fiddle. We made good progress, back and forth from one end of the portage to the other despite struggles with the largest of the canoes, thunderstorms, and two more horses disappearing for a few days. But we found the missing mounts, and near the end of July Gass and Willard headed cross-country with our herd while the rest of us loaded the five canoes and the White Pirogue, which was still in pretty good shape, and started down the river. Now the power of the Missouri was working for us. The Mandan chief Big White had called it a Grandfather Spirit, which made a lot of sense. Since even the Great Mystery couldn't be everywhere at once, family members could share the responsibility. This one had been around for a long, long time. When we'd started up the Missouri, Meriwether had hoped it flowed into something called the Northwest Passage. Instead, it had led us on a winding path of adventure to a high place where the waters turned and ran the other way. Now I had to trust it to bring us all back together. Worried and lonesome as I was, a part of me believed I would see my Master when the river carried us to the assigned meeting place. Hope kept my nose to the wind, always seeking his familiar scent.

That night the men heaped wood on the fire, trying to smoke out the mosquitoes. Even so, the sound of their keening kept all of us awake, and at first light we climbed back into the boats. "Might as well be headed toward home," Goodrich said, yawning. And that was the beginning of an endless day, headed toward Maria's River.

After the long hours, when the sun was as high as it could climb, I heard the rhythm of galloping horses. Could that be Meriwether and his party? Were they in trouble? Then I smelled him, that beloved scent drifting down from the clay bluffs, and launched myself into the river. By the time I reached the shore, Meriwether had reined in his mount at the edge of the bluff, and as Ordway ordered the men to fire a salute, the four members of my Master's party started their spent horses down the steep bank while I scrambled up toward them. Dirt grimed Meriwether's face but I didn't smell any blood. "No time to waste! We may have Blackfeet right behind us!" I'd become enough of a trooper to know that before I could give Meriwether so much as a lick, we had to get away from that dangerous place. In record time the men had unsaddled the horses and tossed the gear into the water. "Turn them all loose!" Meriwether commanded. "We must trust to the river now!"

As soon as everyone found a place in the various vessels, with me pressed up tight against my Master's legs in the White Pirogue and Colter just behind us, we shoved off. Rockfoot brayed once from shore, and then resumed grazing. We sped forward, the men slicing the water with their paddles. Meriwether's breathing began to slow. His hand, which had clenched my neck so tight it hurt, relaxed a little. "These boats were the most welcome sight imaginable. Not just because we were worried that the Blackfeet were trailing us—I feared more that they might have gotten here ahead of us and caught the rest of you in ambush. That's what kept us in the saddle no matter how tired we grew, close to a hundred and twenty miles in twenty-four hours of traveling."

"That's some ridin'!" said Colter. "We ain't seen hide nor hair of any Injuns at all."

"I wish we could say the same." Meriwether didn't speak for a minute, staring back at the bluff and shaking his head. "I had to shoot one of them, Colter, and he was just a boy."

"I reckon you did what you had to."

Meriwether nodded. "But I'm still sorry for the deed. Now any hope of peace with the Blackfeet is surely gone." Then he sat up very straight. "Hand me that extra paddle, Cruzatte. For now, I'll help the current along, and later you'll all hear the whole story."

Even though he looked exhausted, the exercise seemed to do my Master good, but it wasn't until we picked up Gass and Willard, also unharmed, that the worst of the tension had drained from him. By the time we'd traveled a good distance and located a secure place to camp, he was nearly limp. Everyone was anxious to hear about the trip up Maria's River, but Drouillard was as silent as ever and, surprisingly, the Field brothers were, too. "Let the Cap'n tell it when he's ready," Joe said when Colter pressed him for details. "For my part, I was a damn fool, an' there's no hurry talkin' about that."

It rained and hailed so hard nobody got much sleep, but the wet bothered me even less than usual. I had Meriwether back, all in one piece.

CHAPTER SEVENTEEN

The men were aching to hear what had happened on Maria's River, but I was content to stick close to Meriwether's side and wait until he was ready to talk. My Master kept our little fleet moving down the river, now thick with mud and sand, until the second day of August, when the weather turned fair and we located a good camp for drying out our gear. Meriwether occupied himself with preserving the skins and skeletons of three big-horns whose meat had provided a fine supper. Normally he was able to escape the dark shadow when he worked, but that day I could see it perched on his shoulders. Drouillard and the Field brothers went off hunting, returning that evening with several deer. When they'd set the meat to roasting, Meriwether joined the men gathered around the fire.

"I know you're all wondering what happened while we were separated. You deserve the truth." My Master stared into the flames. I leaned against his leg, and his fingers found my fur, but felt heavy, lifeless. "We'd gone as far as planned and had started back without seeing any Indians when I spotted something on a hilltop. With my spyglass I could make out eight war-riors watching us. We knew they had to be Blackfeet. I chose to approach them in a friendly manner, and through sign tried to communicate as best we could. I gave one a medal, one a flag, one a handkerchief. But it was clear we weren't getting anywhere." He was seeing it all again as the fire crackled and sputtered. "Drouillard was out hunting, so Reuben and one of the young Indians went to find him. The rest of the Blackfeet watched us with suspicion, as alarmed by our meeting as we were. Some of them were just boys, and they had only two mus-kets between them, but lots of spare horses." He closed his eyes. "All of us mounted up and rode toward the river, where we met Drouillard and Reuben and the Indian. At the foot of a bluff, the Blackfeet set up a camp and invited us to join them. And we agreed. We ate together. That evening, through Drouillard's hands, we had a long conversation. I learned they were part of a large band camped one-and-a-half day's ride away that trades with the British. I explained we had come from far to the east, but had traveled a great distance to the western ocean and were now on our way to rejoin our party and return home. I said we'd been hoping to meet up, have the chance to convince them to make peace, that American traders would be coming to trade with all the tribes. They said enemies had killed many of their relatives. Those warriors were very fond of smoking, and we passed the pipe until late at night. Then I took the first watch."

Meriwether paused, still staring toward the fire with his eyes closed. I didn't move, even though his fingers dug into my neck. Nobody broke the silence for a long time, but then Joe Field kicked a stick at the edge of the fire, sending a shower of sparks into the air. "I had the second watch. An' while the rest of our side lay sleepin', I let one of those scoundrels grab my rifle, an' Reuben's too." Joe clenched both fists. "I can't believe I done it, but it was enough daylight by then I could see 'em runnin', an' just as I called out two others snatched up the Cap'n's gun an' Drouillard's an' hightailed it up the hill."

"I jumped up out o' sleep an' took off after the one with my gun," Reuben said, "an' Joe was runnin' behind me. We caught up an' started wrasslin' with those two, an' then I had out my knife an' stabbed that fellow to the heart. He ran about fifteen steps an' fell dead."

"I had woken from a deep sleep when Drouillard shouted, 'Damn you, let go my gun!'" Meriwether continued, his eyes open now and night-dark, "and I reached for my own, only to find it gone. Then I drew my pistol and pursued the warrior running off with my rifle, ordering him to drop it—but of course he couldn't understand me. Joe and Reuben appeared with their weapons in possession and wanted to shoot but since the Blackfoot was ready to return the gun, I forbid it. I retrieved my rifle, and Drouillard had regained his, but then the Indians began driving off their horses and mine with them. I told them I would shoot if they did not give back my horse. When I raised my gun, one of them jumped behind a rock and called out to another warrior, who turned and stopped thirty paces away and raised his weapon. I shot him through the belly as he shot back." Meriwether lifted one hand to touch his head. "I felt the wind of the ball through my hair. Then I returned to camp."

Again the others waited for Meriwether to speak. "We rounded up the horses," Joe finally added, "burned the Indians' gear an' took the best of the mounts. Then we made tracks."

Ordway exhaled loudly. "Thank the Lord you all got away."

"I worried that they would seek revenge," said Meriwether, "and had foolishly told them where we were meeting up, so we made all the speed we could."

"So it turned out not so bad," Cruzatte said. "We are back together again."

I felt like Cruzatte, but of course we were only members of the Corps of Discovery. Meriwether had to be our leader. Without his partner there, he had to be twice as strong. His fingers trembled, but he kept them hidden in my fur. "Tomorrow we head to the Yellowstone. Then we'll join up with Clark and his party. Get a good night's sleep. We'll be on the water at dawn."

Despite what he told the men, Meriwether lay awake for hours. I was pretty sure I knew what was going on in his head: *I made a bad decision, and how will I explain to The President*? He wouldn't be remembering how we'd made it all the way to the Pacific, how he'd discovered all those new plants and animals, how we'd mapped the West and made friends with lots of Indians. And Will Clark wasn't there to remind him.

We arrived at the Yellowstone River five days later only to find that Clark and the rest of his party had been and gone. Remnants of a note tied to a piece of elk horn said game was scarce and mosquitoes numerous, which we'd already found out for ourselves. Colter and Collins were out hunting, so Meriwether left them a message and we started down the Missouri again. Then we came upon some elk meat, presumably left for us by Clark's group since the remains of Private Gibson's favorite Chinook hat lay nearby and that meat was still pretty fresh. But every time we hurried downriver, they must have, too, so we couldn't quite catch up. Colter and Collins were still out somewhere, and Meriwether worried that Indians or grizzlies had waylaid the hunters. I figured Colter was just having too much fun hunting his buffs. I also figured the worst was behind us. We'd escaped the Blackfeet, my leg was serviceable again, and soon Clark would share Meriwether's burden. I looked forward to seeing Bird Woman and Little Pomp, even though that meant putting up with Charbonneau (though perhaps he would fry up some *boudin blanc*....)

Goodrich hooked a string of fish, but everyone wanted meat. The best hunters rode in the small canoes, with orders to shoot any game they could. One morning Meriwether killed a buffalo that was swimming the river near the pirogue, but the meat was so poor he left it for the ravens. (I would have been happy to eat more than just the tongue.) Not long afterward we sighted elk in a thick patch of willow. Meriwether invited Cruzatte to join us as we stalked the creatures, staying downwind so they wouldn't catch our scent. In minutes my Master had killed a nice bull, but Cruzatte's shot had only wounded. I was glad to see that both men reloaded immediately. Then we split up to trail the injured elk through the dense growth. Birds twittered overhead, their songs punctuating the incessant whine of the gnats that clouded all around us. The pesky insects seemed to take particular pleasure in tormenting my eyes, and I raised a paw to swipe at them at the same moment another shot sounded. Meriwether yelled, "Damn you, Cruzatte, you have shot me!"

I smelled gunpowder and blood. Six feet away, my Master clutched at his backside, where blood trickled from a hole in the seat of his buckskin breeches. I bounded to his side, hackles at full alert. No one had responded to Meriwether's cry, but the shot had come from nearby. Had the Blackfeet followed us after all? I detected no unfamiliar scents, but someone had wounded my Master.

"To the pirogue!" he shouted. "Cruzatte, we're under attack!"

We dashed toward the river, with Meriwether shouting a warning all the way, though how he could run I didn't know. By the time we came in sight of the boat, the men had heard the alarm and raced toward us, guns in hand.

"We must rescue Cruzatte!" Meriwether panted. "I'm wounded but not mortally. Follow me!"

But by that time his leg wouldn't move at all, so he sent Ordway and the others off in pursuit. With one heavy hand pressing on my shoulders, Meriwether managed to drag himself the rest of the way to the pirogue, where he further armed himself with his pistol and the air gun. "We won't sell our lives cheaply!" He swayed for a moment, and then stood tall and steady. I braced myself at his side, muscles tensed to spring on anyone who dared attack my Master again.

I don't know how long we stood that way, waiting for the onslaught. But no shots rang out, nor could I hear any whoops or screams. Eventually Gass appeared from the willows, with Cruzatte unharmed beside him and the rest of the men close behind.

"No sign of Indians!" Ordway reported. "Are you all right, Captain?"

"I'll live," Meriwether said, "no thanks to whoever fired that shot. Was it you, Cruzatte?"

"I shot at an elk!" he insisted. "It was in zee willows."

"Didn't you hear me when I shouted to you?"

"No, Captain, I hear nothing. Nothing 'til zee men find me."

Nobody said a word, but we were all thinking the same thing. Cruzatte had only one eye with poor vision. Meriwether was dressed in elk hide. And I had scented nothing unexpected.

"I'm sorry Cap'n Clark isn't here, nor young Bird Woman, or even York," Gass said. "I ain't much as a nurse, but I've tended a few wounds in my time, so let's get to it."

Actually Meriwether did most of the tending to the wound himself, though Gass had to help him out of the blood-soaked breeches. The ball had struck neither artery nor bone, only the flesh of Meriwether's backside and on out, so as soon as the men had butchered the elk my Master insisted on traveling, lying facedown in the pirogue. By the time we stopped to camp, he'd grown so stiff and sore that he couldn't be moved. Meriwether dosed himself with bark and spent the night on the pirogue in fever dreams, while I listened to him mumble in his sleep. That night seemed to last a week.

The next morning, we set off downriver in pursuit of Clark. Meriwether's pale cheeks and burning eyes worried all of us, but he wouldn't rest until the Corps was back to full strength. When Willard sighted a small encampment, I hoped it might be Colter and Collins, but instead we met up with two fur trappers headed toward the Yellowstone, the first white men we'd encountered since Fort Mandan, and our fellows all talked at once, seeking news from civilization. The trappers had headed out not long after ourselves, so about all we learned was that Jefferson was still The President, the price of beaver had risen, which was the main reason why these two had started up the Missouri, and that Captain Clark was only a short way ahead of us. We were able to help them out, though, with all sorts of information about what lay ahead, and Meriwether instructed

Ordway to give the trappers powder and lead, which were two of the few things we still had in plenty.

"Why didn't the Captain ask for some whiskey in return?" Labiche moaned.

Colter and Collins had appeared during the conversation, none the worse for their absence, and soon we were speeding downriver again. Our men sweat so much paddling in the heat that they stripped off their shirts, even though the bugs were bad. Gass got sunburned right away. Not long after noon we spotted Clark's party. The Captains couldn't enjoy much of a reunion with Meriwether flat on his belly, but I leapt about and yipped like a pup. Then York carried my Master from the pirogue to a shady spot near the shore, where Clark redressed Meriwether's wound, which was beginning to heal but still hurt so much that my Master passed out during the procedure. When he woke up, a white-faced Meriwether lifted his head to find all of us staring at him: Bird Woman, all three Sergeants, Shannon and the rest. Cruzatte had looked so terrified that he'd killed the Captain that I actually felt sorry for the man.

"Don't I feel like a silly schoolgirl!" My Master's voice was shaky, but he managed a smile. "I've found this position makes it difficult to write in my journal, so I believe I'll leave that to the rest of you for the time being. But first, tell me how all of you fared on your own."

Everyone had something to report. Aided by Bird Woman's memories, Clark's party had crossed the mountains to the Yellowstone. Charbonneau had survived a bad fall from his horse, while Gibson had tripped on a sharp snag that penetrated two inches into his leg. Indians, probably Crows, had stolen half of the horses. The men built two dugout canoes, lashed them together, and hurried down to the Missouri. Pryor and his party had lost all their horses to Indians, which made their mission to the Mandans impossible. The next night a wolf had come into camp and bitten the sergeant while he slept.

"It was just about to attack Windsor when Shannon killed it," Pryor reported. "We were mighty sorry we didn't have Seaman there to warn us. Without horses, we were in something of a fix, but Shannon shot us a couple of buffalo so we could use the hides to rig bull-boats. Eventually we hooked up with Captain Clark's group."

"I wished we'd had ol' Seaman with us when we met up with the Blackfeet," said Joe Field. "He woulda' made a better sentry than me."

I knew Joe felt bad about that, and Cruzatte certainly regretted wounding his commanding officer in the backside, whether he admitted doing it or not, but now the Corps of Discovery was all together and headed for home. That evening after supper the men talked and sang around the fire while the Captains spoke privately. Meriwether insisted on going over everything again, studying each detail of Clark's latest additions to the map with his partner crouched on the ground beside him. "I'm sorry to have missed that country," my Master said wistfully.

Clark laughed and stood up. "Time you get some rest."

"First, could you bring me my journal? I observed a singular form of cherry today, and I want to write about it before— "

"One paragraph," Clark interrupted, his voice firm. "Then you're to expend your energies only in getting well."

"All right," Meriwether agreed.

That night he slept without tossing and turning, and in the morning his fever had passed.

Only two days later we reached the Mandans and the Minitarees, who rejoiced to see us alive and mostly well. Since part of our fort had burned down, we set up a camp not far away, and as soon as possible I sought out Gray Dog and Spotted Dog, who were just as eager as their master Little Raven to hear about our adventures.

"Blackfeet!" Gray Dog growled. "They killed the son of a chief of the Minitarees. I'm sure they were unhappy when your master told them you will trade with Mandans and the lowly Shoshones."

"Blackfeet are as bad as the Tetons," Spotted Dog agreed. "Those warriors don't want peace."

"What your masters don't seem to understand," Gray Dog said, "is that the tribes with the power like things the way they are."

As Clark sat in council with the chiefs of the Mandans and Minitarees, then reported back to Meriwether, it began to sound as if my friends were right. Making peace was a lot more complicated than it seemed. One-Eye, the crafty old chief of the Minitarees, said Sioux warriors had recently killed eight of his people and stolen horses.

"He made it clear," Clark told his partner, "that *he's* done a lot more for his people than any promises we made, since now the Minitarees have a trade agreement with the Cheyenne. As for going to Washington to visit President Jefferson—Chief One-Eye took great pleasure in informing me that when we've made friends of the Sioux, then he might consider a visit to his Great Father in Washington."

"Perhaps you'll have better luck with Black Cat," Meriwether said, reaching back to scratch delicately in the vicinity of his wound. "He's been a good friend to us."

The Mandan chief smoked a pipe with Clark but didn't want to risk his hide among the Sioux either, though he did offer us twelve bushels of corn. Then the smelly old interpreter Jessaume who we'd met before brought news that Little Raven, second-in-command to Big White at Matootonha, had expressed an interest in coming with us. I liked that idea, since Gray Dog and Spotted Dog might accompany their master, and Clark hurried off with Charbonneau to talk to Little Raven. When Clark returned he was smiling. "He has to confer with all his relations, but I think he's willing to come."

But after Charbonneau delivered news from Metaharta, the Minitaree village where he had once lived with Bird Woman, nobody smiled much. Minitaree war parties had ridden out against Ca-me-ah-wait's Shoshones and against the Arikaras. "Were all our diplomatic efforts in vain?" Meriwether wondered. "I just don't understand these people."

"We can't change what's happened," Clark said. "But it makes it that much more important that we put together a real delegation from among the Mandans and, hopefully, the Minitarees."

Chief One-Eye and some of the other Minitarees showed up the next day, which gave the Captains a chance for some last-minute palavering. They decided to present the chief with the swivel gun off our old keelboat, which made the Minitaree's eye gleam, though he didn't like Clark telling him to stop raiding our defenseless friends the Shoshones. Nor would any of his tribesmen agree to travel to Washington until the Tetons made peace.

When One-Eye had departed with his new swivel gun, Clark rushed off to see Little Raven again. I figured Meriwether could be trusted since he had no real options besides lying flat on his belly, so I trotted along with Clark and the interpreter Jessaume, eager to regale Gray Dog and Spotted Dog about the wonders of civilization. But when we reached Matootonha, everything had changed. Big White, the head chief, was jealous that his second-in-command would gain the prestige of journeying with the Americans. "This is ridiculous!" Clark told Jessaume. "If Big White is jealous, he can come with us, too. Tell him that!"

The wrangling between the interpreter and the Mandan chief dragged on. I sat with my canine friends, waiting for the humans to solve their problems.

"I don't suppose you've noticed the surprising amount of young black dogs in our village?" Gray Dog asked, his eyes slitted so he looked very sly. "Funny how they're bigger than the rest of us and spend so much of their time in the river."

"You know," Spotted Dog said, "those pups were born not long after you left, Seaman."

Spotted Dog never was very bright. Of course I'd observed the change in the canine population of Matootonha, which Gray Dog knew perfectly well. I just didn't want to brag about it. I'd also mated again with one of the bitches. Shannon had tried to buy the pup who most resembled me, but the owner wouldn't trade.

Jessaume clapped Big White on the back and turned to Clark. "The chief says he will go with you instead of Little Raven. But Big White must bring his family, and, of course, his friend Jessaume to interpret. And, of course, I must bring my family too."

Clark fumed, but that delegation meant so much to the Captains that he agreed to Big White's terms, knowing that wily Jessaume had arranged matters just the way he wanted them.

"I guess we'll never know what a city is like," Gray Dog sighed.

"It's not so much," I told him. How strange it would be to leave the wilderness. "May the Great Mystery watch over you." *And keep you from the stew-pot.*

The next day we prepared to leave the Mandans. Gass and some of the men bound two of the canoes together with poles to provide a stable place for Big White, Jessaume, and their families to travel. Charbonneau strutted around camp with his expedition pay, amounting to five hundred dollars and thirty-three and one-third cents. It didn't seem fair he got all the money and Bird Woman got nothing, but that was the way things were and she didn't complain. After she bid the Captains farewell, Bird Woman squatted down and whispered in my ear in Shoshone. When Clark offered to take Little Pomp to St. Louis and educate him, Charbonneau agreed to come when the boy was older, so we weren't saying goodbye forever, but it was still hard. We'd traveled together a long time. The soldiers' plans would scatter them all over, so they took turns hugging Little Pomp or throwing him up in the air. The boy laughed and wiggled the whole time.

"Seaman!" he said when Shannon put him down.

The private smiled. "Once more." Then he ran me through my tricks.

"I guess I'll say my fare-thee-wells now, too," Colter said.

The two fur trappers had turned around and accompanied us back to Fort Mandan, and they'd convinced Colter to join their expedition. Actually, he didn't take much persuasion. "I been away too long," he'd explained when he asked the Captains for permission to muster out early. "Feel more at home in the mountains now. I'd just be lonesome in the city."

The Captains had granted the request as long as the other soldiers promised to finish out the expedition, and they'd all agreed. Most of them thought Colter was crazy.

"What about them purty white gals we talked about?" Joe Field asked. "You'll git awful cold out there."

"And you'll run out of whiskey!" Labiche added.

Drouillard didn't say a word, but he watched Colter ride up the river until he passed out of sight.

Lots of Indians came to see us off. All the women wailed as Big White climbed into the double canoe with his family. I guess they figured they'd never see their leader again. The chiefs smoked a last pipe with the Captains. After all his practice, Meriwether had learned to like tobacco, so he propped himself up on his elbows to puff with the Mandans and Minitarees. He seemed a lot happier than he'd been since his trip up Maria's River, for the chiefs made speeches saying they hadn't believed us at first but now they did, and how they'd remember everything the Americans had said and tell their young men not to make war.

"Tell the Arikaras to come and see us," Black Cat said. "Tell them not to be afraid they will come to harm, for we are anxious to make peace."

And then we headed down the Missouri.

CHAPTER EIGHTEEN

When we reached Arikara territory we stopped off for a council. Up on a hillside stood skin lodges that belonged to Cheyenne who'd come to trade for corn, so they were invited, too. We'd met a few Cheyenne during our winter at Fort Mandan, none very friendly, but of course the Captains wanted to make a good impression on that powerful tribe of the plains. Meriwether fumed about being incapacitated, so I stayed with him (even though he was terrible company) until Clark, Big White, and the sergeants returned.

"They didn't mind smoking good Mandan tobacco," Clark reported. "And they sure don't like the Tetons. I got an earful about those 'bad people.'" He shook his head. "Even though the Arikara seem to hate the Sioux, they won't ally with us against them. The Cheyenne chief wouldn't even accept a peace medal, though he was willing for American trappers to come among his people and show them how to catch more beaver."

We were all glad to be on the move again the next morning. The Grandfather Spirit had been busy while we'd journeyed to the Pacific and back. Some of the sandbars had relocated and others had transformed naked beaches to dense low willow. In each canoe, one man assumed the task of bailing, for waves sloshed over the sides and bow. Meriwether fidgeted, wishing he could explore onshore, but Clark said it would be least a week before my Master should try walking. Though I kept hoping we'd stop and hunt the elk and buffalo along the shore, all the men wanted to keep moving toward home, so we ate the Mandan corn and lots of berries, currants, and chokecherries that grew along the banks. Even without meat to fuel them, with sore eyes from the glare off the water, and the current speeding us along, the soldiers paddled hard without any urging. But no matter how fast we went, the mosquitoes kept up. Meriwether's wound was healing. The evening after we'd made sixty miles down the river he hobbled around camp while Clark was out hunting, but my Master overdid it and was so sore neither of us slept well that night.

The next day we entered Sioux territory, where we encountered three Frenchmen who warned us the Tetons were painted for war. They decided to join up with us for safety, and pretty soon we met a few young warriors from Black Buffalo's band. The Frenchmen could speak their language pretty well, so Clark was able to tell the Sioux that he considered them bad people and that we would kill any of them who came near our camp. He also warned them that we had left guns and powder with the Mandans. Big White looked nervous throughout the exchange, and later, when we passed Black Buffalo himself and more of his Teton warriors, the Mandan chief tried to look brave even though his hands were shaking and his wife Blue Corn crouched in the canoe with their son hidden under a blanket. But we passed through Sioux territory without any real trouble.

"Now there's nothin' between us an' St. Louis!" Whitehouse shouted, waving his cap in the air.

Soon we started meeting up with more vessels, and the Captains questioned everyone, desperate for news from the east. By the time we met up with a big Scotsman named Aird, Meriwether could limp around pretty well, so we sat out a thunderstorm in the trader's tent, which actually kept off the rain. Aird reassured Meriwether that President Jefferson was well and safely re-elected. His accent recalled my trainer Fergus. Wouldn't that old fellow be amazed if he heard where I'd been since we parted in Newfoundland! As the three men smoked their pipes, the trader told the Captains we weren't getting along very well with Spain or England, how some general named Wilkinson was now the Governor of Louisiana and two fellows named Burr and Hamilton had fought a duel. Not very interesting, so I went outside the tent where I could breathe and fell asleep in the drizzle. The next morning, Aird presented the Captains with a barrel of flour and gave every man in our party enough tobacco to last until we reached St. Louis. As we started down the river, Gass said, "That Aird's a fine fellow, even if he is a Scot," and spat into the Missouri.

It was three hours later when we reached the place the Captains had named Floyd's Bluff. Even though it was a hard climb, Meriwether insisted on visiting Floyd's grave with Clark, Pryor, Gass, and Shannon. Indians had disturbed the spot, which infuriated the Captains. I guess they didn't understand that it was only Floyd's bones in the ground, not his spirit.

"Our only casualty," Meriwether whispered. "He was a good

man."

My Master's leg pained him for days after that climb, but didn't keep him down long. He insisted on manning a paddle or editing his notes. The Missouri began to seem crowded. We encountered close to one hundred and fifty traders and hunters and trappers, all as eager for information about where we'd been as we were about where we were going. Most people had assumed we were dead. One man named McClellan was so happy to see us alive that he invited the Captains onto his keelboat for wine, while the men received all the whiskey they could drink, which was a lot. York consumed his share, but like Meriwether, it didn't make him silly. Instead, the black man walked up the river and sat down by himself, gazing off to the West. After awhile Drouillard, who wasn't much of a drinker, joined him. I guess they weren't sure how they'd fit in when we reached home. Somebody had already called York "Nigger," and Drouillard, who'd kept us alive more than once through both his hunting skills and his hand signing, was just a half-breed again. Humans put too much stock in bloodlines instead of just accepting a man for what he can do.

Every day we traveled fifty or sixty miles. We still had plenty of lead and powder but the multitude of boats on the river kept the game in hiding, so the men said they'd rather keep moving and just eat plums, which they could gather in minutes along the bank (and which gave me the worst case of the runs I'd suffered on the entire journey.) One morning we rounded a curve in the river to see a cow grazing on a hillside. The men all started cheering. I like beef fine, but it doesn't compare to buffalo hump, so I wasn't sure what all the fuss was about. Soon we came to La Charette, a French village. That was close enough to home, especially for the *voyageurs*, that everyone acted a little crazy, firing off their guns and yelling so much that I caught their excitement and started barking. Those folks had never expected to see us again and treated us like heroes, and when we got to St. Charles it was more of the same. During our last day on the river, the soldiers were all talking about what they'd do when they got to St. Louis. Some wanted women, some more whiskey.

"Gimme both!" Joe Field said.

"Better git yerself a bath first," Reuben said, "or the women'll charge you double."

"I guess yer right," Joe agreed. "May even have to buy a new shirt."

"We are a motley-looking crew," Meriwether said, frowning down at his stained ragged buckskins. The Captains' uniform coats had long since been traded away and the officers didn't look much different than the men. Meriwether had calculated we'd been away two years, four months, and ten days. We'd been subsisting for days primarily on fruit, and I was looking forward to a good meal with plenty of meat—not buffalo, of course, but quantity would have to make up for quality. But what concerned my Master when we docked in St. Louis, with a crowd of more than a thousand residents, the entire population of the city, cheering our arrival after our journey of more than eight thousand miles? He asked if the mail had departed for Washington.

Meriwether had already started drafting his letter to The President during that last hour, agonizing over the perfect words. We'd explored all that new country, but he worried because we hadn't discovered the Northwest Passage and he wanted to let Jefferson down easy. In the end, my Master had to come right out and say that instead of a short and simple portage from the Missouri to the Columbia, a traveler had to walk or ride three hundred and forty miles, two hundred along a pretty good road but the last one hundred and forty *"over tremendous mountains which for sixty miles are covered with eternal snow."* He didn't mention that we'd all nearly starved to death before we stumbled into the Nez Perce and that the trail was, in Joe Field's opinion, "a real ripsnorter we'd jist as soon fergit."

Being heroes was all right, I suppose, since when we climbed out of the boats everybody petted me, clapped the men on the back, and kept making up new cheers in honor of the two Captains. But it was hard work, too, since everybody wanted to hear all about our trip, especially about the furs and the hostile Indians. Meriwether had sent a messenger to hold the post, so as soon as possible we retired to an inn where we devoured a hasty meal, then holed up in a quiet room where my Master could work on his letter to Jefferson and Clark could write to his brother the General and a different sort of letter to the girl for whom he'd named the Judith River. It felt peculiar to be indoors again. Figuring St. Louis ought to be safe enough, I left the Captains with York to guard them and wandered outside.

The city seemed a lot busier than I remembered, with more folks speaking English than before. Though I sought a familiar scent among the local canines, I didn't recognize anybody. Sometimes a human would say, "Isn't that the dog that traveled with the Corps of Discovery?" and I would wave my tail as I continued my exploration. Once I smelled a few of our men, but when I poked my head in the door, whiskey fumes nearly knocked me over. Hall, Werner, and Potts sat with a bunch of strangers, the table before them crowded with bottles and glasses. When Werner called out, "Look everybody, there's good ol' Seaman!" I ducked back outside. The soldiers deserved the chance to relax, but that tavern was no place for me.

Instead, I trotted down to the wharf, where Sergeant Pryor's squad had drawn the duty of safeguarding our vessels and their contents. Though I could tell the soldiers had "wet their whistles," they'd managed to keep the townspeople from rummaging through Meriwether's precious specimens. Shannon, who was trying to convince an old man that the Indians of the plains weren't seven feet tall and didn't eat one another, seemed relieved by my appearance. "This is Captain Lewis's Newfoundland dog," he told the crowd, "who warned us of danger and saved our company many times." His fingers stroked my fur. "I'd say he was one of the most valuable members of the whole expedition. He even has a creek named after him."

I felt proud right then, but a little sad, too, since those adventures were over.

"Them savages have more than one wife?" the old man asked.

"Don't be gittin' ideas!" scolded the woman at his side. "One's more'n you can handle!"

"Many of the Indian peoples do marry more than one woman," Sergeant Pryor said, "but the Mandan chief Big White who accompanied us has a single wife."

Big White, Blue Corn, and their son had gone off with part of Gass's squad, assigned by Meriwether to look after the Mandans and Jessaume's family. If the city seemed peculiar to me, how must they feel?

After a short stay among my friends, I returned to the inn, where both Captains still labored over their letters. Meriwether petted me without really paying attention. I lay down beside his desk. The buzz of a lone mosquito comforted me, somehow, and I closed my eyes, hoping to dream of buffalo hump, but instead I saw the face of a giant who I knew as The President, frowning down at my Master, who was only a boy.

Once Meriwether had finished his letter to Jefferson, dashed off notes to his family, and composed a handwritten testimonial for every one of the soldiers, he relaxed. We enjoyed a good dinner at the Choteaus', and then visited a tailor, for someone had told the Captains they both looked like a fellow named "Robinson Crusoe."

"Shall I discard these buckskins?" the tailor asked, his nose wrinkling as if he smelled something unpleasant.

"We'll be needing them awhile longer," Clark said with a grin, "unless you can sew us into cloth trousers while we wait. They've seen honorable service, and folks will just have to put up with them for awhile."

Sergeant Pryor's squad was happy to be relieved of duty after we'd stowed all the expedition's goods in the Choteaus' secure storeroom. "You men enjoy your leave here in St. Louis," Meriwether told them. "It's time you had a chance to throw away some of your well-earned money."

Shannon saluted. "Yes, sir!"

At the ball held in honor of the partners, I lurked outside, knowing the ruffled women and silk-coated men wouldn't appreciate dog hair decorating their attire. Four musicians played for the dancing. I found myself wishing for Cruzatte's screeching, backed by the rhythm of crickets.

York had spent part of the evening in the kitchen, but now he joined me on the porch. "Mighty strange, ain't it?" York's huge hand could scratch both my shoulders at once. "I been tellin' folks how it was in the Corps o' Discovery, an' they say 'You's just a black slave now, York, same as us. They took yore gun away, ain't they, an' 'spects you to say Massa, just like before you went West?'" His fingers went limp. "But I know I's somebody. Why can't nobody else see?"

Maybe York would find his girl with skin like molasses and be happy. I'd found the local females willing, their bodies soft and welcoming. I received plenty to eat and lots of time off, but St. Louis didn't hold much of a challenge after the Shining Mountains. Civilization would take some getting used to.

The next night the Captains attended a congratulatory dinner at Christy's Tavern, which I spent under the table feeding on morsels passed me by Meriwether. Every time I began to nod off, a toast roused me. My Master had proposed the first, calling The President *the polar star of discovery.* Sixteen more toasts followed, until York had to support both Captains to their beds.

In the morning, though, Meriwether returned to business. Something called the War Department had control of the money he needed to pay off the men and provide the supplies we needed to journey to Washington. Big White was excited about meeting Great Father Jefferson, but traveling in the East took money. We wouldn't have Drouillard along to kill game. I looked forward to being back on the trail, even if it meant going a bit hungry. We could count on the General to put on a good feed when we reached Clarksville.

Weeks passed before we could taste those sausages, though. When at last we set off with Big White, Jessaume, and their families, Sergeants Ordway and Gass accompanied us, along with Frazer and Labiche, but I'd said goodbye to the rest of my friends. Joe Field had tousled my ears and Shannon had promised we'd meet again. I hoped he was right, but we lived in a big busy world. Who could know where we'd end up? In the meantime, we made slow progress, since everybody lit bonfires and held banquets and balls to welcome us. The Captains had new uniforms by then and ladies clustered around them, twittering like birds. I felt a little jealous whenever Meriwether twirled around the room with one of those females in his arms, but was glad to see him smile and laugh.

At last we reached the home of George Rogers Clark, where the food was almost as good as I remembered. The General looked about the same, but Old Bay's muzzle had lost the last of its color and he moved like his hindquarters hurt. "Stove up with the rheumatiz'," he told me. "Yore too young yet to understand."

Eulalie looked as if she hadn't changed much, but when we met out at the barn two bigger dogs flanked her. One wore a patch of white on her chest, while the male was even taller with white legs. Otherwise they were black. "Webbed paws, too," said Old Bay, nodding. "Fine pups you breed, Seaman. Glad those Injuns didn't eat you."

Clark lingered to visit with his relatives before he headed toward Fincastle and the young girl he'd dreamed about for years. Meriwether's friend Chouteau, who had journeyed with us in charge of a party of Osage chiefs, detoured toward someplace called Lexington while we took the Old Wilderness Road for Washington. It didn't feel much like wilderness to me, though, with farms and cabins and even towns with inns along the way. Everyone we met wanted to hear all about our travels in the West, but by late November we reached the boundary of Meriwether's home state of Virginia. Unfortunately, the North Carolinians disputed that border and wanted Meriwether to settle the argument, so he unpacked the surveying tools and found out North Carolina owed Virginia a ten-mile strip. Big White found the whole procedure puzzling, since his people didn't measure the land and try to divide it up. I'd grown to both respect and pity the chief, who stayed cheerful even though he couldn't understand most of what went on around him. Back home he was a leader. Here he had to rely on Jessaume to explain things.

As we approached the wooded hills around Ivy Creek, Meriwether's gelding caught his rider's excitement and started dancing, so my Master left Sergeant Ordway in charge of the Mandans and the goods and loped the last couple of miles. It felt good to bound through the shallow snow beside Meriwether, who had dropped the years from his face until he looked almost as young as the boy in my dream. I was panting as we dashed up the last slope of Locust Hill, and a little worried, too: what if Lucy Marks was the sort of female who fussed about dirty paw prints the size of saucers?

Meriwether's mother was smaller than I expected and smelled like smoked meat. After she'd allowed her son to sweep her from her feet and swing her around in circles, she knelt and wrapped her arms around me in much the same way Bird

Woman had done when we said farewell. "Thank you for watching over my boy," she whispered. Then she let me lick her face.

It turned out Lucy Marks was quite a famous cook—The President bought her hams to serve in Washington City when she could spare them—and the impending return of her first-born son at Christmastime had "provoked a fury of baking and roasting and pickling such as you've never seen," or so Meriwether's younger brother Reuben Lewis explained it. I never got all the relatives straight, but I especially enjoyed my Master's quiet sister Mary and brother Reuben, who looked a lot like Meriwether with the same longish (for a human) nose and upright posture but without the deep-set, shadowed eyes. As for Lucy Marks—well, she fed me so bountifully that I would have grown portly if we'd stayed any longer. Big White enjoyed her cooking, too, and his wife Blue Corn learned how to make something called "trifle" that delighted the chief and his family.

After we said our goodbyes we stopped by Monticello, where The President lived when he wasn't in the capitol. You could see it from Locust Hill, and Meriwether told Sergeant Gass how Jefferson had signaled with a mirror whenever he wanted my Master to ride over and view some new discovery. Monticello was bigger than Locust Hill, and parts of it were really fancy, but one whole room was set aside just for Indian things like bowls and spears and beaded buckskin clothes. Big White grinned when he recognized the string of chief beads he'd sent on the keelboat with Corporal Warfington.

Those last miles into Washington City took forever (not that I was in any hurry to see The President.) Even though it was growing dark, folks lined the roads, cheering for Meriwether and jostling each other for a peek at "wild Indians." Blue Corn and the boy looked scared, but Big White learned how to wave and never let up, grinning at everyone. Eventually we reached a house set aside for our use, where a small, dark-haired woman met us at the door with a kiss for Meriwether that flushed his cheeks.

"It's good of you to wait for us, Mrs. Madison," said my Master. "May I present Chief Big White and his wife Blue Corn?"

She offered her hand to the chief. "People are calling you the King and the Queen of the Mandans," she told him, flashing a smile that dimpled her plump cheeks. "I hope you will call me 'Dolly,' even if the Captain chooses to address me more formally than our friendship warrants. I'm sorry The President couldn't be here himself, but he looks forward to your meeting and hopes you enjoy your stay in Washington."

When Big White said something in Mandan, Jessaume stepped forward to translate; luckily he smelled better now that he'd had some baths and new clothes. "The chief sends zee best of all wishes to Great Father Jefferson."

I spent that night at the foot of Meriwether's bed, and no matter what Dolly Madison said, President Jefferson was right there with us, waking or sleeping.

Washington City turned out to be a lot less fancy than I'd expected. The streets were muddy, for one thing, and some of the people were poor and not too clean. Yet others were polished and pressed and primped. Women dressed in shiny fabrics, with whole dead birds perched on their heads, while men wore lace at their throats and tall hats that smelled faintly of beaver. Now Meriwether fit right in with those folks, and he dressed up the Mandans so they did, too, except for their long black hair. One night they all went to the theater. Dogs weren't invited, but I didn't mind, since it gave me a chance to explore the city and meet a few canines, including one curly-haired bitch with a strange accent. I stayed home during the formal presentation of the Mandans to The President, too, but on New Year's Day, which Meriwether planned to spend with Jefferson, he brushed me till my coat crackled.

"I remember writing in my journal at Fort Clatsop," Meriwether mused, "about where I hoped to be on this first day of 1807." His fingers smoothed the unruly whorl of hairs on my forehead. "It's hard to believe that moment has come at last. One thing's certain: today we won't be eating boiled elk and drinking spring water."

A little elk would have tasted pretty good about then, but apparently none of those delectable beasts lived around Washington, though I had observed (and chased) a few puny deer. The more civilized things got, the less game we'd seen, and I guess Washington City was about the most civilized place in the entire world. "Come, Seaman," Meriwether said, "it's time for you to meet The President."

Jefferson wasn't nearly as big as I'd expected. Some things—like the Great Falls and the Shining Mountains and buffalo—had turned out to be grander than I could ever have imagined, but Jefferson wasn't much taller than my Master or half as fancy as some of the folks I'd met in Washington. He didn't even wear boots, but soft footgear more like moccasins made out of cloth which allowed him to walk without making any noise. I liked the way he squatted down with his hands on his knees to look me right in the eyes. "So this is the dog of the Newfoundland breed," Jefferson said, "which caught those black squirrels migrating across the Ohio River."

He'd read Meriwether's words, all right, and remembered them. I wasn't about to lick the face of The President, but I offered him a paw without any prompting, which he shook solemnly. "I'm sure you were a fine ambassador, Seaman, for all the dogs of America. How I envied you, with grizzly bears, wild rivers, new sights and smells every day." He uttered a deep sigh, and then smiled. "Your Master must tell me all about everything, but first we'll dine together and toast the New Year."

I don't know who cooked those pheasants and the beef in its own juice, but they deserved a prize. The men and women who served the food looked a little shocked when The President had them set a place for me on the floor right next to Meriwether's chair, but they kept my plate as full as anybody's. Dolly Madison and her husband, who wasn't even as tall as she was, ate with us, too, but after the plates were cleared away they left us alone with Jefferson.

"At last!" The President said. "Enough of small talk. Let's adjourn to my study."

That was when I understood why Meriwether loved Jefferson so much. The two of them got down on their hands and knees, surrounded by Clark's maps, my Master's drawings, and the journals, now bound in fresh leather, and went over our whole journey. It was almost like living the adventure again, though Jefferson kept interrupting with questions. I could tell he was as proud of Meriwether as if he were his father.

"Hmmm... China," The President murmured. "A fine market for American goods." He fingered the pelts Meriwether had placed in his hands. The scent of beaver made me salivate;

I'd never tasted any sea otters—probably tasty, also. "No reason we can't assume control of the fur trade, even without the Northwest Passage."

He reminded me of Meriwether then, his hands busy with the soft feel of the pelts but his mind soaring somewhere I couldn't even imagine, as if he could see the future better than most of us see what's right in front of our nose. My grandmother was like that, too. I doubted she'd be especially surprised that I'd ended up in The President's House, sprawled on a patterned carpet.

Those two talked so much their voices grew hoarse. They drank a lot of wine, too, from over in France. Candles burned down, dripping wax onto the polished tables, but Jefferson just lit more. "You say the Nez Perce and Shoshone herds could transport goods over the mountains? I'd like to meet Chief Came-ah-wait. He clearly has his people's best interests at heart."

By the time Meriwether had retraced our route back to Fort Mandan, my eyelids had grown so heavy that I gave in to sleep. The last words I recall hearing were: "Remember those animals you sent me? The little prairie dog survived, and one magpie that nearly drove Dolly mad before I shipped them off to the museum in Philadelphia...."

CHAPTER NINETEEN

I learned my way around Washington, since we stayed in that city all winter, living at The President's House, where I became a favorite with Jefferson's grandchildren. Clark hadn't yet appeared in Washington, since he was busy courting. Meriwether received a letter that read: *"I have attacked most vigorously. We have come to terms."* I didn't know much about the mating rituals of humans, so this sounded peculiar to me, but Meriwether laughed and said, "Good for Will!" As before, my Master seemed to enjoy the company of young females. They all seemed useless, flighty creatures, but I was certainly no judge. Several times Meriwether swore he'd fallen in love, but nothing came of it. "Maybe we're destined to be a couple of old bachelors," he told me.

Banquets continued to celebrate my Master's achievements, and someone wrote a poem in his honor. Meriwether made plans for publishing his journal and commended all the members of the Corps of Discovery in writing once again, except for Charbonneau, who he called "a man of no particular merit." Meriwether sought extra pay for Private Labiche, who had turned out to be useful as an interpreter, and Shields, our gunsmith and best blacksmith. But most of all he praised Drouillard and the Field brothers, who'd gone on the most dangerous missions and kept us from starving. I missed the men, especially Shannon, and Bird Woman and Little Pomp, too, but our lives had changed, whether we liked it or not.

Meriwether fretted until the lawmakers in the Congress passed a bill to pay the men double wages and give them the land the government had promised—320 acres each, and 1600 to Clark and to my Master. I couldn't fathom the size of that acreage, but it sounded like a lot. Meriwether and his partner also received a sum of money, which they planned to invest in the fur trade.

I'd figured they'd talked everything out during that endless conversation on New Years' Night, but nearly every day Meriwether and The President were at it again, rehashing each detail of our journey. Jefferson reminded me of a dog determined to worry every last speck of marrow from a bone, which was probably one reason why he was the leader of the pack. He had a long nose a lot like Meriwether's, but a heavier jaw that reminded me of a bulldog's, and they won't let go once they latch onto something. Even though The President always had a pat for my head and kind words, I felt like I had to be on my very best behavior, with no drooling while I waited for the Cook to fill my bowl.

Late in that gloomy February, Jefferson nominated my Master to be the Governor of the Territory of Louisiana. The President had appointed Will Clark as the Territory's Superintendent of Indian Affairs, meaning my Master's partner would be close by. It sounded like a pretty good place for us to live, since The President said some of that land was "unspoiled country," the opposite of Washington City, which was way too crowded and low on game. Clark had finally reached the capitol, looking pleased with himself and filled out again, as if he'd eaten plenty to make up for all the lean times. York had gone off to the General's, where he planned to marry a woman who lived on a plantation near Louisville, so I figured he'd be pleased, too, and not feel so bad about being a slave. We didn't have much chance to enjoy Clark's company, though, for the husband of Jefferson's daughter became ill and Meriwether insisted on nursing the fellow. We never knew what caused that sickness, but pretty soon my Master came down with the same high fever and then Jefferson caught a cold, so The President's House turned into a hospital. I sat at Meriwether's bedside for hours, my chin propped beside his pillow, and when he stroked my head I could feel the heat in his hand. When Will stopped by for a visit, my Master roused from his lethargy to turn over the land deeds and money for the Corps members and discuss plans for returning Big White and his family to the Mandans. The Captains agreed that Sergeant Pryor, Shannon, and some of our other friends should be part of that expedition. After Clark left, Meriwether dosed himself with Rush's Thunderbolts and improved rapidly. He credited the pills, but I believe his partner's visit did more good. My Master was always better with Will Clark at his side.

Then it was spring. Though I hoped that meant we would be headed west, Meriwether still had unfinished business in Washington. Even though he'd suggested that many of the Corps members keep journals of their own so details of our adventures wouldn't be lost, he grew angry when Sergeant Gass and Private Frazer revealed plans to publish their writings. My Master wanted the public to read the volumes of the two Captains, who were far more educated in geography and the sciences, but Meriwether seldom had a chance to concentrate on editing his words. He stayed friends with Frazer, however, and even loaned him money to return to St. Louis with Clark. Frazer also carried Meriwether's instructions for a man named Frederick Bates, who was governing the Louisiana Territory until we arrived. I wished we were going in person. Civilization wasn't half as good as the West.

At the end of March we left for Philadelphia, where my Master planned to organize the publication of the journals in several volumes. There he rounded up some famous scientists and artists to help. One of the men, an artist named Peale, painted our portrait. I thought he made my eyes too small, but otherwise I looked just as a Newfoundland should. "He left off the gray hairs in your muzzle," Meriwether observed, "and those in my hair. A fair likeness, though."

Was my muzzle really going gray? That winter I'd felt a few twinges of what Old Bay had called the "rheumatiz" in the leg bitten by the beaver and kicked by the horse on the Lolo Trail, but I didn't let it slow down my exploration of Philadelphia. The city had grown since the brief visit of my youth, and by 1807 Philadelphia was almost as civilized as Washington. Though people always asked when the book would be ready and Meriwether spent most of his time on paperwork, he never seemed to get anywhere. The War Department kept pestering him about drafts he'd signed, wanting proof before they paid.

"How am I supposed to prove that I traded my uniform coat

and all that other gear for a canoe and a horse? We needed the means of transportation! Was I supposed to ask the Clatsop chief to sign a chit?" When Meriwether rubbed my ear, I leaned into his hand. "These fellows don't have any understanding of what it was like out there, or what the men went through."

In June Meriwether received a letter from The President, saying he'd called on Lucy Marks and found her in good health after her trip to Georgia. It also reported that twenty-five boxes of specimens sent by boat from Washington to Richmond had been lost, everything except the horns of moose and elk. "All that effort," Meriwether muttered. "You'd think after traveling intact all the way across the continent they could have survived Chesapeake Bay..." He poured himself another glass of ale. With no Will Clark around, Meriwether spent a lot of time with an old friend, a lawyer named Mahlon Dickerson, and returned from their outings with whiskey on his breath. Spirits seldom cheered my Master, sending him into his darkness. Often Meriwether woke the next morning with an aching head, cursing himself for a fool and swearing off drinking. (I wished he'd swear off Dickerson, too.) But nothing changed.

In late July we journeyed to Washington City, where Meriwether met with officials (who he often referred to as "those damned bureaucrats") in the War Department before paying a visit to his mother at Locust Hill. There I had the chance to chase a few rabbits, mate with a young bird dog, and enjoy Lucy Marks' wonderful cooking. Meriwether seemed happier around his mother, the creases between his eyes and around his mouth relaxing so he looked more like the young Captain I'd first met in Pittsburgh. We also spent time at Monticello, where Jefferson's inquiries about the publication of the journals irritated Meriwether, even though he tried to hide it. In July, The President sent Meriwether to Richmond for the trial of a man named Burr, accused of being a traitor to the United States. My Master wanted to leave me behind with his mother, but after I trailed his horse for a few miles and caught up, my tongue lolling, Meriwether laughed. "Still don't trust me on my own, Seaman? It will be hot and dull for you in Richmond, but so be it."

Meriwether was right: Richmond sweltered and I spent most of my time sleeping under a leafy tree outside the courthouse. Frazer, who'd received a promotion, had helped gather the evidence against the traitor, but in the end Burr was set free and we returned to Washington. Meriwether kept fretting about money, though he was drawing his salary as Governor even without being in the Louisiana Territory. Worrying made him drink more, and drinking made him worry more instead of working on editing the journals.

One time I thought Meriwether might get married. In November, we traveled to Fincastle to meet the girl after whom Clark had named the Judith River, even though her name was Julia. Her cheeks glowed and her gentle hands knew just where to scratch. But my Master was too busy to pay much attention, for he'd been introduced to Letitia Breckenridge, the young daughter of a general who lived nearby. Everyone—especially Meriwether—talked about what a beautiful girl she was, but her high-pitched giggle prickled my ears and the powdery scent she wore made me want to sneeze. Every day my Master sent bouquets and letters. Maybe she got scared by the attentions of such a famous man, for she left on a hasty trip to Richmond. For awhile Meriwether drank himself to sleep at night, and then swore off both whiskey and marriage. He never looked at another girl the same way again. But there was always another bottle.

Back at Locust Hill, Meriwether drank less and tried to work on the manuscript of the journals. He wanted it perfect, and sometimes he'd wad up sheets he'd slaved over for hours and fling them into the fireplace. Even though we seldom saw The President during that winter, Jefferson often seemed to be in the room, peering over Meriwether's shoulder. Those long, dark days weighed heavily on my Master. Even if the hunting wasn't much, I wanted him outdoors in the fresh air, but instead he huddled over his desk with that shadow in his eyes.

"He's not happy, Seaman," his mother told me one day as I watched her slide a cake into the oven. "I wish you could have known him as a young boy. Oh, after his father died and the Revolution dragged on, Meri became old for his age, but he'd still hike into the woods with his dogs and return with game and wild stories." She dropped the yolks of half-a-dozen eggs into my bowl. "I think he's afraid he's already lived the greatest story of his life and that nothing half so wonderful lies ahead. Even though I'll miss him, I hope his duties in St. Louis give him a sense of direction."

Lucy Marks was a wise woman. When we said goodbye to her near the end of that winter, she gave Meriwether a kiss, then reached up to tousle his hair in much the same way she'd ruffled my ears. "Off to the West again! You take good care of Seaman, and of your little brother, too."

"We'll all be fine," Meriwether assured her. "St. Louis is hardly the wilderness anymore, and being involved in the fur trade is a great opportunity for Reuben."

Meriwether's younger brother traveled down the Ohio River and up the Mississippi, but we journeyed overland. It took longer, and maybe that was the whole idea. I'd heard enough about the situation in St. Louis to know it would be a challenge, but I think my Master would have preferred to face three grizzly bears and a war party of Tetons. "I know The President intends my appointment as an honor," Meriwether said, "but Governor? I'm a soldier, Seaman, not a politician. I saw enough of intrigue as Jefferson's secretary to know that. How am I supposed to make peace between the old French residents and all the new Americans moving in, not to mention the Indians? Thank God I'll have Clark to help with the tribes. If he ever finishes his honeymoon."

We'd missed Will's wedding to Julia Hancock, for Meriwether had taken sick just after the first day of the New Year of 1808. Maybe it was an attack of malaria. Lucy Marks had doctored him, and my Master had also treated himself, not with Rush's Thunderbolts but instead with laudanum to help him sleep. Meriwether had sent Reuben with our wedding gift: a pair of silver goblets engraved in Philadelphia.

At first I thought Lucy Marks was right, that St. Louis might be just what Meriwether needed. Affairs were in a tangle, and challenge usually brought out the best in my Master. He wanted to improve relationships with all the Indian tribes and build American involvement in the fur trade, breaking control by the British. He proposed a system of forts and trading posts all along the Missouri. That meant advancing into territory inhabited by the Teton Sioux, but Meriwether advocated excluding the Tetons from all trading until they agreed to cooperate.

The city had grown even more during our stay in the East.

Besides the old-time French merchants, the Canadian *voyageurs*, and the Americans, St. Louis was home to Spaniards and friendly Indians, black slaves and even a few that had received their freedom, nearly five thousand people all told. Some folks had built fancy new houses while others lived in shacks or tents. Every night someone held a ball or other festivity, though I never heard a fiddler quite like Cruzatte. The streets smelled of horse manure, which didn't bother me but made Meriwether wonder how Clark's new bride would like St. Louis. He'd found a house he hoped was big enough for the newlyweds, their niece, ourselves, and of course York. "When the babies come it will be too crowded and you and I will have to find bachelor quarters," my Master told me. "Unless you're thinking about settling down with some sleek little female of your own."

Meriwether loved to tease about my "conquests," as he called them. That summer found him in generally high spirits, despite Indian troubles. By the time Will reached us (when we did, in fact, move into bachelor quarters in the home of the Choteaus, since Julia seemed to want Will Clark all to herself, though we continued to take our meals with the couple), the Osage tribe had "cast off all allegiance to the United States." Soon Clark had eighty men ready for an expedition up the Missouri, determined to build a fort along the Osage River. I felt sorry for young Julia, who was already carrying a baby, though nobody said it out loud. She never ate much breakfast, even when York fried up greens with lots of bacon.

In July Meriwether received a letter from The President. Jefferson complained that he hadn't heard from his Governor, which made my Master wince, and asked for a report on how we intended to return Big White to the Mandans, since one expedition had already failed. But it was the last lines of the letter which Meriwether read aloud that worried him the most: "*We have no tidings yet of the forwardness of your printer. I hope the first part will not be delayed much longer.*"

Meriwether really tried to work on the journals. Often, late at night, he'd sit at his desk, turning pages, writing notes, trying to make sense out of old scribblings. But he was stuck, somehow, mired in all those words.

The situation with Big White vexed him, too. Back in the summer of 1807, Pryor, Shannon, and a small company had headed a keelboat up the Missouri with the Mandans and Jessaume's family onboard. But when they reached the Arikaras, the tribe had refused to allow them to pass, angry because their chief who had journeyed to Washington to meet with Jefferson had died of an illness. In the fighting that followed, three of the soldiers were wounded, including my friend Shannon, and the party had to turn back. Pryor figured it would take at least four hundred men to return the Mandans successfully to their people. Now the chief and his family resided with the officers stationed outside the city, but Big White complained that was beneath his dignity, since now he called himself a brother rather than a son of Great Father Jefferson.

As soon as we'd reached St. Louis, we'd paid Shannon the first of many visits. Stretched out on a bed in a military hospital, he'd looked even skinnier than he had after getting lost during the autumn of 1804. His wound just wouldn't heal.

"The doctors keep threatening to take my leg," he explained, "but I ask them what good is a one-legged soldier? Don't look so sad, Captain—I mean <u>Governor</u>. You, either, Seaman. It isn't so terrible, really. I asked if they could find me some books on botany, and after I finished those I started reading the law. Thought I might become a lawyer when they let me out of this place."

"You'll make a fine one," Meriwether said, "and I could use your help about now. Things aren't going so well in the city.... We'll return soon, and I'll see that they keep you supplied with books."

I hated leaving Shannon there, looking so frail and lonesome, but Meriwether was right: we had trouble in St. Louis, and at the root of it was Frederick Bates. The brother of an old friend of Meriwether's, he'd welcomed the new Governor in public, but from the beginning I could tell he was eaten up by envy. With Meriwether in the East, Bates had become more than a secretary, and now he didn't want to relinquish control of things. I despised the way he fawned on my Master to his face and then went behind his back to complain to others. Bates saw plots everywhere, was afraid of Indians, and hated dogs. Once, when someone accused him of trying to undermine the Governor and wanting the post for himself, Bates screamed at him, "If you ever again bark at my heels, I will spurn you like a puppy from my path!" If a single black hair attached itself to his clothes he removed it ostentatiously. Whenever he entered Meriwether's office he detoured around me, but I could tell he would have kicked me if he dared. As the months passed, it was all I could do to keep from growling at the man.

When Clark was around to act as an intermediary, Bates managed to control his venom, though. As before, the presence of his friend and former partner brought out the best in Meriwether. Together they formulated an Indian policy and planned an expedition to return Big White to the Mandans. That winter

Julia had her baby, a boy that they named Meriwether Lewis Clark, which brought tears to my Master's eyes. I thought he was funny-looking, but maybe that was because humans start life with so little hair.

York perked up for awhile after the birth of little Meriwether, but soon turned quiet again. I guess it was hard for him to be parted from his wife, a woman with "skin like molasses." "York's always nagging at me to give him his freedom," Clark confided to Meriwether, as my Master lay in his bed, recovering from an attack of malaria that increased his consumption of laudanum. "This last time, when I explained that I'm used to having him around and need him more than ever, he got downright uppity." Clark frowned. "The Nez Perce gave him ideas. Hopefully he'll get straightened out."

I felt sorry for York, who didn't want a Master anymore, and worried about Drouillard, too. Neither had adjusted very well to our return to civilization. Acting on orders from the trader Manuel Lisa, Drouillard had gone after a French deserter (just as he'd gone after Moses Reed back in 1804) and then ended up on trial for murder, mostly, it seemed, because he was part-Indian. In the end the jury acquitted him, but after that Drouillard stayed away from St. Louis. Maybe he'd hook up with Colter in the mountains and become a trapper. We'd heard that poor Potts had died at the hands of the Blackfeet, Ordway had started a farm, and sometimes we saw Gibson, who'd settled in St. Louis, and Werner, who went to work for Clark. Frazer never published his journals, but Sergeant Gass did. I wondered about the Field brothers and young Bird Woman, who'd promised to bring Pomp to St. Louis when he was old enough for an education.

By the end of the winter, Shannon's leg had grown more shriveled and a new infection set in. During our visit, he told us the surgeon had scheduled him for amputation the next day. "They say I'll feel better without it. Can't say I'll miss the pain, and I guess I can still become a lawyer with a wooden leg."

"You're a brave man, George," Meriwether said, "far braver than I."

Shannon shrugged his bony shoulders. "Things happen, especially to soldiers, and I guess it's our duty to make the best of it." He smiled. "Have I told you, sir, how much your visits mean to me?"

Now it was Meriwether who shrugged. "I wish there was more I could do. Never knew how to chat and make jokes with the men, the way Clark did. Never had the gift for it."

"Don't think we held that against you, sir." Shannon touched Meriwether's arm for just a moment. "Most of us fellows were in plain awe of you. We knew how seriously you took your responsibility. We were proud to serve under you."

Meriwether's smile looked like it hurt. "And I was proud to lead. Just as I'm proud of you now."

Two days later, we returned to the hospital. It was strange to see the outline of only one leg under the blanket, but the fever had left Shannon's eyes. "I'll be up and around in no time. In the meanwhile, I've got plenty of studying to do."

Meriwether was quiet on our trip back to St. Louis. The trouble with Frederick Bates had grown worse. At a ball Meriwether had seated himself near the secretary as a gesture of good will, but Bates stood up and stalked to the other side of the room. That made Meriwether so mad he went and found Clark, saying Bates had treated him with "contempt and insult" and that he "could not suffer it to pass." Clark had tried to patch things up, but the secretary said Meriwether had injured <u>him.</u>

The other big problem facing my Master was money. He'd purchased a lot of land, 5,700 acres altogether, and hoped to bring his mother and his favorite sister Mary along with her family to live in the Louisiana Territory. Meriwether had also acquired a servant, a free half-black man named John Pernia (not near as dark and strong as York), and my Master had to borrow money from Clark when the fellow got sick.

At least we didn't have to worry about Big White anymore. Meriwether had arranged for the Missouri Fur Company, which included his brother Reuben, to transport the chief and his family safely back to Mandan territory, and in mid-May they headed up the Missouri. But nothing else seemed to be going well. Jefferson had retired and we had a new President, James Madison, Dolly's husband. I think Meriwether envied Jefferson, free to study botany at Monticello while Meriwether struggled with Bates and money troubles and the journals. Then, in July, we received word that the new Secretary of War had refused to honor a draft Meriwether had written. When the Secretary refused another of $500 for Indian presents along the route of Big White's return to the Mandans, Meriwether tried to appeal to President Madison, but was told the action had been taken with this President's approval.

Which brought all Meriwether's creditors like a flock of ravens, each trying to snatch a bite before the others. My Master sold off most of his land and paid as many debts as he could, and then gathered up all his receipts and papers, determined to go to Washington City. He planned a trip by keelboat to New

Orleans, then a voyage along the coast to the capitol. I figured time on the water would do us both good, and in Virginia we could visit with Lucy Marks. If Meriwether wasn't reappointed Governor, as Bates hoped, we could stay at Locust Hill for a long time. Clark and two other friends agreed to watch over Meriwether's affairs in our absence. While my Master conferred further with Clark, I poked my nose into York's hand.

"Guess I won't be seein' you for a spell, Seaman," said York. "You take good care of yore Massa, hear? An' maybe when you gets back, I won't have a Massa no mo'. Still hopin' for my freedom."

Late that night I was jarred from sleep by the shatter of glass. Had the Tetons attacked? How could I have let down my guard? But no, we were in St. Louis. In the dark room I could just make out the outline of my Master seated on the bed above me. Not far from my head lay the remains of a bottle and liquid pooling on the plank floor. The fumes seared my nostrils.

"Sorry," my Master said, "didn't mean to wake you." The bottle explained the quaver in his voice, the wobble before he collapsed on the blanket. He'd neglected to change for the night, and I scented saddle leather on his woolen trousers, a bit of dried horse dung on his boots. We'd returned late from a long ramble in the countryside, even though Meriwether had struggled all the rest of that week to put his affairs in order. Glad to be away from town, I was content to sniff at tree trunks, poke my muzzle down fragrant holes, dig halfheartedly after moles, while Meriwether waited, uncharacteristically slumped in his saddle. He'd not taken a single specimen.

"Can't seem to sleep tonight," Meriwether said. He reached down, patted my head. "Glad you're here with me. Just like all those times on the trail. Best friend I ever had. Never once com-plained when I kept you awake." His hand didn't ruffle my ears or scratch between my shoulderblades, but just the feel of his fingers on my fur was worth any loss of sleep. "I've been think-ing about those Watlalas who tried to steal you from me, those damn rascals. Lucky ol' Drouillard was on the alert. Good man. Wonder where he's hunting these days. No St. Louis for him. We're all scattered now, a Corps no more." Meriwether sounded sad so I turned to lick his palm, wishing I knew a better way to cheer him. "Never told you, did I, how proud I am of you? Oh, I lauded you in the journals, but never said how you were worth your weight in gold. Saved us all. Me—most of all." His voice sounded like it was sticking in his throat. "Can't thank you enough. Only try an' make a good life for you."

I didn't need praise, just to stay close beside my Master and keep him safe, now and always. The shadow was in the room with us, that shapeless black with its fearsome weight. I longed for the days when Meriwether was happy, striding into the un-known on our journey West, his eyes bright. Then I heard his breathing change, settle into a snore. But dawn found me still awake, on guard against that enemy with no name.

The following morning, on the day we were to leave for Washington, my Master rose late, turned down the breakfast John Pernia offered but refused to leave the house until I'd finished my own. Then we traveled to the hospital. Shannon looked much improved, sitting up in bed. "Wish you'd been here an hour ago, sir—they're letting me out at the end of the week, so they have me walking around every day, and I met a young fellow who just lost an arm. He wanted to hear all about our adventures in the West and I was telling him about Seaman. Do you have time to let the famous dog of the Corps of Discovery perform his tricks? It would mean a lot to this soldier."

"Of course. You two go along. There's something I need to discuss with the administrators of the hospital."

I followed Shannon down a couple of hallways and into another room, slowing my pace to stay beside him though he could maneuver pretty well on his wooden leg. The soldier, even younger than Shannon when we'd first met, got all excited as I went through my routine, but when Meriwether joined us I thought the boy might faint. "I sure am honored to meet you, Cap'n Lewis—I mean Your Excellency." He grinned. "My pa says yer the best Governor he ever saw."

"I wish the rest of my constituents shared his sentiments," Meriwether said, sitting on the edge of the bed and shaking the soldier's left hand like it was a normal thing to do. "The doctor told me you're quite a hero."

"Wasn't nothin', sir," the soldier told him. "Couldn't let 'em murder that ol' man, even if he was an Injun, but guess I didn't move fast enough to keep my arm." He grinned again. "Mighty lucky I was already a leftie."

Meriwether looked from that soldier to Shannon, and for a moment I thought he might cry. Then he stood up. "I need to be getting back to the city. Could I have a word with you, George?"

We walked together down the hall, slowly, Meriwether with one hand on my head. It was trembling. "I don't plan a prolonged visit to Washington City, George, so I've decided to leave Seaman here in St. Louis. I wonder if you'd look after him? The administrators said he can stay here until you're released—

there are some advantages to being Governor—and then Clark wants you both to live with his family until you're fully recovered."

Stay. That was the word I kept hearing in my head as Meriwether and Shannon arranged my future. He was leaving me behind. Again. This time it wasn't grizzlies or the Blackfeet that threatened my Master, but I could smell the danger. Something was terribly wrong.

"I'll say my goodbyes now."

They shook hands.

"I'm honored to have Seaman with me, sir. Don't worry, we'll take good care of each other."

"I know that," Meriwether said. He knelt down beside me. "It's hard for you to understand, but this is the best thing. It will be the last time I ask you to stay behind." One finger traced the whorl of hair on my forehead. "Be a good dog. Stay." Then my Master straightened, walked down the hall with that ground-eating pace, and disappeared around the corner.

CHAPTER TWENTY

I spent the few days before Shannon's discharge at the hospital, entertaining the soldiers with tricks or simply visiting. It seemed to help them to sink their fingers in my fur, even shed a few tears when no one was watching, and it distracted me, at least temporarily, from worrying about Meriwether on his own. York drove us to St. Louis, not silent now but full of talk and laughter during the jolting wagon ride, for he was too big-hearted to brood when Shannon needed his help. The Clarks welcomed us to their home, where Julia introduced Shannon to Meriwether Lewis Clark, then showed us to the same room where my Master and I had lived before. Even though the linens were different and someone had scrubbed the walls and floors with vinegar, I could still detect Meriwether's scent. Every day we wandered the dusty streets, going a little farther each time, first on foot and then with Shannon on horseback, for he was determined to be independent, even with one leg. In the evenings he studied his law books. I would lie at his feet, just as I had when Meriwether wrote in the journals.

But it wasn't the same. Just like my Master, I'd had the chance to be my best, more than I ever thought I could be. Now I was just an ordinary dog, missing my true Master.

At first, nobody else seemed much concerned about Meriwether's absence, but in October, when we'd still received no word, Clark decided to travel overland to Washington. Shannon had recuperated so well that he was able to attempt the trip, eager to see the nation's capital and the halls of government. He spoke of going into politics someday. The idea of a journey cheered me, too, for I had drooped during the hot, muggy days of late summer, though I tried never to mope in Shannon's presence. I think York understood better than anyone. "You still wants yore Massa, more'n hump meat, even," he told me. "Dogs is different, I reckon. If you runned away nobody'd tie you to a post an' beat you with a whip. Cap'n Lewis should never've left you behind, no matter what. He needs somebody to watch after 'im, an' that Pernia's sure no use. We'll go find the Cap'n."

The autumn woods provided squirrels to chase up trees and deer to flush from cover, but I was just using up the hours. This journey it was East that mattered, and I was most restless at sunrise, anxious to be on the move.

After we reached a place called Shelbyville, Clark rented us a room and stepped out to buy a newspaper. When he returned, Will walked like an old, old man.

"Lewis is dead," he told Shannon. "I can hardly credit it, but the paper says he was found at a place called Grinder's Stand along the Natchez Trace."

"My God," Shannon cried, "are they sure?"

"Apparently he shot himself." Clark covered his face with

his hands. "Oh, Meri, why did you leave us?"

I guess I should have known it all that time. He'd gone off by himself—no Will Clark, no best friend. That dark inside him grew so strong he couldn't see the trail ahead.

It took awhile before we heard the details of Meriwether's death. He'd boarded the riverboat for New Orleans, and by the time they'd reached Chickasaw Bluffs, he'd twice tried to kill himself. The commander of Fort Pickering took Meriwether into custody for his own protection, allowing him only a little wine instead of the whiskey and laudanum he'd consumed since he left St. Louis. My Master had managed to write President Madison a shaky letter, saying he'd taken medicine and was feeling better and had decided to continue on by land, as he carried the precious journals and feared they might fall into British hands. After a week, Meriwether seemed enough improved and so filled with remorse that the commander allowed him to resume his journey, accompanied by a Major Neelly, Neelly's servant, and John Pernia. As they rode toward Washington, Neelly reported, Meriwether seemed deranged. He'd promised never to drink again, but somehow had procured spirits. After two of the horses strayed, Neelly remained behind to search for them, while Meriwether and the two servants rode on until late afternoon, when my Master rented a small log cabin from a Mrs. Grinder. She said he paced in front of the cabin, talking to himself, and then settled in a chair in the doorway, smoking his pipe, watching the sunset and reaching down, over and over, as if to touch something that wasn't there.

Meriwether insisted on sleeping on the floor in a buffalo

robe, while the servants slept in a barn a distance away. Sometime during that night, he rose and shot himself in the head, then in the chest. When the servants appeared, he said, "I am no coward; but I am so strong, it is so hard to die."

His heart stopped just after sunrise on October 11, 1809.

Some folks say Meriwether was murdered, but none of us who knew him best believe that. Will Clark took it hard, cursing himself because he hadn't realized the depth of his partner's despair. Sometimes he'd gaze at young Meriwether Lewis Clark and then close his eyes, remembering. "I loved him like a brother," he said, "but it wasn't enough."

Julia cried when Will spoke those words. "I wish I hadn't raised a fuss about the crowding, back when we were newlyweds. Maybe we could have kept his spirits up...." But it wasn't her fault.

In time Clark traveled to Monticello with the journals. A few years later, Jefferson wrote of my Master: "*Of courage undaunted, possessing a firmness and perseverance of purpose which nothing but impossibilities could divert from its direction...*"

But Meriwether lost his purpose, and he no longer knew where to go.

I remain in St. Louis with Shannon. That was what Meriwether wanted. We have our own little house. Shannon became a lawyer, and people talk of making him a judge. He never asks for more than I can give. Shannon understands that some things don't change with the seasons. There are still times when I want to howl at the moon. It's supposed to be the dog that passes on first, not the Master. But the Great Mystery is just that, and I try to wait patiently, doing my duty, serving as a good companion to Shannon, watching Meriwether's namesake grow in the slow way of humans.

But the bodies of dogs age faster. I'm becoming stiff, especially when the weather turns cold. With my bad leg, it's hard to climb the porch stairs, so often I sleep out in the yard. I dream: one night a great shaggy creature with horns bellows and shakes the ground about me until I wake panting; a winsome bitch howls from across a rushing stream; I even smell the salt of the sea and hear its roar.

There are nights, though, when I can't sleep at all. I gaze up at the sky until I locate the Dog Star. Then I close my eyes, imagining how it will be after I live out my span of years and the Great Mystery calls me home. I will cross over the swift-running river, shake icy water from my fur, and sniff the breeze. Out on the plains graze herds of buffalo. Big-horns pick their way across snow-covered mountains, while beavers labor to build a dam in a creek clear as crystal. Then I catch that scent, and my legs grow strong again, and I bound to meet my true Master....

But until that time, I proceed on.

ACKNOWLEDGEMENTS

Gratitude straight from my heart to:

The members of the Corps of Discovery who shared their observations through their journals—Charles Floyd, Patrick Gass, Robert Frazer, John Ordway, Joseph Whitehouse, William Clark, who never shirked his duty, and, of course—and most of all—Meriwether

The 2001 Rocky Mountain National Rendezvous in Polebridge, Montana, where I met Poredevil, Woodman, Weird Harold, Leprechaun, Dr. Mongo, Captain Billy, and the rest, who made the men of the Corps come alive

Every teacher who shared their love of story and way with words, especially Peg Ellingson, Kim Stafford, Teresa Jordan, Terry Tempest Williams, Sue Armitage, Luis Urrea, the late great Alvin Josephy, Jr., Craig Childs, and especially Lisa Jones, who facilitates "The Heroine's Journey"

Fishtrap Writers Conference at Wallowa Lake, Oregon, for the learning, the inspiration, the landscape, and making me a Fishtrap Fellow

My publishing angel Mary C. Simmons, author of *Corvus Rising*, who designed the cover, formatted the manuscript, and held my hand through The Process—the myriad confusions along the indie publishing trail.

Aziza Theodorou, columnist for the *Bodega Bay Navigator*, who proofed the manuscript and listened to Seaman's voice—just like she's listened to me all these years

The librarians of Ridgway, Colorado, who ordered me the references I needed through Interlibrary Loan, and the librarians of Delta County who never discouraged me from following the Trail, even when it wasn't convenient—thanks, Jane!

All the veterinarians I worked for over the long years, including D.V.M.s Berwyn Richards and Ruth Daniels, on through Bettye Hooley, who always asks after my writing

The compilers of history, who ferreted out the facts that under-lie my journey of imagination—though that's as much about staying out of the way and listening to the dog. In addition to the many versions of the Corps of Discovery journals, I utilized the scholarship of David Lavender, Dr. John Bakeless, Stephen Ambrose, Clay Jenkinson, and especially the insights of James P. Ronda, author of *Lewis and Clark Among the Indians*, who broadened my perspective.

Bill Fischer, whose cabin provided an altitude adjustment when it was most needed—and he let me bring my dog! That second mile high reminds me that I'm a librarian *and* a writer *and* a lover of wild places.

Todd Weber, L&C expert, living history presenter, and educational tour guide at ilivehistory.com, who generously checked the manuscript for historical accuracy and gave me confidence when he told me he cried, and his wife Nadine, for the map on my bedroom wall and keeping in touch, reminding me that the journey matters.

W. Crosby Brown and Colonel U.S. Air Force (Retired) Dave "Preacher" Pohlman, who've attended many a Rendezvous and generously perused the manuscript

Special gratitude to my mountain man who yearns for the sea (and all the places where fish live), that silver-tongued troubadour Harry Harpoon, who always believed

LAURA LEE YATES thrives in a Colorado mountain valley on the west side of the Continental Divide. Returning from an exploration of Montana, she became obsessed with viewing the Lewis & Clark expedition through the eyes of the Newfoundland dog that accompanied the Corps. Currently a librarian but long employed in the veterinary field—always accompanied by large-breed canines—Laura Lee enmeshed herself in the original journals as well as contemporary research to ensure the accuracy of historical detail. An accompanying music CD is available, also titled *Bound for the Western Sea*, featuring Lewis & Clark period tunes as well as original songs with lyrics by Laura Lee, performed and produced by her partner, Harry Harpoon.

Please visit www.lauraleeyates.com for news about Lewis & Clark presentations as well as upcoming projects, including Laura Lee's coming-of-age novel *Moon over the Mountain*, about a homesteading family and Chief Joseph's band of Nez Perce attempting to coexist in the Wallowa Valley of Oregon in the 1870s.

Made in the USA
Coppell, TX
18 January 2021